TRISTAN EGOLF

LORD OF THE BARNYARD

Killing the Fatted Calf and Arming the Aware
in the Corn Belt

GROVE PRESS
New York

First published in 1998 by Picador
Printed in the United States of America

FIRST AMERICAN EDITION

Library of Congress Cataloging-in-Publication Data

Egolf, Tristan, 1971–
Lord of the barnyard : killing the fatted calf and arming the
aware in the Corn Belt / Tristan Egolf.
p.   cm.
ISBN 0-8021-1641-8
I. Title.
PS3555.G37L67   1999   813'.54—dc21   98-35360

Grove Press
841 Broadway
New York, NY 10003

99 00 01 02 10 9 8 7 6 5 4 3 2 1

FOR COLIN EVANS

Stagolee took the pitchfork,
and he laid it on the shelf.
Says, 'Stand back, Tom Devil –
I'm gonna rule hell by myself . . .'

from 'The ballad of Stagolee'
author unknown

PROLOGUE

THERE WAS A POINT AT WHICH, after the Baker/Pottville melee had wound down with the last twenty or thirty handcuffed Sodderbrook poultry-plant wetbacks, Buzzard's-Roost Hessians, Dowler Street trolls, and east-side Baker factory rats being crammed into Sheriff Tom Dippold's departmental paddywagons and sent on their way to the overstuffed abattoirs at Keller & Powell, the trash fires along Main St. had been hosed down and blown apart amid the smoldering wreckage of Gingerbread row, the school gymnasium had been gassed and raided by a poorly equipped and this-side-of-flabbergasted outfit of regional deputies, the general looting along Geiger had tapered off, the 3rd and Poplar riot had been subdued, an outraged pack of coal-truck operators from Ebony Steed's reservoir number six had long-since paid its ill-fated reconciliatory midnight visit to the Patokah-side river rats in a barreling steam-roller procession of Dodge rams, and the rest of the community had become so far entombed in its own excrement that even Pottville 6's newscasters were having to admit Baker appeared to be awaiting the arrival of the four horsemen – there was that point at which, in the full-pitched midst of it all, every cognizant and functioning citizen left in Greene County knew exactly who and what John Kaltenbrunner was all about. One might go so far as to say that in any given household or public tavern the mere mention of his name might've touched off an all-night row, one that could've just as easily dragged on for hours as terminated abruptly in a knock-down brawl. All this literally. By the time John had at last managed to territorialize every hedgerow from one devastated end of Baker to the other, his essence had distilled in the public eye as the orchestrator of a small time holocaust. As the press reported, 'his shadow had darkened every doorstep in town,' his name had become a household word, one generally equated with all that was wrong in creation. He'd become the most controversial figure in Baker's history since that wagon-load of cannon fodder we call founding fathers first dragged their dilapidated ox-carts out of Appalachia and into this valley.

But that certainly hadn't always been the case. Far from it. Contrary to prevailing lore in the local taverns and council halls, John's moment in the limelight was a veritable fifteen minutes, nothing more. The rest of his short miserable existence was spent so far out of the public eye and hell-up-6th-Street in the barnyard that all but a handful of 'expendables' ever even knew he was here. There were only two occasions, each unrelated and distanced from the other by several years, when his name was brought to the community's attention at all. The first was during the ten-week dilemma the *Greene County Herald*'s own axegrinder-in-chief so appropriately and monumentally dubbed 'The Crisis.' The second was by way of a much talked about, though ill-comprehended, shoot-out with area deputies which occurred on the north end of the valley five years earlier. Both events initially fell prey to such extensive revision by the media that now, presently, with a full decade having elapsed and given reign to practically anyone's testimony on either matter, most locals have gotten to the point where they're ready and willing to accept anything they're told. They're inclined to recall the days when John roamed the streets as a rogue virus, kicking over trash cans, accosting elderly widows with tire irons, spearheading labor strikes with a wayward-ho charge, etc. They're even apt to regard the years preceding his arrival as antediluvian somehow – 'preparatorily inconsequential.' For someone who's been lambasted with more posterior defamation, catchpenny character assassinations, and mob-propagated hatchet jobs in the public forum than any other figure in the valley's history, it's amazing just how much of his corporeal existence was whiled away in anonymity.

As the record reflects, there was only one point, outside of the holdout and the crisis, when John managed to make any kind of a name for himself, and even that was marred with slanderous, unsubstantiated gossip. By now it's become common knowledge that more outrageous rumors had come into being and were circulating about and around his existence before he'd gotten even halfway through his sophomore year at Holborn High than had been the case with any other student in living memory. He may not have meant much to anyone else in town, but to his classmates, to those who endured his proximity on a daily basis, he was the notorious *Kaltenbrunner boy*, the kid in room 29, the freak on the tractor, the corncrib fascist, the troglodytic goat-roper from just north of the river – the one who rarely spoke a word to anyone but who, nevertheless, unfailingly succeeded in alienating, revolting, and terrifying just about every living being he came in contact with. That one. Everyone knew his name. Among other things, he was a suspected barn-burner. There was talk of him sodomizing the livestock on his ranch. At one point he'd been arrested for assaulting a member of the Baker General's janitorial staff, and many maintained he'd been one hundred percent guilty of the drunk driving charge leading up to it. And there was other talk as well, some of it partly true, but most of it baseless. Whatever the case, whether you chose to believe one story and not the next, or all of them together and none apart, the end result was the same: namely that by the time John's provocation of the first William Bonney style police holdout to transpire in Pullman Valley in over seventy years was made public, the news can't be said to have shocked many of his peers. By then they were beyond that point. As numerous sources unanimously contend, most of his fellow students may have been in awe that he'd finally gone that far, but none of them would've put him past it to begin with. The holdout was widely acknowledged as an anticipated inevitability, just as its outcome was welcomed with hushed enthusiasm: John was subsequently exiled from the community for several years. Speculations as to his motives and as to the story behind the holdout itself lingered on for quite some time. There was lots of talk. Everyone had ideas, but none of them really went anywhere. The incident eventually died a natural death, as it rightly should have, due to one too many unknown specifics in the case. The holdout and all its main characters gradually but steadily joined the ranks in the elephant's graveyard, so that by the time John did return, with over three years having elapsed in the interim and all he'd gone through having altered his outward appearance beyond recognition, no one could've possibly known he was back. At the age of nineteen he wound up alone and unknown in a town that had never considered him one of its own in the first place. That was the real beginning of his life in Baker. He settled into a pillbox flat on Geiger, got a job at the poultry plant, and started working, drinking, brooding and cahooting alongside of everyone else. And with that began the long empirical initiation to the Cumberland grind that would proceed upward at a slow languorous crawl from the bottom rung of the whole community ladder. It went on like that for years. People don't understand that part. There's a tendency to cling to the idea of John having charged into town from out of nowhere and turned it upside down for a laugh. That's not at all what happened. The truth is, as more than would like to admit are well aware, John Kaltenbrunner was a native, and there was a whole lifetime of accumulated indignity behind his actions. Up until the point when he finally fashioned his vehicle/warhorse, he quietly choked on an ass-end of Baker most area residents are reluctant to acknowledge even exists. He scoured the barnyards and killing floors from the pork shack to the public sewer. He underwent several ordeals that would've outright murdered most locals. His whole life remained an inconceivably bad losing streak by definition. And it went on and on and on like that for years, beyond the point of ludicrous to the brink of near-impossibility, until all the cankered fruit, the poverty and squalor, the endless carousal – every high octane combustible in the cornucopia – at last found an outlet and blew its way all through the countryside. Then there was noise. Then there was a mess. As Wilbur Altemeyer has since stated, the payoff, when it did come, ripped through Baker like a homesick genie on a break from the lamp. Everyone was dragged into it: the press, the authorities, the church, the factories, the schools, the river rats, the Hessians, the wetbacks, the trolls, every family in town, the whole list . . . No one emerged unscathed. Once it hit, it was all across the board, but up until then it remained penned at bay as a quarantined lycanthrope on a waxing crescent.

And the truth is, hard as it may be for most locals to accept, when it did hit, Baker did not hold up. Not by any stretch of the imagination. The Baker Lay were in no way prepared for what was in store. As a way of life, they'd been at one another's throats for so long – backbiting, slandering, mudslinging, keeling for a brawl, snooping around the drainpipe, factionalizing en masse and plowing one another's wives and livestock to the washboard, that when the roof started coming in on the public arena, they, as a group, just couldn't get it together. They didn't know how. Had a band of marauders come charging over Gwendolyn Hill from the north, Baker would have mobilized with ease. That wouldn't have been a problem. But this was different. The crisis came from within, and, as such, called for coordinated internal efforts. Also known as cooperation. Cooperation and accountability. Two of the scarcest commodities in the corn belt. Both were in customarily short supply when the time came for their dispatch. Consequently, Baker took the plunge. For ten consecutive, progressively deteriorating weeks the community's primordial uncarved block was put out on public display. It became a living health hazard. It grew to be the laughing stock of the entire state. For most locals the overwhelming shame and disgrace of this disreputable exposure has left an aftertaste of painful embarrassment.

Understandably enough, it's that part of the story they tend to remember best, or, should we say, that part of the story they have the most difficulty rationalizing. And given the magnitude of the crisis itself, one might even say they can't be blamed for it. For the first few years after the fact, they had trouble even acknowledging what had happened. You could see it in their faces anytime it was inadvertently brought into the course of conversation; a slight tightening of the jowels and an immediate push on someone's part to change the subject at all costs. It was written all over them – the growing suspicion that they'd somehow, unwillingly, been written into a life long revenge letter as down home country-jakes and cricket-bat makers who got everything they had coming to them. They'd been charged with bungling ineptitude, incompetence and all-around malfeasance. And to those charges they'd had to plead incontrovertibly guilty, whether they liked it or not . . . *But for God's sake they didn't have to talk about it!* That's what their elusive demeanors pronounced: it was hard enough forgetting everything as it was. No *aides-mémoire* were needed. Or wanted. The taverns were a whole lot quieter for years.

But eventually the locals realized the whole thing was not about to go away on its own. If any coparcenary peace of mind was ever to be attained, they were going to have to put the crisis into terms they could learn to live with. They were going to have to disfigure and trivialize it into sterility, then chase it out the back door as an unwanted intruder. The very idea that an 'inconsequential' group of trash collectors led by one renegade delinquent had actually gotten the last laugh on their sorry asses in an episode of local history that could never, no matter what anyone did, be renegotiated, was more of an admission than they were about to own up to. It was completely unacceptable. It was out of the question. When they finally did start talking about it again, tempers flared and a not-so-slapstick drove of collective revision commenced. Before long, tavern regulars, whose behavior throughout the crisis was a matter of generally accepted, well-known, and more often than not *documented* record, were conveniently rewriting the course of events to their own benefit. Individuals like Dean Kale, an area electrician who'd been openly witnessed rioting along Main St. with twelve of his compatriots on the night of October 21st, were suddenly laying claim to the role of victim. He hadn't *really* smashed the florist's display window with a Louisville slugger – the police had actually swept him off his feet and thrown him through the glass while he was strolling home. Which would inevitably lead to the 'come-to-think-of-it-I-oughtta-sue' bit. No one really believed Kale's story. But everyone pretended to. Wholesale cooperation was imperative if the slate was to be cleared. As a result, the more outrageous the claim, the more uncontested it went. There was a job to be done. They got to work.

They started off with the melee. They took care of their own corners first, then moved on to the overall picture. Next it was the church. Then the wetbacks, the drowning of Bolling county, the failed tidy war. They whittled everything down to palatability, then pitched it out the window. None of their coverups succeeded conclusively, but with everyone in the game together, an illusory sense of progress was mustered up for the time being.

Before long they were ready to move on to us: the 'Sons of Dr. Katz,' the hill scrubs, Baker's 22. But they didn't know what to do with us. They didn't want to come within a day's march of triggering the whole mess over again, as they knew they would've had they proceeded. So they shied away from us and turned instead toward John. And there they've been stuck ever since.

To start off with, they attacked him on grounds of heritage: *It was impossible that John Kaltenbrunner had been a local. Nothing in Baker could have spawned such an abomination ...* He couldn't have been an intruder from within our own midst, couldn't have crawled up from the cellar and in through the back door unannounced. He must have been from somewhere – or some*thing* – else. It was reasoned. And required. And out of that reasoning and requirement originated a drive to fabricate his existence from its origin. His impact on the community, it was felt, ruled out theories of his purportedly humble origins, denounced them all as a sham, the cold hard facts as fraudulent, a veil beneath which a much more compelling history must lay in wait. And if not, then an open invitation to concoct one.

A few years ago, those of us who knew any better began to get wind of these first revisions. Most of them were just bartalk and grisly fiction that had been whipped up with the latest crop circle: tales of John as the last of kin in a long line that had been dying off since the dawn of the breadbasket, when they were first birthed by a mongrel bitch who got her leg caught up in a barbed-wire fence somewhere out in Utah. Things like that. Hokum and codswallop; ill-conceived and poorly crafted products of a collectively superstitious mind. Most of them were laughable at best. We didn't pay them any mind. It hardly seemed likely that any real threat would ever grow out of them. But had we taken a closer look right there in the beginning, we might have identified the driving force behind these crude prototypes and sensed the mathematical inevitability of their further development. We could have put an end to them right there, but at the time they just didn't seem worth the trouble. We were getting a kick out of them anyway. They were almost flattering.

However, the emergence of the Railway-Miscarriage/River-Rat theory very quickly wiped the smile from our faces; not because it was particularly threatening or that it was any more plausible than the others, but because it appeared to be gaining ground in the taverns. It actually first surfaced in none other than the Whistlin' Dick, Baker's number one swill trough for forty years and running now. Before anyone knew it, it had been well circulated and was panning out to the rest of the bars. That's when we first became genuinely concerned.

The Railway-Miscarriage/River-Rat theory would have it that John was prematurely miscarried into a stainless-steel toilet bowl on a high-speed express train cutting through the woods due southwest of Baker, and that he ended up, battered and disoriented, though still alive, face-down on the Patokah railroad tracks with half a rail tie in his ass and two pounds of afterbirth scattered through the gravel for a mile to the south. His mother, reportedly a wealthy heiress from Chicago who was seven months into term, had gone to the lavatory after developing acute stomach pains. Ten minutes later a passing conductor heard a series of screams and a thrashing about in the commode. After trying the handle and finding it jammed, he kicked down the door. He found the lady in question in a bloody awful mess. She was straining and lurching with one leg hiked up on the sink and both fists wrapped around a pustulating umbilical cord leading from between her drawn legs downward into the bowl. The conductor flew into a panic. He squeezed through the doorway and grappled for a hold on the cord. He could make out the misshapen infant jammed in the chute and howling in a high-pitched wail on the other side of the drop flap, just over the tracks. The screams sounded out all through the passenger car. The mother finally lost her footing in the sauce and pitched over into the hallway. She lost consciousness, leaving the rest in the conductor's hands, literally. The conductor made one last effort at dislodging the maimed infant, but the cord soon snapped, and up came the broken end. It was a terrible scene. By the time the young mother came to her senses with a crowd of passengers standing over her, she wanted nothing more than to turn her back on the whole dreadful affair. Of course, no one thought for a second that the child might have actually survived . . .

But, as the story goes, it did. John was jostled up and lacerated all over, but none of his main cables had given out. He was quite alive. He spent the afternoon coming out of shock in the middle of the trackbed, overlooking a beat-up Studebaker jacked up on wood blocks in a patch of cattails. Two more trains passed over him. The turkey vultures had devoured all the afterbirth along the tracks and were beginning to crane their necks toward him by the time a passing river rat on the way home from the poultry plant stumbled on to him. The river rat did a double take and laughed, then threw John under one arm and carried him back to their trackside encampment. He was placed on a chair at the base of a deteriorated church bus. He was thereafter baptized in a cattle trough and weaned on bastard's supplicant for rabbits until he could damn well function as his own quadruped.

And that was how he came of age, living on catfish and garlic a half-day's journey into the peat bogs with those detestable crop thieves. There was a scrap heap to every millpond up and down the road. The riverbanks were lined with spare tires and axle rods, sacks full of catalogues and hollowed out refrigerators, and the notorious inhabitants themselves: The river rats – seventh generation Cumberland inbreds with sloped foreheads and elongated jawlines. It was open to speculation as to what heathen licentiousness they whipped up around their ceremonial trash fires, but whatever it was, it was reasoned, John eventually brought it all into Baker with him . . .

If left unchecked and allowed further development at this rate, this East Kentucky pulpit dictum will soon snowball into a full-blown monstrosity. It will grow, come into its own, become licensed for endless revision, and ultimately scar beyond recognition everything for which we've worked. All revelations yielded by the crisis will be snuffed out. John himself will be canonized as a stale old Antichrist figure, and we, his apostles, the proverbial hill scrubs. All that we are and all that we've done will become the pre-eminent scapegoat in a mass exodus for acquittal.

Already the Miscarriage/River-Rat theory is well on its way to being taken as scripture. It's even been endorsed by an ailing sclerosis aflictee from Pottville who recently came forward on his deathbed claiming to be the very same rail conductor in question. Others point to the trademark scar on John's left buttock, alluding to the wound received from the rail tie. And still others to his lifelong behavioral patterns, i.e. the river rats. It's not an entirely charmless yarn, but the line has to be drawn somewhere.

First off, John's birth and school attendance are a matter of written record. He was here all along. The scar on his left cheek was nothing more than an old wound received on the farm while doing battle with a sheep. Admittedly, his housecleaning habits may have left something to be desired, but he was no river rat. And realistically, the river rats are loathed through and through in Baker anyway, far too ugly to venture into town, much less hold down jobs in the poultry plant. Time and again these theories fall prey to their own ludicrous incongruities.

And there are others, so many others. John as immigrant. John as fascist. John as homosexual. John as immaculate conception. John as carpenter. John as Hessian. John as pogrom refugee. The list goes on.

Again, maybe the drive to fabricate his origins is unavoidable given the generally dim capacities of the mob in question and the quasi-Biblical magnitude of the crisis; but the truth is, outlandish as it may seem, John, like the rest of us, started out on the farm. That's one thing Baker is going to have to come to terms with. He started and ended right here in Greene County. Period. If more locals were as leatherhanded as they claim, they would have owned up to having been flat-out beaten years ago instead of spending all this time after the fact trying to cover their tracks and save face in the surrounding communities. What's done is done; maybe they'll get that through their heads one of these days and realize there's a lesson to be learned somewhere in all of this. Thus far their attempts to powdercoat the weeping lesion have been disgraceful. They furtherly substantiate the rationale behind the crisis itself. Each and every member of the Baker Lay knows exactly what happened. They were all here. They committed their own indiscretions. And for all their attempts to rewrite the script, they'll go to their graves with that knowledge well intact. It seems the most they can hope for in the interim is to botch the records so irreparably that coming generations won't be able to decipher fact from fiction in the mess left behind. By doing so, maybe they figure, they'll at last have acquired their sought-after pardon.

That's where we come in. It's not that we're necessarily qualified to write an authorized biography on John's life. That's not our intention. Our interest is in preserving the history of an achievement before it's carried off by hill people. With that in mind, a chronological recap of Baker's own past is every bit as central to our objective as John's story will ever be. But it's also impossible to recount any facet of what happened without profiling the most central and indispensable character concerned. That means at least a cursory look at John's life from the beginning. Which is no simple matter. The availability of information pertaining to his existence, outside of a few press clippings, police citations and three or four bogus psychiatric evaluations, is virtually nil. If it weren't for Wilbur Altemeyer's 'balcony memoirs,' we would have next to nothing to go on. No one knows John's life story in full. That's a given. But if there's anyone fit to set the record straight at all, it would have to be those of us who worked at close quarters with him throughout the crisis, precious few that we are.

John's impact on our lives was inestimable. The five months we spent in his acquaintance were crucial on two fronts: for John they saw the payoff of a lifetime, the culmination and fruition of all his previously thwarted energies – retribution well-deserved and long-awaited. For us they provided an equally well-deserved swift kick in the ass; an end to the catatonic stupor, the docile complacency – a wake up call and point of embarkation.

But it's not out of a sentimental affinity for him that we, his unlikely compatriots, are drawing up this account; as those things go we can't be said to have ever gotten particularly close with him. Even when things did get underway, John never really opened up to any of us, with the exception of Wilbur Altemeyer and, arguably, Dale Murphy. It's more out of a profound respect for the change he brought about in an otherwise fossilized community, and, more importantly, the example he set for all with eyes and cojones big enough to see, that we now find ourselves battling the impending avalanche of local revision. It is in the interest of preserving an undiluted account of the extraordinary series of events which rocked Baker to its foundation one decade ago that we're putting pen to paper before it's too late. Admittedly, our testimony will be anything but unbiased. That's out of the question. But at the same time, we won't be caught whipping up this convoluted horseshit coming out of the Whistlin' Dick. To that end we *can* be trusted.

And anyway, all things considered, even a sweeping recap of John's life requires no embellishment to put the most outrageously extravagant of the local opiates to shame.

I

ISABELLE, HORTENSE AND BUCEPHALUS

BAKER IS SITUATED IN Pullman Valley, a twelve-mile pothole which was gutted into the modern-day corn belt by the glaciers of a preceding ice age. The western lip of the valley rises to 475 yards above sea level, with the crowning limestone peaks on the northern end towering an additional 20 yards over all the rest. Between this 600 yard escarpment and the treeless barrens to the northeast lies a maze of knobs and hollows, all thick with saw-briars, sassafras, dogwood and fool's gold. Most of the soil is fairly worn, though it was once among the most fertile in the state. The summers are hot and long, the winters brief, yet occasionally brutal. Positioned at the northeast corner of the town line, almost perfectly centered in the valley – just south of where the Patokah river veers off from its course along the eastern wall and cuts in toward the community – lies Gwen-dolyn Hill, home to the Ebony Steed coal company and probably the greatest key in existence to Baker's muddled past.

Sometime during the postwar industrial mobilization that swept across the corn belt and brought towns like Baker alive with manufacturing plants, a Bostonian entrepreneur by the name of Glendan Castor moved into an old Antebellum home on the north end of town. Castor had purchased three square miles of land in Pullman Valley with the intention of founding a mining operation. It was a fundamentally sound investment, as the land was cheap and the availability of an expendable labor force seemingly inexhaustible – New England money goes a long way in the corn belt. However, what he did not foresee was the endless chain of complications that would come about as the result of his chosen site for operations. Had he known what lay beneath the surface of Gwendolyn Hill, he very well may have packed up and headed back to Boston straightaway.

As it was, the establishment of the company was fraught with disastrous setbacks right from the beginning. Unbeknownst to all concerned at the time, Gwendolyn Hill had been the original site of an early European settlement/trading post, of which most existing records had vanished. In addition, Pullman Valley had been previously inhabited by a tribe of Shawnee Indians. In effect, this meant that encased in the hillside lay a scrap heap of Kentucky rifles, dead Indians, corroded whisky stills, sod houses, busted cooking utensils and grindstones, all of which were deemed 'archaeologically significant' in contemporary legal terms. As standard governmental policy dictated, the discovery of any such find mandated that the respective bureau in the capital be notified at once, and that all operations be temporarily seized. A crew of archaeologists would then be sent in to pick apart the 1.5 mile reservoir with a fine-toothed comb. Which was all good and well for everyone concerned, except the coal-truck operators on unemployment. Castor's original crew had unknowingly inherited a buried pig sty left behind by its forebears.

If a white burial ground was unearthed, the church was called in to exhume the graves. That took two weeks. If an Indian burial ground was unearthed, the bureau of archaeology was deployed. That took up to two months. During that time the company's enormous million dollar coal trucks, each being the size of the average American home, were left unattended, lined up in a row like sick dinosaurs at a watering hole. Their operators filled the taverns, commiserating openly and drinking themselves blind. Before long, they'd become an active public menace. Their behavior was frowned on all through the community. They themselves were miserable and bored. Knockdown brawls resulted. The whole crew was thrown in the county jail overnight on more than one occasion. And no sooner would operations finally get underway again than someone would churn up a section of an old stone wall during a munitions blast, landing everyone back in the bread line for another few weeks. Back to the taverns, back to the public charge. It became a serious problem. Castor's operations started to falter. The company's future was in jeopardy. Some of the operators walked off the job, and, contrary to the way it had been mapped out, they were no longer so easily replaceable.

But the precarious nature of the situation was never more apparent than on the afternoon a routine blast turned up a fully intact, perfectly preserved, calcified skeleton of a grown wooly mammoth. The moment 'exhibit #1A,' as it would later be called, appeared on the southern end of the main quarry, the coal-truck operators leapt out of their rigs and ran screaming along the ledge with their heads in their hands. They swore that was it – it was all over; they would be shut down for the entire season this time. They stood in a flap-jawed row along the drop off, staring down at the half-submerged ribcage protruding from the gravel. Visions of terminal unemployment and public disgrace swept over them. It probably would've been curtains for the entire company right then and there had one man not quietly stepped forward and told them all to keep their hats on. At the time, the head of the human resources department at Ebony Steed was a barrel-chested, charismatic graduate of the university of St. Louis by the name of Ford Kaltenbrunner. Kaltenbrunner, in his trademark levelheaded manner, climbed down into the quarry, threw a black tarp over the latest find, and instructed everyone to take a break. All eyes followed him as he made his way back up the embankment to Castor's office-house.

The outcome of the resulting conference was this: the company's administrators unanimously concluded, under advisement from Kaltenbrunner, that it was high time Ebony Steed took a few basic matters into its own hands. In the interest of self-preservation and at the risk of crippling legal repercussions, it was thereby decreed that, from that day forward, all significant archaeological finds would be handled in a clandestine manner. Kaltenbrunner himself was appointed overseer of the coverup. Beginning with the latest discovery, all artifacts were to be recorded, dusted off, and turned over to him personally. He would then package the material with any pertinent information intact, and store it in a secret, well-concealed location where no one, including Castor, could get to it. The less

5

anyone knew of its whereabouts, the more secure the coverup, it was reasoned.

The new policy was effective immediately. Consequently, the company wasn't shut down once for the next eleven years.

Kaltenbrunner, for his efforts, was promoted and compensated accordingly. He rose through the ranks of Ebony Steed and was soon second only to Castor himself, though in the eyes of the machinery operators he was clearly the most capable man in the company, bar none. He was widely respected and well-liked, seen as a fair man, a brilliant conversationalist, and one of the finest drinking partners this side of the cross. His sway over those around him was widely coveted. He was consulted for professional and personal advice on a regular basis. He was never known to turn down anyone in genuine need of his help.

At the age of thirty-four he was married to an area seamstress of Welsh descent. He and his wife put a down-payment on an estate situated one mile due north of Gwendolyn Hill, just across the river. Ford set up a study in the attic of the farmhouse and soon lined the shelves with long rows of research material pertaining to his archaeological inquiries. His library grew, as did his personal interest in the subject matter. The highly classified evidence from the mine was stored in a hidden location, the whereabouts of which not even Madame Kaltenbrunner was aware. Everything else remained in the attic. A growing collection of textbooks lined the lower shelves of the wall-mounted book rack positioned over the main desk. Information pertaining not only to the heritage and ancestry of the original inhabitants of Gwendolyn Hill, but also further analysis on the settlement and foundation of all of Baker: a chronological study of European migrations to the Midwest, the development of industry in the corn belt, the genesis of waterway navigation on the Patokah, the establishment of the railroads, pre and postwar farm production, the staggering effects of prohibition on a community of drunkards, barnstormings, cornhuskings, quilting bees, revivalism, wood-sawing contests, and even family charts on a good many of the town's oldest residents. Exactly what he

6

was working toward will remain a matter of conjecture, but the fact of the matter stands: Ford Kaltenbrunner probably had a tighter lock on the local populace than anyone in history.

At the age of thirty-eight, when he and his wife conceived their first child, Ford was at the height of his powers. Glendan Castor had become a washed out, embittered old ghost at Ebony Steed, little more than a peripheral reminder that, technically, there was still someone higher up on the ladder than Kaltenbrunner himself. With that in mind, it's no wonder that Ford's untimely demise, which was officially attributed to an explosion caused by a buildup of methane gas in one of the underground caverns, immediately prompted allegations of foul play all through the community.

At 2:30 p.m. on Thursday, September 20, 19—, every operator in reservoir number six heard and felt a sudden explosion where there should not have been one. They all left their rigs at once and began scrambling down the embankment to where an underground entrance lay sealed off by a large deposit of fallen limestone. They spent the rest of the day clearing the mess as quickly as they were able, but by the time they reached the body, it was too late. Ford Kaltenbrunner had been dead for hours.

Madame Kaltenbrunner was said to have never gotten over it. She was six months into term at the funeral and stood in her black combination maternity/mourning garb with a thousand-yard stare roped off behind her drawn veil. She was in shock, they said. She barely looked up all through the service. Afterwards, she left the cemetery without a word to anyone. She spent the evening alone. She didn't appear for the memorial banquet at the American Legion. No one ventured out to the farm to offer his condolences. The coal-truck operators ended up in the gazebo at the town square after midnight, downing quarts of Kentucky bourbon and crying like children. Madame Kaltenbrunner was left to herself.

Thereafter she became an acknowledged recluse. She was only sighted from time to time, moping into the grocery in her beige overcoat. Most locals swore she'd lost her mind.

She never remarried.

Three months later, on December 21st of the same year, John Augustus Kaltenbrunner was born on the fifth floor of the Baker General. He was one week premature, weighed 7 lbs. 7 oz., with sandy brown hair, and type O+ blood. He was released after two days under a vitamin lamp. He and his mother were sent on their way, back to the empty farmhouse on the north end of the valley.

John was a sickly infant, prone to chronic respiratory infections and long illnesses. He was slight of build and somewhat awkward. He always seemed to be stumbling over himself, putting his nose where it didn't belong, prying into things. Madame Kaltenbrunner was as attentive a mother as could be. She listened to old phonographs in the parlor while John crawled around on the kitchen floor, fidgeting with the padlocked solvent covers and cornering mice in the cracks in the wall. He once ate a wild mushroom in the yard and had to have his stomach pumped at the Baker General. Another time he fell from the porch and cracked his skull on a shovel handle. He bled profusely over the upholstery of his mother's wagon on the way back to the hospital. He would later recall the mask coming over his field of vision like a plummeting scavenger as the doctors prepared to sew up his head. He instinctively detested the infirmary from then on.

Outside of those two trips to the emergency room he had very little contact with the world beyond the farm for the first several years of his life. The only visitors Madame Kaltenbrunner ever entertained, or even allowed into the house, were a few of the coal-truck operators from the mine who evidently felt they were paying some kind of tribute to their deceased colleague by visiting his widow and orphan. They were enormous men with wooly faces, Texas-hog belt buckles and stale breath reeking of tobacco and sardines. They would remove their hats at the door and stand over John with an almost apologetic air of reverence and discomfort about them. They would inquire after Madame Kaltenbrunner's financial situation, assuring her that if there was ever any problem with her life insurance benefits they would personally raise Cain themselves. After more small talk in the parlor, most of them would then take John for a ride through the backroads in their pickups. During these outings he was spoonshoveled numerous laudatory anecdotes concerning his father: his father the dragonslayer, his father the genius, his father the benefactor, his father the almighty, his father this, his father that – and what was more, he was assured, he himself would one day grow up to be a hard-driving, fueled, giant-killing sonofabitch as well. He'd see . . .

After their visits, after they'd rolled away and left him standing by the mailbox with his hands in his pockets, John was usually left at more of a loss than ever before as to who his father had actually been. He generally felt he'd spent the afternoon hearing out long-winded, harebrained, entirely pointless confessions which had nothing to do with him. He never said much in response to anyone's claims, and even after many visits over a period of several years, he still had a hard time distinguishing one operator from the next. Try as he did, he couldn't even remember their names. After some time the operators began to pick up on his confusion and wonder what was wrong with him. He was a strange one, they noticed – not much to look at. He was small for his age. He was never seen with any playmates. He seemed to be hopelessly preoccupied at all times, hell-bent on collecting his roadside bottles and tending to that shoddy flock of hens. He almost appeared mildly *inconvenienced* whenever one of them dropped by for a visit, as though he were actually being interrupted from more important matters. They couldn't understand it. Was it possible that the most magisterial individual they'd ever known had spawned a bad apple? Could John, with his father's blood coursing through his veins, really have been all that dim? Eventually it was decided that, yes, he was. He was a cave fish. It was a terrible shame, but it couldn't be denied.

In time, the operators stopped coming around altogether. In all their visits, John had gained no insight of any worth into his father's character. And his mother hadn't helped much either. The only time Madame Kaltenbrunner ever appeared to acknowledge Ford's existence at all was during her occasional late-night scrapbook sprees, which left her slumped over a pile of yellowing photographs and crying into her milk of magnesia.

Otherwise, she was stone-cold indifferent and, for appearance's sake, a-sentimental. It was all a mystery to John.

A long patriarchal shadow had been cast over him from birth, and from beneath its penumbra he couldn't help but feel he'd already been deemed inadequate somehow, that by not immediately following in the footsteps of his father, by not simply existing as an instant carbon copy of Ford Kaltenbrunner to begin with, he was letting everyone down. It left him at a complete loss. He found it hard to believe he was really expected to fill the shoes of someone he'd never known, never seen, never talked to or met, someone who'd left behind only a handfull of photographs, a shell-shocked widow, a few dusty books, and an incoherent drove of bad mythology. To expect him to make heads or tails of this barrage of contradictory input, and then, on top of everything else, to become the next heir to the throne, was an honor he had not asked for and wanted no part of. Anyway, for all he knew his father may very well have been a complete idiot. Thus far he'd seen nothing to indicate the contrary. In the first seven years of his life, he'd seen nothing to live up to at all. If his father had once chosen to go out and play Lord of the hill people, that was just fine, so long as he himself wasn't really expected to follow suit. He had no plans of ever becoming a miner. Even as a child, there were certain outcomes he would have banked on instinctively. Such as: he knew he would never be a university graduate, an athlete, a people-person, a giant-killer, the All-American boy, etc. Just the thought of all those possibilities was enough to make his stomach churn. They were worlds away, and that was for the better. He planned on keeping it that way.

For those reasons, and possibly others, Ford Kaltenbrunner remained an abstract non-entity for the first twelve years of John's life. The photographs depicting him as the vigorous, able-bodied coal kraut with the acute disposition and the all-consuming gaze gathered dust and cobwebs on the black-lacquered stool table in the hallway. His library went unattended. His name became an indeterminate household memory, a dwindling fixture. For John, his father was the former tenant for whom occasional scrap mail still arrived from time to time, the old man who'd once lived in the attic, the one who'd left behind the Winchester and the shack full of tools that came in so handy around the farm. The ornately framed photographs of him as the centerpiece in a rollicking, sweat-soaked bash at one of the local taverns were the same kinds that ended up in a far-off corner of the deceased widow's attic, then anonymous nickel bins at farmers' market and rummage sales, and ultimately forty feet deep in the landfill. The world abounded with them. The world went on without them. John walked right by them every day without looking. They weren't real. His father was a stack of mildewed books in the attic. He himself was too busy building an empire in the yard to pay them any mind.

In attempting to assess John's character in concise terms, Wilbur Altemeyer has often resorted to the following formula response:

John Kaltenbrunner was consistently the best there was at what he did well, but in all other matters he was an oblivious, bungling, absent-minded fool. That is to say, the moment he found his calling there was absolutely no stopping him, but up until then it was always and forever 'lights on but nobody home.' He was driven only by that which transfixed him to the point of obsession. The rest – all the quotidian necessities and requirements – fell to the wayside as peripheral distractions. From the advent of his childhood ranching enterprise to his brilliant orchestration of the crisis fifteen years later, probably his single greatest achievement in life was just managing to keep himself alive through the years.

As an example, the farm, which had deteriorated into an almost uninhabitable wreck during Madame Kaltenbrunner's extended period of mourning, had been systematically pieced back together into a fertile, well-maintained estate over the course of a few short years, while John, the lone overseer of its reconstruction, remained scarcely capable of keeping his own shoelaces tied. From the time he was old enough to walk, he'd been almost perversely fixated on refortifying the homestead to the cornerstone of its foundation. The hours he was required to spend elsewhere – in the classroom, the supermarket, even the dinner table – were small restless eternities in comparison. All other priorities took a designated backseat to his renovational jihad. During classes he stared out the window, pensively reviewing his latest works in progress. At recesses, he sat alone at the edge of the yard while his peers ran circles in a wild pack. At night, long after the rest of the community had turned in, he lay awake, tossing and turning on his boarding-house mattress with a choir of locusts from the orchard drifting in through the open window and the roar of the freight trains sounding out from down the hill and across the river. During all involuntary off-hours, he remained a plugged kettle on the open hearth, waiting, waiting, waiting . . . until finally the bell would ring, the cock would crow, the flag would drop, whatever, and he could at last tear into his work with all the amassed rage of a penned bull. He would stumble from one end of the yard to the other, wielding tin pails, buckets of feed, pitchforks and blow torches, chopping wood and repairing the weathervane, feeding the dogs, patching the tool shack, fixing leaks in the roof. Just about everything needed work. The old farm was in ruins.

He started off by first establishing a base of operations in the barn. He purged the corners of rats and opossums, then cleared off the shelves and set up a work bench for repairs. He gathered-every spare tool from the corners of the loft and the shelves in the cellar. He collected and itemized old tin pails, twenty-year-old cleaning solvents, paint cans, garden hoes, and miscellaneous farm equipment that had been left behind by the former occupants.

Then he got to work on the heavy machinery. He wheeled out an inoperable tractor, stripped it bare, lined up the individual components in the yard, cleaned, polished and replaced any damaged pieces, hammered the frame back into shape, painted the rims, replaced the radiator grill, and called in a mechanic to tune up the engine. Afterwards he wrapped leather bridle reigns in cross stitch over the steering wheel, painted the whole thing yellow, filled the tank with 92-octane premium gasoline, and named it Bucephalus.

Next he uprooted the ragweed, buckthorn, dog fennel, and cheat grass which had choked off the garden over the years, rigged the antique threshers and steel plows left behind in the grain shed, hooked them up to Bucephalus, and soon had a large zucchini and tomato patch underway, in the midst of which he posted a cockeyed scarecrow adorned in feed sacks and rubber tubing. He cleaned up a polluted stretch of the riverbank, where festoons of Spanish moss and disposable diapers were strung out through the bowed willow limbs, and, down below in the mud and motor oil, a discarded septic tank and two shopping carts from the Baker supermarket rose from the current like rotting fenceposts. He dosed Isabelle, the lone sheep on the hill, for stomach worms and liver flukes, dipped her for mange, and kept her nose smeared with pine tar to ward off the grub-in-the-head and nose fly maggots. He removed long blocks of honeycomb from the wooden hive boxes of the bee farm at the edge of the woods, then canned them in old glass jars to line the top shelf in the kitchen. And there was always something more, something new demanding his attention – snakes in the basement, moss in the drainpipes, tent-worms in the orchard, ticks in the bitch's left ear. He saw to it all. He was completely self-taught in everything he did and funded all operations by cashing in wheelbarrows full of discarded bottles which he'd gathered from the roadside ditches along 254.

In the course of a few short years, he'd revamped the dilapidated estate to its former glory, modeling it after an old photograph hanging from the blue-papered walls of his mother's bedroom. John's farm was every bit the homestead it had once been; with the rolling hill behind the barn fenced off for Isabelle, the narrow gravel road from the highway meandering out of the woods and past the two-car garage, between the orchard to the left and cedar-panelled tool shack to the right, the flower garden, the tomato patch, the corn stalks and eggplants, beyond the mailbox and yard ornaments, beneath the giant oak and line of pines, the picket fence by the storage shed, the freshly painted farmhouse with its porch swing and array of wicker baskets, then on down the hill to the northwest in the direction of the neighboring farms.

But he was far from satisfied with just that. He had much more in mind. He'd spent one too many afternoons pacing along the edge of neighboring farms admiring the Rhode Island Reds, Plymouth Rocks, and White Leghorns not to begin tugging at his mother's overcoat for a yard full of his own.

*

14

His mother told him he was ridiculous. He couldn't possibly know anything about chicken ranching, she said. He was a dreamer, very possibly an idiot.

From that point on, he geared all his energies toward proving her wrong.

He decided to ease his way into it by first housing and training a small flock of carrier pigeons. He had it on good authority that introductory, small-scale objectives were preliminarily indispensable to all aspiring stockmen, particularly those entering the field as lone operatives. The most that could go wrong with a flock of turtledoves or domestic quail, for example, paled in comparison with the potential setbacks of a failed poultry operation. The worst-case-scenario profit losses weren't even in the same ballpark. Given the choice, he opted for the carrier pigeons.

He started by piecing together a wire cage from the remains of an old plow that lay rotting behind the barn. What began as a rickety, a-symmetrical lean-to propped up along the orchard fence gradually developed into what Madame Kaltenbrunner would ominously dub 'The Coop.' The Coop, which actually resembled a field-tested air-raid shelter more than anything, was initially equipped with seven perchboards, two porcelain feed dishes, and a jerry-rigged waterline. Although due for several extensive overhauls in the years to come, the original structure did serve its fundamental purpose. The first test-run flock of carrier pigeons John purchased from a bird farm in Pottville fell right into place in its spacious interior and was provided for on every level.

As for the flock itself: John often remarked that the combined intelligence of all sixteen of his 'airborne catfish' couldn't have found its way out of a paper bag. Zero to the power of infinity is still zero. The 'catfish' were far and away the dumbest animals in the catalogue. Also the most unwaveringly obedient.

Getting them situated was the difficult part. The rest was easy. Within a week of their arrival John had gotten his daily itinerary down to a formula. Every afternoon he took the flock into the fields for training. He would stand at the end of a clearing with his father's Winchester in hand to ward off the turkey vultures

15

doing figure eights just over the tree line. The catfish would dart erratically from one end of the field to the other, making a bee line for an empty deer stand, pausing to rest, then returning in unison. He would go home at dusk with four or five of them perched on his shoulders and the rest hobbling through the dirt and stones close behind. Back at the coop he would sweep the floor, fill the feeders, and lock up for the night. The catfish would languish on their scoured perchboards as he set to work on the far end of the yard erecting what would become their open-air roost: the 'Towering Phallus,' a twelve foot dock post embedded to the right of the drive. The first afternoon Madame Kaltenbrunner caught sight of it she ordered him to dismantle it at once. It was *pagan idolatry*, she said: she wasn't about to stand for a blatant mockery of the crucifix on her property. John told her not to be ridiculous; it was a lumber scrap from the dock-yards, for Christ's sake – what was wrong with her? But Madame Kaltenbrunner wouldn't hear of it. She persisted with her demands. John exasperatedly modified the roosting planks until she stopped crying sacrilege. Then he turned toward the flock. He brought the catfish out of the coop and on to the phallus. They assumed position in an unbroken row, eight to either side of the copper-capped support post.

The flock was in place.

With phase one out of the way, he moved on. For ten straight days he spent every afternoon visiting neighboring farms, inspecting coops and stables, and consulting agricultural admin-istrators from all over the valley. Soon enough he'd drawn up plans for a medium-sized layer house and was taking an inven-tory from the lumber in the barn. He quickly assessed his bill of materials. It took the deposit money from seventeen loads of bottles to purchase the necessary hinges, door hooks, mesh poultry netting, perchboards and cement blocks not already to be found in his own cache of scraps. In four months he'd erected the layer house on a flat patch of grass to the north end of the barn, just out of view of the porch. It was complete with a 20′ × 20′ reinforced cement floor, a sloped sheet-metal roof, four feeders, a watering trough, plywood siding, 2′ × 6′ girders, three tiers of 14′ × 14′ partitioned nests, one elevated community nest, and five 40-watt bulbs. Next he fenced off a large pen with a roll of soft-iron chicken wire. Another two weeks saw the arrival of six feed sacks and a bag of wood shavings. After that nothing remained but a small tank of pesticides, recommended worming compounds, and lastly, the flock itself. It had taken six months from start to finish, one bottle deposit refund at a time, but by the summer of his eighth year he'd filed a sizeable flock of second-year leghorns into their new home.

The empirical crash course in chicken ranching followed. His first flock consisted of thirty-four hens and six cocks. If all went according to plan, he could expect approximately 4,500 eggs over the course of the next year. This would require strict dietary regulation, comprehensive sanitation practice, parasite and pest control, and all other necessary precautions to prevent undue mortality. The more unruly hens would have to be debeaked to stem cannibalism. Any of the birds that contracted infectious bronchitis, Newcastle, or fowl pox would have to be vaccinated or removed accordingly. All manure would be rotated on a regular basis in order to reduce the risk of disease and curb fly-breeding. The wood shavings used for nesting would be replenished every week. The eggs would need to be gathered twice daily. Slaughter would be in order in the event of molting. If nothing went wrong, he would soon be providing eggs and meat for himself and his mother, and selling at least six dozen additional eggs to the household consumer every week. It wouldn't be much of a profit to begin with, but it would at least pay for itself and pave the way for the next flock.

John was up every morning running ragged through the barn-yard. The fog would roll off the hill at first light and find him plowing diligently through his list of obligations. He filled the troughs in the layer house while the flock trampled over itself to feed. He unclogged the waterline, cleared out the nests, and took the eggs to the fridge in the pantry. Next he fed and watered the catfish. Then up the hill to feed Isabelle. Then back to the house to cook for his mother. Madame Kaltenbrunner was off to the linen factory by half past six every morning. That left John exactly one hour before school to work on the hover brooder and still air incubator in the barn, the next phase of his plan.

In two months the first wave of chicks had hatched and were feeding beneath a soft-bulbed lamp. By the time he'd incorporated them into the main layer house, the first of the old flock had begun to molt. This called for slaughter. He singled out the featherless, pock-marked hindquarters and dragged them to the block. He chopped off their heads with a hatchet. Each cut was made just below the vocal box so that the head lay squawking in the grass while the body ran through the yard. When it came to rest, it was strung up for bleeding. Then it was scalded for feather removal. Evisceration followed; the body cavity was cleaned of the heart, liver, gizzard, gall bladder, and all fecal matter. The carcass and giblets were chilled in ice water for three hours. Afterwards, they were bagged and refrigerated. The first wave was on the table.

The flock size doubled in the next two months. The freezer was stuffed with more birds than he and his mother could possibly eat. The feed mill's delivery truck began to appear. Poultry catalogues arrived by mail – someone had evidently put his name on a list. He struck up a correspondence with a local distributor. A representative from the household consumer mailed him a book of poultry oddities, the history and folklore of which had soon been well ingrained in his head. He ordered a pair of lavender guineas to ward off hawks, snakes and rats. He even acquired three buff-laced Polish cocks for aesthetic reasons. The farm rapidly evolved into a thriving depository of assorted birds.

John was exhilarated. The moment he accomplished one objective, he moved on to the next, envisioning the day his estate would be coveted the whole world over as the most comprehensive assemblage of domestic fowl in existence, and he himself the self-made coordinator in residence. He pressed on with a terrifying drive.

His mother was astounded. For the first year she didn't know what to think. At nine years of age her son was on a first name basis with the president of the Pullman Valley Hatchery. His operations had taken off like wildfire and given no indication of letting up. It was true, his income *had* long since outweighed initial expenses, and he *was* putting food on the table, there was no denying it – but still, to see him carrying on like this while the rest of his peers didn't appear to have a care in the world seemed decidedly unnatural, to say the least. It was downright frightening. She regretted having taunted him and made a note never to do so again. But the question still remained: what was she to do in the meantime?

Then, one night, John dropped his next bomb. He and Madame Kaltenbrunner were seated at the dinner table after a meal of fried wings and squash. John calmly removed a notebook from his bag and laid it on the table. Then he made his announcement.

He wanted sheep.

Madame Kaltenbrunner nearly fell off the floor. She got up and kicked the wall. She threw the pepper shaker across the room. She began screaming *Sheep?* . . . *Sheep, sheep, sheep!* Was he *completely* out of his mind? Had he lost the few remaining wits he had about him? What was *wrong* with him? It wasn't right! *He* wasn't right! He must have been sick! Normal kids didn't act this way. His teachers had been right. All those phone calls she'd received were true. He was bent. He was *insane*. What would his father have thought? And anyway, had he forgotten about Isabelle? – Wasn't the one sheep they owned already more than he could handle? Hadn't she personally had to rescue him the day Isabelle had rammed him into the corner of her shack and trampled him to a pulp? Hadn't she herself had to pull the pitchfork out of his backside and carry him down the hill in a bloody mess? Was he conveniently forgetting that little episode?

John quickly reminded her that Isabelle was a profound exception to the rule. He pointed out that they were both perfectly well aware of what the old man who came by on shearing detail once a year had always maintained: that in all his years on the Pullman Valley circuit, and through literally thousands of ranches and homesteads all across the state, Isabelle still stood,

19

indisputably, as the oldest, fattest, and by far most foul-tempered animal he had ever encountered. She was more of a devil than a quadruped. There were even tales of her chasing up to three marauding coyotes back into the forest by herself. The whole of the corn belt couldn't have contained one flock of Isabelles; they would've laid waste to the countryside in a fortnight. You couldn't have paid most professional farmhands to go anywhere near her without a comprehensive armamentarium of tranquilizers and stun guns on hand, and even then it would've run a pretty penny in risk insurance, advertising, and manpower. One of the neighbors had been suggesting for years that they just shoot the old bitch and get it over with. But, of course, that neighbor hadn't volunteered to do the job himself. One hard look at Isabelle was enough to deter any executioner. She was in a class all her own. She was in no way representative of the common ewe; it was useless to compare her with the Suffolks he had set his sights on. Besides, he said, he and Isabelle had come to a little 'understanding' years earlier.

He carefully refrained from elaborating on that last point. He knew his mother wouldn't have taken kindly to the fact that after the aforementioned incident he had taken an old axe handle from the barn and whipped hell out of Isabelle something terrible. She had kept her distance ever since.

Continuing on, he recited a list of well-prepared figures which proved his proposal both economically feasible and, ultimately, lucrative. It was exceptionally mapped out. He explained how he'd already cleared out the empty stables in the lower quarters of the barn. The troughs had been repaired, the hay was in place. He himself would foot the bill for all vaccinations and starter's feed. All he needed from her was the initial loan to purchase the first flock of lambs.

Madame Kaltenbrunner stared at him. It took her several moments to grasp the situation at all, several more to overcome her disbelief. Had this impudent little ruffian really just had the unmitigated audacity not only to take for granted her instant approval of his lunatic endeavors, but on top of that to demand her own personal funding thereof? It didn't seem possible. She was speechless.

John could see she was going to need some time. He placed the list on the bureau, told her to think it over, and left her at the table with her head in her hands. He went out to the layer house to de-louse the cocks.

That evening Elias Kauerbach, head of the Pullman Valley feed mill's delivery department, received a telephone call from an hysterical Madame Kaltenbrunner. As he later claimed, she was in a terrible state, raving incoherently about her boy's condition and imploring the mill for help of any kind. He tried to calm her by meeting her halfway and saying OK, yes, first, it was true, her son *was* one hell of an odd fish. He was quite honestly the damndest thing any of them had ever seen. A phenomenological wonder in the strictest sense. However, that wasn't necessarily a bad thing. Though Kauerbach did understand her concern as a mother – Lord knows John was frightening enough – what she also had to come to terms with was that he somehow appeared to know exactly what he was doing. Where he'd aquired his knowledge was anyone's guess, but aquired it he had, and thoroughly at that. At the current rate, Kauerbach estimated, the Kaltenbrunner estate would be on par with national farming standards before John hit his freshman year. There was no explanation for it, but it was true. So – knowing that – Madame Kaltenbrunner really only had two choices: she could either *support* or *discourage* his behavior. They both knew well enough that the latter wouldn't be achieved successfully without physically removing him from the farm. That would involve putting him away in a special school for a while, just as members of the Baker faculty had already suggested. Meaning: money, time, and possibly further psychological damage to his already frazzled mind. None of which, Kauerbach was assuming, was readily affordable at the moment. On the other hand, Madame Kaltenbrunner might opt to rationalize the situation by hoping and praying that John was nothing more than an unforeseen prodigy, a highly unusual case of an early career man – he'd obviously made up his mind right quick – and thereby support his undertakings with the knowledge that for as long as he remained at liberty or at large he *was* going to find some way, with or without her consent, to secure, among other things, his flock. Kauerbach knew it was none of his business, but, since he was being consulted, had to suggest that if it were his son (gulp) he'd go ahead and take out the loan, but *not* without trying to get something out of it for himself along the way.

Make him a deal, was his final suggestion. And that was all he could offer.

Madame Kaltenbrunner, on considering, couldn't help but agree, albeit with lackluster enthusiasm. It seemed there was very little she could hope for other than to turn the situation around so that it at least worked partially to her advantage. In the end, she agreed to draw the requested loan, but on one very important condition: John would first have to promise to pull his act together at school. As she saw it, his academic record thus far was an atrocity. His father had had one of the finest minds in Baker, she said. But John's own record was scandalous, nothing worthy of the Kaltenbrunner character. It was disgusting. Marks like that would get him nowhere. It was almost as though he were intentionally failing to spite those around him. It all had to end. Not only did his marks have to come up, but the phone calls from concerned faculty members had to taper off for good. One of these days, she said, he was going to realize these were supposed to be the best years of his life.

WILBUR ALTEMEYER'S MEMOIRS, from which the majority of the information in this account has been drawn, clearly indicate John's willingness in later years to discuss openly and at length certain aspects of his childhood, while remaining almost completely mute on others. As one example, he would often recount with pride and exhilaration every last detail of that October afternoon when the Greene Ranch stable wagon came bounding up the road with his long-awaited flock of first-year lambs. If encouraged properly, he might have gone on for hours concerning Isabelle's disgust with the whole spectacle; how she'd snapped to attention as the vehicle had come to a halt, had stamped and snorted at the edge of the pasture as it was backed into place for unloading, then broadsided the first lamb out of the hatch at a full-tilt charge. In another context, a full volume might be drawn up on Isabelle alone; the same holds true for the rest of John's life on the farm, erratic as it was. With the proper application and marketing skills, Wilbur's notes might even have all the makings for a Hollywood epic – so vivid and extensive were John's recollections from childhood.

But when it came to other facets of his early years, those he considered to have been empty and meaningless, those without any merit or redeeming value whatsoever, he was a closed book. His experiences at school being the perfect example.

Outside of a few off-the-cuff remarks made from time to time in later years, John's overall commentary on his eleven year run at Holborn (Elementary and High) was limited, almost exclusively, to one sweeping statement. In effect, he claimed he could've mapped out the lay of the land from every one of his classroom windows in graphic detail, but that never in an interminable eon could he have begun to explain what was actually going on in the rooms around him.

The reports from his graduating class concur. As of yet, no one's come forward claiming to have been on personal, or even *speaking*, terms with John. It's a generally accepted fact that he had no friends. His teachers admit to having avoided calling on him whenever possible so as to elude that vacant, reptillian stare that had such an unsettling effect on everyone. He was sometimes known to walk into a room, seat himself, and gaze absentmindedly at his desk top for a full ten minutes before suddenly snapping to attention with the realization that he was in the wrong class. He would then get up and leave, bewildered. He'd spend the rest of the session walking the halls in confusion. That's the Kaltenbrunner most of the student body from Holborn remembers: that scraggly, disoriented barn elf wandering the corridors with his head in the clouds.

We have our own theories on why he didn't fit in, though even our contentions, like all the rest, should be taken with a perfunctory grain of salt. One could just as easily – and inconclusively – argue that John didn't give a damn for any facet of his academic career as say that, had he been appropriately tested, he very likely would have been diagnosed with some obscure, autistic learning disorder. Whether or not he was genuinely disabled is impossible to determine. However, one thing is certain: he was by no means unintelligent. His academic record, as a chronicle of deliberate neglect, is in no way indicative of his true mental capacities. In response to allegations subsequently put forth by the school board, claims of John having been a dim-witted fool, one needs only consider the source.

Baker's 'educational system' – an oxymoron in itself – is a petrified remnant of the Old Deluder Satan law run by post-Scopes Bryanites, cold-war paranoids, and in John's own words, 'casebook studies of arrested development.' Nowhere in the nation is a more antiquated system of old-world work ethics and bogus moral dictum more unconscionably perpetuated than in this cemetery-side Hooverville of mobile homes and crumbling office houses. The existing curriculum has been washed-up and outdated for generations. Most of the textbooks are over twenty years old. The teachers themselves are frequently poorly educated, misinformed, uncertified, and often even oblivious to the most fundamental principles of English grammar. The library is a threadbare dumping ground of dime-store trash, subject to the continual scrutiny of a fundamentalist review board, which is, itself, comprised of arguably illiterate Methodist crones and area Bible thumpers. For all the pomp and panoply surrounding the athletics department and graduation ceremonies, most students leave Holborn High truly believing the dinosaurs are gone because Noah didn't have room for them on the Ark. It only makes sense that any exception to the rule whatsoever would find this environment immediately hostile to his existence. Anyone not hell-bent on pursuing one of two available paths – trade school or the local factories – could be seen as doomed to years of potentially maddening exclusion right from the outset.

But where others would have floundered along through endless identity crises, John had managed to make up his mind pretty early on. He'd been able to put everything into perspective following a single incident which occurred halfway through his second year. As he later recalled, sometime in late November a stray cocker puppy of probably no more than ten weeks of age began appearing from the woods to the east of the highway, just beyond the cemetery, to run with the students during recesses. It wasn't seen as any particular threat for the first few weeks, but by mid-January the teachers had begun to complain. The puppy was showing up on a regular basis, waiting beneath the jungle-gym for hours at a time. It was seen as a distraction and a nuisance. The students were throwing it scraps from the window every time a teacher's back was turned. One afternoon it was smuggled into the main building in a duffel bag and turned loose in the hall. The head principal, a beer-gutted ex-marine by the name of Roy Mentzer, who'd lost three fingers in a chainsaw accident – thus depriving him of his trigger-finger and consequently excluding him from the Baker waterfowl club – thereby tried to remove the animal by force. But in attempting to do so, he was inadvertently bitten in clear view of over thirty students. He was humiliated and embarrassed. He quickly put a call through to the sheriff's department to request assistance. Thirty minutes later two deputies arrived on the scene. By then, the puppy had been returned to the playground, as recess was in session. After five minutes of trying unsuccessfully to coax it into submission, the deputies finally gave up, unholstered their revolvers, and, in open view of two hundred screaming children, shot it dead on the spot.

To the end of his days, John would swear that that was the most white-trash thing he'd ever seen. Which is saying a good deal. He would later excuse unjust accusations from the press, premature dismissals in the workplace, and pandemonious knock-down brawls in the local taverns as intrinsic regional depravities. But he would never grow to accept that afternoon's execution on any grounds. He very quickly abandoned all hope and faith in Baker's educational system. He retreated further into his own netherworld and never lifted a finger in the classroom.

Which is not to say that when the sheep came into the picture, he did not make at least some initial attempt to honor his mother's wishes by bringing his marks up. In all fairness, he did give it a shot. After all, Madame Kaltenbrunner had come through on her end of the deal, and John, always priding himself as a man of his word, was half-heartedly determined to do the same in return. For at least one full month he applied himself to his schoolwork. It took a great deal of effort, but he somehow forced himself to pay attention during classes. He stopped sleeping on his desk tops. He completed his assignments on time. At one point he even brought home a lengthy report he'd passed with flying colors; granted, it was a long-winded dissertation on the history of livestock production in the corn belt – nevertheless, it was something. His mother was pleased. She praised him accordingly. She said she'd always known he had it in him – all he'd needed was a little incentive – and that if he kept up, she might even consider paying off his loan herself. For once, she thought there might actually be some hope for him after all.

But the hope didn't last long. It was right about then that the trouble began. A bad situation would come into being over

26

the next few months, and before it was over John's disdain for the system would be irreconcilably galvanized once and for all.

Statistically speaking, the inordinately high level of alcoholism and child-abuse in Baker is often pawned off on its primarily working-class German heritage. Whatever disputes might be made with the stereotype, it does stand that most of the area's juveniles come from 'troubled' homes, that most of them are of predominantly German stock, that most of them grow up drinking the same domestic liquors their parents consume, upholding identical disciplinary codes, and eventually administering the same beatings they themselves received as children. As a combined result of all these factors, each new generation is often every bit as vicious and combative as its predecessor had ever been. Which doesn't mean every newborn in Baker is imminently doomed to a life of dereliction and villainy, only that, more often than not, he or she is at least bound to go through a period of cold-blooded delinquency along the way, during which time the community on hand suffers everything from crop damage to public arson. Not surprisingly, most of the misconduct tends to taper off the moment each group hits its first drinking year and the vandalism and prowling about give way to hillside hog-roasts and keg-bashes. However, until then it's not uncommon to witness pre-pubescent mobs conducting full-scale raids on isolated patches of the community.

John, for his part, had endured the company of his peers as one of life's unavoidable inconveniences. Throughout his first few years in school, they hadn't really been any more of a distraction than the teachers or the curriculum; they'd just been another part of the backdrop, nothing more. He'd spent most of his time alone anyway, and, that being the case, had rarely been mistreated.

But with the advent of his ranching endeavors that all began to change.

On the average morning, by the time the opening bell sounded at eight o'clock, John had been toiling away in the coops and stables for over two hours already, so that when he stumbled into the classroom in a disheveled mess, stinking of feed and manure and looking every bit the worse for mileage, he became an instant target for ridicule. He often appeared for homeroom sessions with trough hay billowing out of his cuffs. His pant legs were constantly torn and bespattered. The soles of his boots were always caked with two inches of chicken scratch. His appearance, when paired off with that of his peers, openly invited mockery. Which he would have faced sooner or later anyway; as a reclusive, outcast farm boy in Baker he was at high risk of discrimination from the start. But now, looking like *that*, actually substantiating the strikes against him to a tee, he may as well have been an unemployed Jewish wetback surrogate mother. He was in for it.

It started off with little jabs during classes – remarks on his wardrobe, his homeliness, his apparent financial insecurity. The room around him began to hum with muffled whispers. *Lookit the chicken boy!* they'd say. *Dammit if he don't stink!* Quiet laughter, rolling on the desk tops. Then – *Hey, Chicken Boy! Where's yer Pa?* More laughter, followed by a paper clip to the back of the head . . .

It happened every day. They told him he had a face that would stop a clock. They called him a living miscarriage. They posted notes on his back and targeted him with pen caps. They gave him a whole string of degrading nicknames: manure boy, blockhead, swine-herder, nigger-lover. There was no end to their taunting.

After a full day of prolonged excoriation, John would amble home through the cemetery and over the bridge with his hands jammed into his pockets. Once back on the farm, his leghorns, Suffolks, carrier pigeons and even Isabelle seemed like a warm happy family in comparison. He would spend all afternoon tending to them while trying to talk himself down. By dinner time he was usually calm enough to conceal his rage and carry on a semi-unaffected conversation at the table. His mother had no idea of what he was going through at the time. He kept reminding himself of what she'd said, how these were supposed to be the best years of his life.

Some kind of sick joke, he finally concluded.

On the following day it would always get worse. The jeering and laughter would turn into sneers, the insults and jabs to direct threats. The days would get longer and John would grow progressively infuriated. He was soon being pushed around on a regular basis. He was tripped up in the hallway, left sprawled out on the floor. The provocations got uglier every day. He started coming home with black eyes. He was jacked up against his locker and wailed on mercilessly. When he tried fighting back, his attackers would gang up on him, five or six at a time. When he offered no resistance, they would still bear down. They were always bigger than he. Some of them used sticks and rocks. On several occasions they waited for him in groups beneath the power lines on the asphalt macadam. One afternoon they ambushed him in the cemetery and beat him so badly he could barely walk home. On another occasion they left a dead, maggot-infested groundhog from the roadside in his locker. In a few short weeks, he went from being the most low-profile student in school to universal quarry for all so inclined.

None of the faculty was ever any help. No one seemed to care. John would go home at night and stare at the portrait of his father on the wall. All those stories the Ebony Steed operators had told him would come rushing back in one intimidating wave. His father, the dragonslayer, had once singlehandedly dispersed a brawl at the Bloody Bucket by pitching a Pottville construction worker through the front window, then collectedly laying down a wad of bills on the counter top for repairs. Yet now, years later, here was John, the dragonslayer's first born, being fraught upon by every unworthy tavern-rat's offspring in the valley. He was ashamed. He would have to fire off several boxes of shells in the field just to level out.

The situation got nothing but worse over the weeks and months that followed. John would never talk about it afterwards; he would remain steadfastly intent on forgetting the whole thing. But while it was happening there was no avoiding it. It continually headed him off at every pass. Before long he was finding it impossible to make it from one end of the hall to the other without being singled out, run down, and bowled over by several attackers. No one will ever know all the details that went into it, but it must be assumed things got unbearably bad for John along the way. Several of his peers, speaking on condition of anonymity, have since confirmed as much. To this day they reluctantly concede that some of the abuse to which he was subjected was certifiably criminal. There is no record of any disciplinary intervention into these matters on the part of the faculty. Madame Kaltenbrunner did make a call to Roy Mentzer one afternoon after John was publicly beaten with a tire iron in the cafeteria. But Mentzer did nothing about it. Thereafter, John insisted his mother stay out of it. He'd been knocked around, kicked down, was covered with cuts and bruises, and suffering from a concussion for which he never sought treatment. The last thing in the world he felt he needed was the help of a 'concerned parent.' As far as he was concerned, the 'concerned parents' were the root of the problem. He was convinced that the only way to handle the situation was by taking matters into his own hands. For the first time in his life, something beyond the farm had actually gotten the better of him; his peers had succeeded in distracting him from his work. He knew that if things were ever to return to normal, he would now have to resort to drastic measures.

But he didn't know where to begin. He had several ideas. His head was filled with visions of pipe bombs and hatchet racks, Molotov cocktails, sacks full of stable rats, swinging nooses, branding irons, etc. But none of them realistically suited the occasion. None of them really brought him any closer to an acceptable solution. He couldn't very well line up all his peers and gun them down, one by one, he kept reminding himself. It wasn't the worst idea, but getting caught in the act would've defeated the purpose. He knew that much. His approach would have to be a bit more subtle, the calling card left behind every bit his trademark, yet technically inadmissible. At least in a court of law. He would somehow have to pick out one of his peers and use that one as a clear example for the rest to see and understand. But he was still at a loss for a method.

*

Finally, after four long months, an opportunity presented itself, but only by way of an unpardonable trespass on everything he held dear.

One night a group of his peers led by one Brendan Fisher, a notoriously vicious delinquent from north Baker who was to spend most of his life in and out of state penitentiaries, staged a raid on the Kaltenbrunner farm. Fisher was John's absolute nemesis, the son of a suspected hemp farmer of ill-renown, and as good an argument as any that some people are just born bad. Of all of John's tormentors, Fisher stood out as definitive Appalachian sewer-trash. He alone had personally instigated every one of the cemetery beatings. He'd been responsible for the incident in the cafeteria. He'd encouraged others to join in on the attacks. One afternoon he had cornered John in a stairwell, stolen his bag, kicked him down a flight of stairs, and dumped a full trash can over his head. When a passing faculty member had then stumbled on to the scene, Fisher had lied through his teeth and blamed the whole thing on John. John had been heavily chastised for his ineptitude. He was forced to hand-clean the mess, was marched to the office, and beaten by Mentzer with a whiffle bat. As far as John was concerned, Brendan Fisher was an irremediable black mark on the face of the species. There was no place in existence for his kind. He was unworthy of all resources consumed. Just the thought of his presence on the farm was inexcusable.

There were at least six of them on the raid that night. They came out of the woods to the south, sacking everything in their path as they made their way up the hill. They tore apart the coop and drove the catfish into the forest. They left the yard gutted with hoe tracks. They dumped laundry detergent into the well. They ravaged the flower bed and stomped through the garden. They scribbled swirly portraits of ejaculating phalli onto the hood of Madame Kaltenbrunner's wagon with indelible markers. They scattered trash through the yard. They smashed the eggs in the incubator, leaving twenty-two undeveloped fetuses strewn out across the corrugated ridges of the hatching flat. They uprooted the mailbox, cut the porch-swing, shat on the stoop and made off in a snickering pack. The yard was a wreck.

John discovered the mess at 5 a.m. Both farm bitches had been chloroformed to keep from sounding the wake up call. The older of the two was curled up by the woodpile, retching with liver damage from the high dosage. John carried her to the porch, then staggered through the yard in a hateful delirium. He did his best to pull himself together. He forced himself not to think. He tallied the damage as a disinterested tax-assessor in a mudflat bayou. He'd already set to work on the repairs by the time his mother appeared on the porch to inquire about her breakfast. He was vaguely conscious of her screaming something about the pain and humiliation of having to drive across town to the knitting factory with those repulsive heiroglyphs scrawled over the walls of her wagon. He quickly retrieved a can of paint from the barn and gave the vehicle a twenty-minute touch-up. He then sent his mother on her way and got to work.

He missed school that day. He pulled the garden together by noon. There was nothing he could do about the well. Or the hoe tracks. Or the flower garden. But the porch swing and the mailbox were no problem. The incubator itself was intact. The trash in the yard took twenty minutes to clear. The carrier pigeons slowly filed out of the forest and back to the damaged coop throughout the afternoon. The feces on the stoop was the only real problem; that part was *unforgivably* disgusting.

He managed to keep his anger at bay all through the day. Even when his mother returned at dusk, he remained in a quiet void all his own. He was unresponsive throughout the interrogation at dinner. His mother dragged him over the coals, as though he'd been personally responsible for the disaster himself. She demanded a list of names. She demanded all kinds of things. But her demands fell on deaf ears. John wouldn't say a word. He sat over his untouched liver casserole twirling the pepper shaker in his left hand and staring into space. He eventually excused himself from the table and went back to the yard.

He kept working till midnight, securing a temporary pen for the catfish in the corner of the tool shack. Madame Kaltenbrunner could hear him pounding away out there. He was still working at a quarter past when she went to bed. She turned off her lamp and lay awake in the dark, listening to the hammer blows ring through the yard. They didn't stop for another hour.

As members of both the fire department and the Sheriff's league were later quoted as stating, it was *not* due to their own lack of preparation, poor response time, or disorganization that relief efforts were stalled for almost forty minutes after the fire broke out that night. In response to subsequent criticism to that effect, they adamantly maintained the delay had been purely due to the inaccessible location of the blaze itself.

The facts do bear out their testimony. As phone records, official memorandums, and eye witness accounts verify, no sooner had the hillside on the north end of the valley lit up in an orange glow that was clearly visible from every point in town than the first wave of the responding entourage had mobilized and was well underway. The fire was first reported at 3:15 a.m. By 3:25, three fully equipped fire trucks and seven squad cars, followed up by two Methodist mercy-mobiles, five ambulances, the veteran's league chapter van, and somewhere in the neighborhood of twenty unmarked vehicles were witnessed roaring over the 254 overpass, bound for the outlying district commonly known as 'Sparrow's Height.' Five minutes later the procession was temporarily halted in coming upon a large iron gate patrolled by several grown pit bulls and bracketed by a high-voltage electrical fence lining the perimeter of the property-in-destination. After minimal deliberation, Sheriff Dippold gave the order to ram the gate. The trucks went through and spearheaded the rest of the long, winding run up to the estate. On several occasions they were additionally delayed. For one thing, their rigs were too broad for the narrow corridor of overhanging limbs. They were jammed in ditches and pinned down in the foliage repeatedly. The rest of the entourage was sealed off to the rear and couldn't possibly move around them. At another point they were forced to ram a second gate, damaging their radiator grills in the process. All told, the half-mile stretch leading from the highway to the house took over twenty minutes to traverse. Had it been otherwise, it is reasoned, the resulting bust would have been much greater.

As it turned out, the residents of the estate, the infamous Fisher family, were unable to clear even half of the quarter-acre plot of hemp situated to the rear of their burning barn before the entire Baker law enforcement division had arrived in full-force. They were caught red-handed, smeared in hemp oil, charred black, running crooked circles in a furious panic, ripping stalks out of the ground by the fistful and pitching them into the blaze end over end. They were immediately arrested. Seven different family members were thrown into seven different squad cars, while the firemen went to work on what remained of the barn. The whole hill was blanketed in thick black smoke. The air was cut with the sickly-sweet stench of burning sensamalia. The pit bulls were still howling when the press arrived. One of them had been shot in the course of an attack. Over two hundred locals, law-affiliated and otherwise, had responded and were now on hand trying to determine what had happened.

As the *Greene County Herald* was to report, it was the biggest area hemp bust in twenty-four years. When assessed, it was found that what was left of Dick Fisher's crop would've amounted to in excess of eighty marketable pounds of harvested marijuana: an estimated street value, depending on increments of sale, of between $120,000 and $256,000 cash, at going rates. That's to say nothing of what perished with the barn: all the scales, power lamps, phototrons, and no one knows how many drying plants.

And the Fishers' misfortunes didn't end with the discovery of their contraband alone . . .

According to the official report, a small flock of sheep, approximately twenty in number – reputedly maintained only as a front for the family's drug operation – had fled the interior stables of the barn the moment the fire broke out. The flock had then headed down the hill, filed through a gap in the deteriorated wooden fence lining the pasture, charged down the riverbank, over the ledge and into the cold January current of the Patokah.

They'd floated away and hadn't been spotted again until 8 a.m., when seven of their bodies were found lodged in the main drainage valve of a hydroelectric dam located nineteen miles downriver. Repair crews in scuba gear had then been called in from out of town, and all riverboat trafficking temporarily seized. All of which would be added to the Fishers' rising tab.

It was a season-ending disaster for the whole family. What had begun as a restful night's slumber had unexpectedly snowballed into a high-profile nightmare involving the loss of their barn, the destruction of their crop, the drowning of their flock, and front-page snapshots depicting them being led away in chains as suspected, and later proven, drug manufacturers.

In no time at all they would lose everything. They would be castigated and banished from the community for life. The elders would be jailed, the minors interred in juvenile detention centers. Their property would be requisitioned by the state, and no inquiry ever made into their allegations of suspected arson. Baker had been waiting to oust the Fishers for years. The family was despised all through the valley. No one was interested in their alibi. Insist as they would that someone had infiltrated their property, doused the stables with petrol and driven their flock down the hill to the river, their claims just wouldn't hold up in a court of law. Their guilt was *imperative*. They would never be seen in Baker again.

ALTHOUGH JOHN was never questioned, much less officially charged, in connection with the burning of the Fisher farm, just about everyone in town – at least all of his peers, if not the rest of the community – had a pretty good idea of who'd been responsible. Had *any* other family in the area been targeted, he undoubtedly would have been imprisoned for decades. He would have been thrown into a juvenile home, worked over as a threat to society, and expressed to the county jail the moment he came of age. But as it turned out, the exile of the Fishers was deemed too much of a public service to risk introducing any element to the case which might potentially work to the family's slightest advantage. Consequently, the court refused to acknowledge all notions of foul play. In that manner, the whole incident panned out more beautifully than John ever could've expected.

And that's assuming that he was, in fact, responsible at all. To the best of anyone's knowledge, including our own, he never *directly* admitted to his role in the matter. The only time Wilbur ever asked him point blank if he'd done the deed, John had shrugged his shoulders, flashed a quick smile, and moved to change the subject. Which was, of course, his way of saying *yes*. And Wilbur had known better than to ask in the first place. *Of Course* John had done it. It couldn't have been more obvious. He'd taken the two gallon can of petrol perched on the shelf over Bucephalus, footed it through the tobacco fields to the river, followed the Patokah to the south end of the Fisher estate, removed three of the rotting two by four's from the fence lining the pasture, crept up the hill through the crabgrass and ram dung, herded the sheep out of the stables and into the yard, doused everything inside, dropped a match, and driven the flock down the embankment swinging a lit torch in wild circles as he went. We can almost see him there afterwards, crouched in the cornfield laughing to himself as the Fishers ran screaming from the house in their nightshirts, the barn roared out of control, and the sheep bobbed away downstream, a great colony of lashing wool. Of course he'd done it. No one would ever prove it, but he'd done it all the same. There was never any doubt among his peers. Most of the student body at Holborn claimed that after the fact it was written all over him – you could almost smell the petrol wafting up from his shit-kickers – not because he became unusually cocksure or confrontational in the school-yard, but, on the contrary, by virtue of his complete and total indifference to the instantaneous turnaround in treatment there-after accorded him. The overnight cessation of hostilities didn't appear to faze him in the least. The only change his peers could detect at all was a slight alteration in his carriage, a regained composure, a certain poise that had gone undetected before and which seemed to say, yes, that's more like it, *now that we've gotten that cleared up* . . .

It wouldn't be untrue to say that from that day forward John was feared like the plague by *everyone*, including his teachers. He was never again called a swine-herding nigger-lover, or any thing of the kind. He still may have been every bit as loathed and abhorred as before, but, thenceforth, no one dared even look at him the wrong way. It was commonly held that if you're thinking about roughing up the Kaltenbrunner boy, you'd better plan on finishing him off while you're at it; otherwise you, and very possibly your whole family will live to rue the day. It made everyone's skin crawl.

It worked perfectly to John's advantage. Not that he neces-sarily enjoyed the revulsion he appeared to invoke in everyone around him. It just beat out the alternative. Better to have them see him coming and step aside, hush up, shy away, and vacate at the first available opportunity than to be left for dead at the cemetery wall every afternoon. All he'd ever wanted was to be left alone anyway. And that he certainly was. From then on, no one said a word to him. He often fell asleep and snored on his desk top undisturbed for hours at a time. On several occasions he just got up and left the class for no apparent reason. He even started driving Bucephalus to school every morning – across the overpass, through the rail yards, and straight up to the front steps of the building. He appeared to have bought in to some kind of diplomatic immunity. The faculty hated every minute of it, but visions of car bombs and house fires deterred them from taking any disciplinary action. Everyone turned to Roy Mentzer, and Roy Mentzer reportedly turned tail.

By the time John was finally called into the office for a conference, the old man had obviously been racking his brains to no avail for weeks. He was catching hell from the whole faculty on account of John being an all around annihilator of the peace. But for all that, John hadn't *really* done anything – or at least hadn't been caught in the act – and so couldn't be directly chastised on any grounds. Mentzer's dilemma was evident. That morning he was shifty and evasive at his black-top desk as he angled himself off to one side and fidgeted with a pine-cone basset hound while trying to explain, in so many words, that a good deal of concern had been expressed in regards to John's 'disposition.' He stammered on on that note for five terribly strained minutes, at the conclusion of which John, who'd been sitting in a plastic waiting-room chair not saying a word, looked up, shrugged his shoulders and replied with an air of Socratic irony that he honestly didn't understand. He was feeling fine, he said. There must've been a mistake.

The meeting went nowhere. John was excused and went on his way. Mentzer remained behind with his pine cone.

Shortly thereafter, John hit on a system that worked to everyone's advantage. By showing up for his homeroom class exactly five minutes beyond the opening bell every morning, he soon racked up enough tardy slips to land him a permanent seat in room 29, the in-school-suspension quarters. Which suited him brilliantly. It was an unspoken understanding on the part of all concerned that for the common good it should stay that way. The student body would breathe more easily, and John would have every day to himself. It wouldn't exactly work to the benefit of Roy Mentzer's professional reputation, but for better or worse, that was the way it would remain for what was left of

John's academic career. Before it was over he would have more than tripled the school's all time record for hours served in suspension. He would while away hundreds of afternoons staring out the window, watching that decrepit old troll on the cemetery hill digging graves and lining each plot with fresh roses after the funeral processions had filed out of the yard. He would water and cultivate the impoverished cactus on the windowsill while the derelicts all around him snored like tree sloths, faces mashed on the desk tops and tongues lolling out of their mouths. At lunch time they would all file down to the cafeteria together as a pariahcized chain gang. Then back to the $15' \times 17'$ cell for the rest of the afternoon. It would never be the most rewarding way of passing the time; it would still be confinement – there was no way around that. But it *would* win hands down over the standard routine every time. And anyway, boredom wouldn't be much of an issue, as it was right about then when he discovered the vault.

At eleven years of age, John had gotten his daily itinerary down to formula. From bed to trough to kitchen to tractor, weaning to milking to shearing to mutton, hatching to coop to molt to slaughter, everything fell into place right down to the last perfectly timed minute. As was customary, he pulled his second round of feed-and-maintenance detail the moment he arrived home from school. After that he had an hour-and-a-half set aside for miscellaneous details: cleaning, repairing, rigging and contrapting. It was during one of these sessions – as memory would serve, he'd been clearing the rafter beams of scavenger nests – that he came upon the old padlocked door in the corner of the barn's third loft. The door was situated behind a neglected mountain of lawnmowers and cooking grills – which might explain why and how it had somehow, miraculously, escaped his attention up until then. John knew almost every nook of the estate like the back of his hand, and was hard-pressed to believe something so conspicuous had eluded him for that long. He couldn't believe it, but it was also strangely enticing: undiscovered country on the home front . . .

He cleared a small aisle through the trash to the door, then stood looking over the six padlocks and two firmly bolted straight iron bars. There was no way around them. He went down to the main floor to look through his tools. A minute later he came back with a sledgehammer. He spent the next hour breaking down the door. It was unbelievably solid: three layers of reinforced plywood, one sheet of iron plating, and two more bars on the inside. He was half-dead with fatigue by the time the central spread finally splintered and gave way. He discarded the sledgehammer and went to work on two of the bars with a hacksaw. In another twenty minutes he'd bored a hole large enough to crawl through. He climbed in.

The first thing he noticed was a cone of light from where the roof had come in illuminating several thick swirls of dust and outlining a small patch of rotting tile work in the center of the floor. To all sides of the light, numerous indistinguishably oblong shapes draped in old brown sheets were positioned at varying intervals. The objects clustered around the doorway seemed to have been propped up on tables or footstools, indefinable in their shrouded contours. But toward the back of the room, scarcely visible through the dim light, more definite, rectilinear shapes appeared, until, finally, at the far end, situated against the wall, something so enormous it took five or six sheets alone to conceal sat overshadowing everything else. The whole room looked and smelled like a tomb.

He wired a lamp in from the main level and hung it from a rafter beam. He removed all the sheets and placed them in a mildewed pile in the center of the floor. When it was done he straightened up and looked around. He found himself in the midst of a heaping depository of pottery and talismans, flintlock rifles, buckets of arrowheads, bone tools, axe-handles, spade tips, human skulls, wagon wheels, laminated canopies, statuettes, whisky flasks, iron chains, bins of assorted bolts and tools, and along the wall, a fourteen foot femur, a rib cage the size of a gritwagon, a pair of tusks, and the gargantuan skull of what appeared to be an elephant . . .

It blew through him like a high-powered pharmaceutical. He stood there, dumbfounded, half-expecting an orchestra to file into the room behind him and launch into *Tannhauser*. Then the shock pinwheeled into a crippling wave of nausea. He broke out of it. He dropped the lamp cord, crammed back through the hole, staggered out to the loft and lost his footing. He collapsed into a corner. His head hit the wall. He came to rest in a pile of rotting lumber. He remained in that position for some time, trying to pull himself together. He had no idea of what he'd just stumbled on and wasn't entirely certain he'd seen anything at all. He forced the cold sweat to recession, got up, and re-entered the vault. Everything was still there. He didn't know how to believe it. He started rooting through the display for some clue as to its origin. The room was a mess – cobwebs, dirt and fallen rafter beams everywhere. After a minute he found a pile of leather-bound logbooks stacked up on a pinewood desk in the corner. He pried into them.

That's how John discovered the Gwendolyn Hill artifacts, and through them, also and incidentally, how he discovered the only tangible manifestation of his father he would ever know.

He had no way of realizing it at the moment, but this would prove to be the most critical turning point of his life. Up until then he had directed all his undivided attention to the farm; he'd singlehandedly forged into existence a sizeably profitable estate, starting from scratch and ending with a scaled-down regent's manor. His accomplishments as a juvenile, autodidactic rancher/farmer/handyman rank with the paranormal to this very day. They'd required the utilization of every faculty, spare moment, and resource at his disposal, and he'd applied himself as one prompted and motivated by necessity. He'd never thought possible the materialization of any element which might or could conceivably come to stand between him and the farm. The thought had never entered his head. He had known what he wanted right from the beginning; all else had been shrouded furniture, including, and especially, his father. The idea of his own heritage had always been a non-consideration. He had no surviving relatives to speak of: his father's parents had been killed in a boating accident sometime around the outbreak of the Korean war, and his mother had been orphaned at fifteen. He had no grasp on the concept of family ties. He couldn't imagine what it must've been like to have an uncle, a step-sister, three or four cousins, a next of kin. He'd become convinced that none of those things really existed, that they were lies invented by people like Roy Mentzer – people who insisted blood was thicker than water. People who threw cookouts on Sunday afternoons and railed one another in gin-fueled deliriums. People who went to jail together when their barns burned. People who had every reason to hate and destroy one another, but who somehow stuck together anyway. All of it had always seemed a rogue virus to which he himself would never play host. No vestige of his own heritage worth pursuing had ever presented itself to him. Until now.

One of the first things that entered his mind when he finally managed to calm down was the idea that someone out there might be coming up the road to repossess this mess. A whole range of possibilities occurred to him at once: someone in the valley must have been aware of the vault's existence. For legal reasons they probably wouldn't be too keen on the idea of John chancing upon it the way he just had. All it would take would be one phone call. They must have known that. Wouldn't they then be coming to recover everything? Wouldn't they send men, if they hadn't already? . . . If they hadn't already. . . Come to think of it, he seemed to remember some of the Ebony Steed operators snooping around the barn on their supposed 'friendly visits.' Hadn't all their 'friendly visits' in fact been a sham? Hadn't they been prying for something the whole time? Weren't they all in league against him? Weren't they? . . . An emphatic yes! They were! He had to do something about it . . .

With the benefit of hindsight, he would later admit to having overreacted a bit. Even if the Ebony Steed operators *had* made an initial attempt to locate and requisition Ford's archives, they would've long-since given up the search by the time John was eleven. They would've either found what they were looking for right off the bat, or would've come to rest assured that if nothing had turned up in the first few months immediately following Ford's death, then nothing was likely to surface over the course of the next lifetime. They would have gone on their way, trusting the artifacts had been stashed away in the forest somewhere, down on the riverbank, off in a cave, far out of anyone's reach. End of story.

But that's not the way it occurred to John at the time. His first reaction was instinctively protective. Priority one: fortify and conceal.

He spent the rest of that first afternoon piecing the vault back together. He cleared out the fallen lumber and pitched it from the loft. He removed the padlocks, unbolted the bars, and soon had the old door in a pile on the ground floor. He hand-washed the sheets and left them on the line to dry. He repaired the hole in the roof. He patched up the floor. He cleaned out the rats' nests, then swept the floor and ceiling. He hauled up a trapdoor from the second level and reinforced it with chicken wire and tin plating. By early evening the new door was secure. He added three new padlocks and one sliding bar. When the sheets had dried they were thrown back in place. He finished by barricading the entrance with all the mowers and grills on the loft. He then locked the barn and ran up to the house with the logbooks under one arm.

He was going over everything at the main desk in the attic when Madame Kaltenbrunner arrived home from the factory that evening. The room around him was a testament to neglect, cobwebs and dust, busted furniture everywhere . . . The antique recliners at the top of the staircase were draped in crumpled black tarps. Piles of books, old records, gun racks and sewing machines were heaped up beneath the windowpane along the wall. The desk had been left untouched, as though not a day had gone by since his father's last recording. An empty cast-iron safe was mounted to the top of the bookcase, next to which sat the twenty-year-old bottle of Scotch whisky which, Madame Kaltenbrunner had informed him, was to be handed on to him when he came of age. Following it down, each of the four shelves over the mahogany desk top were packed with reference books pertaining to every fathomable aspect of life in the corn belt from time immemorial. Beneath the underside of the bottom shelf, a ceramic vase jammed full of dried ink pens sat next to a copper-plated ashtray and a disconnected telephone.

John had already gone through the two manila envelopes and was now paging through the logbooks. Some of the material had been damaged by rain water. A few of the pages had bled and washed out, and a good deal of the paper had begun to yellow with age. But most of the entries were still perfectly legible. The first envelope had contained a collection of family trees, which were individually color-coded so that each page could be laid out beside its counterpart, one after another, until the finished product resembled a misshapen succession of pyramids stretching from one end of the floor to the other. Included were birth dates, criminal records, denominations, military rankings, and occupational notes on most of Baker's oldest families. With all the German blood in the community, it almost read like a Bavarian telephone directory: Kohls and Heitmullers, Dotterweichs, Offenbachs, etc. The second envelope had contained a pile of scrap papers, blotchy notes and memorandums, none of which had made much sense. He had pushed them to the side and moved on to the seven logbooks. Within minutes he had discovered what his father's official capacity with Ebony Steed had actually been: Ford Kaltenbrunner had been in charge of covering up a trove of archaeological relics from the bowels of Gwendolyn Hill. And these were his scrupulously compiled records pertaining to every last spade tip and arrowhead unearthed over the course of nine years. There were literally thousands of entries. Each article was prefaced with a preliminary rundown including date and circumstance of discovery, depth readings, surrounding mineral deposits, suspected rate of decay, and speculated origin. Each article was then individually detailed and referenced at length. Many of the textbooks lining the shelves had been categorized according to the sequence of the logbooks. The organization was impeccable.

John had to leave the study to prepare dinner halfway through the fourth book. Once downstairs, he could barely keep his hands from trembling over the frying pan. During the meal he managed to feign indifference while posing a few direct questions to his mother: what had been his father's job at the mine? What had he done? How long had he been there? . . . Within minutes he was comfortably convinced Madame Kaltenbrunner knew nothing about the existence of the vault. He relaxed a bit.

They finished dinner with a short discussion about the weather. And that was about the last rational conversation they had for the next three weeks.

The last sound Madame Kaltenbrunner heard before driving off to work the next morning was a chainsaw roaring away in the barn. When she returned at dusk it was still going. She practically had to march John down to the house at gunpoint for force-feeding and a change of attire. He was smeared in motor oil and smelled like a goat. He wolfed down his meal, threw his overalls back on and returned to the barn. The chainsaw resumed and didn't let up till midnight.

It started again at 5 a.m. Madame Kaltenbrunner tried to summon him from the barn, but he'd locked himself in and couldn't hear a word she said over the roar of the motor. She left, feeling nervous and apprehensive. When she returned, once again just before dinner, John and Bucephalus were gone. She ate cold leftovers in the parlor. John returned after dark trailing behind a wagon load of lumber and odd looking equipment. He blew right by her on the way to the basement, not even stopping to say hello. He looked worse than he had the day before. She could hear him cursing and throwing objects around down in the cellar. When he emerged, he was carrying an axe. He went back out to the barn.

By the next night she noticed the barn was shaping up in leaps and bounds, with every six or seven hour interval bringing it one step closer to resembling a fortress. John wouldn't even look at her. There were long rips in his pant legs. His arms were cut and burned. He was swearing incessantly, and Madame Kaltenbrunner could've sworn she'd seen a cigarette dangling out of his mouth at one point. She listened to him stomp back and forth in his room all night, mumbling something about a blow torch.

On the fourth evening, when she went to retrieve him from the barn, she unintentionally set off a newly installed alarm system. The moment she stepped across an unmarked line on the gravel drive, a howling siren and a rack of multi-colored floodlights bore down on her in a panoramic assault. She cowered. John came charging out of the barn swinging a crowbar and looking unspeakably disgusted. She barely recognized him where he stood. He screamed at her to mind her own business and to get out. She ran back to the house in terror. She locked herself in her room for the rest of the night.

Madame Kaltenbrunner was convinced that was it: John was finally cracking up. She'd heard about this kind of thing before – the Midwest being the number one breeding ground for mass murderers and serial killers in the country. And her son had become one of them. But more than that, the whole farm seemed to be coming alive around her, as though it were operating as a living, breathing organism all on its own. Every evening she came over the hill and approached the house at a slow crawl. At the first turn the catfish, lined up on the phallus to the side of the drive, would take flight and follow her all the way in. She could see them to either side of the wagon, careening back and forth like a regimental escort service. Once she was parked, they would veer off and return to the other end of the field to await further disturbances. As she stepped out of her wagon four or five of the cocks would herald her arrival. The rest of the flock would dart to the fence and peer out at her. The racket in the barn would let up only long enough for John's head to poke cautiously out from the main door and look her over. Then he would disappear and the pounding would resume. Up the hill, Isabelle and the bitches would be working side by side, rounding up the Suffolks and keeping them in check. The bees in the hive would appear at the forest's edge as a self-contained cloud. The cleaned remains of one or two leghorns would be chilling in ice water on the porch, as though accepting their appointed slot on the food chain without complaint. Even Bucephalus, angled in the drive, seemed coiled to strike. Madame Kaltenbrunner was a stranger in her own home.

John continued on in the barn. He sawed out the ladder leading to the loft and installed a sliding rack ladder system which was only accessible by code. All deteriorated sideboards were replaced. The main hatch leading to the stable was permanently sealed. The loft was fire-proofed. The ceiling was insulated with fiberglass mats. The vault door was fortified with an array of combination locks. All windows were boarded up. The main door was barred. The exterior was given a fresh coat of paint. The whole building was exterminated for termites. Every corner, perchboard and windowpane was rigged to a tee.

On the seventh morning a squad car came up the road on behalf of the school board. John had exceeded the standard allotment of unexcused absences. Two deputies had orders either to acquire a legitimate doctor's excuse, personally escort him to school, or arrest Madame Kaltenbrunner as an inattentive guardian. John scoffed with indignation. He threw his tools to the side and locked up the barn. He climbed into the squad car, covered in two days of sawdust, housepaint and manure. When he arrived at the school, Roy Mentzer was there to turn him right back around for breach of dress code. John threw up his hands. He stomped back over the bridge, up through the woods and into the house. He pried into the downstairs closet for something to throw over his back. These were the circumstances under which he first pulled on his father's leather mining coat, the one which would become his trademark in time – the one garment solely responsible for the 'John as fascist' post-crisis campfire creation theory. With this broad-shouldered, low-riding munitions coat in place, it is true that his overall appearance took a turn for the purge. In one movement an instantaneous transformation occurred: his whole aura, his gangling stride, the coarse ragweed hair hanging over his forehead in a tangled mop of knots, the way his eyes rolled back and forth in those cavernous, unibrowed sockets, his stoop-shouldered gait, everything – his entire carriage, as a diminutive echo of Ford Kaltenbrunner – came flying out of the woodwork. His father's coat would rarely leave his back from that day forward. The 'corn-crib fascist', they would call him. The Lord of the Barnyard.

Fortunately, most of the repairs on the barn were completed before further truancy was eliminated as an option. There were a few more minor adjustments to be made, but for the most part, he could rest-assured any prowling intruder would have to leave the premises empty-handed, or, if persistent enough, be hauled away in a meat wagon. The barn was a live wire. No one would come within sniffing distance without risking gratuitous bodily harm.

The only other thing that remained was the attic, and that took less than a day to pull together – lime water and wet-rag treatment, followed by sweeping and mopping. More than half of the trash was cleared out in ten minutes. The bottle of scotch was removed from the shelf and placed in the downstairs cupboard for safe keeping. The logbooks went into the safe. The combination code went into a hole in the wall. From start to finish it took one afternoon. The whole renovation had been completed by the first of the summer.

John never intended to share the vault's existence with anyone. The artifacts and logbooks were *his*, and that was the way it was going to stay. They were worthy of preservation in and of themselves, but also, for John, who'd never heard his own father's voice, had never known anything concrete or dependable about his old man at all, they were the only substantial remnants of Ford Kaltenbrunner in existence – the last vestiges of his earthly endeavors. They would become the divining rods in an otherwise ambiguous martyrdom. Without them, no more than two decades would've been required to bury all traces of his existence; his living memory, as the memories of countless generations before him, would've dissipated into nothing. He would have been lumped together with the rest of the forgotten. John couldn't bear that thought. Through the artifacts, he would somehow become convinced his father had been a great man, and thereby look upon himself as the sole trustee and inheritor of an empire.

As for similarities between the two of them, from what we've been able to ascertain, Ford and John, father and son, shared as many traits in common as points in contrast. Both were uncannily driven by nature. Both could be seen as tactical geniuses at utilizing minimal resources. Their scrutinizing gazes were all but a blueprint of one another. Their powers of observation undoubtedly stemmed from the same source. And they physically resembled one another as well, though John was much more slight of build, certainly not the Titan incarnate. But Ford ended and John began in the public relations department; that is to say, in terms of interacting with other living beings, they were, for all practical purposes, polar opposites. There was Ford the exhibitionist, John the introvert. Ford the conciliator, John the intolerant. Ford the crowd-pleaser, John the misanthrope, etc., none of which John may have actually picked up through his discovery of the vault alone. For all we know, the artifacts may not have brought him any closer to his father's real character than before. As we understand it, no real opinions were expressed in any of the logbooks. In terms of revelation, they weren't on par with a lost diary, for example, or a pile of manuscripts, a stack of film reels, a journal. In the time Wilbur knew him, John only made occasional vague references to his father as an individual. He mentioned the logbooks, he discussed the artifacts openly, but only up to a point. He was wary of divulging too many specifics. His father's memory seemed to be something he guarded with a good deal of suspicion, mistrust and even hostility. It was the same with the logbooks, which, despite their lack of confessional overtones, appeared to provide him with some genuine, authentic key to his father's character, one he'd been deprived of all his life.

John rarely talked about the rest of the study, but two factors in particular lead us to believe he must've spent a considerable amount of time chewing through several, if not all of the textbooks lining the shelves. For one thing, many of his peers and two faculty members from Holborn have attested that for the next four years, as he remained holed up in the suspension room, he was never once seen without a book in his hand. He reportedly kept a small library in a blue duffel bag at his feet and pulled from the stack at random, all day long, day in and day out. He never slept at his desk. He stopped only for lunch, to water his cactus, and to fill out any test forms that were sent up from his teachers, most of whom he'd never seen. He failed just about every exam he ever took. He didn't even look at the questions,

he just circled multiple choice answers at random, pushed everything to the side, and went back to whatever he'd been
researching. He was initially held back for two grades, then the
faculty began passing him, fearing he might actually acquire
some initiative one day, actually make an attempt to reintegrate.
If he did so, it was reasoned, the further along on the ladder he
was, the less the faculty would have to deal with him in the long
run. The second factor has to do with his intellect. Although
none of us ever saw John read more than a newspaper, and
though he couldn't possibly have learned much of anything in
school, he somehow, if and when he talked at all, had: 1) an
extensive vocabulary, at least for this area, 2) a formidable understanding of particular societal functions, the comprehension of
which would require at least minimal preliminary groundwork,
and 3) a familiarity with local affairs, historical and contemporary, that so far transcended common knowledge it often left
many of us thumbing through encyclopedias and almanacs to
verify.

In any case, he never talked about it much, just as he refrained
from comment on the majority of the first four years immediately following his discovery and fortification of the vault.
During that time, there were plenty of unrelated livestock stories
– the time Isabelle attacked the mail carrier, the time the vultures
descended on the coop, the time a muskrat tripped up the barn's
alarm and brought John racing out of the house in his underwear
with a shotgun in hand at 4 a.m. – lots of stories, but most of
them have no place here. After all, these were the good years –
Madame Kaltenbrunner's 'best years' – and so, call for very little
comment. Throughout everything, all of John's interests
remained the same. His plans were still intact: he would quit
school on his sixteenth birthday and expand operations on the
homestead to full force. In the meantime, the existing livestock
count would have to be held down to a manageable capacity, for
practical reasons. The only thing that had really changed was the
introduction of Ford Kaltenbrunner and the Gwendolyn Hill
artifacts into his life, and by virtue of the same, a realignment of
his previously indivisible priorities.

THE TROUBLE BEGAN with the death of Isabelle. As the overview runs, that was clearly the point at which everything started to fall apart. Looking back on it now, it's almost as though, with the unexpected passing on of one brittle-hoofed old Suffolk hag, the Kaltenbrunner estate suddenly had the trapdoor pulled out from under it. It was a strange set of circumstances. Almost like a curse, as though Isabelle herself had been the only mortar in the homestead's foundation. She wasn't gone for more than a day before everything started going over like a row of Douglas Firs on a strip-mining campaign.

There's really no subtle way of documenting the following events. As it is, we don't have proper insight into most of what happened to do the final outcome any more justice, or damage, than the press already has. Venturing upon conjecture would only erode the story's already dubious standing in the community eye. All we can plausibly hope for is to bring to light a few basic facts which have either been withheld from the public, or were never ascertained by any party other than our own to begin with. By so doing, by at least laying the groundwork with all available factual and first-hand testimony, some conceivable explanation for the much-talked about – by now infamous – holdout that followed might be made available to anyone wishing to inquire beyond the popularized misconception that John was just a psychotic farmhand with a lifelong penchant for annihilating everything he laid hands on. It's been said by the select few who've since been clued in on the full story that, all things considered, given the force, magnitude and rapidity of the misfortunes that descended on his world that autumn, it was highly remarkable he survived at all. Burt Clayton has claimed he personally would've hauled down the rifle from the rack on the wall after the first week; with everything moving so quickly, with it having been literally one thing after another – not on a daily, but on an hourly, sometimes a *momentary* basis – the way it was, even (and especially) a sharp-witted individual like John could've very easily been sucked up in the overwhelming incomprehensibility of a single sixteen hour stretch. From morning to night the hours would begin to drift apart as individual installments in an increasingly muddled overall picture. The noonday hours would seem distant and irretrievable, free-floating episodes and voyeuristic discharge, when recalled at dusk, as though a long sleep, an intercontinental voyage had separated the two: like waking up in Tulsa and lying down in Bangkok with a great blur of country roads, taxis, airports, customs officials, time zones, jetlag, culture shock and language barriers in between. Thirty different worlds in the course of a day – one day after another – with the events of the previous week seeming farther off still, and everything before that falling right out of existence altogether.

Isabelle's death itself was hardly unlikely; *surprising* maybe, even a bit unfathomable for some, as her constitution had continually left members of the Pullman Valley shearing circuit at a complete loss. For as long as anyone could remember, she'd been *the* focal centerpiece of the estate. Elias Kauerbach had been calling her old before Ford Kaltenbrunner first inherited her with the farm twenty-one years earlier. Her age had by now surpassed estimation. She must have been one hundred and seventy-some-odd years old in human terms, and for all but the last three or four days of that time she kicked and lashed like a mountain ram.

Which isn't to say she hadn't aged – as that goes, playing host to the demonseed *had* exacted its toll on her frame. Her fleece had grown coarse and brittle, only sprouting up in random patches over the length of her back. It was economically worthless. Had she been led to the block, the resulting mutton would have been tainted beyond palatability and probably would have left any consumer in the throes of an explosive fit of vomiting and flatulence.

Isabelle's body had endured on command of will alone: *You cannot kill that which refuses to die.*

Which also never lasts.

It was a Sunday afternoon in late August. John was fifteen. He'd just finished a round in the layer house and was making his way up the hill to disperse the group of Suffolks congregated in the doorway of Isabelle's shack. The flock scattered as he approached, leaving only the bitches poking their heads inward. Inside, Isabelle was keeled over on one side ramming her head in agitation at a cloud of encircling nose flies. The movement of her skull, in contrast with the bivouacked dead weight of her grotesque body, made for the overall appearance of a cornered company of foot soldiers in the last doomed stages of an impending siege. As Madame Kaltenbrunner and a few of the more conniving associates with whom she would soon be in acquaintance might have soliloquized: it looked as though the Lord Jehovah was finally on his way to take Miss Isabelle across the River Jordan. But one look at Isabelle herself told John the River Jordan wasn't big enough. An object in motion tends to stay in motion, and this was one categorical God damn it she was not about to take lying down.

The prognosis was evident. Isabelle had been dipped and vaccinated for every liver-fluke and sheep-scab in existence. She wasn't falling prey to internal parasites. She was just dying. Old age. Her machine had finally outrun itself. There was nothing to be done.

Over the next three days, John spent several hours with his back to the wall in her shack. He picked ticks from her neck and fed her sweetcorn from the pantry. She would ram her head against the foundation pipe when particularly bad waves came over. John would then be given to understand that he was being dismissed. He would leave her there in the corner and go to the house for a while. On returning he would find her one more step along.

On the final day, she made a last attempt at getting up. John would never forget the way she rocked on her haunches, straining to one side and lurching to the other, trying to work up

53

enough momentum to get one hoof to the floor. She got about halfway up. Then she wobbled and pitched back over into her bed with a crash. A look of absolute contempt spread over her face.

For her efforts, he fed her a pound of chocolate that night. He knew she would probably be gone before it had a chance to wreak havoc on her digestive system. She chomped and slobbered without shame. And in the morning she was dead.

He dug a hole at the top of the hill. He dragged her body by the stiff hindquarters through the sudan grass and sweet clover, gutting the earth along the way, leaving a thirty yard toboggan ditch of torn wool and dirt. He threw her down in the hole. The bitches ran circles around him as he refilled it.

Less than twenty-four hours later the radio came alive with an emergency storm warning. John was sitting in the attic when the sky outside went black. The wind picked up from out of nowhere. Madame Kaltenbrunner screamed in the kitchen. He ran down to see what was wrong. There was a tornado watch in effect all across Pullman Valley, she said. A twister had been spotted in Pottville and was reportedly gaining momentum as it pushed through the river gap, heading straight toward Baker. A crew of forecasters were transmitting live pursuit-coverage from the cockpit of a meteorological van moving along 254. John listened to the commentary for a minute. Then the radio went dead. The lights went out. The house started to shake. He thought of the vault. He ran out to the yard. The wind almost threw him over. The forest's edge was lined with bowing oaks. Dirt and scraps were flying by to every side. He tried to push his way toward the barn. He was clipped by a fence post in midflight. He went down. Through the noise he could hear his mother yelling to him from the front porch. He looked around. Her silhouette was framed in the doorway. Her dress was blown up all around her. The door behind her was flapping on its hinges. Her voice was lost. He got back up and continued toward the barn. Before he was halfway there, the sky went dead black. The roar from over the hill doubled in pitch.

Down on the riverbank the twister appeared. It had torn a

path through the woods from the north, touching down at intervals as it went. When it had hit the Patokah, instead of blowing across the water, it had clung to the bank and followed it west, straight toward the farm. John only laid eyes on it for a second. It came around the bend gutting up the ground, destroying everything in its path. Tree limbs were being torn from their trunks and thrown over the length of the field. The yard came alive with flying objects. He dove to the ground. A picnic table sailed by. The porch swing soared a hundred yards into the woods. Several leghorns were lifted into the sky. The barn's frame rocked on its foundation. Hinges blew off like notebook paper. A limb from the main oak smashed into the house. Power lines flapped loose. John remained sprawled out on the ground with his hands behind his head and every muscle tied into a tense, anticipatory knot. Every object around him was lifted from its place and incorporated into the pounding hailstorm of wicker baskets, yard ornaments, dirt, limbs and vines, all sailing by in a deafening roar.

When it was over the yard fell silent. The twister died out down river. A film of dirt began to settle over the field. Every living creature on the estate quietly poked its head out from whatever hole it had crawled into. John, still face down in the gravel, checked himself over for damage. As far as he could tell he was all right. He got to his feet. He made a panning sweep of the wreckage. The yard was totaled. He crawled through the scattered remains of the wood pile, made his way under a torn drainpipe hanging by a thread from the roof trim. He climbed through the doorless archway. He walked down the hall toward the kitchen. He found his mother curled up in a fetal knot beneath the coffee table. She was frozen stiff with terror. He dragged her out from under the table. She crawled back into place, whimpering. The windows above her had blown in. There was shattered glass over the floors and counter tops. The dishes had been swept from the rack. Large clumps of mud from the window-side tomato garden had been hurled through the open frame and caked along the opposite wall. Everything had been ripped to pieces.

It wasn't any better outside. Most importantly, the barn was still intact; but just about everything else had been tossed to the dogs. What was left of the bee farm was scattered for two miles into the woods. The oak limb that had smashed into the house was lodged firmly into a mangled windowpane on the second story. The power lines along the ground were dead. The rear wall of the layer house had been completely ripped apart. The leghorns were wandering aimless through the fields – one of them would later be found in the chimney chute, lodged in the ventilation duct with a broken neck. The incubator shack had collapsed. All the equipment inside had been destroyed. Isabelle's shed was blown all over the hillside. The phallus had been snapped in two. The garden and flowerbed were uprooted. The Suffolks were huddled in a mud-stained pack by the overturned grain shed. The coop was leveled. The catfish were nowhere to be found. The list went on. The Kaltenbrunner farm had been all but annihilated. In the course of less than a minute, a full decade's worth of labor had been turned inside out, leaving only a razed pit of mud and trash.

John didn't know where to begin. He sat down on a log and tried to shake the dirt from his hair. Then he just stared into space for a while. His final year at Holborn was to begin in five days. He was four months away from his birthday, one hundred and fifteen days to the finish line. The paperwork for his holiday flock had already been filed, the increase in stock and production mapped out to the last detail . . . But now, with this mess . . . It would take months just to put everything back together, and another year to fix and replace the damaged machinery. And then there was the question of credit. A loan would need to be taken out. He wasn't insured. Nothing on the farm really was.

Holborn High's fall term opened in mid-week. On Thursday afternoon, John pulled Bucephalus into the drive after school to find his mother's wagon back from the factory several hours early. He cut the engine and went inside to see what was happening. Madame Kaltenbrunner was marooned on the couch with a wet rag over her pale, swollen face. She complained of headaches and dizzy spells. She'd been having random blackouts for about a week now, she said. She was weak and having trouble keeping food down. That afternoon she'd lost consciousness at her machine and had awakened to find a crew of stitch-hands standing over her, their faces blurred and unrecognizable at the end of a long dark tunnel. A yellow and green cauliflower bruise had spread out over her backside at the point of impact. She was in low spirits. John draped a blanket over the shattered window to the right of the couch to block the draft. He turned on the radio and heated a cup of milk, then sat on a footstool watching her drink it. She was asleep in twenty minutes. He crept out of the room and went back to work in the yard.

An hour later he heard an unexpected cry from the house. He dropped everything and ran inside. He found Madame Kaltenbrunner on the floor, retching uncontrollably and pulling herself along the rug toward the kitchen. She'd broken out in a heavy sweat. She was babbling nonsense. He picked her up and carried her to the couch. He straightened up the room, then sat down and looked her over. Her chest was heaving. She couldn't seem to breathe. This time he mixed her a gin sour and remained in the room after she'd fallen asleep. He placed a tin pan at her side. He waited. She slept straight through the night, moaning from time to time with her eyes darting back and forth beneath the clotted lids. At 3 a.m. a rifle shot cracked out through the woods to the north, waking John with a start. Madame Kaltenbrunner didn't move. Her breathing was shallow and erratic. He walked around the room thinking everything over. He couldn't settle down. His mind wouldn't stop. There were poachers in the woods. He sat on the porch smoking cheap domestic cigarettes and watching the 2,800hp diesel locomotives on the opposite riverbank pulling long lines of freight cars to the west. At dawn two groups of Canadian geese pushed by overhead, angling their Roman numeral fives to the south toward the piping chimney stacks of industrial Baker. He was still wide awake.

When his mother hadn't moved by noon, he broke down and called for a doctor. A German M.D. with a nickel-rimmed monocle and a bad limp showed up after an hour. The M.D. took his black medical bag into the living room and gave Madame Kaltenbrunner a five minute exam. *Nervous breakdown*, he concluded. Nothing serious. 75 dollars please. John threw him out of the house without offering up so much as a dime. He could go to the filling station for advice like that, he screamed. The M.D. drove away empty-handed.

John paced the room for a while. Then he called for a second M.D. This one was so short-sighted it took him three hours to find the farm. When he finally did arrive, he'd been to every estate on the north end of the valley in search of the correct address. John was seething with impatience. This time his mother's diagnosis was simply 'fatigue.' 135 dollars. It was everything John could do to keep from fetching the Winchester. He told the M.D. not to insult his intelligence and to get the hell out. He quickly realized he could expect nothing from these mail-order homeopaths. He may as well have thrown his mother into the Wapiti sweat hut to bleed out her carnalities. It was unbelievable.

Madame Kaltenbrunner was in and out of consciousness for another night. When she did come to, it was only to mumble some half-delirious proclamation concerning her black Singer with the gold-leaf trim. John kept her down and full of alcohol. She wouldn't eat anything. As she slept, he carefully looked her over in hopes of determining what was going on with her system. Some kind of change was coming over her – her physical appearance had altered somehow, though the alteration was creeping in from around the edges and was not immediately discernible. He couldn't put his finger on it. Her face seemed to have softened into a gelatinous paste. Her skin was hanging loose from the bone, spread out from her frame and flattened into the sofa cushions. She looked heavier than what he remembered, but he couldn't quite tell. Nothing was visibly discernible at first.

But when he woke up the next morning it was clear. Madame Kaltenbrunner's condition had unmistakably taken a turn for the worse over the course of a few short hours. It was as though she'd been quietly gestating into a rutabaga all night. It was nauseating. It was time for the emergency room.

The telephone lines were down again, as they had been on and off since the twister came through. There was no telling when they'd be repaired. The situation couldn't wait. He cleaned out the back of his mother's wagon and escorted her, with one arm thrown over his shoulder and the bulk of her weight leaned against him, down the stairs and into the yard. The wagon had a stick shift. He had never driven it. He'd never driven a real car in his life. He was not yet legally of age. He pondered the gears while laying his mother out in the back seat. He threw a blanket over her. He thought of an account his father had kept of a wood cutter who'd been trapped under a fallen tree and had sawed off his own pinned leg at mid-thigh, crawled up a four hundred yard hill to his truck – a stick shift – and driven himself to the nearest hospital, thirty-two miles away. If that wood cutter could do it with one leg in a duffel bag and every nerve ending in his body in a world of indescribable agony, then so could he, he told himself. He fidgeted with the ignition. His mother mumbled in the back seat.

He stalled out twice on the gravel road leading to the highway. The right front tire got caught up in a ditch at one point, causing the whole vehicle to lurch and jam. He angled the wagon back on to the drive and continued on. Once on to the highway, he followed a trailer full of swine across the overpass into Baker. The trailer veered into a docking bay halfway through town, leaving John unescorted. He made it through the next two red lights without any problem. Everything was going fine. It was just like driving Bucephalus, only a bit faster. He made it past the 11th St. intersection and was just about to pull into the final stretch leading to the hospital when the trolls appeared.

The old jacked-up Studebaker with a tangled mess of cane poles and tin buckets protruding from its open trunk launched out of the gravel drive from the Baker Bait Shack without any warning. John heard the oncoming driver scream over a back seat full of children just before the two vehicles collided. The thunderclap boomed out for miles. John's head snapped forward on impact. His face went through the windshield. Madame Kaltenbrunner was pitched into the back of his seat and lodged at an angle on the floor. He felt a hot rush spread out over his face, tasted the unmistakable salt of his own blood. Beyond the spiderwebbed pattern on the windshield, a blanket of thick black diesel smoke was piping out of the trolls' battered engine block. Through the smoke he could hear five or six of them crawling out of their wagon and fighting amongst themselves. He kicked open his door. He crawled out and went to the aid of his mother in the back seat. All her parts were still intact. He pried her from the floor and carefully tucked her back into place. One of the younger trolls loomed up behind him as he did so. John turned around, his face and shirt soaked with blood. The troll took a step back, hesitated, then started spewing venom.

The rest of them flew into a fit. The smaller ones shrieked and ran circles around the car. The father spat and cursed with his lower lip flapping loose, a pair of shopworn electrical goggles knotted into his greasy black hair, and his corpulent mayonnaise and catfish gut roped off at mid-bulge by a cracked vinyl belt. He looked like a genitally infected tree monkey in the throes of a masturbatory frenzy. One of the youngest in the bunch retrieved a fish net from the trunk and jabbed it threateningly toward John. The rest just kept screaming and wiping the dirt from their faces. John couldn't understand a single word they said. He gave up on all hopes of communicating with them. He leaned back and pressed a rag to his gushing forehead. The aboriginal theatrics continued all around him.

To either side of the road packs of locals were gathering, pressed against their windows and milling around on the sidewalk. The doorway of the 7–11 was filled with older women. The men from the hardware shop were talking amongst themselves, gesturing up and down the road. The cashier from the Bait Shack was the only one to approach. Her fingers were soiled from churning up nightcrawlers. John asked if she'd seen anything. She hadn't. He was *doomed*.

The police arrived. The trolls gathered around the two deputies, flailing their arms in John's direction. One of the deputies came over to question him. John responded that he would give a full report as soon as he could, but first he needed an ambulance for his mother. The deputy ignored his request and demanded a driver's license and registration. He had neither – all he wanted was an ambulance. The deputy turned him around and patted him down. The crowd went wild. The group at the 7–11 was growing by the minute, their faces lined up in a row, hands gesticulating, jaws flapping. The second deputy pried into the wagon to remove Madame Kaltenbrunner. She thrashed wildly. He persisted. She caught him across the face with the heel of her shoe. He staggered backwards, clutching his mustached lip. He went for his gun. She started screaming and pounding on the seat. Her cries went up and carried through the street like an air horn. The general commotion ceased. The chatter from the crowd fell off. Even the trolls piped down. It was suddenly very quiet. There was just that bloodcurdling scream emanating from the backseat. Everyone looked at John. Once again, he told the deputy he needed an ambulance.

Five minutes later the medics arrived. John had been hand-cuffed and thrown into the back of a cruiser. Outside in the road, several operators from the junkyard were hooking up Madame Kaltenbrunner's wagon for towing. The air stunk of overheated engines and hot rubber. Three medics were bickering back and forth with the deputies beneath a traffic sign. At the conclusion of their dispute, John was transferred to the ambulance. He watched the trolls disappear from the rear window as he was driven to the hospital. He sat directly over his mother for the duration of the ride – monitoring her breathing, watching her face, and wondering, above all, how he'd gotten them into this situation.

When the vehicle arrived at the incoming gate Madame Kaltenbrunner was strapped on to a blue roller cart and wheeled off toward the emergency room. John was escorted, still in hand-cuffs, to the lobby.

The waiting room was heavy with the wafting odor of cleaning solvents and disinfectants – that nasty, all too familiar stench of ammonia and toilet cleansers that burns its way through the nasal tracts to the brain and reduces the passage of time to a dyspeptic crawl. John always maintained it was that smell more than anything that made one hour in the Baker General equal to six in the real world.

He was seated on a rack chair near the gift-shop window with a display of plastic orchids staring him in the face. The upper half of his body was soaked with thick black globs of coagulated blood. The room around him was filled with unsuspecting relatives and acquaintances of interned patients. They regarded him nervously and asked the deputy standing guard why he hadn't been tended to. The deputy laughed and made a few jokes. John couldn't tell exactly what was said, but he distinctly overheard one jab about drunk driving and having ruined several lives. The deputy then told everyone not to worry, *the criminal minded got no special treatment in Baker*. Which quickly dispelled all sympathy for John's condition. Whatever it was that had been said, the crowd had apparently bought it hook, line and sinker, as within minutes they were all glaring in his direction from every corner of the room. The animosity was overwhelming. He looked around and tried to grasp the situation, but he just couldn't bring himself to accept the testimony of his own senses. This couldn't really have been happening, they hadn't actually *believed* that line about drunk driving. Had they? He looked around again. Everyone was still staring. It was incredible. He did his best to appear unaffected, but he had trouble concealing his utter astonishment.

One family in the far corner was particularly bad. From what he gathered, one of their brothers or sons or uncles had had a bike wreck earlier in the day and was now being treated for a concussion. They'd been sitting there for hours, fidgeting with their soda cans and poking at one another. They were bored out of their minds. John was the best thing that had happened to them all day. The mother wasn't so bad – she didn't really seem to care about anything. She just sat there chain-smoking Virginia Slims and looking grey as old liver. But the father and the two boys were irascible. The father started by delivering mock-sermons on the hazards and consequences of drinking old paint thinner from the cellar. *Just look what it did to that bastard*, he would say, motioning to John. They would all laugh. The older boy then got stuck on the phrase of the day, which he repeated over and over, *ad nauseam*: *It's one nation under God, one nation under God, one nation under God* – whatever that was supposed to mean. All three of them continued, coming up with some of the most idiotic, convalescent wisecracks John had ever heard in his life. They couldn't get up to go to the water fountain without making some remark on the stillborn in the corner. The deputy on guard eventually fell into the rapport as well. Pretty soon the whole room was in on it.

It continued like that for over an hour, getting worse as it went. At some point a cleaning lady waddled out of the hallway and scolded John for soiling the chair with all that blood. Her remark sent ripples of satisfied laughter all through the room. Everyone got a kick out of it. It served him right, they said. *Filthy degenerate – probably from Pottville. A Pottville degenerate, even worse: the worst strain of filth in existence. No doubt unemployed. Probably on welfare too... Looks like a river rat. Disgusting...* They laid into him. The cleaning lady picked up on all the excitement and assumed center stage. She became a third-rate show girl, the waiting room a vaudevillian drunk pit. They ordered him to head back to the outhouse. They called him a freak. They implored the deputy to give him a slap, knock him around a bit, *club him...* They kept going, trying to outdo one another. The receptionist joined in. Then a passing Methodist crone, the florist, another maid: *even the janitorial staff was getting corrupt...* John still couldn't believe what he was seeing. The cleaning maid was twirling around with a mop in her fist. Whole families were doubled over and flushing with laughter. The deputy stood gazing smugly over the room and its yakking occupants, their dentures chattering, toupees shifting, pacemakers straining, intestines churning. It was unbounded ridicule – as John coined it, 'anthropoid malfunction.' He started yelling back at them, saying they didn't understand. No one listened to him. They threw plastic cups and made faces. The deputy told him to shut up.

When the cleaning maid finally jammed her mop in his face, he could take it no more. He kicked her in the crotch. She went down. The lobby exploded. Before she even hit the floor the rest of the room was on top of John. He fell to one side and pulled the cuffs up over his face. Someone kicked him in the ribs. The deputy's nightstick came down on his back. The cut on his forehead reopened. Feet, fists, and furniture slammed into him from every side. He tried to crawl under the chair. They got a hold of his feet and dragged him back to the center of the floor. They beat the hell out of him. He lashed on the carpet. Someone spat on him and told the deputy to kill him. A public hanging was in order, they said – go ahead and finish him off. *No jury would convict.*

He was eventually peeled from the floor and pitched out the door. He was ushered to a cruiser with the mob at his heels. He was thrown into the back seat and expressed to the Sheriff's department. The deputy on guard didn't let up for one minute the whole way through town. He rattled off a list of charges that would be brought against John, the latest of which included assault and battery. The mug shots later obtained from police files depict John with a deer-in-the-headlights look plastered over his ravaged face, his collar and neckline a blood-sopped mess, a bulging lavender shiner on his left cheek. The dark cell they finally threw him into felt like a sanctuary in contrast with the world outside, the twelve-year-old mute crop thief within, an angel. He would have just as soon stayed there for the next week; with any luck, he hoped, the charges would all go through and he would have no choice.

But that's not what happened. As it went, he was released after nine hours. Sheriff Dippold announced that they couldn't very well starve him to death, but that he wasn't worth his weight in plumbing expenses. He was thrown out of the station in the middle of the night. The crop thief was left behind to rot. It was 3 a.m., September 7.

He walked up 254 in the dark, stiff and shivering. The highway was empty at that hour. The few passing freight runners must have done Hail Marys all the way down the road at the sight of him. He hadn't been fed a single crust of bread in the holding cell. He was still in his bloodstained clothing. He got home to discover that a pack of wild dogs had come out of the woods and made off with six leghorns. Blood and feathers were scattered all through the yard, testament to a prolonged struggle. Both farm bitches were heavy with litters and hadn't been able to hold down the perimeter in his absence. Several raccoons had cleaned out the community nest and were now sacking the kitchen. Bags of half-devoured bread and corn meal were splayed out through the hall. His mother wasn't home. The power was out. The phone was still down. He half-expected the frame of the house to come down on him directly. He would have let it.

The rest is pretty simple. He rummaged through the blackened kitchen, found the only bottle of liquor in the house, set up a candle on the living-room table, and proceeded to knock himself out with drink as quickly as he could. It took about twenty minutes. All he remembered from that time was staring vacantly at a photo of his father on the table. Otherwise, he just sat there taking long sickening hits on the bottle and watching the candle light flicker through the room. Every bone in his body felt broken. The events of the day had left him in a state of psychological and corporeal shell-shock. It was odd to have a moment to himself – not just one moment, but a roomful of ongoing moments, and none of them out for his throat. Had he been able to, he would've gathered a few of them together and stored them in a pill box, for future use.

BAKER'S METHODIST CRONES have probably always existed in one form or another – their lateral equivalents run like cancer through every society. But the particular troop of basket-wielding sociopaths John would come to know all too well following his mother's admission to the Baker General was unified and patented in the wake of a postwar legal dispute between the Baker city council and the B&L railroad company.

Topographically, the Patokah-side railroad tracks veer south from the riverbank just beyond the southwestern support beam of the of the 254 overpass. They continue on, by and through the grain mill and dockyards in the north, cutting a twenty yard diagonal swath through the northeastern quarter of Baker, from 1st to 4th St. During the postwar industrial expansion, the rail yards in Pullman Valley had been a hotbed of regional trade. Baker was *the* central port of exchange to Tanner, Bolling and Cooke counties for eight of the busiest years this area of the country has ever known. Overpacked freight trains, some of them stretching for up to seven miles in length and dragging along at a snail's pace, regularly sealed off one end of the community from the other for well over thirty minutes at a time. As a result, there were numerous instances when ambulances from the Baker General responding to medical emergencies on the north end of the valley were delayed *en route*, sealed off from their point of destination, with often grave, even fatal consequences for the patients. A legal battle ensued. Before the court ultimately imposed a series of injunctions limiting the length and speed of all incoming and outgoing freight traffic, a network of 'first responders' had founded its opening chapter in Baker – most of it being comprised of elderly women from the Methodist church. Hence the Methodist crones. The group quickly grew into an organization. Its members were initially trained in first aid and kept on call throughout the valley in continual shifts, so that if and when an authorized rescue crew from the Baker General was thwarted by a passing train, temporary relief would only ever be moments away. Ideally, at least one emergency responder would be on continual standby within two minutes of any address in Baker north of the railroad tracks at all times. That was the crones' original directive. But as their membership grew, their duties were eventually expanded. In time they started spending the bulk of every day going door to door to hospital to funeral home, delivering canned peas and whipped potatos to the all but vegetable remains of the town's afflicted. Over the years they learned to straighten hairpieces, remove dentures, change diapers, run errands, deliver flowers, provide spiritual counsel to those in need, and alert the hospital when meals-on-wheels recipients were no longer responsive to their doorbells.

As charitable as their endeavors may appear on the surface, there *is* another side to the picture. John's lifelong aversion to the crones may have been based on gut-feel alone. That very well could be. But he also may have been keen on a few basic facts which have been relatively well safeguarded from the public. Such as: since the advent of the 'first responder' campaign, over eighteen and a half million dollars worth of property and life-insurance proceeds have been requisitioned by the First Methodist church of Pullman Valley. The majority of those proceeds have been acquired – signed over to Rev. Terrence White – through questionably unethical deathbed consultations with the diseased or terminally ill. As it works, Rev. White keeps a tight lock on the Baker General's registry at all times. The moment any case is pronounced terminal – with all clinical verification intact, of course – he rounds up a group of crones and assigns them to post. They begin by appearing at the appointed bedside bearing gifts of flowers, oat cakes, and coffee-table-inspirationals. Over the course of the next few weeks, a trust is slowly established between themselves and the sedated aflictee, after which they do a sudden turnaround and set in to coaxing, beguiling, and if necessary, intimidating said aflictee out of as many of his earthly possessions as he is willing to forfeit on penalty of hellfire. By the time the case comes to its natural end, it's not uncommon for Rev. White to leave the memorial court with an entire homestead in his possession. A week or two after the funeral, a county-wide auction is held and widely attended. All proceeds go to the church, and as such, go untaxed. Once again, that's eighteen and a half million dollars in just over four decades: twice the equivalent gains of the area Baptist and Catholic churches combined. Time and time again, the Methodists have come into thousands of dollars worth of merchandise, farm-equipment, machinery, jewelry, and property. Their crowning achievement stands as the acquisition of a functioning dairy farm legally entitled to an Alzheimer patient by the name of Blair Kuntz. At the time of Mrs. Kuntz's imminent demise, she hadn't been involved in her own family operations for years; she was by then slumped over in a wheelchair in the Greene County retirement home. She hadn't spoken a word in seven years. Nevertheless, the crones arrived on the scene the moment her prognosis was announced and, over the last week of her life, somehow managed to acquire several important signatures pertaining to the disposition of her estate. After she'd passed away, her unsuspecting family had taken to the courts to sort out the mess, but to their boundless outrage and disbelief, being that all the appropriate paperwork was in order and that Rev. White held considerable sway over the judge, jury and general staff at the town hall, they ended up losing every square foot of the same farm on which they'd been born and raised. When they were all uncompliant with the resulting order to vacate, they were systematically warned, fined, threatened, and, in the end, forcibly evicted. Two of them were even subsequently jailed for excessive resistance. And afterwards they were stuck with an avalanche of court fees that would take years to pay off. They'd been swindled at every turn. And there have been other homesteads as well. Many others . . . Each case is a matter of written record. John's aversion, again, was probably more instinctive. He always considered the crones closet-case necrophiliacs above all, *then* evangelical racketeers. He believed their financial motives were secondary, that there was more than just money involved in their operations. There had to be. *They were volunteers.* They were feeding something more hideous and insatiable than the reverend's pocket book with all their missionary zeal. Their labors may have been performed in the name of Christian charity, but as John saw it, their real drive was to bear witness to all that withered and died.

So it follows that he knew his mother's condition must have been serious when he woke up the next morning to find one of the crones standing over him.

There was an early light coming in through the window and bathing the scattered contents of the room the moment he woke up. He opened his eyes, having stirred to consciousness with the strangely uneasy feeling that he was being watched. Beyond his own torn pant legs and the toppled bottle of sloe gin on the foot stool, a broad-shouldered, somewhat heavy-set woman in rouge polyester was gazing down on him with a medium-sized glass bowl in her hands. Inside the bowl, a lone goldfish was swimming circles. It darted back and forth against the overblown backdrop of blouse seams. John looked up at the woman. He knew she was a crone right away – the predatory, canine angling of her brow was a dead giveaway. She was a trademark first responder, with all the ill-concealed cunning intact, though she wasn't quite as old as the rest. Probably in her early to mid-forties. She'd gotten her start with the church pretty early on.

Hortense, she said. Her name was Hortense.

She stood looking him over for a minute, then set the bowl on the table and sat down next to him. She removed a large envelope from her purse. There were several medical papers inside. She spread them out on the table. He looked at them.

Apparently, Madame Kaltenbrunner had been diagnosed with 'Cushing's disease', a syndrome 'resulting from hypersecretion of the adrenal cortex in which there is excessive production of gluccotinoids.' It was presumably 'caused by either a tumor of the adrenal gland or excess stimulation of that gland as a result of hyperfunction of the anterior pituitary.' Symptoms included 'protein loss, adiposity, fatigue and weakness, osteo-porosis, amenorrhea, impotence, capillary fragility, excess hair growth, diabetes mellitus, skin discoloration and turgidity (plethora), purplish striae of the skin . . .' He didn't make it any further. He put the papers down and asked if any of that was really supposed to make sense. Hortense said she thought he might feel that way – in fact, that was why she'd come along, to put everything into layman's terms for him.

Cushing's disease, she began, was a very difficult syndrome. She'd seen it before. It was ugly, physically devastating, and highly unpredictable. She set in to outlining the dexamethasone test Madame Kaltenbrunner had been administered the day before, and the registered results from the lab that morning. Although her file had been turned over to a specialist for further screening, chances were she did indeed have Cushing's disease. She would need a complete endocrinology workup, with elab-orate urine and blood tests, etc., etc., etc. . . . John still didn't understand. He had no idea of what it all boiled down to.

Then came *the pitch*, after which he understood perfectly. Hortense started off by saying the months to come were going to be very difficult for everyone. Things were going to get downright unbearable pretty soon. His mother would be almost too painful to look at in another week. He had to understand that. They would all have to stick together and trust in Lord Jesus if they wanted to pull through . . . *but*, she said, turning toward him – and *here it comes*, he thought – *but*, unfortunately, it was going to take more than just Lord Jesus to make up for the practical expenses. Much more. What John had to realize was that these tests were costly. Madame Kaltenbrunner's health insurance policy, as far as they could tell, wasn't going to cut it. That's when she asked to have a look at the family financial records. *If* John didn't mind.

He threw her out of the house even faster than he'd ejected the M.D.s two days earlier. Later on, he would acknowledge that he'd have probably done better by himself and everyone involved to have just shot her on the spot and gotten it over with. *Better to be judged by twelve than carried by six*, as the colloquialism goes. But he didn't shoot her. Instead, he only

70

chased her to the Methodistmobile and drove her off the property in a barrage of threats. There was no place for vampires on his estate, he screamed. They'd picked the wrong address for once in their lives. He was not to be tested, he was warning her. *Never* come back.

On the way out, she rolled down her window and looked at him. She suggested, in a sedate, monotone voice, that he was just upset. It was understandable. By the looks of it he was in bad need of a shower anyway. He'd feel better later on. In any case, not to worry, they'd be seeing a whole lot more of one another soon enough. They were family now. And speaking of family, *Did he have any idea how much he looked like his father?*

John froze in his tracks. He felt his jaw drop, his brow arch. He saw Hortense examining him with a cold smile. It took a minute for his mind to catch up. That last remark wouldn't fully register. It couldn't find a way in. He felt as though he'd been sucker-punched and was now being sized for fit on the uptake. Hortense kept staring. She wouldn't let go. She appeared to have just found what she'd come for. She lingered on for another minute. Then she snapped out of it, looking strangely self-satisfied. She rolled up the window and drove away. He watched her go. Once her car had disappeared, he was left alone in the demolished yard with her final statement echoing through his head.

As might have been expected, the goldfish didn't make it through the afternoon. Without any proper food or vegetation, it was little more than a 25-cent time bomb. John was convinced its expiration had been intentional, that Hortense had deliberately planned it that way. He took it as a forthright, albeit elusive insult; message received. How typical of a crone to deliver one of God's creatures to your doorstep on its dying breath.

He went to the bathroom to flush it, only to find that, in addition to the phones and power being down, the waterline had been ruptured. The plumbing was out. No shower. He went outside. He walked down the hill to the river. The aftermath of the twister was still clearly visible to all sides. Three or four trees were down. One of them had been torn in half and was hanging by a thread from its trunk. A large ditch had been blasted into the bank. All around its ridge the vegetation and overhanging limbs were permanently bowed back in windswept arcs. The rest of the farm was much the same. He had only just gotten started with the general repairs when the trouble had begun.

He dumped the fish in the river and watched it bob away. Above the tracks on the opposite bank, a line of trees was sprawled out toward the foot of Gwendolyn Hill, on top of which several bulldozers were plowing through the dirt. One of them was poring over the blast site where the valley's first Christian church had been hastily erected. The original red tiles from the cupola were sitting on a shelf up in the vault. The rest of the building was somewhere off in the capital. It had been founded in 1787. Which meant absolutely nothing. It made about as much sense as Cushing's disease. It all seemed useless.

He threw himself into the water. The current wrapped around him like a cold wet glove. He came up shivering. Clouds of mud churned up at his feet. The grime and blood from his body drifted away in an oily film. The water soothed the aching in his ribs. It was a momentary reprieve.

There was no word on Madame Kaltenbrunner for the next six days. In that time, John did his best to work the property back into shape. But as he proceeded, it seemed that every time he made one repair, something else would immediately fall apart, and that the ruin was beginning to outrun the reconstruction. It was as though every standing object on the estate had been joggled right up to its breaking point, and was now just waiting to be tipped over by the first autumn breeze. To every side drainpipes were falling, windowpanes crashing, pictures dropping from the wall. At one point a section of the roof suddenly collapsed, bringing the black chimney-side weathervane down in the middle of the attic. The hallways were filled with an intermittent ensemble of crashing objects. He couldn't keep up with it.

When a repairman came out on the second afternoon to look over the waterline, John warned him to watch out for falling objects while he worked. The repairman emerged unscathed, but he exacted all the remaining funds John had stashed away in the cupboard. There was no cash left in the house. The plumbing was back in order, but the phones were still down. The layer house was fortified against further attacks, but the coons had descended on the kitchen in greater numbers. The grain shed was full, but the troughs had been destroyed. The leghorns were molting, but John was in no mood to put the hatchet to the block. The gash on his forehead closed up, but he had to reopen it with a butter knife to remove a shard of the windshield which was still lodged under the skin. The bitches were swelling to term. The catfish were becoming ungovernable. Isabelle had been gone for fifteen days and the whole estate seemed bent on driving itself into the ground in pursuit of her. It was a nightmare.

The deterioration continued.

By the seventh morning, John had once again exceeded the standard allotment of unexcused absences at school. The same deputy who had stood guard in the hospital lobby appeared at the front door in a wafting trail of knee-highs and moth balls. As John pulled on his father's mining coat he took a look around and wondered if the house would still be standing when he returned later in the day. He watched its dilapidated frame disappear from the back of the cruiser over a garbled transmission of honky-tonk and blue-collar radio.

Roy Mentzer was waiting for him when he arrived. John barely made it through the front door of the main building before he was summoned to the office by the secretary. He was pointed through a pair of double doors. Inside, Mentzer was in a tither. It looked as though the old man was finally putting his foot down in the name of his professional reputation. *John Kaltenbrunner had become the chancre sore of his career*, he proclaimed. He wasn't going to stand for it any longer. He didn't care if John was in the final stretch or not – with this new police report which had been hand-delivered to his desk the day before, he himself had been made the laughing stock of the whole faculty. He was being called an incompetent ass. He was being openly ridiculed for not being able to keep one lone student on a leash. They'd even slandered his virility. It was inexcusable. It was all going to end right now. From that day forward, he said, either John straightened up his act, or he would be recommended for expulsion. And that would leave him Pottville bound. And he knew what meant, didn't he? Pottville. The Hessians. Those derelicts would have him hanging from the flagpole inside of a week. He would never hold up. It would be his end, didn't he see?

Mentzer got up and stormed through the room. He kicked his desk. He threw his arms around, fit to be tied. He went on to outline their new policy. John's ongoing holiday in the suspension room was *over*. It didn't make the least bit of difference if he was closing in on his sixteenth birthday or not, he *would* make a concerted effort to integrate. Or at least appear to do so. His own well-being was at stake. From then on he would fall into place as a normal student. He would never speak unless spoken to. He would straighten up or perish. Refusal to comply would only greatly complicate his own life.

On that last point, John had to concede, the old man was right, whether he knew it or not. The prospects of having to spend the next three months in Pottville, the idea of nosediving into any new system as a complete unknown while potential disaster was brewing back home was not something he relished. The possibility of the crones creeping around the property while he was off at school was bad enough. But if he was forced to commute back and forth to Koll county on a daily basis – a ninety minute drive alone – and to weather the inevitable rites of initiation and enrollment into a new system, the farm would be left wide open to attack. Impossible as it seemed, Mentzer actually had the upper hand in the situation.

John had difficulty even reading his schedule. He hadn't attended a class in years. He didn't know the names of any of his teachers. He barely knew what grade he was in. He'd forgotten how nauseating the lime-green walls and pink tiles were – the paste-up weather charts and filthy blackboards, undernourished geraniums, hissing gas heaters, Disney posterboards, branded oak plaques with their coined adages, the heinous apparel donned by his peers. Memories of the toll this optical bombardment had taken on his mind in the past came rushing back in one putrefactive wave. It was like sitting on a loud, neon-lit avenue all day long. Even the farm, in its current state of disrepair, was less psychologically damaging to regard. Anything would be. From the walls of Mt. Rushmore to every bombed-out wharf hovel the whole world over, nothing had in its appearance more power to clone a reich of eunuchs than the revolting fanfare of mid-American whimsy plastered over the walls of Holborn High. It made him sick to his stomach.

His peers were terrified at the prospect of his reintegration. All through the first day they fidgeted nervously at their desks, throwing sideway glances in his direction. No one heard a single word spoken by the faculty in any of his classes. The air was impossibly thick with tension. The teachers were met with undivided questioning looks which seemed to say 'What is *He* doing here?' He destroyed all semblance of order without even opening his mouth. Everyone wanted him out.

But Mentzer was determined. He was going to see his plan through, regardless. Right from the first morning he personally took to keeping watch in the hallways outside of John's classes. He would poke his head around the corner without warning. He would peer out from behind open locker doors, follow along between classes. John would be seated at a desk staring at the wall, when out of nowhere the old man would suddenly pass by the door, leering in his direction. He would stand there for a few seconds. Then he would disappear. Class would continue. The teacher would talk on. Ten minutes later he would be back. He would make another pass, gliding along with his brow screwed up and both arms locked at his sides. And once again, he'd disappear. He appeared and reappeared that way all day long. He did nothing but add to the existing tension in the classrooms. John left school that afternoon feeling as though he'd been hounded by a prowling warlock for the last seven hours. He half-expected to spot Mentzer creeping along the edge of the road behind him on the walk home.

*

The house was still standing when he arrived. As he approached from down the hill he could see that a shutter had fallen from its hinges on the second story. Everything else appeared to be in order. No cars, no sign of intrusion. The barn was untouched.

It wasn't until he stepped through the front door that he knew someone had been there. Angled on the footstool to the right of the doorway, a glass bowl with a new goldfish was propped up below the coat rack. The fish was already half-dead, swimming slow circles on its side. He stooped to inspect it. He gave it a quick shake for no particular reason, then stood and headed toward the living room. When he rounded the corner his mother came into view.

He didn't see her right away. On first glance, it just seemed that the general layout of the room had been altered somehow, that an object had been added, an old piece of furniture hauled up from the cellar maybe. Then something moved. He narrowed in on the couch. He saw an arm come to rest on a polyester fabric. He followed the fabric up to a pair of eyes staring in his direction. He made his way out from there. Then it hit. He had to stifle his immediate urge to scream: seated on the couch with her back to the blanketed window, what had become of Madame Kaltenbrunner was situated like the remains of a bloated piñata that had been dragged from a septic pit. She was unrecognizable. Her swollen face was covered with porous black bruises and stretch marks. An enormous double chin had ballooned outward from her neck, past the jaw line and over the grotesque buffalo humps on her shoulders. Her abdomen had become as large as a grit ball. Her forearms were gutted with pustulating acne. Every visible inch of skin on her body had sprouted coarse black hair. She looked to be tranquilized on several different barbiturates. It was difficult to tell if she even recognized him at first, her eyes were set so far back in the mess and her gaze seemed to be coming from worlds away. After a minute she lightened up, if only for a moment, and in a deep, wavering voice, spoke his name.

His initial impulse to scream turned to an urge to vomit.

At that moment, he probably could have lost what little remained of his self-control. Had the events of the previous few days not battered him half-senseless, his reflexes might have sent him tearing into the forest with his head in his hands. As it was, he kept it together, but just barely. His heart raced, but didn't blow. His knees buckled, but didn't give out. His lungs heaved, but didn't burst. The thing on the couch kept staring at him. The room was overheated with a cryptic stench.

His heart rate eventually leveled out. Madame Kaltenbrunner's book of financial records was sitting open-faced on the table. The moment he realized it had been pried into, his senses returned. He snatched it up. Several notes in red ink had been added to the most current figures. He flew off the handle. He demanded an explaination without yet knowing if his mother was capable of responding . . . What had those parasites done? How many of them had been there? What had they said? Had it been that Hortense? Had that one been in the house again? If she ever came back around he would draw and quarter her conniving reptile ass with his tractor and a pile of log chains . . .

Madame Kaltenbrunner silenced him. She wouldn't put up with it, she said. That kind of talk was inexcusable. He should've been ashamed – those 'parasites' had been taking good care of her over the last week. Which was more than could be said for *some* people. They'd helped her along and kept her good company. He was never to speak that way again.

John told her she was terribly mistaken, that she had no idea of what she was talking about. Didn't she realize she was playing right into their hands? Didn't she realize those vipers were going to suck her dry for everything she had? Didn't she understand? She had to listen to him. The Methodists were sick. They didn't mean her any good. He knew what he was talking about, she had to believe him.

But Madame Kaltenbrunner wouldn't hear of it. She said he was talking crazy and that he ought to have his head examined. And once again, for the umpteenth time, *what would his father have thought?*

John screamed back that he knew *exactly* what his father would have thought. He so much had it in the old man's written word, (Unverified) something along the lines of the crones being 'back-alley panty sniffers for the sweet smell of decay,' 'jacked

77

up on their haunches over bedridden aflictees,' 'basking in the stench of it all, waiting for the cardiograph to sing . . .'

Madame Kaltenbrunner screamed. She clamped her hands over her ears and kicked her feet, refusing to hear more. Her striae glistened. Her face flushed over in hot streaks. John kept going. He told her they would poison her. He said they would throw her in the closet and take her wardrobe to market. They would strip the farm bare if she let them. They didn't care. They'd do whatever they had to do. Why wouldn't she listen to him? He was the only one who could help her. Didn't she see?

Neither of them budged. They stood their ground, each a lacerated cross-hatching of cuts and bruises, as two poorly preserved medical abnormalities in a heated screaming match. Somewhere in the din a vehicle pulled into the drive, but its arrival went unnoticed. Madame Kaltenbrunner had wailed herself into a gurgling choke. Her body looked as though it might burst. John was still going, stomping in and out of the doorway rattling off a long list of episodes to support his claims. He was in the midst of recounting the church's alleged requisitioning of a feed distributor in Tanner county when Hortense stepped through the front door. He turned and looked at her. She scowled at him. He scowled back. From where she stood, out of view of Madame Kaltenbrunner, all the unadulterated malice was plastered over her face. It was unmistakable. She harbored no shame in its exposure. On the contrary, she seemed to revel in it. They stood there, caught up in a whirlwind of mutual recognition. There it was – the essence and epitome of all he despised. He wanted to tear down the wall and reveal it to his unsuspecting mother. That would have shown her.

But Hortense was one step ahead of him. She was far too experienced in these matters. She knew what she was doing better than he knew what he was talking about.

Her face softened the moment she came around the corner. She stood in the doorway and beckoned to Madame Kaltenbrunner. Madame Kaltenbrunner let out a cry of relief. Hortense rushed to her side, got down on her knees, and threw her arms around Madame Kaltenbrunner's cyclopean girth. They both started crying. Madame Kaltenbrunner was slobbering uncontrollably. Hortense yelled at John to look at what he'd done. Didn't he have anything to say for himself?

John couldn't believe what was happening. He stood in the doorway looking down on them, disgusted to the point of heartbreak. It was the most appalling spectacle he'd ever laid eyes on. It made a firing squad seem rational. He couldn't bear to stand there and look at it for another second. He had to get out, had to save himself if no one else. He'd just been forcibly excluded from the argument anyway. He could no longer contend. Not on those grounds. The code had been changed. He'd been eliminated. He was an exiled monoglot. There was nothing he could do about it. He left.

That night it rained. Hortense and Madame Kaltenbrunner stayed up in the living room while John sat with his back to the wall in the vault. He was crushed. As he ran his gaze over the artifacts, he couldn't help but feel that he'd let his father down; that Ford Kaltenbrunner, a man he'd never known on a one-to-one basis, but a man for whom he'd nevertheless cultivated a good deal of respect, must've been rolling in his grave at John's inability to handle the situation. John had never felt so ineffective in all his life. When he finally drifted into an uneasy sleep, he did so with a feeling of shame and unworthiness gnawing at his insides. A collage of jumbled images coalesced in his mind's eye. He saw himself at the helm of Bucephalus driving a terrified pack of naked and enslaved Bakerites across a plateau. He was bathed in an ethereal glow with the Winchester thrown over one shoulder and his steed roaring like a Howitzer. To all sides, the mob scurried before him in buck-naked profusion: beer-gutted deputies from the Sheriff's department stumbling over fallen cleaning maids. Hairy-backed trolls bounding along in quivering rolls of free-swinging celluloid. Crones with bowls of dead goldfish scampering over the sick and dying, stopping only to rob them of their jewelry and lap at their wounds. Roy Mentzer on all fours being openly sodomized with garden tools by the chain-gang in suspension. The student body from Holborn bleeding from every orifice, crawling along on their hands and knees, being trampled underfoot, tearing and biting at one another, pulling hair, gouging eyes, all fleeing in an obscene bow-legged panic toward the edge of a cliff. And John driving them forward as the shepherd in residence, Bucephalus screaming, the Winchester pounding, bodies falling, the terrain being marred, and finally the whole convalescent lot of them being driven straight over the edge. And their bodies falling like feed sacks against the open sky before being impaled, pounded and blown to bits on the escarpment of jagged limestone columns below. And John plodding along on the ledge high above, the panoramic display of the open sea stretched out and cascading before him, the dead mob strewn out along the beach having finally gotten its cue and gone silent.

LOOKING BACK ON EVERYTHING five years later, John would recall the last leg of the downward slide with relative imprecision. The events of that particular autumn, as they would remain preserved in his memory, would lack any semblance of chronological order, existing only as a botched cluster of random images interspersed and condensed within a single time frame. As they originally transpired, they were so tightly knit and inter-coordinated, they almost appeared to function as a cooperative whole; but in retrospect, from a safe distance, their interplay would grow more and more incomprehensible, leaving John to wonder exactly if and when reality had ended and its alternative begun.

To start with, just as he'd feared, Madame Kaltenbrunner soon forfeited all financial control of her estate to the Methodists. In effect, her decision threw open the gates to every first responder in the valley. Hordes of crones began rolling up the drive in caravans of four or five at a time on a daily basis. Within a week they were coming and going as they pleased. They were showing up at all hours. Some of them were camping out in the pantry for days at a time. Others would only appear while John was off at school. They lined the shelves in the kitchen with plastic daisies. They doled out lemon meringue pies and Spam in the can. And every day they brought goldfish. And every day the goldfish died.

John stood by and watched everything unfold all too predictably. As it proceeded, he got a close, first-hand look at the crones themselves, individually and on the whole. Before long he had distinguished a few basic divisions in their ranks.

As a common thread, they were all melancholic. They hovered over a progressively deteriorating Madame Kaltenbrunner like alley dogs over a side of beef, eyes agog and protuberant with ravenous exhilaration. Regional lore has it that the first responders capture each of their victims' dying breath in a cannery jar to be pried into like a box of smelling salts at a later date. It's even rumored that somewhere in the most remote, far off corner of one of the church's subterranean storage vaults a whole gallery of such jars – all collected from over the years and aging to perfection – is kept under lock and key, primed for the air strike. The crones were carrion mongers all around, with no exception. That they shared in common.

But he quickly realized that some of them were more dim-witted than others, and that among the most dim-witted in the bunch there was no capacity for genuine cunning or prowess. He made no mistake about it: there were undoubtedly those who truly believed they were paying their dues through missionary charity and who were probably even less cognizant of the dark underbelly of their own operations than someone like Madame Kaltenbrunner. However, as John saw it, those few were not to be pardoned for their obliviousness, only weeded out and set apart from the others on account of it. The others were much worse. Among the higher echelon of the first responders, there was that select handful who, one and all, were so conniving, lecherous, and deceitful, that they actually knew their roles as would-be extortionists and embezzlers and played them anyway. None being a clearer example than Hortense.

Hortense Allenbach, as the crones' unspoken leader and wiry-headed Gila monster extraordinaire, was ineradicably unconscionable – so flagrantly corrupt she made Baker's founding fathers look like communal philanthropists. From the moment she got her claws into the Kaltenbrunner estate she proceeded to filch and appropriate every last object she was able to lay hands on without ever exhibiting the slightest outward indication of remorse. She'd obviously been through this routine a thousand times before. She had highway robbery down to a science. She paced operations in perfect synch with Madame Kaltenbrunner's rate of deterioration, taking the emergence and development of all anticipated symptoms as her cue to move on to the next step of the plan, the next set of demands. In that respect, she was a marvel to behold.

But in other regards, in *so many* other regards, she was a floundering idiot. What really got John more than anything about her was that, for all her sway over his mother and the rest of the crones, she really wasn't *that* convincing. When it came down to it, she was actually just a bad actress. She would've been booed off the stage as a third-rate parlor floozy in any back-alley showhall in the state. Under normal circumstances she never would have gotten to John. She wouldn't have been able to. She just wasn't that good. However, in this situation, probably the only plausible one of its kind, he was legally powerless to put a stop to what she was doing. And unfortunately, she was tampering with his own hard-earned livelihood. She was butchering the sacred cow. That was the most difficult part of it: to have to sit by and watch everything for which he'd worked fall into the hands of an adversary so blatantly unworthy of his most fundamental respect, much less his heartfelt contempt.

But it was more than just the presence of the crones that contributed to what would gradually become John's overall breakdown, both mental and physical. Every other aspect of his life had become a tragicomic impossibility as well. His forced attendance of Holborn High was marred with the continually lurking apparition of Roy Mentzer. The castigation and disdain from his peers continued. A court date for the Bait Shack/Troll disaster was set for December 1st. A bill for the removal of his mother's wagon arrived by mail. Then came the first of the hospital charges, medical expenses and overnight lodging fares. The Pullman Valley hatchery wagon stopped coming around. Half of the remaining leghorns were molting. Two of the three buff-laced Polish cocks were killed by coyotes. One of the Suffolks contracted anthrax and had to be quarantined and slaughtered to prevent further contagion. Madame Kaltenbrunner grew a full-length beard and bloated like a fat grape. She was placed in a wheelchair. She would no longer even look at him – Hortense had poisoned her to her own son. The crones cleaned out the freezer and stole off with all the birds. The catfish apparently grew tired of waiting for things to return to normal and disappeared into the forest for good. The house kept falling apart. A plague of termites was hollowing out the walls. About the only thing that remained intact the whole way through was Bucephalus.

John's nerves were shattered. His appearance had gone to seed. He was having trouble keeping food down. He couldn't stay asleep for more than an hour at a time without drifting into one recurring night terror or another. He was chain-smoking over two cartons of cigarettes a week. His lungs were tight and congested, his palate stale, his throat raw and raspy. His blood pressure was through the roof. He could see his heart pounding away beneath his shirt pocket, his pulse rippling through his cuffs as he sat in class. He could even make out a drastic decline in the legibility of his penmanship due to his ongoing bouts with the shakes. He lost ten pounds in two weeks. Before long his skin was wrapped over his bones like heated cellophane.

To add to everything else, during the third week in September both farm bitches delivered their long-awaited litters at once; only the litter produced by the younger of the two was hopelessly worm-ridden and diseased – half of the pups were stillborns, the other half caked in some milky-white fungal residue. It was a Methodist crone's wet dream. John knew there was no hope for the afflicted pups. As was customary, he wrapped them in a feed sack and tossed them into the river. That was probably the beginning of the end.

The visions began three nights after he'd dispensed with the litter. As he recalled it, he was lying in bed after midnight, drifting in and out of a restless sleep when a grinding noise started up in the hallway outside of his door. He sat up. At first he thought it was one of the crones snooping through a closet. But after a minute something told him no. He got up and unfastened the padlock. When he opened the door he saw it: there, on the far end of the hall, a waterlogged stillborn dragging its corpse along the floorboards, trailing behind a thick streak of sludge. He slammed the door and fell into a corner, screaming. Hot needles pricked into his face. Pinpoints of light danced through his field of vision. It took him several minutes to pull himself together. When he finally looked out again, it was gone: no sludge, no corpse, no nothing. Gone. He sank into his bed trembling. He stared at the wall, almost without blinking, until 4 a.m. He eventually managed to drift back into a semi-slumber, but within minutes of doing so he was reawakened, this time by a piercing uproar coming from outside, down the hill. They were howling on the riverbank in an anguished choir. There must have been ten or twelve of them. It was horrible. He got up and ran out into the yard. But before he reached the Patokah, the racket had died out. He found himself alone in a pit of mud with an oak two by four in hand. The sun was coming up. His head was pounding. He returned to the house and drank a pot of coffee.

After that, the stillborns very quickly became a permanent fixture, not just in his bedroom, not just in his dreams, but everywhere he went and in all states of mind. He could hear them scratching at the windowpane every night. He heard them moving around in the attic. They kicked up lumber scraps in the cellar. He had difficulty differentiating between their presence and the coons in the kitchen. He was soon catching sight of them on the fringes of his periphery, always lingering just out of direct view. They perched up on Bucephalus in a sorry little row. They darted out of lockers at school. They peered at him from sewer ducts and potholes on the street. At length they were everywhere – in the roadside ditches, behind the tombstone in the cemetery, at the foot of various faculty members, in and around the Methodistmobiles, all through the barnyard, all hideously ugly, some snapping their jaws, others whimpering, a few of them dead to the world, the rest jammed in the gas stove and the chimney chute.

John knew he was in serious trouble. He was well aware that his mind was coming apart. He understood that. He didn't know what to do about it, but he understood it. He really had no option but to stick it out. He had to keep it together. He couldn't leave the farm. He couldn't leave his mother. He couldn't leave the vault to the crones. He couldn't admit himself for treatment – if anyone found out what was going on in his head, he'd be dragged away for months. And he couldn't afford that. Not yet. He was still needed. What was left of the farm was depending on him. He *had to keep it together, had to keep it together, had to keep it together . . .* Over and over he repeated it. It became his mantra. It was his life raft. He told himself he could still function for as long as he remained cognizant of his condition – could keep it together for as long as he remained aware that he was falling apart. When the howling ended, then it would be time to worry. Until then, the pain would have to keep him in check. The pain would have to serve as his emergency indicator, his safety net, his last lock on himself. His continuing susceptibility to, and awareness of, his own distress would have to testify to the lingering sovereignty of his reason. He would endure for precisely as long as he was able to hurt.

For the moment, he knew he was still in control, but even that knowledge began to dip in and out of uncertainty as his agitation increased. It was like a snake devouring itself into a vanishing point: the waterlogged stillborns drifting into the Methodist crones, the crones to his mother's plummeting condition, Madame Kaltenbrunner to a perpetually outraged Roy Mentzer, Holborn High to the homestead, the foiled house repairs to the airtight vault, then back to the stillborns for another round all over again. His head became an open forum of free-floating information, with all the formerly categorized data from the logbooks having blown loose from its file cabinet in one sweeping blast. Individual statistics ricocheted through his mind faster than he could pinpoint them. He began to hear a resounding B flat wherever he went. *Had to keep it together, had to keep it together, had to keep it together . . .*

While all that was happening, the crones pushed on from one phase of their operation to the next. The first article of furniture to go was the antique oak-framed bureau from the living room. The proceeds from its sale were to 'cover basic expenses,' John was told. And that was about the only attempt at an explanation he ever received. After that no one paid him any further mind. He was never again consulted, or even informed, on any decision. However uncompliant and potentially volatile he may have appeared, the crones knew he had no legal entitlement to the farm and therefore represented no real threat to anyone. Madame Kaltenbrunner had been sold on their intentions. That was all that really mattered. The looting began.

They were somewhat less bold with their demands at first. They had to keep the trust intact and on course with the lady of the house in order to proceed. They buttered her up with flowers and egg nog before breaking the news that the family couch had to go. Madame Kaltenbrunner never doubted their intentions for a second. She was saddened to learn that the sale of her cherished marble footstools and dressers was now imperative to cover accumulating medical expenses, but Hortense would rationalize each decision with such saccharine-sweet overtones that by the time the movers had packed up the minivan and gone on their way, Madame Kaltenbrunner would have dried her eyes and begun condoning the latest theft as a just and necessary sacrifice.

After initially testing the waters and finding her unwaveringly tolerant of her losses, the crones abandoned all discretionary tact and got down to business. They dove in. Their modest requests for single furnishings became authoritative demands for the contents of entire rooms. They no longer asked for permission to cart off huge loads of merchandise; they just took what they wanted and left the explanations to Hortense. Hortense, in turn, stood guard over Madame Kaltenbrunner with a clipboard in hand, 'supervising,' as she termed it. The big furniture went first: the bureau and dressers, the dinner table, the felt recliners. Then came the bed frames and mattresses. Then the chairs, the pillows, the wall hangings, tapestries, cabinets and wardrobes. They tore into everything. Once they got started, nothing stood in their way. They were like a group of car thieves stripping a deserted Lincoln. *Ruthless* efficiency. John had never seen anything like it. They turned the estate upside down. They were in the bedrooms and closets, out in the yard, down in the cellar. One afternoon they brought in a tax assessor to examine the property. On another occasion, John came home to find the work bench and half of his tools from the basement gone. It was all happening too fast. They were covering ground at an alarming rate. The halls were soon emptied out. The kitchen was cleared. Before long, the reverberations from a single hand clap were carrying from the far corner of the upstairs bedroom to the foot of the staircase in the cellar . . .

But they had a problem with the attic. The door to the top-floor study was locked, bolted and barred to the jambs. No one could seem to locate the key, and it was suspected that *he* had it. They couldn't get into the attic and they didn't have a chance in hell with the barn. They didn't know what to do. The son was *definitely* a problem. He'd been exceedingly uncooperative at every turn. They couldn't get close enough to talk to him without running the risk of invoking his wrath. He cursed them repeatedly. He often barged in and forcibly expelled them from a given room. One afternoon he'd locked himself in the kitchen and cooked up the last of the leghorns from the icebox without offering to share it with anyone. They'd tried to force open the door, but he'd told them to go away. His mother had refused to intervene. It was out of her hands, she'd said. They'd then run to Hortense, but Hortense had fared no better. John had remained holed up in the kitchen yelling unprintable attacks on their gender while finishing off what he called *His own God-damned chicken*. Hortense yelled back that he was a vile beast. The rest agreed.

John kept the keys to the attic and the combination codes to the barn on his person at all times. And he *never* let Bucephalus out of his sight. It took approximately five weeks for the crones to clear out the rest of the house. The few belongings he was able to salvage from his room, along with a handful of photographs, antiques, two family lockets, and a smattering of sentimental oddities from the cellar were kept under lock and key in Ford's study. Everything else went. Madame Kaltenbrunner didn't seem to care anymore. Her eyes had glazed over. She was left unattended in her wheelchair by the parlor door for hours at a time. John had tried to get through to her on several occasions, but she wouldn't even look at him, and every time he drew near to her, Hortense, wherever she happened to be at the moment, would snap to attention, come flying out of the hallway, and intervene.

He started missing more school. The police had to drag him out of his bedroom on three separate occasions. The crones did their dirtiest work in his absence. He was intensely aware of that fact as he sat at his desk at school. By the third week in October, once the rest of the house had been pretty well sacked, he was convinced he had no more than four or five days left before the crones managed to worm their way into the attic, and, by way of the attic, the vault. He turned all his attention toward the fortification, or, if necessary, the *removal* of both.

That's pretty much everything that's known of the events leading up to the holdout. The church's legal testimony on the matter is, for obvious reasons, highly unreliable, just as John's own version of the story was limited and inexact. His peers have maintained that in the weeks immediately preceding his exeunt from the community, his already frightening appearance became down-right deathlike. He was rumored to have been diseased: he looked delirious with fatigue and malnutrition. He had developed a severe twitch in his shoulderblades. He spent every day with his gaze locked on his desk top and that blue leather coat wrapped over his famished body. One of his homeroom peers claimed he never blinked. Others swore they saw him talking to himself. He was never seen eating food. Once the day was over he was witnessed, hunched over the steering wheel of that enormous yellow tractor, chain-smoking his way across the overpass as a disconsolate zombie.

That being said, nothing remains to the story but the last twenty-four hours.

At 9:05 a.m. on Wednesday October 21st, John was seated in a third-row desk of Susan K. Detweiller's English class. He'd come into the room three minutes late. He was just in time for the handout of quarter-term literary reports which had been collected a week earlier. Roy Mentzer loomed up in the hall just as he received his paper. Class commenced.

John was slumped forward in his seat as Miss Detweiller went around the room questioning individual students on various aspects of their assignments. He wasn't listening to her. His report was sitting face-down off to one side on his desk top. He was wrapped up in finalizing a plan he'd hit on the night before, still trying to figure out how he was going to get the schooner wheel down from the loft. He'd had problems with the pulley system and had had to reinforce the rafter clamp with twelve-inch bolts. He wasn't certain it would hold for the heavier artifacts. He had a few ideas, but nothing on which he could depend. He needed to get home and run some tests. *He needed to get home and get to work, period.* All this niggling around in the classroom was wasting precious time.

At some point he became vaguely aware of a momentary break in the chatter around him. A hush had fallen over the room. He looked up. Everyone was staring at him. Mentzer was watching from across the hallway. He looked around. He suddenly realized he'd been called on. He turned toward Miss Detweiller. She was motioning to him from the end of a tunnel with a pink bow in her frosted hair and a diseased stillborn strewn out across her desk. From what he gathered she was questioning him on some aspect of his assignment. He asked her to repeat herself. She did so, but her words took some time to connect. Apparently, she wanted to know where he'd gotten his information on this outrageous report paralleling classical themes in the *Red Badge of Courage* with scalp diseases and infant mortality among nineteenth-century potato farmers in east Kentucky. It was excellent work, she said – but he'd included no references.

References? He flipped his paper over and looked at the title page. He could barely remember having written the report. He'd lifted the majority of its contents straight out of one of his father's textbooks. The whole thing had taken twenty minutes to draft, word for word, after which he'd inserted a few quotes from Crane, and turned it in, as is. It had been flat-out plagiarism. It had only been intended to keep Mentzer off his back. So what was she talking about, references?

Then it hit him: Miss Detweiller was asking him to cite volumes from his father's library. That's what she was getting at. She was jockeying for a way into Ford's study. The crones had infiltrated his alma mater and were now fishing for the keys to the attic through this miserable old harlequin wench.

He straightened up and told her to know her place. Miss Detweiller did a double-take. Everyone in the room froze.

Roy Mentzer came pounding in from the hallway. He reared up along the front row. He *Double-dared* John to repeat that last statement. *Double-dared*, he said it again. This was the opportunity for which Mentzer had obviously been holding out: a shot at redeeming his badly tarnished reputation. He looked as though the release papers from his own private hell had finally come through.

John went pale to the neckline. He looked around again. Everyone was still staring, all eyes boring in. He was suddenly convinced they were all in it together, every one of them, that they could hear what he was thinking. They knew what he was up to. *They were going to cut him off and hold him there while the crones cracked the code and finished off with what was left . . . This was it . . . This was the end . . .*

He couldn't take it anymore. He shot out of his seat. He blew by Mentzer, clipped the door frame, and stumbled into the hallway. Voices boomed out from the room behind him. He took off toward the main office. A row of olive-drab lockers shot by to either side. He reached the main door, forced his way through the enclosure, and took the outside staircase in one leap. He ran past a gardener. He continued in the direction of the third parking lot, out toward the property's edge, out toward Bucephalus. He heard Mentzer screaming somewhere behind him. He didn't look back. He reached Bucephalus. He climbed up and started the engine. He took off across the front lawn in the direction of the cemetery. Mentzer ran after him. He floored it on to the highway and leveled out on the divider strip leading to the bridge. Mentzer sputtered out and collapsed at the macadam's edge.

There were four Methodistmobiles parked in the drive when he got home. Several crones were chastising two hired movers for their ineptitude in maneuvering the broken player piano out of the parlor and on to the porch. Everyone stopped and stared as

John drove by. He rolled up to the barn. He climbed down from Bucephalus in front of the main doors and began decoding the various combination locks. The crones went wild. They scattered in every direction. One of them ran inside to alert Hortense. The rest fluttered about in an excited pack. As John pushed the swinging door inward, he could see them all gathered around on the porch motioning frantically in his direction and straining for a glimpse of the barn's interior. He climbed back up on Bucephalus, drove inside, hopped down from the driver's seat, and slammed the door. He put the straight iron bar in place, then got to work.

He'd been up all night preparing for this moment. The Gwendolyn Hill artifacts had been packed up in wooden chests and turkey crates, then set out on the loft in an accessible pile at the top of the ladder. The blue tractor cart he used for repairs had been angled at the foot of the ladder base, just below the overhanging system of ropes and pulleys. He deactivated the code and brought the sliding staircase down from where it was consolidated, high up on the rack. He climbed up to the loft. The arrowheads and bone tools were already packed away in the first chest, sealed in an airtight lining of plastic and padded with newspapers and styrofoam peanuts. Laminated data sheets pertaining to the whole collection were included in every box. He'd also sealed the logbooks.

The night before he'd told himself he would remain calm when the moment came to go through with the burial. He'd tried to talk his way through it beforehand, tried to brace himself for the coming instant. But as he started tying up the chests and crates and lowering them into the tractor cart below, his equilibrium was reeling out of sheer anguish. He couldn't help it. He hated having to do this, and couldn't pretend otherwise. He felt he'd done nothing to deserve it, that it was flat-out wrong no matter how one looked at it, and that all the right people never got what they had coming to them. As he continued working his remorse turned to anger, and his anger eventually to hatred.

At some point, the alarm suddenly went off. He scurried down the ladder. He threw open the door and ran out into the yard swinging a pick axe. The four or five crones who'd been creeping through the shrubs at the side entrance went fleeing down the hill. He screamed after them that the next one who came within a cock's run of the main door would have her spine ripped out of her back with a crowbar. He warned them not to put him to the test: they were all going to die soon enough, but if they needed any help cutting straight to the chase, he'd be only too willing to oblige. He shot a quick, hateful glance all around. Then he went back inside to turn off the siren.

He kept working. In two hours he had the loft cleared of everything but the mammoth, the schooner wheels, and three funeral caskets. The cart was packed. He threw a tarp over the outer railing and tied it up. He hooked the wagon to Bucephalus and angled them both toward the door. Everything was in order. The artifacts were sealed. The vault was empty. He climbed up on Bucephalus and smoked his way through the next six hours, doing his best not to think.

Shortly after sundown, the last of the Methodistmobiles left for the day. John crept up the hill and scanned the perimeter. After finding everything clear, he went back to the barn and opened the doors. He pulled Bucephalus out into the yard and drove to a plot he had dug somewhere in or around the six-acre lot which was once the Kaltenbrunner estate. He lowered everything into place. Then he went back and got the rest. The rafter clamps held.

To this day, the whereabouts of the Gwendolyn Hill artifacts remain unknown. John took that secret with him.

That night he built a fire on the riverbank. He piled up the remains of Isabelle's shed, along with a load of timber, part of the grain shack and a section of the layerhouse wall. He doused everything with lighter fluid, then sat on a pile of rubber tires watching it burn.

He was exhausted. He was convinced his life was finished. With the farm on its last legs, his mother all but dead, his expulsion from Holborn official, and the artifacts having been returned to the earth, the open road stretched out before him was leading nowhere; there was no point of destination or embarkation, no visible hazard zones *or* open retreats. He'd been stripped of all purpose. Everything for which he'd worked had come to ruin. Nothing remained, only a quiet, anonymous, undocumented expiration in the middle of nowhere. 'The short, worthless existence of a Greene County peasant bastard,' it would read. He could see it on billboards and storefront windows all through the corn belt. The ticket sales wouldn't amount to a hill of shit. Before long even the stillborns would jump ship, leaving him a broke, homeless orphan bound for Pottville.

At half past eleven a Methodistmobile pulled into the drive. He watched its high-voltage headlights pan out over the field in a wide arc, throwing silhouettes of crooked tree limbs over the trunks of the surrounding oaks and poplars. The lights continued their sweep until the car came to rest, lighting up the southern facade of the house in a pale glow. The engine cut. The lights went out. From down the bank he could see Hortense step out of the driver's seat. All the implacable revulsion she'd invoked in him only the day before, even that morning, had settled to a sterile, semi-disinterested loathing. As he watched her walk across the yard toward the house, he could no longer seem to muster anything but a vague acknowledgment of her presence, and, at best, a subtle feeling of contempt. She didn't really matter anymore. Nothing did. He turned back to the fire to listen to a decayed oak beam full of termites crackle and spit in the flames.

For the next few minutes he seriously contemplated killing himself. He tried to walk through it one step at a time – he would go up to the house, load the Winchester, lock himself in his room, and lodge the barrel in his throat. He would sit there sweating over his bedsheets with the cleaning oil settling into his gums, coating his tongue and tonsils, burning his nose – his front teeth chattering over the iron pipe as he stared at the wall, counting individual termites on the baseboards, running his gaze over the room until hitting on number thirteen, lucky thirteen. Or maybe he would pull out the gas stove from the hallway closet instead – snuff the flame and lock himself in the cellar with a flint kit. Or go the bathroom cabinet, find a length of twine in the barn. Asphyxiation. The possibilities were endless. He thought about it all for quite some time. But he eventually gave up, having begun to feel like a complete ass. Even the prospect of suicide failed to get a rise out of him. There was neither hope in eluding it or terror in succumbing to it; he lacked the necessary impetus to act toward either end. There was now only a decelerating vacuum in place of the previously indomitable will; a dull, wintry absence where before the hairtrigger would have cracked and blown without respite. Even the backdrop on hand had unexpectedly ceased in its role as would-be executioner. Plate-glass windows were no longer there for the storming. The Patokah had desisted from beckoning at depth. Brick walls had fallen off as collisionary bulwarks. The set had lost its backbone. The possibilities were endless, but the real options were nil. He ended up right where he'd started from – staring at the fire with no particular reason to move.

Somewhere along the way his thoughts were interrupted by a noise from up the hill. He looked up to see a figure cutting toward him through the dark. Even before she stepped into the light with her hair frilled up and hanging over her pin-rigged sequoia blouse, he knew it was Hortense. He'd been expecting this visit all week. The crones had phoned the school board following his return that morning. They'd wanted to get him out of the way via the usual means – two deputies and a pending arrest warrant – but had been told that John's enrollment at Holborn had been officially terminated. The paperwork for his transfer was being drawn up, but it would take some time to go through. Meaning, the crones were stuck with him for a few days. Meaning, there was no way around him into the attic. Hortense had finally come for the keys. But the keys, very sadly, were in the river.

She stepped into the clearing and lit up like a roving mackerel. He could've seen the softened look on her face coming from a thousand miles away, that sham-theatrical honeysuckle pathos to which only a Methodist crone with an ulterior motive would have the gall to resort. It was unbelievable, really, that she would still try it on him. Their cards had been all over the table from their very first encounter. Theirs had been the only honest rapport Hortense had maintained with anyone. She couldn't *possibly* have expected this sudden turnaround to work . . . She really did take him for an absolute moron.

He told her to speak and be done with it.

She edged over toward him. She leaned against a tree and cocked her head to one side. She looked at the river for a minute. Then she spoke.

She started by saying she thought it was high time they had a person-to-person talk. There were too many misunderstandings between them, she said, and it pained her to think that two reasonable individuals couldn't sort out their differences to the benefit of everyone. Although the threats John had hurled toward 'the girls' that afternoon had been cruel, immature and horribly unfair, he had to know he'd been forgiven by everyone for his understandable confusion. After all, his mother was going through a terrible ordeal, and he must've been under his own pressures too. Everyone had been so busy attending to Madame Kaltenbrunner that they had unintentionally neglected his needs and requirements for consolation as one of God's creatures. She had come to apologize and allow him the chance to speak his mind. He deserved it, she said. He had the right. And he just might've found, as well, that she had a good ear for these sort of things, contrary to the way it may have seemed. There were so many things he couldn't have possibly understood, so many things he needed help with. He was just a boy. This situation with his mother would've put any loved one's nerves to the supreme test. He probably just needed a good shoulder to cry on, a hand to hold . . .

John told her that if she laid a finger on him he would throw her into the fire.

Hortense drew back, caught off guard. The individual components of her profile took a vaguely discernible strain, as though momentarily fumbled by an arthritic puppeteer. But she somehow managed to retain her overall composure without breaking character. . . . She told him not to get excited now. He was angry. Anyone would be. She had expected this. He really had to understand that she had come to make peace. Honest. In all sincerity. Despite what he may have thought, her heart really was in the right place. She'd given her life to those in need. And she cared about him too. It tore her to pieces to think of the pain he'd been going through, all alone and by himself. She'd come to clear the air. But she wasn't fool enough as to expect him to welcome her with open arms. It would take time and effort for them to work things out. An honest exchange was in order, no matter how difficult the task. Knowing that, she had taken the liberty of bringing along a token of her sincerity which, with his approval of course, might clear the air and help the conversation along toward a mutually beneficial end. She knew it was a bit unconventional, him being only fifteen and all, but the current circumstance might allow for an otherwise dubious proposition . . .

She reached into her bag and removed what John instantly recognized as his father's bottle of scotch whisky.

As she understood it, she said, this bottle was to be handed on to him when he came of age. It was a family heirloom. She knew he wasn't supposed to touch it for a few more years, and she was perfectly ready and willing to honor that expectation without question . . . But on the other hand, it seemed to her – and maybe she was wrong – but it seemed to her that with all he'd been through of late, one might have considered him to have come of age prematurely. Practical experience had wizened him beyond his years. If they were to break open the bottle at that moment, it might help them to stop leering at one another like forest wolves. It was entirely up to him, but it seemed to her that a more perfect time to imbibe and clear the warpaint would never be. And anyway, as twenty-year-old scotch from three decades past, this must have been the finest bottle of whisky in the valley. Fifty years old!

John snatched it out of her hands and told her to cut the shit. It was making him sick. She could go ahead and pour as much of the family heirloom down her nasty little gullet as she damn-well pleased, so long as she stopped patronizing him. He had no objections to cracking the bottle, he was just surprised she and the grotto hags hadn't hocked it already. It might have brought top dollar in the local taverns. And anyway, he said, twenty-year-old scotch, once bottled, will never be anything more than twenty-year-old scotch. There seemed to be no end to her blundering.

He cracked the seal and tipped it for several long gulps. He came up coughing. He spat to one side, wiped his mouth, and thrust the bottle toward Hortense. *Drink it and shut up*, he said. She sat down on a torn Goodyear next to the fire and drank. John went into a fierce coughing fit. He hacked up large balls of phlegm, spat them into the fire, retrieved the bottle and took another sickeningly long pull. It tore through his insides. He dug his fingers into the tire beneath him. Hortense kept drinking at a less alarming, yet steady rate. Fifteen or twenty minutes passed in silence. Then the bottle was empty. He threw it into the Patokah and watched it float away. So much for the family heritage.

He turned back toward the fire and announced that, all right, maybe he would humor her ridiculous request for an open forum by starting out with the fact that she was the most hypocritical, dirty-legged peddlesnatch cum bitch-in-heat he'd ever had the misfortune of encountering. Not since the days of gin-cellar speakeasies had a more avaricious bull-harlot wandered the streets of Baker in the guise of a law-abiding citizen. She was a sham and an imbecile, and she grossly underestimated his common sense. To hear *her* talk of God's creatures was even more nauseating than her hot-gospelling street pimp of a reverend's shameless exploitation of the carpenter and his apostles. Everyone knew that to the Catholics, Jesus was Mary's boy, to the Baptists he was the savior, to the Jews he was nothing, but to the Methodists he was a tax deduction. Had she really bought any of her own text she would've been overcome with enough guilt, shame and self-contempt to have flagellated herself to an early death years ago. She was a liar and a thief, and she had dragged her carcass into the only neck of the woods that publicly subsidized such iniquity. She had found a host in Baker. They deserved one another. It was the only spot on the map where she could laugh her way to the bank as a pillar of the community through burglarizing every diseased, senile, bedridden invalid in town. And probably live to a ripe old age doing so. For as long as she remained in place, there was no justice left in the world, and she knew exactly what he was talking about. Because that was the thing: even if he was the only semi-perceptive being she ever encountered, even if she lived out the rest of her days among the God-fearing pecksniffs and foxhole yokels of Greene County, there were still individuals out there, individuals like himself, and like his father, who knew her and her kind for the cold-hearted, necrotic, grave-robbing two-dollar whores they were. Everyone had to dance and fart before the king sooner or later. He could see right through her, and they both knew it . . . And *really* . . . Trying to get him *drunk*? . . . Trying to capitalize on his *poor, fragile uncomprehending mind* with a bottle of whisky she hadn't even had the decency to go out and buy herself? *Jesus* . . . That just about said it all, didn't it? She was a *real class act*. Both cheap *and* unoriginal, she'd broken all the records this time . . .

But then again, really, all cards on the table, they both knew perfectly well that she couldn't have cared less for what he thought of anything. And where was the shame in such limited exposure anyway? She and her coven had gotten everything they'd come for, with or without his consent. They'd won. They'd stripped the farm. The only thing that remained was the attic and the barn. So, if she was done with the charade, she would find the keys somewhere along the riverbed about twenty yards from shore. Otherwise, there was no point in continuing this discussion. Meeting adjourned.

John leaned back on his tire and waited for her to leave. Despite the intensity of his attack he had really just been blowing hot air, and to him, it was embarrassingly evident. He was so hollowed out with fatigue and resignation, that he'd had trouble putting words together at all. The majority of his tangent had been extracted from a much lengthier indictment that had been germinating in his mind for weeks. A few days earlier, its delivery might have set the valley on fire. He could have whooped it up on any soap box in town and had the locals in a frenzy. It would have been something to see, had he been standing behind it . . . But now it had lost its edge. It had come off empty and, in the end, anti-climactic, with all the eminence of a washed-up orator's last crack at the platform.

But Hortense didn't take it so lightly. To John's surprise, his words actually appeared to have gotten a rise out of her somehow – something he hadn't thought possible. An unexpected change suddenly came over her. The concerned look vanished and gave way to the familiar old lycanthropic contours. Instead of bowing out and scuttling away up the hill as he'd expected, she hunkered down right where she was, shifted on her Goodyear, and, appearing ultimately unimpressed with his outburst, though unquestionably infuriated at having been called on her bluff, poised for her retort. John looked up to find the Hortense he knew and loathed sitting before him in all her undisguised treachery.

All right, she said, if that's the way it had to be. He was pretty quick for a snot-nosed little bastard, so she'd drop the act and give it to him straight.

She started off by saying that, in a way, he was almost to be commended for his efforts. He'd managed to make a considerable nuisance of himself – a problem she and her associates rarely encountered anymore. In fact, if it was any consolation, they quite honestly hadn't dealt with a more ceaselessly irritating pain in the ass in years. They'd almost forgotten what it was like to have one of their clientele put up a good fight. A little spunk added flavor to the game every now and then, it was true, and he'd certainly done his part as far as that went. But it was just a good thing – and he ought to have been thankful, for his own sake – that no one *gave so much as a rat's ass* for what he thought. Otherwise, she would've had to have gotten ugly. They had ways of dealing with his kind. They'd seen this situation before. He wasn't the first black sheep to try to hold out. But he had to understand that nothing ever stood in their way for long. There had been 'problem cases' in the past, but none of them had warranted anything more than a temporary delay. The final outcome had always been the same. God goes a long way in a town full of ammo-mag junkies itching for a hit. Had he been a few years older and posing any real threat, he might've found himself waking from a chloroform blackout one night, bound and gagged to a moving incinerator belt at the Bolling County refinery. As it was, such steps were not presently in order; as it was all he really needed was a quick sobering up on a few key points. Which she herself could provide without further delay. In fact, it would be her distinct pleasure.

To start with, John's assessment of the situation was impressive, she said. In another time and place he might've actually amounted to something by then. Ironically enough, part of her opening spiel *had* turned out to be true: he *was* wise beyond his years. He had a pretty good lock on everyone for such a little shit. There was no doubt about it. He had big eyes for his age.

However, when it came to his father, that ox-felling colossus lining the walls of his mother's parlor, he had another thing coming altogether. Oh yes, he was in for a *big* surprise. She realized he'd grown up being force fed all that garbage about how magnanimous his old man had been; how, when push came to shove, his father had coaxed the ranks into submission as a cool, calm and collected local hero with all the world in the palm of his hand. But the truth was, dear boy, in spite of everything he'd been told, the truth was, *dear, dear, dear boy, Ford Kaltenbrunner had been a crooked, manipulative, womanizing, alcoholic sonofabitch who'd made deadly enemies of almost every soul in town.* He'd been far and away the most hated man in all of Greene County in his day. He'd swindled more locals out of their pay checks, nest eggs, and life savings than John ever could've imagined. He'd slept with every farmhand's wife for miles around, and that *fat, heinous thing with one foot in her grave that John called mother* had never known about any of it. Madame Kaltenbrunner had been the laughing stock of the whole town in her younger years. Ford had repeatedly put her down in public, and had probably gotten more of a laugh at her expense than anyone. The *Ovarian Cyst*, he had called her . . . The *Concubator* . . . And he'd berated the rest of his associates no less. By the last two or three years of his life he'd aced himself out of every corner of the community. He'd bruised his way into so many bad situations, had alienated and estranged so many tavern regulars, town locals, and law enforcement officials, that no one in the area would have so much as lifted a finger to stave off his untimely demise. Even his colleagues at the mine turned on him in the end. That was another thing John didn't understand – that 'cavern disaster' story surrounding his father's death had been a coverup. It was pure bullshit, and everyone knew it. The truth was, Ford Kaltenbrunner had been organizing an oncoming labor strike at Ebony Steed at the time of his death. He'd been plotting to oust Glendan Castor and take over the company himself, only Castor had gotten wind of the plan beforehand and had launched a counteroffensive. One after-noon Ford had been sent into an underground cavern for inspection. The moment he was well inside the tunnel, two of his supposedly trusted cohorts had given the signal to a munitions man on the hill, who threw the switch and blew the cavern all over the reservoir. *Ford Kaltenbrunner had been murdered in cold blood.* And no one ever made an inquiry. By the time of his funeral, something more along the lines of a celebration had been in order. Only those sorry bastards who'd spent the first few years of John's life paying visits to the Kaltenbrunner farm har-bored any good memories of him whatsoever, and that was only because most of them hadn't had wives he could plow to the washboard on a nightly basis. John was going to have to accept the fact that his father had been anything *but* the local hero. His father had been a crafty, evil-hearted criminal with no loyalties to anyone. Whether or not John chose to believe it, it was true, every word of it.

And she wasn't finished with just that. She stood up and continued rattling off an obscenely long list of indiscretions committed by his father that would have put a troll to shame. She worked herself into a craze, towering over him, spitting in his face, grabbing at his shirt sleeves, unloading one grisly detail after another. It got worse by the minute. John could no longer hear her voice over the screaming of the stillborns. His mind had collapsed. Hortense had destroyed him. He was a dead man. . . But she still wasn't finished. She wanted even more. She wanted to batter, maim and disfigure him, then trample and desecrate his grave beyond recognition. She was on a killing spree. She seized him by the collar and threw him to the ground. She tore open his trousers. She hiked up her dress and lowered herself on to him, snarling and hacking into the dirt. She ripped a clump of hair from his scalp. She tore at his skin, clawed his chest, his face, his arms . . . He was pinned down in a paralytic trance. He couldn't move. Her hair whipped over his face. She bucked and writhed, hissing through clenched teeth. He felt as though he were being smothered by a pustulating maggot. The stillborns pushed into a crescendo. She clutched at him, arched her back and shuddered, then fell over to one side. She was back on her feet immediately. Her chest was heaving. She looked down on him and scowled. Pathetic, she said. She kicked him in the ribs. *Pathetic.* She walked to the edge of the clearing and turned for one last jab. Maybe he didn't have anything to worry about though, she said. Maybe he wasn't so much like his father after all. *At least his father had known how to satisfy a woman. . .* But him, she said, looking down in disgust – *He was nothing but a goatboy . . .*

With that she disappeared. She faded out of the light and slunk away up the hill. He heard her footsteps diminishing through the maze of ditches and fallen limbs. A car door opened and closed. The headlights shot back over the field. The sound of an engine moved off down the drive. Then it was gone.

He remained on his back in the dirt with his belt line at mid-thigh. The firelight lit up an overhanging shelf of limbs. He absentmindedly allowed his gaze to wander over and through the foliage and lock on a spot just over a fork in the trunk. He stared at that spot for what felt like hours, dipping in and out of awareness. Hortense's final words echoed through his head as a thousand doors slamming in one empty hallway. *Nothing but a goatboy, nothing but a goatboy, nothing but a goatboy . . . A Goatboy.* She was right. He was. A goatboy. And he feared she may have been right about a good deal more than just that. She may have been a liar and a thief, but her attack on his father had been spat forth in blood. That much he could tell. He didn't want to admit it, and he probed for any way out, but he couldn't dismiss the agonizing suspicion that at least part of what she'd said was true. He doubled over and curled up in the dirt.

Some time later a church bell tolled out across the river. It rang three times. The fire was almost dead. Only a bed of coals remained. He pulled himself up from the ground. He staggered up the hill toward the house. He reached the porch. He climbed the staircase. He fell off the ledge while rooting through the corner in search of a sledgehammer. His ankle twisted beneath him when he hit the ground. From where he lay groping in the yard he could see the indicator lights of a jet plane cut slowly across the belt of Orion. He watched the lights go until they cut behind a cloud and disappeared. He pulled himself up again and hobbled back up the stairs. He found the hammer behind a pile of broomsticks. He picked it up and went inside.

It was only fitting that he ended up being the one to break down the attic door by force. He had done everything short of booby trapping the staircase to bar it against forced intrusion, only to have to resort to forced intrusion himself. Yet another touché for Hortense. He started chopping. The hammer blows reverberated through the halls. Madame Kaltenbrunner screamed from her chair on the ground floor. He could hear her flailing in her Bankroft down there. He ignored her and finished off the door. He ripped it from its hinges and dropped it toward the closet behind him. He went up.

Once in the attic he made straight for the cast-iron safe on the top rack of the bookcase. He pried it open and removed the few remaining contents that hadn't been buried with the artifacts. He disregarded the loose scraps, focusing his attention instead on the one manila envelope which contained those strange scribblings that had never made any sense. He pulled the papers from inside and spread them out on the desk. He lit his butane lighter and looked at them.

In less than five minutes his suspicions were confirmed. There before him, lined up in perfect order and just shy of complete, were all the plans for a full-scale labor strike on Ebony Steed, with Ford Kaltenbrunner's John Hancock over every page in the bunch. Hortense had been right. His father had been organizing a general walkout at the time of his death. All the signatures were there, everything. But the strike hadn't gone through. That meant it had been headed off. That meant his father *had* been murdered. That meant Ford Kaltenbrunner really *had* been a son of a bitch.

He closed the latch on his lighter and leaned back. He was able to drift for one moment before the sickness hit. Then he shot forward and slammed his head on the desk top repeatedly. It all registered at once. The dragonslayer had been a clip artist. John had sanctified and venerated a known degenerate. The vault had been his whole life, but the vault had been a lie. Both he and his mother had been rightly played for fools. All the world was corrupt and obscene, *and he was nothing but a goatboy . . .*

It took ten minutes to demolish the study. He swept the textbooks from the shelf with one arm. He tore out pages and ripped up covers, pitching them in every direction. He smashed the bookcase with the gun rack and threw the desk down the stairwell, then stumbled back and forth through the mess. His mother could hear it all from her corner in the living room. The last she'd seen of him, he'd been plodding up the staircase with a hammer under one arm. Then the rampage had begun – pounding and smashing and cursing, glass exploding, wood snapping. The walls around her shook with the impact. She called out for an end to it. She was ignored. It went on for quite a while. Then it suddenly stopped. Silence. Not a sound in the whole house. She called up. No answer. She wheeled her way to the foot of the staircase and called again. Nothing. She rolled back to her corner and sat wide-eyed in the dark, listening for some sign of activity. It was *too* quiet for the next hour.

Then, at four thirty she heard a noise. He was moving around again. She could hear papers rustling, floorboards moaning. Footsteps started coming down from the attic. A minute later a thud directly overhead. More footsteps. Down the staircase. Around the bend. He stepped through the doorway with a knife in one hand. She stared at him. He looked as though he'd been hit by a truck. He didn't look at her. He turned and started prying a wire loose from a row of staple clamps lining the door frame. Several termites fell from the ceiling around him. They tapped on the floor and scuttled away. He continued working the wire loose. He cut it. He discarded the knife, then disappeared again. She heard him walk down the hall toward the kitchen. The cellar door opened. He went down. Metal and lumber rattled around in piles. He was looking for something, rooting through the house fixtures. She had no idea of what was going on. She looked up at the door frame and tried to understand. The wire he'd cut was hanging loose, snipped and curlicued at mid-length. She followed one end of it to where it disappeared into a hole in the ceiling. She went back and followed the other end, down the frame, along the baseboard, over the floor and up to the telephone. She wheeled over and lifted the receiver. The line was dead. It had taken three weeks to get the phones back in order, and he'd just knocked them out again. She panicked. None of the girls were there – there were no beds left to sleep them in. She was trapped on the ground floor, and he was acting crazy. The footsteps started coming back up. She wheeled into the corner and froze. She saw him go by, limping toward the front door with a paint can in hand. The door opened. He went outside.

Out in the yard the first suggestions of dawn were bleeding through the forest. One of the bitches was suckling her pups by the mailbox. John walked to the side of the house. He pried into the can with a putty knife. A wave of fumes wafted out. The paint inside was over twelve years old, black, caustic and noxious. It had long-since congealed and separated from its base. He stirred it with a stick. He removed a stiff brush from his belt loop and dipped it in. He slapped a patch between two windows on the southern wall. It had an instantly corrosive effect on the existing whitewash. Several beads bled down the paneling and went rust brown around the edges. He stepped back and took a look. It was hideous.

He spent the next twenty minutes slinging thick black globs over the exterior facade of the entire house. Every wall sized up to a nightmarish scribble drawing – erratic swirls tapering off into pencil thin strokes, then leading into gigantic dripping pools. His skin and clothing were splattered. The hair on his forearms was clotted together in hard knots. When all but an inch of the supply had been used up, he filled the can with tap water from the outside faucet. He swirled it around and dumped it over the porch. He went back into the yard and looked over everything. He stood there for a minute. Madame Kaltenbrunner watched him from the window. He threw the bucket to one side and went into the house.

He walked to the kitchen. He pulled a two pound bag of sugar from the cabinet and emptied it into a pot. He'd read about this in the James Porter guide to home maintenance. He filled the pot with hot water. He stirred the mixture into a thick paste. Starting with the kitchen, he smeared it over every wall with his bare hands. He mashed it into the ceiling mats and flung it into the corners. He lined the interior of the cupboards. He coated the windowpane. After a minute the termites began appearing from the cracks in the corners. They crawled into the paste in a ravenous army. Before he'd even finished with the ground floor, they'd blanketed every inch of the ceiling and were moving downward. He went upstairs and continued.

It was dawn by the time he'd finished off with the attic. He dropped the pot and wiped his hands. He picked up a pipe from the corner. He went down to the second floor. It took two or three minutes to smash every remaining window in the house. With each new crash, Madame Kaltenbrunner's voice went up in a shrill cry. Her screams rolled through the halls. He made no attempt to placate her. She kept screaming. He didn't say a word. He finished with the windows and headed for the gun rack.

There were four boxes of lead shot left in the cabinet. He thumbed one shell into his back pocket and dumped the rest into a pillow case. He tied the top end of the case to his stained belt loop. He loaded the Winchester and went into his room. He looked around. A framed portrait of a young Ford Kaltenbrunner hung directly over his mattress. He blew it through the wall. Plaster and glass exploded over the floor. Early morning light spilled through the hole from outside, illuminating braided rivulets of gunpowder smoke and dust coursing through the room. Madame Kaltenbrunner went into overdrive. Her screams intensified and curdled. She lashed in her wheelchair, calling for an end to it. John pumped the Winchester. He shot the light fixture. A shower of sparks sprayed over the bed. He pumped again. He unloaded two more shells into the walls, opening new gaps and hazing up the room. Chunks of plaster came down on his head. He reloaded. He walked out into the hallway. He blew a hole in the ceiling. A patch of insulation opened up, exposing a seared network of electrical wiring. He went on. On the way to the bathroom he stopped to level the only article of furniture left on that floor – the oak-top Davenport with the copper trim. It was reduced to a pile of lumber in one direct blast.

Inside the bathroom, he stopped to regard himself in the full-length mirror along the wall. He barely recognized the face staring back. The emaciated figure with the sallow, cadaverous complexion and the crooked posture was slightly elongated by the bowed contours of the mirror's frame. Death eating a cracker. He blew it to a thousand pieces. He took out the cabinet mirror with the butt of the gun. He shot the toilet. A geyser of plumbing water surged from the mangled pipes and spread out over the floor. He reloaded. He could hear Madame Kaltenbrunner over the ringing in his ears.

He went on to her bedroom and did the same – one shot through each wall, one through the ceiling, one through the door. He turned around and looked down the hall. By carefully angling himself in the doorway, he was able to tear a single expanding strip along the Victorian papered walls, all the way back toward his room. He blew a hole in the closet frame, then turned toward the attic.

He obliterated the desk lodged in the stairwell in a single blast. Another shot went into the steps. Once upstairs, he put five holes in the roof and one through each wall. He smashed the light fixture with his fist. Already, as he turned his back on the devastated study to make for the ground floor, the whole house had been rendered unmarketable.

Madame Kaltenbrunner, by then, was expecting to be staring down a loaded barrel. She was coiled up in her Bankroft with her swollen hands wrapped over her skull. Her face was tight with the tracks of her tears. John came plodding down the staircase. She watched him walk by. He was reloading the Winchester on his way to the kitchen. Four consecutive shots boomed out. She heard a cupboard drop from the wall. The dish cabinet went over with a crash. The unbroken plates were stomped to pieces. The icebox door was blown from its latch. The footsteps made for the parlor.

She cried out, imploring him to stop this madness. He'd lost his mind, she said. He had no idea of what he was doing. He was to *stop, stop, stop at once*! She got no response, just a few hushed mutterings between gun blasts, something about woodrunner's justice and being the last outpost of reason. She heard her washbasin go. Then another door. She screamed and screamed and screamed, but it did no good.

At that moment a car rolled up in the drive. Madame Kaltenbrunner maneuvered her way to the window and drew back the blind. It was the first of the girls, right on time. She tried to yell out a warning. She wasn't heard. The crone in the wagon remained seated behind the wheel, gaping at the exterior of the house. Madame Kaltenbrunner yelled again. She wasn't noticed. Then she heard John coming out of the parlor and running for the door. She pleaded for him to stop. He didn't listen. He pushed out on to the porch and leveled the gun at the vehicle's windshield. The crone screamed. She slammed the car into reverse. He blew out her left front tire. The vehicle dropped to one side and continued lurching backwards. It fishtailed around the wood pile, then opened out along the drive. It disappeared, veering wildly around the bend on three wheels and one rim.

Madame Kaltenbrunner tried to change her approach by scolding him. *Now he'd done it*, she said from the window, *he'd open fired on a law-abiding citizen. The police would be coming out for him shortly. If he had any sense left he'd stop while he was ahead.*

It did no good. He didn't even turn to look at her. She watched him set the gun down in the yard and walk to the side of the house. He got up on Bucephalus. He started the engine. He turned and drove up the hill toward the barn. Halfway up he turned around. He started coming back. He went into a straight downhill run toward the house. Just beyond the wood pile he locked the throttle to the floor with a two by four and jumped off. Bucephalus pounded over the gravel. It shot up the bank and slammed into the wall. The radiator tore through the paneling into the kitchen. Part of the ceiling collapsed. The sink and counter exploded. The bulk of the tractor's frame lodged into the wall, with the forequarters squared away in the kitchen and the back wheels churning up mulch in the flower garden. The engine eventually jammed, locked up, and died with a crack. A cloud of diesel smoke piped into the kitchen.

That's when Madame Kaltenbrunner became convinced he really *had* lost it, for good this time. That tractor had always been his pride and joy. She remembered all those afternoons when he'd taken long trips to the hardware store for spare parts. He had loaded up on 11th St., then dragged everything back in a roller cart, all the way across the river. Afterwards, he'd even come up with some ridiculous pet name for it, though she couldn't remember what it was. In any case, he'd been obsessively attentive to its upkeep ever since. No one had gotten near it for a second. And now, he'd just driven it through the kitchen wall.

John reloaded the Winchester and shot up the yard. The mailbox went down. He put two gaping holes in the porch. He shot the power lines from their pole clamps. He walked down to the barn. He unfastened the locks and went inside. Twenty or thirty blasts resounded from the interior and carried over the hillside. He came back out. The alarm went off. He turned and blew the electronic horn from its nook beneath the drainpipe. It fell two stories into a patch of weeds. He walked back toward the house. The Winchester was searing hot in his hands. The whole estate looked like a breeding ground for Appalachian cannibals. He stepped on to the porch just as the first of the squad cars came screaming around the bend at the end of the drive.

Madame Kaltenbrunner watched him come back in. He locked the front door and walked into the den. She saw him rooting through a foot cabinet along the wall. He pulled out a half-empty bottle of gin from inside, stepped back, and pumped two shots into the collection of empty fishbowls lining the lower

110

shelf. He tucked the Winchester under one arm. He came back through the doorway.

Outside in the yard the squad cars ground to a halt. Several doors flew open. Voices went back and forth. A bullhorn came alive with spaghetti-western one-liners. Several demands were leveled at the house. John pulled the curtain back and looked out. More engines sounded from down the drive. He released the fabric and stepped back. He pulled up a chair. He sat down.

For the first time all morning he looked his mother straight in the face, and for the first time in longer than both of them could remember, she looked back. He handed her the bottle and said it was rightly hers. She took it into her trembling hands while he removed the last four shells from the pillowcase. He loaded them. He laid the Winchester across his lap. He looked at her again. Then he spoke.

He said there was no time for explanations. He knew she didn't understand the first thing about what he was doing. He also knew she thought he was crazy, and no one could ever blame her for it. But he was *not* crazy. He knew exactly what he was doing. He didn't expect her to believe it, but it was true. She was better off not knowing why. The only thing he wanted her to understand and remember was that he had never meant her any harm. He was only doing what he *knew* to be the right thing, outrageous as it may have seemed. If and when the time came, they would both end up on the right side of the fence, and then he would explain everything, not to worry. But for now they were out of time. The only thing he asked was that she get his Suffolks and leghorns into the hands of Elias Kauerbach at the feed mill, as he hadn't had time to make the necessary arrangements.

Madame Kaltenbrunner begged him to stop this horrible talk and go reason with the police. It was all so unnecessary, she said. He hushed her up and said it was too late for that. He got up. He walked over to the window and yelled out that he was sending his mother to the door. A garbled response shot back. He stepped away from the window. He pumped the Winchester. He walked around Madame Kaltenbrunner and angled her Bankroft toward the door. She started screaming. He pushed

111

forward. She groped at the walls and the door frame as they went. He pushed her into the hallway. She implored him not to do this. He unlocked the door. She latched on to the handle. He pried her fingers loose and told her to stop it. She pleaded. Tears gushed over her bloated cheeks. He opened the door and yelled out to come get her. The deputies crept through the yard. He leveled the Winchester. They hopped up on to the porch and got a hold of the chair. They lowered her from the ledge and wheeled her across the lawn. He threw the bottle of gin after them. Madame Kaltenbrunner looked back, screaming uncontrollably. He gave her one last look. Then he shut the door.

He fastened the locks and walked upstairs. He sat down with his back to the wall in the hallway. He could hear his mother and the bitches howling over the bullhorn. He looked around. A line of termites was coming through a gaping crater in the wall. He watched them drop into the plaster and glass along the floor. The air was thick with smoke from Bucephalus's engine. The closet door was hanging by one hinge. The toilet was still surging over the floor. His own ravaged figure seemed right at home in the mess.

After a while his mother's voice was gone. He had to assume she'd been taken away. He leaned the length of the gun barrel against his forehead and tried to forget about her. She'd be better off now anyway. The hospital would have her. And with a little luck she'd never discover the truth to any of this. She deserved a quiet ride from there on out. As long as she remembered the flocks as he'd told her, she could bow out with as much dignity as was left to be salvaged from the situation. Things actually could have ended up a lot worse, considering. He thought about it. His only real regret was that he wouldn't get to see the look on Hortense's face when they told her that what was left of the farm wasn't worth shaking a stick at. In this condition, it was actually a liability. With any luck, maybe the church would even have to foot the bill for the cleanup itself, it being the legal heir to the estate and all . . . Maybe . . . But probably not. If he knew well, Rev. White would somehow manage to snake his way out of it. That was usually the way these things worked. The only thing John had *really* done was managed to cancel the upcoming auction. In that light it wasn't much, admittedly, but at least it smacked of some sense of authorship. At least he'd finished the farm himself, being that, apparently, it had had to go in one way or another. No one could take it away from him now. There was nothing left to take. That was more than could be said for the crones' former associates. He allowed himself that. And anyway, if nothing else, the stillborns had stopped screaming . . .

He got to his feet and inched over to the window. He looked out. There were nine cruisers in the yard. He could hear the deputies creeping around on the porch. No crones. A lone squad car was sitting unattended by the wood pile. He looked around. No one had spotted him. He braced himself against the window-pane. He lined up with the vehicle. He fired. The windshield exploded inward. An immediate barrage of shots went up in response. He fell back into the hallway. What sounded like ten thousand rounds tore into the walls above him. He slid away from the window on his back. An expanding patchwork of black holes blossomed over the ceiling. Paint chips and hunks of plaster rained down on his head. He yelled at the top of his lungs. His voice was lost. He unloaded his last three shells into the wall. The Winchester went dead.

Someone called for a cease fire. The shooting stopped. The general roar panned out to the valley walls and was thrown back, criss-crossing and ricocheting between the opposing cliffs like a waylaid artillery attack searching for a home.

The deputies yelled back and forth again. He heard one of them fall in through the pantry window downstairs. Then one in the kitchen. He thumbed into his back pocket for the final shell. He got a hold of it. He opened up the magazine. Something dropped through the window to his left. He looked down. A cylindrical canister was sitting at his feet. A small rod ejected from one end. A thick stream of purple gas began hosing over his legs. He kicked at it and tried to scramble free. His eyes, nose and throat started to burn. He got up and stumbled toward the end of the hall, coughing and hacking. He felt his testicles strain toward his thorax. He tried to load the Winchester. His fingers seized up. The shell dropped to the floor. He reached for it. His legs gave out. He fell. He could hear footsteps charging over the floorboards down below. He collapsed and lashed out at the wall. A closet door fell over him. The last thing he heard was a voice over the bullhorn saying something about him being only fifteen.

II

BAKER

THERE'S NEVER BEEN a consistent methodology to Baker's judicial system. From the homiletic rulings of the valley's first council to the modern day courts' enforcement of a *regionally prioritized* derivative of national law, it seems that for as long as any legislative body has been in place, all the right people have, indeed, gotten all the wrong treatment. And vice-versa.

In October of 1871, a tobacco farmer from Sparrow's Height was convicted and sentenced to life in prison for the murder of a prominent Greene County plantation owner. Remarkably enough, there were no actual witnesses to the crime and all existing courtroom testimony amounted to almost comically unreliable hearsay. All the same, the sentence was passed, the case was closed, the defendant jailed. Several years later a deathbed confession was obtained from a known rival of the imprisoned farmer, who owned up, in his eleventh hour, to having committed the murder himself. But when brought back to the court's attention, the confession was deemed inadmissible – the self-professed culprit having passed away before his admission could be verified – and the convicted man lived out the rest of his days behind bars, despite substantial outcries of protest from the community.

Then, in contrast, less than ten years later – while the former defendant's appeal was still pending – a reputedly notorious town bully was witnessed by no less than fifty locals in the fatal shooting of an area shopkeeper. The murder occurred in broad daylight on the corner of 4th and Poplar, yet of all those bystanding witnesses, no one could be brought forward to testify – presumably out of fear of the gunman's associates. No charges ever materialized. The killer served no sentence.

In June of 1932, a local shoemaker was denounced as an incorrigible degenerate and sentenced to twenty years in prison for impregnating his fourteen-year-old niece. The court's alleged intolerance of pedophilia and incest was widely publicized throughout the case. However, two days after the trial's conclusion, its residing judge attended a family wedding at which the four hundred relatives in attendance were to be identified by one of four color-coded pins signifying their respective family links to either the bride or groom's parentage. A quick tally of everyone in attendance then exposed the entire proceeding as a hotbed for several generations of inbreeding, with some relatives sporting all four color-coded pins, and the judge himself wearing three.

Municipal justice in Pullman Valley, or the evident lack thereof, had made little marked progress in terms of consistency by the time of John's arrest. The Greene County prison was full of grown men serving two-year terms for possession of as little as one gram of marijuana, while chronic reports of spousal battery and inveterate child abuse went unheeded by authorities on an hourly basis. If and when arrested in Baker, there was really no telling what one might face. The local courts were notoriously dismissive of alcohol-related offenses, public disturbance cases, domestic disputes, and license violations. On the other hand, they were inordinately harsh on flag burners, crop thieves and homosexuals. John, in his case, might have just as easily been imprisoned for life as committed to a psychiatric ward for countless rounds of shock treatment.

But as it was, he did have one thing going for him: of the fifteen deputies in attendance during the holdout, one of them had been a state – as opposed to a local – officer, and as fortune would have it, it had been that one officer's patrol car upon which John had open fired. That necessarily brought the affair to the attention of the state, as a *state* concern, to be handled in *state* courts, by a *state* judge and, if necessary, a *state* jury. Which was probably the only thing that saved him from a hasty mock-trial and subsequent banishment to a dank cell in the county jail for the rest of his life. He'd chosen his quarry well, whether he knew it or not.

After two days of lithium-induced catatonia in one of Sheriff Dippold's holding cells, John was transported from Baker to a high-security juvenile branch of the state penitentiary, where he was kept under close observation in an isolated ward for the next two weeks. He was diagnosed with suicidal tendencies and heavily medicated with lithium, Xanax and Laudlin up to and through mid-December. The mug shots from the Bait Shack/Troll disaster, when paired off with the state crime-lab photos from the holdout taken only six weeks later, reveal an unbelievably drastic deterioration in his overall appearance. The wall-eyed, deer-in-the-headlights look of the first set give way and pale in comparison with the pathological, Texas-axe-murderer leer of the latter. On first glance, it would appear that several years had elapsed between the two pairs of exposures, or that the characters in print were not even one and the same.

After rigorous psychiatric evaluation, his case was handed over to a review board. Despite the panel's uncharacteristically liberal consideration of the mitigating circumstances behind the holdout, i.e., the defendant's ailing mother, his status as an only child in a one-parent family, the consequential lack of supervision, etc., the overall leniency of its ruling was still probably more of a bureaucratic slip-up than a humanitarian gesture. One can not generally rely on such humane treatment anywhere in the nation, particularly when charged with flagrant assault of a public defender. Baker would have jailed him for no less than a decade for the same offense. But the state was less severe. In the end, John was sentenced to three to six years of work release as an unpaid deckhand on a rivergoing freight barge.

Two days after the sentence was passed he was released from his cell, escorted to the docks of an upstate river town, and boarded on to an 8,400 hp triple-screwed Lower Mississippi towboat. He was led over the main deck, down a staircase and through the crew's lounge to a supply closet. The other deckhands' rooms were occupied, he was told. This hole in the wall, with its overhanging transducer cords, coiled steel cables, fire-axes, and one petroleum-stained burlap cot in the far corner, was to be his home for the next three years. During that time he was to work continual shifts, six hours on, six hours off, seven days a week without variance. He would never be permitted on shore, except to tie a line to the bank. He would drink no alcohol and ingest no illegal substances, on penalty of immediate return to prison in the capital. He would receive no pay, but in time, pending good behavior, he would be allotted a meager credit line with the incremental economy boats. For all this, he would be afforded the privilege of working in the open air, as opposed to confinement in an eight by ten, and granted the opportunity of serving out his sentence as a 'productive member of society.'

Once again, he could've done much worse. Life as a deckhand would prove to be no easy ride – the labor was brutal, the food disgusting, and the crew a group of barbaric plow dogs – but he would manage to remain left alone, and the practical experience of working the river did have certain advantages over the range of alternatives.

For one thing, he didn't have to worry about being raped by some five-hundred pound gorilla in one of the shower rooms. Which is more than might be said for any of the correctional facilities in which he might've otherwise wound up. There are distinct advantages to homophobia in certain contexts. The rest of the men on the boat, as agents of their own free will, were clear to sign off in any given port for a weekend of whoring and carousal anytime their own sideway glances toward crew mates became anything more than casual. John saw more turnovers in staff, for that reason, than he could soon remember.

He was also aware that, for himself at least, just about anything beat imprisonment. Even at the beginning, when the hundred-pound packing ratchets had dug permanent grooves into his shoulders, and the ceaseless demands from the captain were leaving him so worn out and exhausted that he felt his ravaged body might just disassemble right there on the gunwale without notice, he knew that instead of careening over the deck in a slave-driven delirium, he might have been vegetating in a dark hole somewhere without enough floorspace to pace. For that he felt genuinely fortunate.

And what was more, he never went hungry on the river. He could eat all the food he wanted at any hour of the day. The grueling nature of the work quickly hammered his frame back into shape. His appetite increased daily. His muscles toned and insinuated to definition. His shoulders bulked up, his torso hardened. He came to know the invigorating effects of intensive physical labor as he'd never experienced before. For probably the only time in his life he adopted regular sleep habits.

But by far the greatest advantage of all was being out of Baker, away from the incubus of crones, trolls, deputies and schoolrooms. He'd been placed on the river with no tangible link to his past, no idea of what was going on back home, what had become of the auction, the farm, the flock, etc., no letters in the mail, no school, no hospitals, no fine print, no press clips, in effect: *no history*, other than his own head full of memories. He'd been temporarily relieved of everything. But there still wasn't an hour that went by over the next three years that he didn't relive every step of the holdout in graphic detail.

While mopping the decks with the eddying river water cascading over the steel rim of the bow and rolling down the slope of the deck, he would stare out across whatever terrain confronted him, whether the dense tree-lined forests along the banks of Illinois, the erect stone chimneys of the power plants in Detroit, the pale yellow carbon arcs and coal docks in Louisiana, or the endless chain of river-rat camps in Kentucky, he would square himself off toward the sky-line and instinctively know, like a setter to the woodcock, the general direction of Greene County. He would almost be able to hear its roar coming through the forest, as though it might hike up its skirt at any moment and come stomping through the countryside to squat its rank, festering hindquarters right back down on top of him. It never left his mind. His past was canonized in his isolation. Baker, as a backdrop, swelled in his memory, martyred itself in his absence, until the whole thing had metamorphosed into an overblown freak circus in which vampires and cattle thieves roamed the streets in infected packs. It may have been a thousand miles in the distance geographically, but it was never really any farther off than his next moment alone.

After every shift of wiring timberheads to pelican hooks, packing ratchets, straps, chain links, shackles, pins, jackstaffs and cheater pipes, he'd sit alone in his dingy supply closet listening to the boom and crackle of the wheelhouse bullhorn, the hiss of the air clutches, the 2,800 hp engines mired in their pits, and over 300,000 gallons of diesel fuel sloshing around in the tank just below deck, and through it all he would strengthen his resolve, for better or worse, to start all over someday, to return to Baker and get it right the second time around.

John worked the river for just shy of three years. During that time he took to the post with all the vigor and resilience of even the burliest of his crew mates, all of whom, incidentally, were at least twelve years his senior on every boat. He never voiced any complaints concerning the work. He kept quiet and did as he was told. Several interesting stories came out of his experiences. As an example, there was one evening in a lower Mississippi tributary when the operating pilot got drunk on Old Crow and did $75,000 worth of damage to an overhanging interstate bridge. Among other things, the pilot was subsequently stripped of his operating license, the company was sued through the roof, and the interstate was closed for the season. Another time a crew technician who was lowered into the current to pull a midnight dive for emergency repairs was unexpectedly met with the fright of his life. As it worked out, he went down without cause for alarm, but he wasn't submerged for more than thirty seconds when his belt line started jerking and slapping wildly against the hull. A moment later he resurfaced in a wild panic, screaming to *Pull him up, pull him up, pull him up now!* Five deckhands hoisted him out of the water at once. When the captain finally managed to calm him down, the technician came out with a haunting report of a Mississippi catfish of no less than seven feet in length having loomed directly in line with his aquatic flash beam. And certainly the one that took the cake was the tale of the 'unfortunate deckhand.' The unfortunate deck hand was an ex-shop assistant from West Virginia who, while in a sleep-induced stupor one night, got up from his cot to relieve himself and unknowingly walked right by the same OUT OF ORDER sign that had been temporarily hung from every bathroom door on the ship. The sign apparently escaped his attention. He used the commode, unaware that the crew disposal engineer was at work two decks below connecting a filled-to-capacity forty-gallon septic tank with the vessel's main pressure generator and the sub-waterline discharge valves used for the routine unloading of accumulated waste. When the deckhand finished off with his business, he stood up, zipped his pants, hit the flush lever, and was blown off of his feet by the last four days worth of fecal matter from the entire crew, from the lowliest dock rat all the way up to the captain himself. There were hundreds of pounds of pressure per square inch behind the blast. It blew into every corner of the room. It filled the sinks, tore the mirrors from the wall, clogged the towel dispenser ... The rest of the crew heard the explosion and came running to see what in God's name ... They reached the lavatory doorway to find the deckhand wallowing blindly and thrashing about in a sprawling bog of pestilential excrement. He'd almost been scalped by the blast; the feces had packed into his gums, had jammed under his eyelids, had blown up his nasal tract, down his throat, into his lungs and stomach. The captain quickly radioed ahead to the next town so that an ambulance was waiting on the docks ten miles upstream.

The river abounded with similar anecdotes. There was no end to them, and John, being the avid raconteur of lengths-gone-to that he was, brought back his share, like everyone else. Wilbur still has a good number of them on file. They all might be considered noteworthy in some other context, but realistically, they're not central to our objective and would serve very little purpose here.

The important thing to bear in mind is that by the end of his term John looked and felt a whole different person than when he'd begun. Three years had elapsed since the holdout. He was now nineteen. He was much bigger in both height and stature, though a good deal of his bulk was only temporary and relied on continual exertion for its upkeep. His hair was cropped short. His appendages had thickened and taken on definition. Facial hair was coming in. At nineteen, he looked twenty-five, and few bartenders in town would ever take the time to card him for identification. The goatboy from the hill was gone, rendered unrecognizable through thirty-five months of hard labor.

The Baker he was returning to, on the other hand, hadn't changed a bit. Gingerbread row, with its novelty shops and trinket bins, was a calling-card replica of its former self. There were still no bookstores in town. There was still no musical outlet for thirty miles around, save for the jukeboxes in the taverns. John's own graduating class had moved on in accord with the provincial maxim: 'The rich man goes to college, the poor man goes to work . . .' The unavoidable gossip surrounding the holdout had gradually died away and been replaced with other postal-ballistic episodes of renegade assembly-line workers running rampant and driving stolen oil tankers through highway-side Baptist churches. No one remembered John on a one-to-one basis. Only his name had survived, and even that had begun to fade from public memory. Most locals remembered him only as 'The tractor boy.' *Whatever happened to the tractor boy?*, they would ask. No one knew. No one had ever known him in the first place. He was on his way back to a community that couldn't have seen him coming.

Madame Kaltenbrunner was long dead. Four months into his sentence John had gotten word by way of an express-telegram that after six days in a deep coma, she had finally slipped away for good. In the weeks immediately preceding her death she was found urinating in the janitor's closet and eating handfuls of crabgrass from the hospital courtyard. John had been formally barred from attending her funeral, which had saved him the trouble of having to decline the invitation. The house had been leveled. The land had been bought by a power company, an electrical generator erected on the spot where the barn had stood. The Suffolks had been culled after contracting anthrax; Elias Kauerbach was never contacted, for one reason or another. The last anyone had heard of Hortense, she'd been Tennessee-bound with a cancerous widow's enticing dossier tucked under one arm. Roy Mentzer had retired early and was said to be living in a trailer park just outside of Pottville. Some of the main characters had moved on. But the crones were still around. The trolls would always be there. The factory rats still poured into the Whistlin' Dick every night of the week. Baker was pretty much everything it had always been, just a few more inches around the equator.

John was released shortly after his birthday on the condition that he seek gainful employment in the community and attend a bi-monthly psychiatric consultation program for the duration of one year. A small apartment near the corner of 3rd and Geiger was secured for him in advance. Both his windows overlooked a filling station and a yard full of porcelain Baptist ornaments. A family of trolls lived just down below on the ground floor, with their hubcaps, skateboards and busted slingshots lying around on the lawn. The hallway outside of his door was cluttered with used tires and spare auto parts. The room itself was roach-infested and poorly lit, with a crumbling plaster ceiling that hadn't been repaired since before the war. Just upstairs lived a middle-aged garbage collector who would later enter the picture under more pressing circumstances, though for the time being, said collector and John would remain total strangers.

All in all, it was an anti-climactic return. John had expected, maybe even hoped for, a little something more to herald his arrival – some burning crosses or lynch mobs on the lawn, a coven of Methodists to picket his re-entry, a banner-wielding committee from the school board, anything at all. But to his disbelief, he found the streets quiet and empty. If any of the locals did know he'd returned, they didn't appear to care. He felt more inconsequential than ever. Three years of anticipatory apprehension deflated right out of him within his first few hours back in town.

On the second morning he jerry-rigged a bed from a nylon mat he'd found in a dumpster. He bought a footstool from the thrift shop and stole a radio from a neighbor's porch. With that, his room was furnished. He had one bag of rice, one fork, a saucer, a half-empty salt shaker, an alarm clock, and two dollars in change to his name. He was ready to start looking for a job.

That's how he wandered into Sodderbrook.

THE SODDERBROOK POULTRY PLANT is a long, rectilinear tin shed positioned at the southwestern base of Gwendolyn Hill, an equidistant stone's throw from the Ebony Steed reservoirs and the highway. The plant was established by a prominent seaboard industry in the mid-fifties. Its construction was overseen by a local committee of arguably shell-shocked war veterans whose seal of approval was deemed imperative any time a new industry made a pitch for nesting grounds in Baker. The main building, which has since been widely expanded and re-equipped, originally took eight months to construct, in which time the first wave of Mexican and Central American immigrants poured into Baker in response to a state-wide labor call. In essence, the need for an expendable work force brought the first of the 'wetbacks' to Baker, and the completion of the poultry plant, under their backbreaking efforts, paved the road to keep them coming for years on end. Most locals tend to cite this event as the beginning of some kind of end, though contrary to prevalent stereotypes, the Sodderbrook wetbacks have always been the most docile bunch in town. They live together on the outskirts of the community, up to eight or nine families at a time, in burned-out tenement houses leased by area slum lords. Their weekly paychecks from Sodderbrook and the sanitation department, meager as they are, can often support an entire family living south of the border for over a month. Regardless of the plant's dubious renown as 'the asshole of all creation,' the wetbacks apparently find life in Baker far preferable to their own hometown realities, and, that being the case, are almost always on best behavior beneath the watchful eye of regional immigration officials. They've gone to every conceivable length to get as far as they've

127

come and are not about to blow their increasingly favorable prospects of acquiring citizenship for nothing.

The building itself accommodates over seven hundred employees at full force. Almost five hundred of them are incrementally spaced out along two one hundred yard elevated evisceration tiers stretching from one end of the building to the other. Above each platform, a hook-lined belt runs along the length of the ceiling, from which the incoming gobblers hang suspended for various stages of disembowelment. At the farthest end of the plant the kill room is situated behind closed doors. As the belt emerges from the kill room flaps, it forks and proceeds over a colonnade of one hundred and eighty gallon scalding vats, along the tiers, and ultimately through to the finishing rooms, where the packaging workers seal and wrap the final products. There's also a storage house situated thirty yards from the main building, which is put to use primarily during the holiday seasons when excess production brings in almost 36,000 birds a day and the standard trailers can no longer house the surplus. The loading docks on the eastern end of the building cater to outgoing supply trucks and are always manned by the hardiest wetbacks in the fleet. All in all, the plant is one of the largest and most prosperous in the area, and, though situated outside of the main perimeter of production plants on the south end of town, is nevertheless a distinguishing hallmark of the community, to the eternal chagrin of most locals.

It was the height of the holiday season when John first came through the field, across the pickup-jammed asphalt lot, past the docking bay, and into the brown-carpeted applications office on the south end of the building. He looked out of place sitting there in his riverboat pants and his blue mining jacket (the only article returned to him from the estate). He waited on a plastic chair in the lobby amid eight or nine wetbacks lined up at the bathroom door for their arbitrary urinalysis. The room around him was filled with the stench of death, just as the air for a mile to any given direction of the plant was heavily laced with the aroma of blood and evisceration. Now, seated within earshot of the steady hum of the cleaning belt and the grating whine of the roller carts and rotary blades, he felt he was entering the belly of the whale itself. It didn't particularly frighten him so much as it began to corroborate the contentions of various firearms and game advocates who adamantly maintain that the due processes which put meat on our boards ultimately make the packs of heavily armed trolls roaming the forests in reckless hunting parties look like concerned humanitarians. Which is true enough, in spite of the general simian-mindedness of most huntsmen; just as it's necessary to 'separate the man from the artist' on occasion, so it is equally essential to credit an appropriate conclusion, regardless of the apparent spiritual or intellectual incapacity of its author(s).

When the time came, he was motioned toward a single door on the far end of the room. Once inside, he was seated at a long black table facing a spotty-looking poultry wench in a hair net. The poultry wench grilled him with a preliminary questionnaire, hovering over her clipboard and striking off appropriate boxes as she went. Did he have any severe allergies? Did he have a workable knowledge of the Spanish, or any other Latin, language? Did he have any history of mental illness? *Did he have any objection to working with a knife?* Was he willing to testify under oath to all of these claims? etc., etc., the standard rundown. All went well until he was questioned on having ever been convicted of a felony, at which time he fell silent and produced the rehabilitation papers as he'd been instructed. There was a tense moment of silence as the poultry wench went over the information with one raised eyebrow. When she finally broke out of it, she reached for the last of four red-ink stamps and slammed a block-capital KILL ROOM label on the face of his application. Without further comment he was dismissed to the urinalysis line.

He was 'zippered for the Gipper,' administered rubber hip boots, a hair net, overalls, one pair of elbow-length gloves, and a fourteen-inch carving knife with a newly sharpened blade. He was led down a hallway in the company of six similarly bedecked wetbacks, then escorted into the main room, from which the clutter and racket of high-powered machinery was emanating. As he came through the doors alongside of the others, he stood still for a moment to run his gaze from the center of the pipe-lined seventy-five foot ceiling above, down the grey walls with the host of repairmen on ladders tending to a ventilation fan, over a maze of cross-hatched fire escapes from the offices in the upper quarters, through the piping steam from the scalding vats, all the way down to the line of faces turned momentarily in his direction from the evisceration tiers. It was not unlike an incoming grunt's initiation to the troops in a full-scale conflict. Someone hollered at the wetbacks on the tiers to get back to work. The row of faces quickly melted into a sea of turned backs. The neverending hacking, chopping, gutting and cleansing on the belt continued.

The group John was with was quickly dispersed. Two of its members were sent to the packaging room, three to the second tier, one to the scalding vats, and John himself to the kill room. He plodded down the appropriate staircase and knocked on the door. An older wetback in a face mask who stood at about 4′ 11″ peered out, offering up a pair of safety goggles and a wool jaw strap. A stifling wave of hot air filtered out from the room behind him. The door opened. John went in.

Several months later he would learn that the kill-room wetbacks had been placing bets on how long he would last for over twenty minutes preceding his arrival that morning. As a rule, no one ever rated spats and a walking stick at Sodderbrook until he'd clouted the anvils of the kill room and lived to tell. As the record reflected, most white boys ran screaming from the building inside of the first ten minutes, if they even made it through the door at all. The odds had come to rest at 6–1 that he'd be gone by lunch.

On many days, as on that morning, the iron drainage ducts in the corners of the room were so clogged with coagulated plasma, feces and scorched feathers, that the entire 16′ × 25′ floorspace was backed up in a shin-deep lake of gore. The six cleaving altars, three to either side of the overhead belt, rose from the murk like stilted oil wells. The walls were permanently stained a deeper shade of crimson from floor to ceiling, and could even be peeled from it in brittle, semi-transparent layers which, according to wetback lore, were highly hallucinogenic when orally ingested.

Regardless of the two high-powered ventilation shafts set back in each wall, the overwhelming stench of bloodshed was almost unbearable.

The belt fed in forty grown turkeys of varying domestic strains per minute. The way it worked from start to finish was this:

Each incoming trailer was first backed into dock and locked in place. The doors were then thrown open so that the crews on hand, with their cod nets outstretched and body armor intact, could storm inward to round up all rogue gobblers. The turkeys themselves were pharmaceutical monstrosities; born and bred on massive cycles of steroids, housed in overpacked assembly cages, and transmogrified by dietary impurities that rendered them hostile to virtually all outside forms of life. When cornered, they often put up a terrific fight, but all were eventually subdued, hoisted upside down, and clipped by the ankles to the moving belt running along the ceiling. They thrashed, flapped and squawked all the way into the electrocution box, where they received a two hundred watt jolt that tore through every corpuscle in their bodies and left them spent and lifeless when they came out on the other side, straight into the kill room. And there the four to six knife-wielding wetbacks would stand, ankle deep in blood and feces for nine hours a day, cutting throats, one after another. There were six second intervals per person between each passing bird. Any gobbler which somehow survived both the electrocution box and the kill room was sure to perish in the scalding vats, the next stop beyond the rubber flap door on the far end of the room.

During the holiday season 25,000 birds on average were killed, cleaned and packaged every day. The increase in production called for a corresponding increase in temporary employees, among whom John was initially ranked. He started on a 'prove-your-worth' trial run basis. At the end of the holidays, if he'd been deemed a boon to the industry, he would be signed on permanently; if not, he'd be sent on his way at the first of the year with an eighteen pound turkey tucked under one arm as a token of the company's appreciation. That meant he had approximately ten minutes to seal his fate – first impressions count for everything at Sodderbrook.

He assumed position next to a fifty-something, battle-wearied looking wetback widely known as 'The Zombie.' The Zombie, as the second-to-oldest resident employee in the company, had been manning the kill room for seventeen years and counting at that point. He had all the air of a dead man about him. His systematic knife strokes were slow and devoid of hesitation. His movements were rigid, as though restricted by acute whiplash. His face was pale and drawn, his eyes hollowed and sunken as to resemble a callowed old whisky priest distributing communion wafers with an aura of devitalized sanctimoniousness. He was the most lifeless looking individual John would ever lay eyes on.

At the turn of the century a wave of progressive legislation had been passed to limit the number of hours the slaughterhouses' administers of death could be legally required or allowed to perform their duties without rest. For example, the steer droppers were prohibited from manning the blocks for more than two hours without taking a mandatory forty minute break. This was intended to preserve their psychological well-being, or at least to avoid the complete deterioration thereof. The new policies undoubtedly served their purposes for the beef industry. But somehow, separate and distinct legislation had been drawn up for the poultry plants, so that the employees in kill rooms all across the state – their duties somehow being considered less psychologically taxing than those of the bull-runners and steer-droppers (evolutionary ladder of life: mammal vs. fowl)—had been exempted from eligibility for similar mandatory reprieves. Consequently, most every poultry plant and fish cannery in the nation had its own token handful of employee breakdowns marring its history. In the case of Sodderbrook, there had been two severe episodes in the past ten years. The first involved a renegade wetback who'd gone into a hyperventilatory fit in the kill room, driven everyone out, and, in a psychotic frenzy, gutted and trampled what amounted to sixty-two incoming gobblers. He was eventually restrained and institutionalized, thereafter deported from the country. The second was a swan-dive/suicide into a scalding vat by a female employee who'd been transferred from the packaging room to the tiers after eight years of reliable service. Everyone agreed that the gruesome, taxing nature of the work could often drive a reasonably sensitive soul to the brink of madness, particularly when deprived of ample breathing time. But in other cases, when concerning more calloused, downtrodden souls like the Zombie, the result was often more akin to drug-induced anaesthesia than pressurized revolt. Individuals like the Zombie, and at least two hundred others along the tiers, were left as hollowed-out automatons who, after so many years, could scarcely register the light of day any more.

John would quickly recognize the essentially therapeutic value of his few incremental breaks. By his first lunch hour he'd singlehandedly cut three thousand throats. Though he had foiled all existing wagers as to the brevity of his endurance, he had nonetheless gone into uncontrollable vomiting convulsions after the first ninety minutes on line. All the gastric acid and half-digested beans from his stomach could still be seen bobbing around in the blood. As he pulled off his mask and stepped outside into the crisp morning air, he realized he had just been inundated with a concentrated dose of a far-off corner of reality most of the nation was not even aware existed. It shed a whole new light on his conception of packaged holiday turkeys lining the shelves at the supermarket. He thought of families all across the nation, rich and poor and all walks of life alike, meandering through candy-coated meat departments beneath soft lighting and holiday muzak. He wondered how many of them would remain carniverous if they were to be driven into the hack and splatter of the kill room for even five agonizing minutes of their lives. In John's own words: most of the nation lives far outside of having to stare its meal square in the eye before plowing in.

The thirty minute break in the parking lot, with the long line of wetbacks casually smoking on the steps and platform of the docking bay, slipped through his fingers like that much sand. The screeching of the belt, which had ground to a halt and given way to an ominous calm, still rang through his head in nerve-shattering repetition, just as the stiffening in his right hand from maintaining the grip on the cleaver all morning only commenced to crawl upward into his forearms with the temporary inactivity. It seemed he barely had time to walk to the edge of the lot and have a smoke of his own before the bell sounded out, signalling everyone back to post. The whine of the belt resumed and fell right back into place in his head, where it had never missed a notch to begin with. He pulled on his mouthguard, unsheathed his blade, punched back in on the clock, and descended into the pit once again.

He had marched through the fields to the plant before dawn that morning. When he finally punched out for the day, there was less than twenty minutes of light left in the sky. By the time he'd footed it across the highway, through the woods, beneath the water tower, and up the length of Geiger to his small red-brick apartment building, it was completely dark. Once inside his room, he hit the light switch and saw a drove of large black cockroaches scatter across the walls. He pulled off his father's coat and made a bee line for the mattress. He collapsed and didn't make a sound for the next hour. In all that time, it was everything he could do just to pull off his boots and feel his feet throb in the drafty, unheated matchbox of a room.

Downstairs the trolls were in the throes of a heated dispute. As per norm, he could hear them going back and forth over the dinner table as to various *faux pas* and breaches of etiquette. Their television was blaring so loudly he was actually able to follow the airing sitcom's plot over the ensuing argument. Sometimes in the late hours he could hear the mother and father caterwauling great cries to Allah while copulating with an all too visual zeal. He knew that with an upbringing like that, having sprung from a gene pool *that* polluted, and with the vices of their forebears so thoroughly impounded and secured right from the outset, all troll children were imminently doomed to perpetuate the lineage, *ad eternitum*. They didn't have a chance. They never would. As it was, their parents' excessive profanity and intermittent outbursts of violence threatened to infect all within earshot, family related or no.

134

At some point, after the trolls had finished their meal and moved operations from the room directly below his, John came out of his trance filthy and ravenous. He put a pot of water on to boil, then trudged out to the hallway water closet to wash up. By the time he made it back to the kitchen, the water had evaporated, as he'd spent over twenty-five minutes with his back to the wall on the shower floor scouring the dried turkey blood that had spilled into his boot and clotted into the hairs on his ankles. He'd rubbed his skin raw with a used Brillo pad that had been left behind with the toilet. This ritualistic cleansing was to become as much of a nightly staple as the pork flavored instant-noodle dinner on the fire escape and the subsequent five minute walk to the liquor store for two 40 oz. bottles of malt liquor. John's lifelong bouts with insomnia were to reach an all-time high throughout his stay at Sodderbrook, and without that cheap beer to take the bite out of the grind, to ease the pain in his ankles, and to keep the soundtrack in his head at an endurable minimum, he probably would have aged a full ten years over the course of the next two.

That first night he lay awake in the dark hearing the slosh of turkey blood, the popping of the electrocution box, and the screaming of shackled birds in the same manner others hear register keys and the clanging of dishracks long after the day's end. He drifted into an uneasy sleep some time after 3 a.m. with the events of the day having become distant and horrific to the point of impossibility. Then, at 6:15 a.m., his alarm clock rattled to send him back through the fields for another go.

Six days later, on receiving his first week's paycheck, he found that his already pathetic final figure had been docked a full day's pay for his required apparel. He was initially outraged over the additional charge, but he was eventually forced to accept it, knowing it meant he'd been approved for permanent employ and would outlive his fellow temps beyond the holiday season. He had withstood the demands of the kill room with uncommon fortitude, and for what it was worth, someone up in the castle had taken note. It was vaguely comforting.

For the first two weeks, the hours at the cleaving altar dragged by at a torturous crawl. John was off at dawn and back at dusk with nothing in the interim but an unrelenting litany of bloodshed that would've reduced most Pottville highwaymen to tears. His life was an ongoing lament of jammed drainpipes, severed jugulars, screaming turkeys, and thunderclaps from the electrocution box. The disgracefully inadequate pay rate was, in terms of insufficiency, rivaled only by the company insurance policy's myriad of loopholes which rendered the standing five hundred dollar deductible 'safety net' an illusory joke. He'd seen one too many wetbacks hauled off in stretchers after crippling falls from the tiers not to begin to realize that their never being seen or heard from again indicated Sodderbrook's refusal, on grounds of one vague technicality or another, to foot the required medical bills. This was apparently acknowledged as standard policy by both administrator and employee. In the event of an injury, the belt was rarely even brought to a halt. The natural human inclination to gather around the latest casualty in an inquiring pack was eradicated by the howling reproaches of the foremen. Ideally, when an accident did occur, everyone continued working without missing a single hack, stroke or thrust. Before the victim could be strapped into place by responding medics, a pitiless traditional Mexican death chant would go up all along the tiers, as though to say, from those left standing to him in the crypt, 'so long, pendejo, and give my regards to the family.' The singing welled up in the expanse of the main room like a lakeside Baptist choir railing at the heathens on the opposite shore.

Back in the kill room John was stuck with the Zombie – who never said a word – and two younger wetbacks who spoke no English. In a staff of seven hundred, those four had been appointed to the cleaving altars. They rarely had cause for dispute. There was really nothing to fight over, and the existing communication barrier limited their infrequent exchanges to sporadic guttural mutterings. They each took turns getting down on all fours in the murk to unclog the drains with a common toilet plunger. They were very democratic about it. They even had a laugh from time to time, at least John and the younger two:

as the closing hour approached and the punch-drunk delirium set in, they would take to lobbing off heads in one clean stroke and angling their chops so as to clip one another with the severed projectiles. They kept score in that manner, though all were too poor to wager any real money on the game. During one of their bouts the younger of the two wetbacks, who had, incidentally, played the role of Christ in his home village's annual live re-enactment of the crucifixion some years back – and even had the scars in each hand to show for it – accidentally lodged his knife into the vertebrae of one of the birds during an unsuccessful cut. The belt carried his blade away, and it ended up at the bottom of a scalding vat where no one could reach it. The wetback was fined $47 for its replacement and reprimanded for his ineptitude. Strange as it sounds, it was the only laugh to be had in the kill room.

The rest was an unrelenting nightmare. Once the holidays were over, the more inefficient temps were sent on their way. John was left behind at the altars as a new addition to the perma-nent staff. Almost half of his earthly existence was whiled away as a sweat-soaked executioner, sinking his blade into the quiv-ering gobblers, one after another, day in and day out. The charge from the electrocution box often singed the feathers and brought the stench of scorched quills wafting into the room to com-mingle with the already caustic odor of blood. It stank so badly that even the Zombie, after seventeen years of steady service, was still prone to occasional fits of vomiting. Vomiting was never regarded as a black mark on one's virility; on the contrary, it was seen as a lingering testament to one's residual, albeit withering, humanity. One hurled and was done with it. The others covered for him in the meantime.

Most of the Sodderbrook wetbacks were blithering alcoholics. Their circuitous route from time clock to tavern, then home to bed seemed like the only reasonable option left – other than maybe stealing off with a lime-green Kawasaki, donning a sombrero and a Superman cape, and driving straight through a department store window at 90 m.p.h. – for anyone working in the plant. It was a difficult pattern *not* to follow, and John soon found himself stricken with his share of the *thirst* as well. His own footsteps began leading him in an involuntary march for the Whistlin' Dick at the close of every shift.

BEING THAT THE BETTER HALF of Pullman Valley's existing populace has a history of heritage-in-residence almost predating the birth of the nation, and that, by nature, most of those families have steadfastly adhered to the fundamental values, beliefs, and objectives of their forebears throughout the centuries, paralleling historical and contemporary realities often delineates many of the same peculiarities akin to Baker's founding fathers and subsequent settlers which are evidently manifested in the carriage and conduct of its modern day residents. In an age when the rest of the nation may be undergoing its much talked about 'loss of family values,' its 'moral breakdown,' etc., the citizens of Greene County, tucked away in their remote, insular outback in the corn belt, continue poll-parroting the behavior of their ancestors to a tee. As such, the consumption of alcohol in almost any form is, historically and contemporarily speaking, as inseparable to the genealogy and heritage of the Baker Lay as its deep-seated creed of envy, mistrust, and contempt for one's neighbor. The two are, in fact, interrelated and run hand-in-hand all through Pullman Valley's post-European migratory history.

The first known European explorers to appear in this area were the 'coureur des bois,' – the French/Canadian wood runners – who, in the first quarter of the seventeenth century, came plowing through the unexplored wilderness from the north with satchels full of brandy thrown over their shoulders and all due intentions of establishing trading posts with the natives. The none too friendly tribe of Shawnee Indians they found parading around an enormous village at the foot of Gwendolyn Hill quickly offered up more beaver pelts than the wood runners could possibly haul in exchange for all the brandy the white men had in their possession. For the next six days the Shawnee drank themselves into an uninhibited frenzy. They scampered through the fields and threw one another into the river. The wood runners, having completed their transaction, hastily departed for fear of being ambushed once the supply had diminished. They went on their way and did not return. No white man was spotted in the area again for the next century.

Then, in 1769, the notorious 'Long Hunters,' the pioneers of the wilderness road, came forging over the Blue Ridge Mountains, through the Cumberland Gap, and down into the plains. Once again, dubious trade relations were established with the natives – the mountain men offering kettles, trinkets, pistols, and, of course, whisky, in exchange for otter and beaver pelts. The Long Hunters returned to the coast with cart loads of precious hides and tales of deer at every salt lick, flocks of wild turkeys in the trees, lush land for the taking all around, and a tribe of filthy bare-asses with an uncanny hankering for watered-down rotgut. The news tore through the seaside colonies like wildfire, enticing whole settlements of transient wastrels, pogrom refugees, chronic alcoholics, escaped criminals, exiled illiterates, and several thousand German mercenaries, or *Hessians*, left high and dry after the revolutionary war. Within a few years the wilderness road had been well worn by droves of livestock and Conestoga wagons drawn by three to six yoke of oxen a piece. In Pullman Valley the settlers descended on Gwendolyn Hill *en masse*, erecting a rickety village walled with slate and limestone overlooking the Shawnee camp.

As the few documented Shawnee accounts indicate, area tribes had been elaborating on rumors of fabled gods from the east arriving by sea in chariots of gold and ivory for generations preceding the appearance of even the wood runners a hundred years earlier. By the latter half of the eighteenth century their expectations had reached an all time high. A whole new legion of Patagonian oversouls had been envisioned, the arrival of which would mark the end of an age of sickness and confusion, and signify the dawn of a new era of prosperity. It had been foretold and awaited for generations.

So, naturally enough, it was to their profound disappointment that they found the first wave of 'new gods' to be the most debauched, repulsive mob of cut-throats and degenerates they had ever imagined possible. It was as though some hair-shirt gollem had unexpectedly vomited all over the valley. The settlers forded through the river gap in what the tribal elders took for sick buffalo. Their children were inexcusably foul tempered and were frequently witnessed battering one another with garden tools. The women were bloated around the middle and adorned accordingly in what appeared to be dried coot gut. The men had filthy faces, were unabashedly cantankerous, dug into their rectums while intoxicated and brawled amongst themselves continually. And with each new wave of settlers came more sickness and disease – strange new infirmities that left over half of the Shawnee bedridden for weeks. There was vomiting and death in every camp.

But the settlers didn't seem to give a damn. The European diseases raged through the tribe while the settlers themselves threw riotous bashes and fellated one another openly. Casks of moonshine were erected on stilts. Cottages and sod houses were built. Churches shot up. The men fired off their rifles from the hillsides around great bonfires every night. The village was filled with trash and cooking utensils. The settlers gutted up the ground for no apparent reason, ran screaming through the streets in bald packs, spewed venom from the windowpanes, beat one another mercilessly, and were swept away by camp-meeting fever which left them speaking in tongues and convulsing in quasi-epileptic fits. It didn't take long for the Shawnee to realize these were no gods at all; on the contrary, these were exiled kitchen scullions from some faraway and undoubtedly cursed nation of hobgoblins, where their chief or king or leader, or whatever it was that governed over them, had emptied out his jails and driven off all the undesirables in the land. As such, full-scale confrontation was imminentized.

The common historical inquiry as to why the settlers and tribes could not peacefully coexist is a useless, untenable approach to the matter; the real question should be – how and why were the respective groups able to endure the proximity of one another for as long as they did. As time passed the initial tension between them was only exacerbated by numerous infractions on the part of both camps, not the least of which involved the birth of a half-breed to one of the settler's wives, and the unearthing of a tribal burial ground during the settlers' rerouting of an irrigation ditch along the banks of the Patokah. Realistically, war was inevitable long before it broke out, but interestingly enough, it wasn't until a group of Shawnee braves crept up the hill one night to torch the inn – the *only public saloon* – that a decisive catalyst was produced and the settlers were prompted to retaliate with a full-blown attack. Their liquor had gone up in the fire, and they were left stone-cold murderous on the hillside, frantically pitching buckets of water from the river up the makeshift daisy-chain to the blaze.

The standard massacre followed.

Over the course of the next few weeks the Shawnee were systematically driven out of the valley. Their camps were burned, their hunting grounds poisoned, their braves hounded down in packs, their women raped and killed. The settlers moved in to stay. What was left of the tribe moved on forever. Before long it was as though it had never been there.

The settlers lost sixty-seven men and a small cache of Kentucky rifles in the conflict. Afterwards, there was an abortive attempt to reconstruct the inn, but halfway through its completion a long rain began, and before the downpour subsided a landslide on the north end of the settlement brought sixty yards of the village wall down into the river. After that, many of the sod houses began to collapse. Even the church, with its solid oak frame, fell to pieces. The village had become uninhabitable. A meeting was called, a motion was made, and without further delay the settlers packed up their belongings and moved down the hill to begin construction on what would eventually become Baker as we know it. The remains of the original settlement were left behind to rot on the hillside as a prolonged, one hundred and seventy-five year compost experiment to be handed on to Ebony Steed in the middle of the twentieth century.

The river was as central to the existence of the early European settlers as 254 is now vital to modern-day Baker. A small colony of log cabins and stableyards was built along the banks of the Patokah, two miles to the southwest of Gwendolyn Hill. By the turn of the century, flatboats transporting twenty hogs heads of tobacco, logs, pig iron, lime, slaves and hog meat were embarking for New Orleans every day. A group of burly Dutch and English dock workers set up in tin shacks and lean-tos along the banks. The community river raft which transported cargo and lumber from one shore to the other was replaced by a stone bridge, two ox-cart lanes wide. Every afternoon, local farmers brought their crops into port to stand in line alongside of lumbermen and miners from all over the valley. Baker, as a functioning colony, had been established.

The growing community soon saw the arrival of missionaries and pastors. The First Methodist Church was built along a gravel road which would eventually become Main St. The church stood alone on an oak-lined lot with a stone wall and garden of petunias surrounding it. The bordering forest was cleared, a road was carved out, and a line of balloon-framed houses was built to either side of the courtyard.

Three decades after the church's construction, the first great wave of European Immigration was under way. Before it was over, Baker, like most of the corn belt, would inherit a throng of predominantly German and, to a lesser degree, Scandinavian castaways, all fleeing political turmoil, feudalism, poor harvests, and overwhelming oppression overseas. Once again, these settlers were not comprised of the moneyed, affluent, well-to-do citizenry of leisurely, upper-class Europe, the way nationalist historians may contend, but rather of the poverty-ridden, uneducated, woebegotten dregs of the peasantry. The poor huddled masses. The white trash. On the whole they were a combative, vulgar, ignorant and hopelessly superstitious people. They brought with them a system of old-world work ethics sure to perpetuate itself for generations to come, and the obstinacy to stand behind it all to the bitter end. As in the case of

Baker's original founders, behind the new wave's guise of diligence and thrift lurked a propensity for indulgence and expenditure, just as behind its facade of Christian harmony lay an inexhaustible reservoir of seething and contempt for one's neighbor.

By midway through the century an eastern railroad company purchased a strip of land through the northern half of Pullman Valley and began laying down a set of tracks along the right bank of the Patokah. A grading crew of German and Irish laborers used picks, shovels, and scrapers drawn by horses to level the roadbed. Five 'Iron Men' were assigned to each 700 pound rail tie, to be followed up by ten spikers and clampers. It was a rough, indefatigably vigorous crew by nature. The men and their temporary directors were housed in local inns during the construction, and later on, after they'd moved on, they were quoted as stating that in all 500 miles of their work-related journey, they never wandered into a more volatile community of lunatics and drunkards than Baker. *Those people are insane*, they were prone to repeating. Leatherhanded as the crew may have been, they couldn't wait to get out of the area.

In 1857 the rail line was completed. J.B. Turner steam engines were soon rolling through the valley around the clock. Their conductors and crews made regular stops at the grain mill on the north end of town. The freight cars were backed into place beneath elevated grain silos, locked, loaded, and sent on their way. By then most of the nation's corn, wheat and wool was being produced on this side of the Ohio, as more than half of the country's citizens were living west of Appalachia.

Baker prospered. The town hall was built. Antebellum homes replaced the log cabins in the north. Tobacco warehouses came into existence. A limestone courthouse was built along Main St., itself now a thriving 350 yard outpost of exchange. There was a public bank, a school, an infirmary, a network of roads, and enough taverns to spoon-feed four battalions of pub-sots. The turn of the century saw the community well on its way. And the Germans kept coming.

Farm income rose by a third during the First World War,

but afterwards operating expenses went up and overproduction decreased prices. Many locals emigrated to the cities during the twenties as a result of the economic crisis, leaving Baker behind, a notoriously 'wet' community in the throes of the national prohibition. The age of bathtub gin and bootlegging began . . .

Anyone familiar with this region and its people would have to concede that the very concept of imposing sanctions on 'friend alcohol' in a place like Pullman Valley is on a par with plotting to strip a pack of forest wolves of its fresh kill. Nowadays even the *thought* of it might ignite a civil war. It was bad enough back then, when the churches were openly endorsing the injunctions and the law was obliged to follow suit. For thirteen long years whisky stills abounded in corroded tin sheds all through the valley. Poisonous brews of sourmash and corn whisky blinded, crippled and dropped locals dead in their tracks on street corners and porch stoops. Governmental raids turned the community into an open war zone. There were shoot-outs in the hills. There were random attacks on public defenders. There was widespread dissension in the ranks among local smuggling rings. All of Greene County was thrown into a paranoid craze, one which culminated in the widely publicized fatal plane crash of a barnstormer who was four score to the billygoat at a public exhibition. In all of Baker's history, no single decade has been more turbulent or disastrous than the 'roaring' twenties, and it all stemmed from the inception of a policy which the powers-that-be should've known better than to have seriously considered implementing in the first place. It was a bad idea from beginning to end, and before it was over, it had successfully threatened to tear the whole nation apart at the seams in the same manner it had the corn belt.

But the prohibition eventually ended. The national depression brought many farmers back to town. But it wasn't until the advent of the Second World War that the agricultural dilemma was resolved. The government moved to subsidize the cost of fertilizer, and universities sent agents to instruct farmers in building up the eroded land. Thereafter production soared. The war put agricultural products in high-priority demand, and by

1945, farm yields and income had more than doubled. The war ended with the ball in the farmer's court, and the farmer himself back in the valley to stay.

The depression was over. The troops came home. A nation-wide industrial mobilization began. All across the country towns like Baker came alive with production plants. A network of highways swept across the corn belt. In Baker, it was 254 around which the entire community would soon base its existence. From the Sparrow's Height stableyards to the hospital-side trailer park, 254 ran from north to south like a central nervous system, up and down the expanding backbone of warehouses and manu-facturing plants. The streets fell into a horizontal grid, split down the middle by the highway, from the St. Francis of Assisi resting ground on 1st Street, through the town square with its gazebo and public fountain, and out to the community hospital on 13th. The majority of the factories were clustered together on the south end of town. Their gravel lots and docking bays held over five hundred cars and trucks a piece on average. The fac-tories collectively released over two tons of environmentally toxic hydrocarbons into the air every year, thickening the valley with a full-time stench of burning plastic. There were novelty warehouses with towering aisles of baby Jesus, velvet Elvis and poker dogs to be shipped off to the nation's social security recipients and patrons of Jimmy the Greek. There were pressing plants that pumped out everything from compressors, screws, clothing, furniture, caskets and church steeples to cherry-wood reproductions of Victorian bureaus and multi-colored motel bill-boards. There was a sanitation department, a pork shack, a truck stop, and a landfill. There was 'Main' – or 4th – street, 'Ginger-bread Row' with its utility and trinket shops, spiraling barber poles and cigar-store Indians, circa 1952, at every corner. Baker was a prospering coal-town and postwar time capsule, a defini-tive blue-collar labor base with all the production plants and red brick houses to boot. That's what it had become, and that's what it has remained.

Presently, every morning at 5:30 a.m. 254 comes to life with bleary-eyed machinery operators and factory rats mobilizing in somnambulistic succession, pickup after gun rack after confederate flag in a row. And behind each windshield another baleful countenance lighting up with the glow from three or four cigarettes to be washed down with a breakfast of soda and potato chips in the dark. They pour into town by the thousands every morning before dawn. They toil away at their respective trades all day, then head home long after sundown, leaving behind the stark little community of just over four thousand residents, all of whom could be packed into the school gym in the event of an air raid.

In Dale Murphy's words, the Baker Lay are a hard-driving, insatiably melancholic mob of sectarian-minded patriots who'd just as soon see their own beloved neighbors strung up with turkey wire and swinging from the high-frequency light poles all the way down the road to work. This is the land of Jesus on a gun rack, where the church is the linchpin of daily life, the make of a man's automobile is more of a status symbol than his wife, and family roots run, and sometimes intertwine, as deep as spring water. The community revolves around weddings, funerals, school athletics, the perennial maxim that 'shit won't happen if I just work harder,' and the nightly downing of as much domestic swill as one can possibly imbibe.

Year after year Greene County is consistently among the top five in the nation in terms of per-capita alcohol consumption. Almost everyone in town drinks out of a terrifying necessity. Most young men aren't considered as having come of age until they've wrapped at least one pickup around a telephone pole in a drunken stupor. The school board is comprised of notorious drunks. The youth throw keg bashes in the hills only to be chased off into the forest, inebriated and half-naked, by beer-gutted ex-marines now serving as defenders of the public trust. The factory rats are born with sourmash in the flask on hand. The trolls are even worse. Even the bartenders quaff a few on the sly. It's a community of lushes and no one would ever argue otherwise.

On the inside wall of the men's stall at the Whistlin' Dick, it's all been summed up in a nickel-whittled Hail Mary:

147

THE BOTTLE, THE BOTTLE, THE BOTTLE BLESSED BE,
THE BOTTLE-BEARING EARTH BOUND CHARIOT
BY ALL WE HOLD DEAR, LET IT NEVER RUN DRY . . .
GIVE US THIS DAY OUR DAILY DRAM
AND LEAD US NOT INTO SOBRIETY,
BUT DELIVER US FROM DROUGHT
IN NOMINA DOMINI, BY ALL WE HOLD DEAR,
LET IT NEVER RUN DRY . . .

Author unknown. It could've been any tavern regular who scrawled out this notorious beershit epitaph during a round at the porcelain altar. Most locals know it by heart and are given to group explications of its indubitable wisdom during late hours at the Dick. Though there are several other swill troughs in town – most notably the Bloody Bucket, the Drop In, Bob's Good Time, and, of course, the truck stop – the most cavernous gullets in town regularly convene in the Whistlin' Dick as the number one preferred tavern in the area.

Situated three doors in from the town square in the two hundred block of Main St., the Whistlin' Dick was founded in the mid-fifties by an elderly German couple who later sold out to a one-time pipe organ tuner by the name of Dick Fisher. Thus, the Whistlin' Dick. The Dick's ownership has since changed hands many times over, but somehow the name has always stuck. The building was originally the only theater house in town, which explains the plummeting downward slope of the floor and the enormous, curtain-drawn stage in the back room. Over half of the available floor space is closed to the public, but the remaining room, on its eighteen-degree angle, is often said to leave patrons feeling as though they're drinking on a wheelchair ramp.

A long peninsular counter extends outward from the west wall into the 40′ × 75′ space of the main room. Several black and white photographs hang slightly cockeyed in pine frames high up on the wall next to an old wooden rowing oar mounted over the register and a rack of whisky bottles. The room is furnished with overhead fans, neon beer signs, a row of hubcaps along three separate shelves, a twenty-year-old jukebox, and more mounted bucks than might appear in the Tanner county emporium of taxidermy. The walls are marred with live wires running over graffiti and beer stains that haven't been cleaned for the better part of three decades. Positioned next to the business hours card and facing outward on the front door hangs a license plate logo with a pencil portrait of a smoking gun, which reads: WE DO NOT CALL 911.

Most of the factories let out between 3 and 5 p.m. The Whistlin' Dick is on its way by early evening, roaring by nine. The majority of the locals make a nightly bee-line from the plant lot to the tavern, and, as such, it's only on weekends that they appear geared in anything other than factory apparel and soiled jumpers. The pitchers roll at all hours and don't let up until closing time at two.

John usually arrived with the Sodderbrook crew just before six. Although not legally barred from entry, most of the wetbacks knew better than to stick around the Dick for more than an hour. Out of an instinct of self-preservation they downed their first round in the early hours and cleared out before the night got underway. Most of them then headed for the truck stop or Bob's, where the proponents of open-season on all first-generation immigrants were comfortably outnumbered. John, as a white boy, didn't have the same worries. His concerns lay more with dodging flying chairs and steering clear of the numerous confrontations sure to surface throughout the evening.

He would quietly seat himself at a single table in the far corner which is still regarded as 'Dead man's lair.' He always ordered one double shot of Jose Cuervo and three pints of beer all at once, so as to avoid contact with the bar staff for the next hour. After a full day in the kill room it took the whole of his first round just to level back out. In retrospect, some of us seem to remember having spotted him there in the early days, sitting all alone in the dark with the overhead low-powered lamp bulb throwing long shadows over his exhausted countenance. He was there almost every night. But none of us knew the first thing about him at the time, and he was never seen in the company of others. His solitary hours in the Dick were spent winding down

149

from the job and watching the regulars steadily metamorphose as the night wore on.

Evenings at the Whistlin' Dick proceed in three phases, the first of which, as the preliminary setting for the rest of the night, is relatively low key and uneventful. On average, phase one could be taken for any other Podunk tavern's happy hour in the corn belt, just as, other than their intrepid apparel and questionable genetic deficiencies, the Baker Lay, on first impression, look to be run of the mill American gothic. Between five and eight o'clock, no one ever makes much of a fuss. Actually, no one really even talks. The jukebox remains disconnected until after the grill is shut down at seven. Factory rats from all over the valley file in to set up at their tables and disinterestedly converse while power-chasing literally hundreds of gallons of draft beer from the taps with a quiet, somber air of determination about them. As ferocious as their preliminary intake may sound, early hours in the Dick are always the quietest of the evening, really nothing out of the ordinary. Most of the regulars are just trying to come back around to what passes for levelheadedness in Pullman Valley, and they do so by efficiently knocking back enough tumblers, cans and bottles to overload the first two or three sixty-gallon trash bins and send them on their way to the dumpster in the alley.

At some point after eight, things begin to take a turn. The onset of phase two is much like an unseen blanket slowly settling over the room – the lights going down, music starting up, after-dinner crews pouring in, and the stool huggers who've been at the bar since five having suddenly attained 'coal rat's bliss' through the downing of the first half-case. There's no real way of picking out the moment it hits – one usually just looks around at some point along the way to find himself immersed in an enlivened phase two. The indications are clear to every side – faces flushing over, sweat beginning to roll, beer calls becoming more frequent, urgent and impassioned. The whole room starts to reek like a vapid Schlitz fart on the break from the communal rectum. Every table load reels its way through a round of self-congratulatory group triumph. Jaws flap loose, laughter goes up. Card games hit the tables. Drinking contests are held. Everyone has a go at the day's toll by upping the watermark a notch. In these moments the regulars are in the 'good old boy' phase. They're the good old boys for an hour or two, and there's never much to fear from the good old boys. They usually do no harm to anyone but themselves. A good old boy is different from a redneck. Despite all confusion on the matter, there *is* a difference. A good old boy is different from a redneck in the same way the rednecks are different from the white trash. Though they may all seem one and the same to some people, the three faces of eve to others, and torn somewhere between two indistinguishably horrid extremes – the river rats and the trolls – to those who absolutely do not know their knee-highs from moon pies (damned yankees), anyone in the area would have to agree that the good old boys will always be the least threatening of the lot. They're generally not out to cause any trouble – they just want to blow off some steam – and anyone this side of the ACT-UP swat team, the Schnellville tree-huggers association, and the friends and advocates of the Reverend Jesse can still make it through the next two or three hours without much of a problem. Once again, if the evening were ever to end on this note, the Whistlin' Dick could easily pass for any working man's dive in the nation. But this is Pullman Valley, and phase two rarely outlives midnight.

After that, one begins to get some feeling for the chill that must have shot through the hearts and minds of the Shawnee two centuries ago when that first boat load of European scalawags came charging through the river gap and into the valley. It's usually that one beer, that one line-breaker that goes down a few minutes after the hour which bridges the gap between this-side-of-inebriated and nasty-violent drunk. It's that one beer that unexpectedly transforms the main floor of the Whistlin' Dick public tavern into the upper loft of the Pullman Valley Stable Yard Inn, circa 1789. It's almost as though all the malevolence of our forebears had been distilled for time-release impact in the current house whisky. Phase three is when the good old boys die. It usually originates and breaks loose from one particularly rowdy table. No one ever sees it coming, and with hindsight, no one ever knows exactly what touched it off, but once it does hit, there's absolutely no stopping it.

To understand phase three in full, one should first be given to understand that on general principle no one ever walks away from a direct challenge in Greene County, no matter how out-numbered or in the wrong he may be. It just doesn't happen. Physical injuries heal with time, but being blacklisted for cowardice in Pullman Valley is a lifelong stigma. No one walks away from a pointed threat. Particularly when he's power-saturated twenty beers and five shots of whisky, and the room around him is every bit as ready to blow as he'll ever be. When someone tells him where to get off, he responds in kind (classic: 'Fuck you' – 'No, Fuck *you*!'). Which inevitably leads to *What're you gonna do about it?* And there's obviously nowhere to go from there but down. All it takes is one little gaff to set the stage for an all out pipe-wielding feud in the streets. One of Baker's most notorious knock-down brawls – the October of '74 blitz – originated with an argument over a basket of pretzels. It doesn't take much to set the regulars off. The brawls are really just waiting to happen. Most locals would probably define them as good clean fun more than anything. Which still doesn't mean it's not a miracle no one's ever been killed in one of them . . .

As it goes, they're usually touched off by two or three isolated individuals who inadvertently stumble into a dispute over one thing or another. Their argument remains self-contained, off in one corner, and goes back and forth for a minute or two until additional parties eventually begin to catch on and join in. After that it's only a matter of moments before the whole thing is panning out and sweeping the room like a rampant epidemic. Table loads take off like rivaling sports teams. The furniture workers, for example, need no prompting to lay into the crew from Keller & Powell. The cannery rats have always despised the DMU group. The Pollenderry lumber men have it in for the Dairy Queen staff. Etc., right on down the line: everyone hates the hill scrubs, few care much for the staff from the Dollar General, and no one in his right mind – which, of course, is no longer a consideration at this point – will ever challenge the coal truck operators from Ebony Steed (they've got that crazy Evans sonofabitch who just doesn't know when to quit). Before anyone can move to stop it, the whole room is teetering on the brink of collapse. Groups are tearing into one another, voices going up, fists pounding on the counter tops, threats being made. The bartenders often try to intervene but are personally insulted in the process and thereby dragged into the dispute as active participants. Direct challenges are soon issued. On most evenings, the staff can successfully reroute the bulk of the ensuing battle to the street without having to pull out the artillery. But on other nights, the insults run too deep to avoid the outbreak of an all-out knock-down brawl right there on the floor. There's really nothing in the world that can compare with the collective spontaneous combustion of a room full of shit-faced Greene County factory rats. Other scenes of pandemonium may measure up to and surpass the Baker melees in terms of magnitude and body count, but nothing compares with a Dick brawl on grounds of pure ineradicable havoc. Once it starts, the room is reduced to a bomb-swept disaster area in seconds – chairs flying, tables overturning, bottles smashing over heads, fists pounding, etc. – one battling mass of humanity surging for the doorway in a deafening ensemble of bone on bone. At that point, if any disinterested party happens to be on hand, meaning if anyone was actually dumb enough to see it coming and didn't clear out while he had a chance, the only real option, as a non-participant, is to take haven in the far, back left corner of the room the way John used to, and watch out for flying objects. On a good evening the bartenders can usually empty out the room – with the help of the loaded 12-gauge from beneath the counter – within a minute. But once outside, the battle resumes with loud hosannas. Trash cans are pitched end over end, flower pots smashed, cars crawled over, packs of the vanquished stampeded through the streets and into the fields on the edge of town.

John, in his day, almost always managed to make it out of the tavern unscathed, and even on the few occasions that he did not, it was only to the tune of a blind sucker-punch or an unintended blow from a random projectile. Otherwise, he remained all alone in his corner and maintained his neutrality as a lone, inconsequential Sodderbrook employee with no sworn allegiance to any group. From time to time he was briefly acknowledged as the turkey boy in the corner who never seemed to say a word and drank as much as any wetback in town. But once the brawls were underway, he was forgotten. No one paid him any mind.

Over the following seasons he must have been on hand for at least thirty Whistlin' Dick brawls of varying severity. He studied and reveled in them with the same initiative that brings lettered men to the corridas, sociologists to cockfights, and all good patrons to the coliseum's edge.

JOHN WAS DUE FOR his first psychiatric evaluation by the second week in February. On the morning of Sunday the fourteenth he crawled out of bed at 7:15 a.m. – his one day off and he still beat the sun – to foot it across town to the social security building on 12th St. He was dressed in the standard-issue reintegration suit granted him on release from the river. Wandering up the highway in that stiff-collared polyester dress coat and those pleated slacks, he might have been taken for any wayward churchgoer on the Lord's day.

The night before had been something else ... There had been three unrelated incidents leading to arrest in Baker alone, and the Sunday morning paper, along with police scanners all across the county, was reporting similar, no less wild and bizarre behavior from the surrounding communities as well. The first arrest to be made was that of an area welfare-recipient whose checkered past with substance abuse had resulted in the revocation of his driver's license, banishment from almost every tavern in town, three citations for lewd and lascivious behavior, and the total breakdown of his fourth marriage. Being technically deprived of legal driving privileges, he'd then taken to tooling through the streets on a common John Deere riding mower. On the previous evening he'd drunk his existing reserve of homebrew and gone pinwheeling into a four-way intersection on his mower, jamming the Saturday-night traffic flow at 9th and Poplar for over twenty-five minutes. He was eventually beaten by frustrated commuters, thereafter arrested on four different charges.

It didn't get any better on the outskirts of town. At 9:06 p.m.

155

an area resident phoned police to report that an unidentified man in a blue rain coat had broken into her barn and was molesting the heifers. Sheriff Dippold immediately dispatched an officer to the scene, where the report was soon confirmed. But the intruder, having spotted the deputy on arrival, fled the barn on foot, clad only in a pair of rubber galoshes and a dog collar. The deputy gave chase and apprehended the suspect in a ravine two hundred yards from the scene of the crime. The suspect's name and address were being withheld for reasons of 'public interest.'

The final arrest was that of an area munitions worker who, on briefly returning to his home in the midst of an all-night pub crawl, had found his homestead vacant and went on to suspect some levantine deviltry in the works between his wife of twenty-one years and a nearby shopkeeper. He'd then stormed to said shopkeeper's establishment and singlehandedly smashed two full-sized storefront windows with his bare fists. On being apprehended and sedated, he'd had nothing to say for himself. His wrists and forearms were badly lacerated and gushing. He was driven to the emergency room. His wife, who, incidentally, had run to the market for lunch meat five minutes earlier and had returned to find the kitchen overturned and the front door ripped from its hinges, stated that 'Stanley's a bit excitable from time to time, especially on account of the moon.'

Which was probably true enough. Moon sickness, as an enigmatic ailment, has always affected Greene County in a manner statistically transcending mere superstition and continually putting skeptical members of due medical professions to the test. The moon had been full the night before, and the inordinately high level of acknowledged misconduct was only a vague indicator of what had really been going on behind closed doors. For every registered arrest there was sure to have been a slew of similar infractions which went unreported.

John himself suffered from moon sickness to some extent, but he never took to screwing house cats or torching dumpsters as a result. He was more subject to all night bouts of maddening insomnia. The evening before his evaluation had been no different. He'd slept three hours in the past seventy-two and was now walking down the road, therapy-bound on the morning after. He was delirious with long-term sleep deprivation. Which may have had something to do with the disastrous scenario that followed.

He reached the social security building at 8:05 a.m. He was seated with a counsellor by a quarter past. He quickly realized that the young, well-trimmed university graduate who was to conduct the interview had at his command about as much intuitive understanding of human behavior as a fourth generation river rat. 'The Graduate,' as he would be remembered, was the most pathetic social cripple John had ever seen. It was hard to believe such a fidgety, pencil-necked nincompoop, one who probably could've been reduced to tears in two or three direct words, had actually been appointed to deal with ostensibly reformed felons. It didn't seem possible. Anyone, closet-case misanthrope or no, could've breezed through the following exchange with the absolute bare minimum of tact. It was more like applying for kitchen work at a Dairy Queen than being evaluated as a potential threat to society.

He was given a preliminary rundown of yes/no questions, including inquiries on his health, his religious denomination, his current wage, his relations with neighbors, any recent dabblings in illegal substances, etc. He was then asked to produce proof of his running employment status. He handed over a pile of paycheck stubs. The graduate pored over them, nervously pairing off with his own notes while chewing on one end of a yellow fountain pen. John still couldn't believe what he was seeing.

Next came the formula confession – the sensitive part – the 'one-to-one reflection and consideration' which the graduate had obviously been dreading all morning.

When asked if he could briefly reflect on any progress he felt he might have made toward becoming a respectable member of the community, John had to consider his options. He knew that if he phrased his response accordingly, said only what he knew the graduate needed to hear, he would be on his way in ten minutes. But a part of him wanted to state otherwise. A part of him wanted to say Yes, his reintegration was proceeding brilliantly – since his release he'd learned to sever an electrocuted jugular from every conceivable angle, to speak a smattering of profanity in street Spanish, to purge his roach-infested apartment with boric acid, to hand-clean his blood-soaked laundry in a shower basin, to prepare microwave dinners in a conventional cooker without scorching the whipped potatoes, to rattle off a handful of working-class puns, the lyrical content of the current country top 40, that all negroes have such big noses because God had to step on their faces to rip their tails off, that man's job was to answer to God, but woman's job was to answer to man, that Pottville Hessians ate their children, that it was better to see your wife run off with a Jew than to see your boy on a Jap bike, and that, come to think of it, the Japs were getting altogether out of hand again – time to nuke 'em, that all foreigners ought to be banished to a remote coral reef and fragged into oblivion, to vote Republican or die, that there's nothing better for the soul than a hard day's work, that the only good queer is a dead one, to knock himself out with drink as the only viable ticket to sleep, and that, if the truth be known, as long as things kept up at this rate he'd be completely reformed in no time at all. Pretty soon he'd be living in some troll-infested trailer park and shooting up the neighbor's yard with a .45 automatic. Yes, he was definitely making progress, he wanted to say. He'd become fully convinced that every well-adjusted, God-fearing citizen in Baker persevered with all the characteristic resilience of a sewer rat in the face of a nuclear blast. And he'd be one of them soon enough, he would. He wanted to say . . .

But of course, he didn't. Instead, as much as it pained him, he stated very simply that everything was going fine, which, just as he'd expected, pleased and relieved the graduate to no end. With a mutual nod of the head, there was no further discussion between them. Moving right along, the only thing that remained to their meeting was a small stack of papers that needed signing, after which John would be free to leave. He initialed every page in the bunch with little more than a casual glance at each. He probably would have finished the whole stack in two minutes had something about the second to last form not suddenly caught his eye. He slowed down to look it over. From what he gathered it was a life insurance policy of some kind which he knew nothing about, but which nevertheless smelled offensively Methodist. On closer examination, his suspicions were confirmed. He turned the page over. He found a pre-existing signature in bold red ink in an adjoining column on the lower half of the page, which read, plain as day: Hortense Allenbach.

John snapped forward and demanded an explanation. *What the hell is this*, he screamed. The graduate turned pale and started shuffling through his papers. He found something and looked at it. It took him a while to comprehend. Then he began to explain something to the effect that following John's release, according to legal procedure, Hortense Allenbach, as his *sworn guardian*, was due to receive monthly funding to assist with his upbringing until he reached the age of twenty-one. It was all there in black and white. Madame Kaltenbrunner's own signature had sealed the policy.

At that point John lost his head completely. What had opened and proceeded as a tolerably inconsequential exchange between two total strangers concluded with a nonsensical rampage that could've very easily landed John right back on the river to serve out the remainder of his maximum penalty sentence. As it went, he lunged across the table, grabbed a fistful of the squealing graduate's hair, and pinned him to the desk with threats to leave him wandering the highway with a fire poker in his ass. He screamed that they could put him back on the river, they could throw him in a cell, they could slander his name all over town, but he would *never* in a hundred thousand centuries be caught dead signing that paper. It was out of the question. They'd have to shoot him first. They could hack it up, burn it up, tear it up and shove it – take that paper along with the viper, every crone in the valley and the church itself on a flying screw to the moon. He would *never* sign it. He ripped it up and stormed out of the office, kicking over an aluminum can in the lobby as he went.

Halfway up the road he came to his senses. He found himself standing on the corner of 8th and 254 with a line of church-bound Lincolns pushing by to either side. The realization of what he'd just done began to hit. He went in to pacing circles around the corner phone booth, torn between a reawakened hatred for Hortense and panicked disbelief in himself for having blown his lid at the precise moment he could least afford it. He realized that if he didn't pull himself together and make some hasty amends, he might very well be holed up in the capital in the company of hardened criminals by that hour the next day. He could picture the resulting press, hailing him as another casualty 'on account of the moon.' It would be a terrible way to go.

All these combined considerations sent him footing it into the supermarket to purchase a token of his apology. After some deliberation, he settled on an expired fruit cake from the damaged rack. He paid for it with the last of his wages, then headed back toward the social security building. But once there, the secretary at the main desk informed him that the graduate was not taking visitors. He'd locked himself in his office, she said. He'd locked himself in his office and would see no one. John could picture the sorry bastard sputtering over his files in there. He left the fruitcake on the counter and crept out of the building. He was *screwed*.

No one really knows what happened with the graduate. As could have been expected, he didn't last long in Baker. After six weeks on the job, he applied for an out-of-town transfer and, to the best of anyone's knowledge, was thereafter bound for an office job in Missouri, never to be heard from again. But his transfer doesn't account for the sudden disappearance of John's case. Nothing really does. In the end, not only was John never charged for his outburst on the morning of the fourteenth, he was never contacted by anyone in the agency again. He received no letters, no visits, no follow-ups or phone calls, and never had another psychiatric evaluation in his life. It doesn't make the least bit of sense, but that *is* what happened. Either someone lost his file, someone dropped his case, or the graduate was genuinely touched by the fruitcake, some slip-up that no one can rightly figure transpired along the way, the end result being John's complete dismissal from the state's attention.

After a week of walking the floors and throwing paranoid glances over his shoulders at every turn, it became clear that he was not being sent for. And as another month passed, then another, and finally a third without any word on the matter whatsoever, he realized that, amazingly enough, his bungling mismanagement of the mandatory evaluation had somehow brought his three-year sentence to an abrupt, miraculous and not altogether legal end. Surprised as he was, it was an unexpected gift horse he was not about to stare in the mouth. In effect, he'd become a free man with all the legal rights and entitlements of the average citizen, and, more importantly, he'd been granted the option of quitting the poultry plant, or any other barnyard he ended up in, if and when it became too unbearable. He was back in the world with no little green men at his heels, no chimeras on his back. Impossible as it seemed, the long, drawn-out nightmare which had begun almost four years earlier with the death of Isabelle had finally come to an end.

On the positive side, this granted him some much-needed leverage at Sodderbrook. Had his legal status as a trial-release felon remained in effect, as it should have, he would have had no real say in his everyday appointment to post. He would have been in no position to make demands of any kind, and all potential causes for reprimand would have brought him within a hair's breadth of invoking the dreaded phone call to the state correctional administrators. But, that no longer appearing to be a primary concern, one of the first things he did on feeling comfortably in the clear was get himself out of the kill room. The endless repetition of his hours at the cleaving altars had become a quotidian dead end. Every hour of every day it was one hairpin stroke after another at the same fixed pace. It was going nowhere. He was accomplishing nothing.

On resolving to put an end to it, he left his post in mid-stroke one afternoon, climbed one of the steel mesh fire escapes to the main office, and entered the human relations room with demands for a reassignment. His forwardness apparently left a favorable impression, or possibly left no room for dispute, as within the hour a spot had been cleared for him on the first evisceration tier. He saw to it directly. But after two days of removing gizzards and cleaning body cavities at the same deleterious rate as before, he was back in the office with renewed demands. He wanted a spot on the docking bay, he said. He wanted a spot on the docking bay, and if the company knew what was good for it, they'd give it to him. Consequently, his cleaver was taken in exchange for plastic body armor and a four by six cod net. He was marched down to the platform and turned over to the operating foreman to join the hardy, barrel-chested wetbacks on the incoming docks. It may not seem like much of a promotion, but working the docking bays – in contrast with the uninterrupted lull of the kill room – afforded John the first opportunity he'd had in years to prove his worth. He was at last in a position calling for personal skill, dexterity, and technique, and as might've been expected, he proved to be the most valuable employee on the payroll within the first week. In no time at all, raiding fecal-blasted trailer cabins with his cod net outstretched and the gobblers scattering in every direction before him became second nature, just as the pustulating hack marks from beak and claw lining his forearms became signifying trademarks of his profession. After the first month he was singlehandedly performing the equivalent labor of four grown men. He put the wetbacks to shame. It was said to be almost embarrassing. He was unquestionably the finest turkey chaser in the plant, and, all things considered, the attainment of his new appointment to the post could be indirectly traced back to his uncontrolled, moon-sick outburst in the social security building on February fourteenth. In many ways it turned out to be a blessing in disguise.

But in other respects, the consequences of his only meeting with the graduate had a proportionately adverse effect. Most notably on his personal life. With the newly acquired and sickening realization that, after all the time that had elapsed since the holdout, Hortense Allenbach, the viper omniscient, was still cashing in on the plunder and destruction of the Kaltenbrunner homestead, the very same past which John had done everything in his power to categorize, bury and forget over the years was irreversibly brought back to center stage. The idea that not only had the crones razed and desecrated his estate via public endorsement, but that they were still, years later, after all that time, being so much as governmentally subsidized for it made

John realize, once and for all, that the past was not over, that the chicanery continued, and that forgetting about anything was no longer an option. Try as he had, he'd never really gotten over the loss of the farm anyway; he'd only learned to live with it as a dull, steady ache that could be held at bay with the required effort. Had there been no further installments, he might've even come to terms with it in time . . . But that was out of the question now. He would never be able to rationalize this latest development. Madame Kaltenbrunner was dead. The vault had been plundered, John had been sentenced, the farm had been leveled, and Hortense, wherever she was, was receiving a monthly paycheck for her part in it all. Any way he looked at it, it was unforgivably disgusting.

One of the advantages to working the trailers during that period of his life was the general inability of any dockhand to loaf on the clock. From the moment the iron gate was thrown open at dawn to the final turkey's shackled disappearance into the kill room at five, the docking bay, as the plant's lifeline, was constantly swarming with high-powered activity. Darting back and forth from a trailer load of screaming cargo to the overhead clamping belt with the entire line's rate of operation hanging in the balance left not a moment to be spared on anyone's part, least of all John's. It was everything he could do to keep from charging into the parking lot in a bounding series of pirouettes during break time (again, an object in motion tends to stay in motion), much less to find a free moment to stand idly by on the clock. For as long as he remained at Sodderbrook, the rigorous demands and responsibilities of his post nullified his tendency to wax reminiscent.

But even during the holiday seasons when the call for overtime took the clock into the late hours and left most of the wetbacks dead on their feet, no amount of expenditure or fatigue could've stemmed the resurgence of memories sure to ensue the moment John was left alone with himself. It would begin the second he set foot into the fields after work, and wouldn't let up until he was back on the clock the next morning. In the interim, his pot-pie dinner and a round at the Dick would set the stage for the late night pacing to come. Long after the rest of the world had turned in and the highway had quieted down to an occasional roar from an out-of-town freighter, he would find himself walking the floors of his apartment, cutting back and forth through his own docking-bay stench, until the bottles started rattling and falling from their shelves down below in the troll kitchen. The two light bulbs in the center of his ceiling threw multiple shadows of his passing form along the wall as he moved. He was soon well acquainted with every spot in the room where the two shadows would converge, one would give way to the thickening shade of the other, one would fall off, pan, lengthen and recede along the floor, then swell and darken again at the expense of its companion. Time after time, pass after pass, hour after hour, he and his shadows reeling through the room, fueled on by a synthetic octane of alcohol, nicotine, MSG, and undiluted primordial anger. He often felt that the systematic rages he worked himself into actually fed on themselves biologically, that by carefully recollecting every given disaster his mind's eye could conjure – the twister tearing a hole through the estate, Madame Kaltenbrunner's catatonic obesity, Roy Mentzer creeping through the hallway, careening trolls in uninspected wagons, bleeding into a pool of himself in a dark holding cell, Ford Kaltenbrunner's forever indeterminate alignment, and always, without fail, Hortense's Parthian shot before slinking off into the night, all of it, every wrong that had gone unredressed, everything that had become a distant, incomprehensible nightmare that was so consistently bizarre it *had* to have happened – he often felt that by dwelling on the big picture in its entirety, the hypersecretion of some rare internal gland was actually brought about, one which, had it been extracted, purified, mass-produced and administered to a company of front-line grunts in a clandestine governmental experiment, would have indisputably proven to heighten aggressive instincts to the point of homicidal mania.

He would spend drifting eternities staring at the cracks in the ceiling, seeing the winding tributaries of a river down below from a bird's-eye view of planet earth. Passing headlights would send the silhouette of his windowpane panning over the length of the room in long arcs. Sometimes he would take to the streets to meander over the asphalt in the dead of night. He would follow Geiger north, past the Methodist church, along the row of houses with their wind chimes clanging and their blinds drawn. He would cut east across the highway, always alarming the golden retriever at the corner and leaving it straining on its chain. He would climb the craggy embankment to the cemetery, scale the wall, make his way up the hill, and come to rest with his back to the crumbling headstone of a governmental official who'd been beaten to death by 'Peace Democrats' while issuing draft notices during the Civil War. From there he would have a clear view of the entire valley, with an electrical storm of fireflies blanketing the fields across the river to the north, and the flood-lights and porch lanterns illuminating the roads of Baker to the rear. On clear nights, the moon and overhead constellations would light up all of Gwendolyn Hill. The line of trees running along the Patokah was clearly visible down the bank from where the farm had stood. Which would invariably bring to mind the afternoons he'd spent cleaning up the riverbank, hauling shop-ping carts and carburetors out of the mud and towing them down to the dockside dumping grounds with Bucephalus. Or looking out across the river to the Ebony Steed reservoirs every morning. Or burning Isabelle's shack and pitching his father's bottle into the current . . .

Sometimes he remained in the cemetery for hours. He once fell asleep and woke up in a thunderstorm, covered with hill snails. He later remembered that evening as one of the finest of his life. Something about the storm clouds pushing by just over-head and the wind rolling up the hill from the south to meet them, while he stood there in between, shaking off the gastro-pods from his rain-sopped jeans. There were a handful of nights like that, most of which he spent perched on gravel mounds in the dockyards with the waves lapping gently at the support beams of the outbound pier. Several locomotives would push through the yards behind him, rolling by, high up on the trackbed, dragging behind an uninterrupted line of freight cars, until the spent lavender cabooses would loom into view, veer by, disappear around the bend and continue on their way. And staring out over the film of petroleum on the surface of the Patokah to where the cornfields began their long stratified run toward the valley walls. And the wild dogs in the forest sounding off to one another in sustained howls, while the locusts hummed on and the hoot owls went into dive bombing runs along the banks. There were those nights when he almost managed to forget about everything, if only temporarily. One of the most ironic things about Pullman Valley is that, all marks of civilization aside, the landscape really is beautiful. On select occasions, with an emphasis on select, John almost felt as though he were a part of it all.

But those few moments were annihilated the second he set foot for home. Even as the community slumbered in the pre-dawn hours and the street lamps clicked off for the duration, all it took was one glance in any direction to remind him that, in Baker, goatboys running their paralytic mothers to the emergency room were broadsided by trolls, denied required medical attention, beaten to within an inch of their lives and incarcerated in unmopped cells, while just outside every white-trash/pit-bull combo in town hooted at mud football matches between the sheriff's league and the fire department. Try as he did, he just couldn't shake it off. There were too many *aides-mémoire* to every side, too many props still on the set. He was in residence at the scene of the crime, and there was no escaping it. Like any reasonably sensitive soul born to a falling off in the road, ostracized as a fool, branded an idiot, a loser, and a freak by a confraternity of goosestompers and wife-beater-born-to-the-plow, he soon cultivated an irrevocable hatred not just for Hortense, or Mentzer, or any group of individuals in particular, but for the community around him as a faceless whole.

Which could lead to the question: *Then why didn't he just leave?* If he had no family in the area, no friends, nothing but bad memories. If he really held down one of the worst jobs in the nation and was terribly underpaid for his services. If he had no vested interest whatsoever in being or becoming a part of the community, then *Why Stay?* It doesn't make the least bit of sense. One of the first things that ought to occur to anyone as impossibly out of his element as John Kaltenbrunner was his whole life through is that you *get yourself out, and you never, never, never come back for as long as you live*. John wasn't the most practical-minded individual ever to grace the valley, but certainly that conclusion, more than any other of its kind, had to have occurred to him on a regular basis.

Yet stay he did. And not only did he remain in residence, he threw himself headlong into the epicenter of local affairs. The taverns were the hotbed of Baker behaviorism. For that reason they would've seemed the last place in the world to find John on any night. He would've had no reason to immerse himself in the company of those he most despised had he not been working toward something all along. Had he only wanted to drink, he could've gone to the liquor store and spent the rest of the evening in his apartment, in the cemetery, the coal yards, any-where but the Dick. Yet night after night there he sat, intently running his gaze over the crowd. There had to have been some reason.

We believe that what it comes down to is this: John was too far into his own history in Baker to pack up and leave. He probably never would've been able to live with himself had he left town without first incinerating a few hundred bait shacks. There were too many loose ends to his existence. Too many matters had been left unresolved. He'd lost one too many battle and made several thousand too many mistakes to back out without first taking a shot at evening up the score. Anyway, he couldn't do any worse than he already had. He'd reached rock bottom, or so he thought. Things could only sink so low before they began to come back up.

So he stayed on. He kept going, studying the locals, walking crooked circles, looking for an opening, something, *anything* that might work *for* instead of *against* him for once in his life.

WILBUR ALTEMEYER was born and raised on a pig farm in a corn-producing region of southern Wisconsin. At the age of twenty-three, as a stocky, well-fed farmhand with no current academic enrollment, he was drafted for a tour of duty in Vietnam. With the customary bluster and support of his home town spurring him on, he, along with seventeen other locals – ten of them volunteers – was set to take to the bush in defense of the body politic. A farewell parade was thrown in the town square. All respects were paid, all parting sentiments exchanged. Then, without further delay, the eighteen young men in question were shipped off for Fort Banning in an olive drab personnel bus. Which should have been the end of that. However, to the overwhelming shame and disgrace of his family, Wilbur alone was subsequently pronounced unfit for active service due to his poor eyesight. He was shipped back home within a week of his initial departure. He returned to the community as an acknowledged outcast. He remained in town for three weeks of public excoriation until, finally, he could take it no more and left.

He spent the next seven years operating as an all-night freight-truck driver, hauling eighteen-wheeler shipments from coast to coast on sleepless, three-day excursions. It was during one of his later runs when he got his first look at Baker by way of the all-night truck stop just north of town. There he met a young brakeman's-daughter type by the name of Leslie Verkamp, who was working behind the coffee counter. He and Miss Leslie hit it off immediately. Wilbur began making somewhat less than practical detours on his weekly runs in order to pay visits to the girl he was convinced would someday be his wife. Finally, one afternoon, after several months of these erratic visits, he sauntered into the truck stop, got down on his knees, and announced in tones loud enough to halt the course of conversation at every table in the dining area, that he was prepared to renounce the callings of his trade if only she'd consent to be his in wedlock. Miss Leslie accepted his proposal without hesitation, and, with a foot-stomping ovation spurring them on, they left the building in full-stride. Three days later Wilbur turned in his trailer and secured his last paycheck. He and Miss Leslie became Mr. and Mrs. Wilbur Altemeyer one week later, and with Wilbur's life-savings in a bundle they lit out for an extended honeymoon in Baton Rouge.

It was a common, Arthurian enough opening to the average life in matrimony. But what followed was not in keeping with the same . . .

While moving south through Louisiana on the third day of their trip, the new Mrs. Altemeyer came upon dreadful misfortunes in a rest-stop lavatory somewhere along highway 61. Apparently, earlier on in the afternoon of the day in question, a swamp moccasin of no less than three feet in length had made its way into the highwayside sewer system and slithered up through the septic pipes, so that by the time Mrs. Altemeyer seated herself on the commode, it was coiled up in the bowl and waiting in a thick, repulsive knot below the surface of the water. The investigating coroner later found no trace of venom in her system; evidently, she just parted her legs, saw a pair of beady eyes staring back at her, and went into immediate cardiac arrest. The officers responding to the emergency were said to have spent a full ninety minutes trying to pry the tattered and thrashed remains of the snake from Wilbur's fist after he'd locked himself in the room and horsewhipped the mirrors and dispensers from the walls in a maniacal frenzy. He was kept under close observation for two weeks, then sent home to drown in his sorrows for the rest of his life.

He came off of the three-week drunk that followed penniless and unemployed. At the age of thirty-one and three months he secured a job with the Baker disposal company and settled into a dimly lit chamber near 3rd and Geiger. The walls of his room became a shrine and testament to Miss Leslie. Next to the long row of framed snapshots from their wedding ceremony hung a long lock of her hair which had been laminated in sheet plastic. For as long as he lived, Wilbur swore he would never find another like her. Like Madame Kaltenbrunner, he never remarried.

At forty-three he was squat, pot-bellied and balding – the portrait of a middle-aged trash man in black-rimmed spectacles and faded overalls. He lived on a steady diet of nightly rounds and televised sports events. He finished off every evening with nine or ten cans of cheap beer, then cleaned off the counter, emptied out the ashtrays, and turned into his oak-framed military surplus sleeper. There was nothing particularly noteworthy to Wilbur's outward appearance. He was a good enough character – harmless, dependable, and efficient – but realistically, there were millions of others just like him all across the country. Had he never crossed paths with John, he probably would've lived out the rest of his days as a relative nobody.

In over twelve years in residence on Geiger, Wilbur had seen just as many tenants file in and out of the room directly beneath his own. As an unrenovated rat's nest, the whole building should have had a higher turnover rate than it actually did. But as it was, the trolls on the ground floor had been in residence for six years, and being that Wilbur himself had revamped his own quarters to suit his needs well into the next millennia, it was only the second floor chamber which saw the change of faces that might've otherwise been expected.

The latest transient was John Kaltenbrunner, though for John's first fourteen months in residence, Wilbur didn't even know the name. For practical reasons those two had lived out of sight and mind of one another for all that time. They'd been barred from frequent contact through conflicting work schedules; Wilbur was always off for the nightly rounds the moment John arrived home from Sodderbrook, and though the two of them had passed in the stairwell once or twice, no real exchange had gone between them. Wilbur's only impression of his downstairs neighbor up until then was that of an angry young recluse who probably thought too hard for his own good.

The first occasion on which they had cause to interact was a cold Saturday morning in early March. John was just out of a two month stay at the Baker General, where he'd been treated for massive injuries sustained in an accident on the job. Over the Christmas holiday, he, as a 'valued employee,' had been assigned to the storage house at Sodderbrook to herd and assemble the surplus stock – anywhere from 2–10,000 turkeys were syphoned in and out of the building every day during that particular season. John had been appointed overseer of ground floor operations. He'd been assured a substantial hike in pay and a Christmas bonus for his services, though the corresponding call for overtime had effectively rendered all proposed benefits illusory. Nevertheless, he had accepted the promotion without complaint – he couldn't have borne to see the job fall into someone else's hands – and, as operations had proceeded under his directorship, all had gone well.

But two weeks into the season disaster had struck.

Shortly after midnight on December 13th an overstuffed storage coop on the edge of the main loading pen had suddenly wobbled and collapsed on its foundation without warning. John, who had been driving gobblers through the scratch and rot down below, was flattened by two stories of plummeting perchboards and iron plating. Three or four wetbacks from the graveyard shift had immediately come running, but given the structure's eight hundred pound frame they were unable to pull him clear. He remained pinned to the floor for the next twenty minutes as the turkeys in the fallen coop scrambled and shat over his prostrate form. When the fire department finally arrived he was unconscious. They pried the coop away and pulled his gurgling body, with the chicken-wire mesh print over one cheek, from underneath. This was followed by a mad dash to the hospital, anaesthetic blackout, and waking up in a body cast with a televised Hee-Haw Christmas Special looming over the foot of the bed.

It was a miracle he had survived at all. His two front teeth had been knocked out. His right lung had collapsed. He had several fractured ribs, a broken arm, a broken leg, a busted cheekbone, scrapes and contusions, bruises and cuts, on and on . . . The eve of his twentieth birthday and he'd been virtually paralyzed, laid up in traction and put on life support. Both arms had been suspended in stirrups. He'd been plugged with catheters in every orifice and hooked up to something resembling a soundboard. A tight-fitting cast had been wrapped around his torso and midsection. A bedpan was hanging from the wall. The panel-operated comforter bed beneath him had been jacked up in a debilitating, zig-zag configuration so that his outstretched leg, suspended in stirrups, had extended overhead at a forty-five degree angle, as though being launched from a stunt ramp. He'd been completely immobilized, no more able to dig into the hot, irritated skin beneath the casts than to commandeer the television's remote from his sitcom junky/accident victim of a room-mate.

The month that followed, as every claustrophobe's worst nightmare, had been the most consistently horrifying experience he would ever know. It was even *worse* than the month leading up to the holdout. Day after day of being strapped up in traction and watching every moment drag by at an agonizing crawl – without being able to move, without being able to breathe properly, without being able to perform the simplest, most rudimentary bodily functions without coming to terrifying terms with his own mortality – had put his every threshold to the stake. His head had been filled with visions of throwing himself from the open window, ending it all with a flare-gun from the janitor's closet, dosing himself into lethal paralysis with the high-concentrate elixirs kept under lock and key at the nurses' station . . .

Before long he and his room-mate had been forcibly separated and relocated after an afternoon's exchange of literal death threats which both had been too incapacitated to act on. He was later reprimanded for accosting a doctor, two nurses and a window-washer in the same manner.

On Christmas night a troop of Methodist crones had gone fleeing from his room, swooning and retching, after he'd projectile-vomited over the holiday cake they'd delivered as a token of 'good faith and seasonal cheer.' They were shuffled away by the nurse on duty, leaving John behind with the crackling police scanner they'd brought by – purportedly to keep him informed on local issues during his stay. For the next two hours he had listened to active correspondence between the Baker fire department and the local police, who were at work trying to extinguish a four-alarm blaze raging in two separate hog houses on the south end of town. The ongoing dialogue of panicked demands amid the surging water hoses, roaring flames, and screaming multitudes of roasting swine was interrupted when a Methodist country-gospel quartet known as 'Brother Love and the Obedients' had suddenly burst into his room with a nauseatingly ethereal rendition of the 'Good Old Country Baptisin' Down At The Creek' (pronounced 'crick'). At that moment he felt more of an affinity for the scorched hogs giving up the ghost in the sub-zero yuletide night than for any living creature that had ever walked the earth.

And the misfortunes had done nothing but continue. One week into the new year John had received a letter from Sodderbrook informing him that not only were his services with the company being terminated, but that, according to clause IV3b-i of his insurance policy, his 'reckless mismanagement of duties in the workplace' – whatever that meant – had formally annulled his eligibility for financial assistance and medical benefits. In other words, he'd slipped through one of the notorious 'loopholes.' He was on his own.

He knew that even if he'd somehow been able to coerce one of the wetbacks into testifying as a witness to his defense, he would've lost hands-down in the local courts, and would've been furtherly buried in legal fees. He knew a lost cause when he saw one. There had been nothing left to do but sit there and take it like a dupe. Which is what he did. But nothing could have kept him from hating every minute of it. Yet another name had been added to his ongoing shit-list.

Day after day he'd remained in bed drawing up an infuriated inventory on the community. He'd spent hours on end staring out the window over the variegated plateau of cabin tops in the Linkhorn trailer park, imagining every natural disaster in existence tearing through the ugly conglomeration of tin sheds and troll shacks in view. As time passed, he had alienated every one of his attendants, had had the television switched off for

173

good, had managed to ward off any prospective room-mates after the relocation of the original, and had settled down to a quiet seething all his own. The weeks had pushed on. The long catfish whiskers lining his upper lip had curled downward and dangled into the gap where his two front teeth had once been.

Eventually, after what seemed like a Biblical eternity, the casts had begun coming off like old snakeskin. One afternoon his head had been wired with an architectonic skullcap of some sort, after which an orthodontic surgeon had set to work implanting two oblong ebony fangs into his gums. The implants were then filed into shape with an electric drill which filled every corner of the room with thick, black enamel smoke. He had emerged with a full set of teeth, but once again, no way of paying for them. He'd kept his mouth shut and continued waiting.

In another week all of his appendages had been released from the stirrups. He'd become fit to sit up and move around at will. Two days later he'd managed to walk a crooked circle around the bed. After another few days a therapist had been appointed to revive him as a functioning biped. His release had become imminent.

On February 26th, he was at last released from the Baker General with one aluminum hand-crutch at his side and the promise of many high-digit medical bills to come. He hobbled out of the waiting room into the cold morning air, then made his way up the highway through Baker, headed for his apartment building. His stay at the hospital had come to an end. But the recovery had only begun.

One week later Wilbur was returning home from an early morning trip to the hardware store through the grey, snow-lined streets to the north. As he rounded the adjacent building's facade, he came into view of his own yard just in time to witness someone on the tail end of a bad fall from the top of the main walkway's staircase. Whoever it was had apparently gotten one leg caught up in the trolls' garden hose, which was frozen stiff and strung out over the walkway like a petrified serpent. The figure was now groping in the mulch and spewing profanity. Wilbur rushed to lend a hand. He retrieved a battered crutch from the sidewalk, then climbed the staircase. The fallen figure rolled over and got halfway to his feet before Wilbur realized that this frail, trembling cripple was none other than his downstairs neighbor. Wilbur couldn't believe his eyes. The same kid he remembered as the tough, resilient looking dockhand with the borderline athletic build had somehow been reduced to a spent, splotched and wheezing skeletal wreck with a bad case of the shakes and scarcely enough strength to remain upright. He was almost unrecognizable. The only visible trait that allowed Wilbur to make the connection at all was that unmistakable unibrowed scowl. The rest had been ravaged for all it was worth. The blue leather coat hanging from his shoulderblades was the only article of clothing on his whole body which didn't appear to be falling apart at the seams. He had a bad cough which sounded more like a damaged engine block rattling away in a cardboard box than a natural biological function; every time he hacked a network of veins strained and bulged beneath the diaphanous skin wrapped tightly over his bones. Wilbur could see he was sick and, more likely than not, starving. He immediately resolved to do what he could.

From that day forward, Wilbur Altemeyer was to remark at length, both privately and publicly, that though he always found John to be the most authentic, capable, trustworthy, intelligent, and, in his own strange way charismatic individual he ever had the good fortune of knowing on a one-to-one basis, it still couldn't be denied and left one to marvel that he was also consistently plagued with the most outstanding bad luck imaginable. As so many locals have repeatedly emphasized, John was 'born under a bad sign,' he was 'a hard luck case of a higher order,' 'misfortunes hounded him down in packs,' etc. Despite the obvious shortcomings of all these clichés, anyone who ever knew John personally would have to concede, at least partially, to their circumstantial validity. The situations he somehow managed to end up in by way of means entirely beyond his control could very easily persuade one to believe that he was, indeed, operating under a lifelong curse.

Consider his condition on the morning he and Wilbur first

met: at the time, not only did he look to be at death's doorstep, but almost every facet of his financial and societal well-being was equally shot. The first of the medical bills which would eventually amount to a figure in excess of $16,000 – thereby qualifying him for bankruptcy – had begun to arrive in the mail only the day before. In addition, a pile of legal notices had accumulated on the front stoop in his absence, informing him that he was almost three months behind on rent and would soon face forced eviction if not immediately compliant with the realtor's demands. His electricity had been cut during the second week in January, and he'd been forewarned to expect the same with the gas at the first of the season.

And those were just the bills. That's to say nothing of the practical expenses. It's difficult to take a five digit number to heart when one's been relegated to sifting through piles of dirty laundry in search of loose nickels. Wilbur would later discover that during John's first week after being released from the hospital, he'd been eating out of the bakery dumpster and combing the public fountain floor for wishing-well change at three in the morning. He'd spent every evening eating cold pork and beans straight out of the can and smoking cheap, generic cigarettes in the dark. He'd refused, on principle, to go to the welfare office. His financial dilemma had nothing to do with an inability or refusal to work. Just earlier on in the morning of his and Wilbur's first encounter he'd been turned down for employ at the Dollar General for failing to produce a high-school diploma. Most every factory and production plant in town had given him a flat out No, or, at best, a suggestion to come back when he'd recovered from his injuries. All his meandering up and down the highway had come to nothing.

And though it's true John was in the midst of an unusually brutal losing streak at the time – perhaps the *epitome* of everything he'd sworn off the season before – what Wilbur was to discover on further inquiry was that a good deal of his past had been no less disastrous. And even more than that, his inordinate susceptibility to misfortune would be additionally corroborated in the months to come by the disastrous ends to which every one of his ongoing endeavors would come.

A few examples:

—On initially trying to help out, one of the first things Wilbur did while John was still recovering was land him a job his condition would allow for. One of Wilbur's acquaintances owned a grown Rottweiler which had a tendency to tear apart the furniture when left alone for the afternoon. Wilbur therefore suggested the most obvious solution, and two days later John was officially dog sitting at $3 an hour. It wasn't much of a career move to start with, but it would at least pay enough to put food on the table for the time being.

However, the way it worked out left him unemployed again in less than a week.

On the third morning of his new job, he let the Rottweiller out on the lawn to do its business. He stood around the front yard – barefooted, puffing on a cigarette, leaning on his crutch – while the dog combed through the bushes to the rear of the house. He finished off his smoke and threw the butt into the gutter. On his way back to the front door, the Rottweiler suddenly appeared from a row of shrubs with the trolls' family rabbit, torn to pieces and dead to the world, clamped tightly in its jaws. John flew into a panic. He pried the rabbit loose, hustled the Rottweiler up the stairs, and locked himself in his room. It took a full twenty minutes to scrub the dirt from the rabbit's fur beneath the running faucet. Afterwards, he threw it into the hallway dryer and listened to it bang and rattle around inside the machine for another half-hour. When it emerged, it was in a static-charged, poofed-to-capacity state of rigor mortis. John cursed the shamefaced Rottweiler to no end. He dropped the rabbit into a brown paper bag. He crept down the staircase and into the yard, made his way along the hedge to the rabbit's storage pen, and, as quickly as he was able, tucked the corpse back into a corner of its cage. He hid out in his room for the rest of the day.

When Wilbur got home from a trip to Pott's county that afternoon, he found the troll standing by the pen in the yard, scratching his head and looking bewildered. When Wilbur asked what seemed to be the problem, the troll replied that it was the damndest thing he'd ever seen . . . Apparently, he said, at some point that afternoon their rabbit – *the one that had succumbed to a prolonged illness and died two weeks earlier* – had been dug up from the mulch. But not only had its body been exhumed, someone had gone to all the trouble of cleaning it up, and placing it back in its cage as well. The troll was spooked. *Sick people running around nowadays*, he said.

Wilbur left him to ponder the mystery and made for the fire escape. He was halfway up the ladder when John suddenly came bursting out of his window on to the landing, looking to be on the tail-end of a three-hour anxiety attack. There was no time for explanations, he said. He wanted this dog out of his life at once. Wilbur half-heartedly conceded, and the next day John was unemployed again.

—Two weeks later he landed a job at the gravel refinery collecting and sweeping loose piles of cinder from the well-worn bulldozer path. Not much to report there. On the second afternoon, a veteran employee capsized a forklift into a drainage ditch and emerged to blame the whole thing on John – the 'greenback.' When called in for questioning, John, who had actually been on the other end of the yard at the time of the accident and knew nothing at all about anything, couldn't understand what his accuser was talking about or even that he himself was being accused. But it didn't seem to matter to the foremen. He was fired anyway. He never even received a first paycheck for that one.

—Over the Easter holiday he was commissioned as a delivery boy for the pork shack on 7th and Poplar. Though barely off of his hand-crutch at the time, he was ordered to run fried pork-strips in gravy to various spots throughout town. The delivery bike was a rickety old banana-seated Huffy with a hub-clamped Confederate flag and poor alignment. He wrecked it twice. In the evenings he was ordered to scour the day's accumulation of deep-fryer accessories piled up in the dingy, grease-splattered back room. He detested the owner from their first encounter. Tensions mounted and eventually came to a head when John was clipped in a hit and run while out on delivery one afternoon. The moment he hit the pavement the plastic carrier bag strapped over his shoulder was torn loose, throwing his delivery of piggly-wigglies all over the road. He got up in time to see a blue Volkswagen fleeing the scene. It veered wildly around the bend before he was able to make out the license number. He hobbled back to the pork shack, where all the owner could do was scream about the bike. The situation ended with a toppling soda rack and a fifty pound bag of flour in mid-flight. And then he was out of a job again.

After another week he came into service with the Westpoint temporary employment agency. Westpoint was and still is commonly considered the end of the line – most temps are ensured little more than intermittent one-shots at the garbage-scow branches of every factory in the valley. But it does at least guarantee semi-dependable employment for those on the outs, and given John's financial quandary, he really had no choice.

—His first appointment was a two-day run at Bob's Discount Pet ('Pet' being singular somehow) where, dressed as a six-foot cocker spaniel with a blue-ribboned collar, he was to wave at passing traffic along 254. It was the most degrading thing he'd ever done. He turned in his gear after being bombarded with rotten cantaloupes by a carload of factory rats. His total hours on the job numbered two.

—The next two appointments were one-day affairs and weren't much better. The first was an afternoon of shoveling dog shit from the sidewalks with a garden hoe. The second was a four hour spree of collecting golf balls from the two hundred yard strip at the country club's driving range, where he tooled back and forth in a bobcat thresher beneath a storm of 90-compression balls being driven in his direction by a group of drunks on the tee-off. Both jobs paid a heavily taxed minimum wage, plus commission.

—Next he was sent into the sewers for rodent extermination. He spent two indescribably wretched six hour shifts clubbing rats with a lead pipe beneath the streets of central Baker. He was first administered two inoculations, issued a thick, plastic one-piece sanitation suit, a mouthguard and goggles, the pipe, a battery-operated lamp, a pair of clippers and two burlap bags. He was then lowered through a grit-lined manhole on Main St. to spend the afternoon sloshing around in an ankle-deep current of granulated feces with a crew of fifteen or twenty wetbacks. As Wilbur later tried to assure him, he was *not* dismissed on grounds of poor performance. Quite the reverse, as his netted loads had more than tripled the base-wage quotas and had towered over everyone else's, it was clear that he'd put the company's roundabout method of fulfilling its minority employment obligations in jeopardy by cleaning out the sewers *too* fast, which then necessarily would've required the department to take on wetbacks in the office place. On those grounds, had they been clearly stated, his dismissal might've been taken as a compliment (overqualification), but, unfortunately, the department had chosen to cite 'Insubordinate Behavior,' or something along those lines instead. John never really got over that one.

—The next job lasted for a record-breaking three weeks. John was sent to a convenience store on the north end of town to mop and stock the back rooms during the graveyard shift. He was given a blue, mustard splotched apron, polyester pants, a bow tie and a tub of styling gel for his hair. The styling gel, when applied, hardened into a plastic helmet with the individual teeth marks from the comb running all the way over his skull in little trenches. In the mornings, when he stumbled home to wash, the gel would end up tearing clumps of hair out by the roots and clogging the shower drain. As time passed he started skipping the showers altogether and simply collapsing on his mattress every morning, fully-clothed, dirty apron and all. The styling gel left a brown ring on his pillowcase which gradually darkened as the weeks passed. His face took on a pasty hue. His two false teeth in front went uncleaned so that he could run his tongue over the enamel and taste the last hot dog downed, the last smoke intact and preserved for hours to come. During off hours he wasn't much to look at. People saw him coming or caught a bit of him downwind and moved to the other side of the road. But back in the arena, situated in his element, on his own stomping ground behind closed doors, he was Lord. He out-stocked, out-swept, out-priced and outmaneuvered circles around the entire staff. Ripping through the fruit case, slapping together liverwurst and onion sandwiches, and mopping the floors into the ground with that filthy apron wrapped around his waist like a soiled tourniquet. He was the most efficient worker the store could've dreamed of hiring, but a holy terror to everyone nonetheless. He did what he wanted, when and where he wished, and listened to no one. He drank all the coffee and grubbed all the lunch meat, took smoke breaks in the street and carried home bags of food for the sheer gratification of not being questioned. He threatened customers and wrote his own schedule. He arranged for the dismissal of any employees who rubbed him the wrong way. He redefined the dress code. He came to work drunk. He reorganized the stockroom and eliminated complete lines of products, replacing them with others that suited him better. He skipped mandatory store meetings and was never questioned for it. He arranged for the replacement of the Muzak box. He had new furniture for the lounge shipped in at the company's expense. He demanded a raise. He got one. He heaped insults on the cashiers. He sabotaged the sausage machine beyond repair. He found a stray dog and built a home for it in the back room, charging all of its medical bills to the store and feeding it steaks from the deli. He spat on the floor. He overturned a soda rack. He stole from the register, stomped through the back room, cursed the locals, smoked all the cigars, and horrified everyone he came in contact with. He was finally dismissed when the owner put a call through to Westpoint's personnel department, claiming John was the single worst thing that had ever happened to their business . . .

Including the latest installment, he'd now received four official reprimands for inappropriate behavior, yet his attitude had shown no signs of marked improvement. The agency was fed up. They wanted no more of it. Of all the locals they'd ever signed on, and that meant over twenty years worth of the most burdened dregs of Anglo-Saxony in existence, they'd never received so many complaints in regard to one individual. Their associates were railing John as an impertinent beast, and random citizens having nothing to do with anything were posting urgent requests for his immediate removal from their vicinity. The agency was through with him. A brief letter of dismissal was drawn up and hand-delivered to his mailbox on June 2nd. He was now officially *blacklisted* from Baker temp work for life.

And it wasn't only in the work place that things went to seed all around him; it was in everything he did on an hourly basis. Where a normal person would walk into a room, close the door, and sit down at a table without cause for alarm, John, in attempting the same, would inevitably snare his pant leg on the door frame, tear the seam from toe to crotch, damage the wall while trying to free himself, and finally sit down in the chair, only to have one leg give out from under him. Wilbur had seen it happen a thousand times. He would have banked on it regularly. If only one individual in a crowd of fifty were to be shat on by overflying gulls, it would've been John, every single time, without exception. No one had a greater knack for being in the wrong place at the wrong time.

But that's just one way of looking at it. The whole thing might just as easily be turned the other way around. It would be no less appropriate to say he was a living disaster area as to point out that he was also one of the most extraordinarily capable individuals in the history of Pullman Valley. Wilbur picked up on that right from the start; one's intuition had to be on par with that of the Baker Lay not to sense it. The better Wilbur got to know John, the more deadset convinced he became that behind that ravaged exterior there was a mind capable of almost anything. His current position, Wilbur believed, was just a matter of having been waylaid by circumstance.

It's really not at all surprising that those two hit it off as well as they did. Despite their obvious difference in age, they had several points in common from the start. Both lived alone as hopeless bachelors. Both had grown up on farms. Both had bizarre family histories. Both were outcasts in Baker, and though

Wilbur couldn't hold a candle to John in terms of ongoing misfortune, both had taken enough steady beatings along the way to share a certain ground in the world around them. Within twenty minutes of their first meeting, they were going back and forth on the pros and cons of still-air incubators vs. battery-powered hover brooders. Within an hour, before Wilbur could even clear the empty plates from the table, the first of the balcony/barnyard sessions was underway.

After that they quickly got their routine down to formula. Every night, within five minutes of Wilbur's return from the rounds, John would make his way up the fire escape to come knocking. Wilbur would throw open the door, turn and plod over the floors, still geared in his bespattered jumpsuit and steel-toed work boots, to retrieve a case of beer from the icebox. They would then adjourn to the balcony. They would kick back in their plastic lawn chairs, prop up their feet on the black iron railing, and look out over the tree-lined expanse of Geiger running north and south to either side, with the soiled asphalt lot of the filling station across the way as a centerpiece. They would generally open proceedings with a round of livestock anecdotes, which then had a tendency to develop into long-winded debates on the virtues and merits of domestic leghorns vs. Rhode Island Reds, Cheviot ewes vs. Corriedales, the cutting of standard feed with linseed vs. soybean during mating season. This could then lead to further discourses on preferred bulb wattage during incubation, effective means of pest control, and, on more than one occasion, standard shearing techniques. They sometimes managed to put away a full case of beer while wrapped up in these preliminary discussions alone. One marathon spree on the value of community nests vs. sectioned tiers went on for three nights, only to terminate, hopelessly deadlocked, in slight favor of John's case, i.e., the tiers.

Wilbur was in awe of John's extensive, almost encyclopedic familiarity with breeding and ranching techniques at such a tender age, to say nothing of the fact that he appeared to have been entirely self-taught and, what's more, hadn't spent a day on a farm in almost five years. It didn't seem possible. During their sessions, his recollection of the most minute details from childhood made it seem as though not an hour had elapsed since his last round in the layer house. He had an unbelievably concise memory – very possibly *too* concise for his own good. His response time was immediate. He was able to assess, evaluate and act on impulse in one fluid motion. His native intelligence more than compensated for his lack of formal education. He was articulate, quick witted, unapologetic, and, needless to say, uncompromisingly strong willed. All of which Wilbur coveted to no end.

But what Wilbur was to discover in time was that, not only had John never had occasion to exhibit or utilize most of these abilities publicly, he'd never had a single friend in his life. Wilbur alone was catching a glimpse of something no one had ever seen. This was probably due to the fact that he was the first person John had ever been comfortably convinced was not out for his throat. Once the trust between them had been established, a side of John appeared which most locals still don't know ever existed: the side which, believe it or not, was capable of having a good laugh from time to time. During their sessions he would lean forward in his chair with a Cheshire grin wrapped over his scruffy, unshaven face, a can of beer in one hand, and the other arm waving free as he launched into one of many crazed narratives on an episode gone by. Sometimes he upset a pyramid of empty cans at his feet in the process, and went on, following through with a sweep of his hand crutch, to send five or six of them falling over the edge of the balcony into the yard. He and Wilbur would cackle and hoot and try not to think too hard about the troll down below, then resume right where they'd left off without missing a single point. In those moments John was like one liberated, fresh out of cell block five. But it was only in Wilbur's presence that those moments occurred at all. Had anyone else walked into the room, John would've seized for the duration. Wilbur and possibly Dale Murphy were the only individuals John ever trusted.

Wilbur doesn't exactly know what prompted him to start taking notes. At that point in his life he'd never kept, and never expected to begin keeping, a personal diary. He wasn't a deep thinker by nature. His sum-total philosophy to life – if it can even be called that – was well in place and going nowhere.

Nevertheless, within two weeks of meeting John he'd bought a spiral notebook from the Dollar General and had begun jotting down brief recaps of their balcony sessions over coffee every morning. It was probably just a matter of having been temporarily inspired. He certainly wasn't intent on proving any point, and he most definitely never intended to share his notes with any outside party. He knew well enough that if prying eyes were to stumble on to his memoirs, *as prying eyes tend to do*, he and John would be summed up as washed out farmhands who'd been bored to tears on small town evenings. It would make for some excruciatingly tedious reading. And anyway, who would ever possibly care? His original initiative to put pen to paper was casual and devoid of any conscientious motive; but ironically enough, it is to that same initiative that we owe the precison of a good deal of this account.

As has already been mentioned, most of Wilbur's notes have no bearing on the crisis. In addition to the early pages being filled with off-the-cuff remarks, many of them scattered and incomplete, Wilbur himself was practically illiterate when he first started writing. It's only by halfway through his third book that the penmanship becomes legible at all, and even then entire passages are marred with so many ink blots and coffee stains that next to nothing is clear. The few points that have been salvaged reflect more of Wilbur's unbounded admiration for John as a character than any speculations as to his origin. The opening pages coin him a 'prodigy fallen on hard times,' a 'bona fide case of royalty in exile, the royalty being inherent, the exile complete,' etc. It wasn't until much later that Wilbur would set to work gathering information pertaining to John's life from the beginning. The earliest notes often ran as such:

May 2 – 0:30–4:15, case Ribbon. Cornish X, Rock. Expelled 15. Balls.

With an emphasis on 'Balls.' Wilbur repeatedly noted that it would be interesting to know how John might've fared on the other side of the hill, 'in a different circus-tent' as he put it, away from Greene County. He was convinced John had been dealt a bad hand and actually belonged elsewhere, felling giants by the cadre. As it stood he was a monument to destitution. But that never could have curbed Wilbur's affection for him in the least.

John, for his part, may very well never have made it through the season without Wilbur. It's almost certain he would've been evicted, if nothing else. Thereafter, as a homeless, unemployed cripple in a community of terminal work rats, he would have been forcibly exiled. Knowing that, Wilbur had snuck into town one morning and paid off enough of John's rent to keep the landlord at bay for the time being. He had also hocked two repaired televisions and a radio from his treasury to load up on groceries. John was averse to hand-outs by nature and was even more embarrassed than Wilbur had expected when he found out. But Wilbur told him not to worry. He knew John was doing everything he could to land a job. He assured him they would settle up in time.

Three months later they were in the exact same predicament. Shortly before noon on the morning John was finally dismissed from the temp agency, Wilbur jolted awake on hearing a series of crashes from the room down below. He pulled on his trousers as quickly as he could and ran downstairs to find John sitting on his mattress with the room around him looking like a typhoon had just ripped through. He had gone on a tear with his discarded hand-crutch. He'd broken most of his dishes, put two holes in the wall and cracked the porcelain basin of the toilet bowl in the corner. He was now slumped over on his bed soliloquizing that nothing ever worked. He looked like a broken down gutter-tramp without a prayer in the world. Wilbur fished for an explanation.

On discovering what had happened he lightened up. *To hell with Westpoint*, he said. Temp work was for trolls and everyone knew it. No one worth a damn had ever fared any better going sink to grit wagon like that. If John had really needed a full-time job he should've just said so in the first place. *Not to worry*, Wilbur assured him, temporarily forgetting everything he'd seen over the past few months – all of John's foiled endeavors, from the pork shack to the pet store, the refinery to the driving range.

186

Not to worry, he said, without hesitation, without thinking, without pausing to reflect for one moment on the potential consequences of his actions. *Not to worry*, thereby committing himself to an obligation that would keep him on pins and needles for weeks to come, kicking himself for his excessive generosity and wondering if his own recommendation would ever hold water at the landfill again – *Not to worry, he would go have a word with his employer that evening . . .*

III

HILL SCRUBS

As in the case of numerous provincial aberrations, corn-belt deathbed confessions, like 'meals on wheels' and Baker charity drives, are frequently an outgrowth of age-induced fear of hell-fire. A growing terror of being cast into the infernal lake for a lifetime of unrepentant depravity prompts the yokel into chilling, long-winded admissions of misconduct the moment he takes ill. Each of these admissions is a last-legged bid for salvation, and, as such, often makes for an uncomfortably hostile funeral service afterwards. Brother Dick, before passing on, owns up to having buggered Cousin Ed's wife for the past twenty years, then, at the last minute, kindly asks Ed's understanding and unconditional forgiveness. It's a tense moment for Cousin Ed, as his every faculty for self-restraint is put to the supreme test. It's even uglier in the rare event of Brother Dick's miraculous and unexpected recovery to full health, upon which he finds himself estranged from Cousin Ed, the subject of widespread public scorn, and worst of all, hated and abandoned by the betrayed mistress he needs now more than ever. It's an age-old phenomenon – at least in this area – one which, if compiled in even a fragment of its entirety, would make for one of the most lapidary pabulums of treachery and betrayal on file.

The third and final deathbed confession to be mentioned in the course of this account is one of Greene County's most notorious and, coincidentally, pertains to our very own landfill. Twenty years before John Kaltenbrunner first appeared at our gates, a retired mail carrier by the name of James Kopp was diagnosed with terminal brain cancer and given six months to live. As it turned out, he lasted no more than four, but the Baptist minister tending to his bedside during those final hours quoted

Kopp as saying it didn't really matter – he would've needed at least another year to own up to every crime he'd committed over the course of his lifetime. He went to his grave less than halfway down the road to absolution, leaving behind a highly incriminating chronicle of local-based racketeering and felony. A partial record of his confessions was then somehow leaked to the public, by means which remain unknown to this day, and hit the community like wildfire. Kopp's confessions were an overnight sensation/disaster, and though they drew bitter outcries of libel and slander from every corner of the county – thereby posthumously memorializing Kopp himself as a pathological pseudologue – many public figures never fully recovered from the scathing insinuations put forth in his final hours. He may have been blasted as a compulsive liar, but he was one compulsive liar everyone seemed privately inclined to believe. The accused, while rigorously denying their own culpability, consistently put enough store in the allegations pertaining to those around them as to suggest that their own charges-faced had hit entirely too close to home. Regardless of the unanimous contempt invoked by the mere mention of his name, Kopp's deathbed confessions were soon being swallowed as fundamental scripture, to the expense of just about everyone in town. The Baker Lay buried themselves in it. The mayor was a speculated pedophile. A catholic priest screwed sheep. A district court judge was involved in drug running. Two school teachers were candlewax sodomites . . . etc. Some or all of which may have been true, but certainly none of which had ever been intended for public circulation. No one benefitted from the storm of gossip that followed. It was South Dakota voodoo unbridled, and everyone got a pin in the back. It took three or four years, for some individuals more, for the community to recover; Kopp's admissions linked him with every den of wolves in the county.

One of his more grim testimonies was to having taken part in the suspected murder of Dr. Bartholemew Katz, a resident pediatrician whose unexplained disappearance over thirty years earlier had gone unresolved and kept most locals baffled to no end. As Kopp's version of the story went, Dr. Katz, along with several pominent area figures, had gotten involved with a local counterfeiting ring. A deal had been struck up between three separate parties, but Katz, following a heated argument with one of his accomplices, had refused to follow through with his end of the deal. He'd then seized control of the main printing presses, and gone into hiding, threatening to expose his associates if they persisted with their demands. After some time, Kopp and two cohorts were contracted by said associates to 'resolve' the dilemma quietly. The three men tracked Katz down in forty-eight hours. They manhandled him out of his Lincoln on a back road, shot him dead, and drove his body to the Pullman Valley landfill – then in only its third week of construction. There, with the consent of the landfill's original director, they sealed the corpse in the compacted clay and high-density plastic lining the bed of the reservoir. The burial began at midnight. By 8 a.m. the next morning no visible trace of their activities remained. There was only Dr. Katz's Lincoln on a backroad with one door hanging wide open to account for his disappearance. The resulting investigation yielded nothing.

Over three decades later when Kopp confessed to his role in the murder, there was little talk of reopening case. To be sure, it caused a stir in the area; it appeared to offer a tangible explanation for an unexplained mystery . . . But most locals, in the meantime, were so tied up in dealing with their own butt-ends of Kopp's admissions that no one had time to pursue claims that a good doctor of one too many years past had once gotten involved in a situation he couldn't rightly handle. It was ancient history by then, and anyway, if Kopp's contentions were true, it was felt that Dr. Katz had probably gotten what he deserved. No one pushed for a subsequent inquiry. As with all of Kopp's claims, there was a looming fear that the moment one case was reopened, the rest would naturally have to follow. There was no way to confront one head of the hydra without tackling the entire beast, and the Baker Lay being, figuratively speaking, armed with only sticks and stones, opted to dodge out and let the whole thing trample over the community as quickly and painlessly as possible. Which is what happened. Personal and professional reputations were damaged beyond all hopes of recovery, but no one went to prison. For that everyone in the area was grateful. In a few years, the only traces of the exposure that lingered on were a handful of bad relations and a jackpot of superstitious folklore/paranoia. In the case of Dr. Katz, it became commonly accepted that his body was encased at the bottom of the landfill and that on certain foggy, moonlit evenings, etc. one might catch sight of his phantasmagoric apparition wandering the labyrinths of rot and debris, muttering lamentable entreaties for retribution. It was even said that once every two or three weeks an ectoplasmic orb resembling his pained countenance could be made out in the flames from the twelve foot methane torch on the north end of the yard. And to top it all off, even now, almost sixty years after the alleged murder, several of us, on more than one occasion, have heard bartalk of John Kaltenbrunner having been the hell-bent incarnation of Dr. Katz come back to take vengeance on the community . . .

Yet another drove of Baker lore which will never be resolved. All the answers are gone. The landfill's original founder is thirty-five years dead at this point. None but the oldest on our crew can even vaguely remember the days when Baker disposal workers were referred to as the 'Sons of Dr. Katz,' and Dr. Katz himself, if he is down there, is buried under a mountain of compacted rubbish so extensive and impenetrable that even the most colossal bucket auger in the nation would fall thirty yards shy of impacting with his corpse. None of us have ever seen his ghost. The methane torch on the north end of the yard is no longer even operable. And John Kaltenbrunner, if he was the incarnation of anything, was more likely the chieftain of some cattle-raiding hill clan than a doctor of medicine.

The landfill as it stood on the day of John's arrival, had long-since grown to be the largest human-made monument in town: a sprawling three and a half acre plot of refuse burrowed over one hundred and fifty feet below ground level and towering over the highway in seven, impermeable clay-capped plateaus. Three successive generations of Pullman Valley residents had contributed over 85 percent of their daily disposables (about 3.2

pounds per person) to its girth. From an aerial view it had the appearance of a devastated hamlet in the wake of a hack and burn campaign. A limestone drainage ditch paralleling a twelve foot barbed wire fence lined the perimeter of the yard with incremental contamination-monitoring wells spaced out along its base. The bulldozer path running from the front gate, up along the first incline and across the one hundred and fifty yard stretch to the latest dumping site was easily broad enough to accommodate two compactors side-by-side for its entire length. From the highest point in the yard, a sixty foot tabletop-mono-lith on the eastern end, one could look out on a 360° panoramic view of all of Pullman Valley. The only higher point in Baker was the northeastern reservoir at Ebony Steed.

The company was equipped with three iron-treaded bull-dozers, two mini-plows, two eight-wheeler dump trucks, one excavator, four forklifts and a small fleet of green compactors. Most of the machinery was in a continual state of disrepair.

There were twenty-two full-time employees on the payroll – most of us middle-aged, heavyset, and perpetually dog-tired – all operating under one foul-tempered creature by the name of Jeffrey Kuntsler. We worked 45-hour weeks on average with a base wage of $217 all across the board. Most of us had been employed by the company for more than a decade. In that time we had received one substantial hike in pay, and that only in compliance with a legal mandate intended to compensate for inflation. We weren't due for another raise for the next six years. Our insurance policy operated with a $700 deductible, meaning we might very easily blow two weeks pay out of our own pockets, with no financial assistance whatsoever, in acquiring the medical excuse required by the company in the event of anything exceeding a two-day absence. Which doesn't even touch on the issue of injuries sustained on the job – several years of slinging furniture, rusty iron tools and hundred-pound bureaus had resulted in numerous slipped disks, hiatal hernias, and broken bones. It was nasty work, and everyone who'd been doing it for more than a year had endured several debilitating mishaps. If and when injured, one was often left just as high and dry as John had been following his accident at Sodderbrook. In our case, we simply felt fortunate in having a job to come back to at all. Given the nature of the work, the insurance policy, like the pay, was a sham. Even Pottville's landfill provided for its employees on more humane terms.

But of course, we'd never actually *done* anything about it. We'd done lots of talking, yes; for as long as anyone could remember we'd adjourned to the Whistlin' Dick or the Bloody Bucket after hours to rail Kuntsler as a foul old sonofabitch who would've just as soon cut his own mother's throat for a quarter as done anything to improve our situation. Time after time we'd whooped it up in the taverns, resolving to head in to the landfill the following afternoon and lay the old bastard out for good – kick his teeth in and leave him slumped over in the gravel. Sometimes our resolve had even lingered on through the following afternoon, as we amped ourselves for the kill over one or two pots of coffee and a round of Hank Jr. But by early evening it was always the same story: we'd roll into the yard, convene by the row of plastic barrels, and have the old man come tearing out of his office brandishing threats of termination for loafing on the clock. On that we'd scurry in every direction. Fifteen minutes later we'd be back on the rounds, too ashamed to look one another in the eye. And later on we'd find more excuses for it. All our talk had come to nothing. The truth was, Kuntsler was stronger than we, and everyone knew it. We were humoring ourselves by even dreaming of ousting him. We had nothing better to do. Our after-hour plotting was testament to our inability to converse on any other level than one of unrestrained commiseration. We wouldn't have known how to live without it.

Kuntsler himself was quintessential high-powered white trash with one of the most rancid dispositions to be found under any flag in Christendom. He was a fifty-six-year-old Dutch-blooded parrot fish of modest stature – standing at about 5′4″ – with a windswept balding head, a deviated septum, a furrowed brow-line, scoliosis of the right shoulder, and disproportionately thin hands. To the everyday outside party, he would've appeared to be stricken with some involuntary bodily tremor which was only worsening with time: what had begun as an occasional twitch of the shoulderblades had steadily crawled upward and developed into a grimacing facial tick. This was generally attributed to an overabundance of bad character. For twenty years he had ridden herd tyrannically from a roadside mobile home jacked up on a stack of cinder blocks to the left of the main gate. At any hour of the day he could be found seated behind his black enamel desk with a fat cigar jammed into his mouth and gigantic piles of paperwork heaped up on the chairs around him. A bold plaque on the wall indicated his full birth name – Jeffrey Harker Kuntsler – in gilded calligraphy. But he was *Mr.* Kuntsler to the rest of us – *Mr.* Kuntsler, the logorrheic old phrasemonger whom all dutifully served in the workyard while collectively pipe-dreaming his overthrow into oblivion during nightcap sessions – *Mr.* Kuntsler with his bad temperament and shrouded past, pacing through the landfill at high noon and jabbing his bony forefinger toward the forklift operators on duty – *Mr.* Kuntsler with his mildewed family photos from some indeterminate number of years past propped up beneath the desk lamp for all to see – *Mr.* Kuntsler with his tendency to speak in haiku: *Murphy, you shit! – You shit, Murphy!* – always proceeding to the statement's conclusion, then backtracking to its source. Wilbur was insistent that the old man had never gotten over being rejected for military duty and that he remained holed up in his office all day long watching old war footage from the battle of Stalingrad in preparation for the arrival of the second shift. Which was probably true, though no one knew for certain. Others swore he was infertile, possibly even impotent and had only conceived of his fabled offspring by artificially inseminating his now-deceased wife with a turkey baster. Another theoretically plausible explanation for his demeanor. Whatever his full story may have been will remain unknown, but one thing is for certain: at the time of these events, Jeffrey Kuntsler was unequivocally the nastiest human being any of us had ever encountered.

Every evening before we headed out, he would invariably come storming out of his office in a pungent trail of cheap tobacco and aftershave to proclaim us all the most pathetic lot of Appalachian porch monkeys that side of apple pie. He would flail his arms and stomp back and forth through the gravel with a wobbly-kneed stride which threatened to give out beneath him at any minute. He was prone to throwing unannounced fits and kicking over aluminum drums. He often boxed our ears at random and dared us to retaliate. On Friday evenings he would open his office door and disgustedly pitch a sack of paychecks into the yard for everyone to look through himself. He would remain in the doorway for a minute, craning over our group like an emaciated turkey vulture, then whirl back around, step inside, and almost slam the door off of its hinges.

As for us – the 'Sons of Dr. Katz,' the 'Green Niggers,' the 'Hill Scrubs,' the 'Sultans of Slag,' 'Baker's 22', John being 23 (Law of fives) – we were broken men with checkered histories as assistant morticians, grocery clerks, fieldhands, and toll-booth operators. Most of us had been born and raised in the area. Over half of us were high-school dropouts, the others low-ranking graduates or GED recipients. One of us, that being Steven Curtis, had been locked away in a cellar for the first nine years of his life – à la Kaspar Hauser – and had only been brought to the school board's attention as an unregistered mute when his father had suddenly passed away, leaving the Methodists to prowl through his house on property assessment detail. He was pulled out of the cellar, pasty-faced and emaciated, then integrated into school on a mentally handicapped level. His education lasted for seven years. He then quit to go to work for a glass factory, at which point he was arguably capable of reading a STOP sign.

Don Bailer was no better. Ten or eleven years prior to John's arrival, Bailer had been dismissed from a linen factory for unwittingly registering himself as a negro on his tax forms for six straight years. When the IRS finally caught on, the company was heavily fined for perjury. Bailer's superiors refused to accept his claims that he'd been oblivious to his misdeeds. As he rationalized it, the 'jokers on the day shift' had been calling him a 'nigger' for so long, and he 'didn't read too good anyhow,' that when it came time to fill out his annual claims, he hadn't been able to check the appropriate box. The company had chased him away, then filed a request with the IRS to reformat the W-2 declaration term from 'Negro' to 'African American,' thinking that would somehow eliminate the confusion, even though Bailer was about as Anglo Saxon as they come.

There was one genuine university graduate among us. Dale Murphy, the fifty-two year old compactor operator, had received a B.A. for horticulture from the university of West Virginia. He was the brightest in the bunch – which, admittedly, isn't saying much – but his past as a convicted felon had sorely limited his opportunities for upward mobility in the workplace wherever he went. Murphy's mind had been badly jumbled throughout two voluntary tours of duty in Vietnam. Following his return to the States, he'd gotten involved in an alleyway knife fight with two drunks in Chicago. He'd then served twenty-seven months in a Illinois penitentiary for third degree murder, and another six thereafter for violating parole. In spite of his docile, almost bovine demeanor, Murphy had a head full of broken gears. He'd had several extended bouts with alcohol and was seasonally plagued with recurring night terrors which left his nerves on end and his capacity for exchange in the rut. He was, nevertheless, the most alert, if not practical-minded, individual among us.

Probably one of the strangest life stories in the group was that of Burt Clayton. Clayton's birth and upbringing, in terms of the tragicomic, ranks right up there with John Kaltenbrunner's. Burt's biological mother had been a part-time counter girl by the name of Emily Fisk. One afternoon during her seventh month into term, Ms. Fisk suddenly went into an unexpected epileptic seizure while driving across a river bridge in Tennessee. She lost control of her vehicle and sailed over the railing into the current. By the time the responding rescue crew had dove, dislodged her body from the driver's seat and dragged her to shore, she was dead beyond hopes of revival. But an area surgeon who was on hand with the ambulance crew chose to attempt a seemingly foolhardy post-last-minute Cesarian section to save the unborn child. To widespread astonishment, the operation was successful. Burt Clayton was prematurely removed from his dead mother's womb, and after two months of intensive nurturing had recovered to full health. Officials were incapable of locating his father. His mother had been unmarried and was apparently set on raising her child as a single parent. Burt went up for adoption.

He was raised by an elderly couple in a riverside cabin three miles from his unlikely birthplace. All through his life he'd been labelled a liar whenever he recounted the circumstances surrounding his birth. Even when he produced the appropriate news clippings, people called him a tabloid monger and a dolt. He was no tabloid monger.

And then there was Dennis Stauffer, the indubitable Dennis, probably the most outstanding wreck to whom we had the dubious honor of laying claim. Dennis's full story would take hours to go into at length, but a brief summary of his fourteen year bout with substance abuse should suffice . . . Dennis began using methamphetamines at the age of seventeen. By twenty he was hopelessly hooked, and not just on speed or coke, but on anything and everything and as much thereof as one could place in front of him. There was *nothing* Dennis wouldn't take. On average he remained awake for literally five days a week without a single hour's sleep. He was pencil-thin and bug-eyed raving all through his daily seventeen hour shifts as a forklift operator at a diaper production plant. On the weekends he would go home to his cramped apartment on 11th and Snyder, mainline a $10 bag of heroin in the bathroom, drink two six packs of beer, pass out on his bed and fall into a deathlike coma for the rest of the weekend. On Monday morning the factory would ring at 7:00 a.m., on which he would rise, fix up a new spoonful of crank, and head back to work for the next sleepless five day run. Week in, week out, for fourteen straight years, absolutely no variance. One might cry bullshit and cite medical impossibility, but anyone who worked with Dennis at the time would have to admit that, yes, it was true, every bit of it. Dennis's brain had been fried to a crisp. He had successfully doped himself into dyslexia. His inherent stupidity was probably the only thing that had kept him from suicide. He had eradicated all capacity for despair. He was eventually arrested on a multiple-possession charge. When admitted to a clinic for detox, he was chained to a bed frame by all fours. His withdrawal was so severe – purportedly the worst case the clinic had ever seen – that after three days of violent, non-stop convulsions his stomach had ruptured from the enormous strain. He did survive the detox, but during the subsequent two-month recovery program that followed he was told that if he ever drank another beer in his life he would die. Since then Dennis had gone clean and taken up amateur bike racing. His crowning achievement as an athlete had been a third place victory in a three mile run (there were five contestants), even though the award ceremony had ended on a quirk, as his prize trophy had been handed over to him, inscribed in last-minute block lettering – DENNIS STUFFER. At thirty-four, he was the second-to-youngest employee in the yard, though he looked to be not a day under sixty.

And so on with the rest of us. The eighteen other employees at the landfill not mentioned had similar life stories of varying severity. As one casualty begins to lead into the next, it ought to be clear that the landfill was generally something men (there were no women) were driven to, or that they arrived at, after all other options had fallen through. As Curtis says: it was a last-resort hotel, and the tenants fit the role. The average 'green nigger' was no longer even particularly discouraged with life. He was simply finished. He had few, if any, remaining aspirations. Repeated failure had beaten him back for long enough to make the weekly acquisition of the bare essentials a triumph in itself. That's the way Kuntsler picked them. Which could lead one to wonder how John ever managed to slip right by unnoticed.

THE FIRST STANDOFF between Kaltenbrunner and Kuntsler – the one Wilbur feared might easily erupt on the opening night – actually held off for almost three full weeks. Granted, neither of them spoke a word to the other in all that time; the preliminary calm was actually just a lack of exchange. Nevertheless, considering all that could have gone otherwise, it was amazing nothing happened any sooner.

After hiring John at Wilbur's behest, Kuntsler remained holed up in his trailer, as usual, appearing only for what we referred to as 'Roll Call.' Roll call was the old man's nightly moment at the podium. It usually lasted for two or three minutes, but had been known to drag on for up to an hour on occasion. Every evening, after we'd filed out of the locker room and lined up in the gravel in a broken row, he assumed position on his cluttered porch stoop, took a quick head count, then proceeded to cry to Jove and rail our current performances into the ground. In these moments he was like one possessed, a bastardized hybrid of a bereaved drill sergeant and a soap-box minister from East St. Louis. The rest of us had long-since grown indifferent to his tyrannomania. Kuntsler had been carrying on like this for years. All his acrimonious assaults and excrescential diatribes no longer even fazed us. But it would take some time for John to comprehend the situation, and a whole lot more to adjust to it. With the exception of their brief opening interview, these outhouse sermons were the only words he heard the old man speak or spew in his first three weeks on the job.

One minute into his first roll call John had suddenly turned to Wilbur in a panic and asked why everyone was just standing around. The old man was obviously having a seizure, he'd said.

Why didn't we *do anything*? Wilbur had whispered back that this was standard routine; in all his years with the company he'd never once seen Kuntsler break character. The old man was as real as the McCoy could ever possibly get. John had then asked if he was a Tourettes afflictee or something, genuinely concerned. Wilbur had told him to put a lid on it.

At that point John had barely gotten over his shock from the opening interview. Wilbur had tried to forewarn him that the old man was a crazed, book-burning tunnel dwarf with an unprecedented Napoleon complex. To which John had replied that he was sure he'd seen worse. But he had *never* seen worse. Their opening encounter had been disastrous. Wilbur had tiptoed into the office trailer with John at his heels to find Kuntsler poring over some vague discrepancy in one of his logbooks. The old man had kept his gaze locked on his paperwork all through Wilbur's nerve-racked introduction of John as a guaranteed asset to any organization, a hard worker, a dedicated young man with a reputable character, etc., etc. When he'd finally concluded, Kuntsler had briefly looked up through his fogged bifocals to remark that whatever else John may have been, he was still uglier than a Jew out of Treblinka. Wilbur had hastily thanked him, claiming he wouldn't regret his decision, then backed out of the office at an awkward stumble. But John had remained behind, more astonished than anything. He'd stood there with his hands at his side and a Y-shaped rut carved into his brow. A moment later Kuntsler had looked up again, asking if a close-captioned cue card was in order. Wilbur yanked John out of the office before he could reply.

By the end of his first call John was visibly shaken up – not so much by the old man's bombastic diction as by the deadset seriousness of his delivery. Impossible as it seemed, it was apparently no joke. It was sick, John said. It was *unbelievable*. Wilbur told him not to worry about it – what he'd just witnessed was bad, true enough, but it was the most they'd be seeing of Kuntsler on any given night. And that had been the case.

Kuntsler had remained in his office all through John's first few weeks in the yard. As a general rule, the old man had no idea of what was going on with the rest of us. Not only had he never pulled a single round in his life, he'd never laid eyes on the majority of his own routes, much less discussed their particulars with any of his employees. He was completely in the dark concerning the hands-on nature of our work. He had no informers. He was detested by everyone. We could've been running guns from the roof of each compactor right under his nose and no one would've said a word. He had no wormtongue to boot. But he didn't need one. He knew us well enough not to worry about a thing. His fear of dissension in the ranks was non-existent. His concern for group morale was nil. He'd never lost a minute's sleep for fear of an ambush. He didn't need or want to know anything about our nightly activities; so long as he received no complaints and the job got done, he couldn't have cared less what we did. His policy was simply to keep us down in the hole where he found us – an easy enough task with a few choice words – and to be sure to spurn all prospective applicants not already marooned at a stone's throw from the end of the line. Such had been his first impression of John: a bit young maybe, but battered enough – no threat – give him to Bailer and Murphy. With that he'd gone back to his work and only thought about John insofar as his respective column on the payroll.

Our first impression had been considerably different. As group memory serves, the first night we laid eyes on John seven or eight of us had just suited up and were waiting around in the yard for the others to arrive. The sun was hanging heavy over the valley. The whine of the bulldozers was drifting through the lot. Clayton was badgering an inspection officer who was going over compactor number four with a check-off sheet. Curtis was teasing the yard bitch with a mop end. Murphy was standing with his back to a pole, arms crossed. Everyone else was still inside.

The landfill's main gate is situated in clear view of 254. From where we stood that evening we were able to see five hundred yards up and down the highway from across the scrap-lined overpass field. We could spot all last minute stragglers rolling in long before they reached the small ramp exit leading to Donnerville Road, and from Donnerville Road straight into the lot. At some point one of us commented on Wilbur's approach, as in those days Wilbur's old Ford was easily identifiable at great distances. Curtis mumbled something cryptic and continued working the bitch into a tither. The rest of us waited.

Wilbur slowed to a stop on the other side of Donnerville. Through the sparse flow of traffic dividing us, we could see he had a passenger along with him. He pulled through the gates and parked on the far end of the lot. The engine cut. He got out. From out of his passenger seat hopped a scraggly looking young man in an eccentric get up. The first thing we noticed was the coat, the way the blue, thigh-level tails were parted and drawn up by the arms, the hands being jammed firmly into the pockets of a pair of badly java-stained painters pants. Under the coat there was an off-white undershirt, on the feet, a pair of black orthopedic shoes, for the overall effect of a waylaid aerial bombardier behind enemy lines. As he approached at a stoop-shouldered swagger, the last thing to come into clear view was his face. His cropped hair, with the random hack marks from a steak knife, was gutted in bald patches. His skin was a living testament to battery – multiple scars and puncture wounds old and new. And by far the most disturbing thing was the eyes, that unibrowed, deep-socketed pair of ice-blue orbs darting back and forth over our group as they approached. By the time he'd loomed directly into view we were already being stared down. Most of us turned away, feeling as though we were being evaluated somehow. It left us very uneasy.

Those two walked by, climbed the staircase to Kuntsler's office, and disappeared inside, leaving the rest of us to wonder what kind of urban degenerate street trash Wilbur had dragged into our midst. We figured we'd find out soon enough.

Which we did. Immediately.

After the rounds that night Bailer came out with an alarming report from the fifth route: The new kid, the one Wilbur had signed on – the Cutler-blower guy with the funny haircut – had *more* than held his own throughout the evening; so much so that from the moment he'd gone on gate, with Murphy at the helm and Bailer to one side, he'd followed through with all the fervor and dispatch of a seasoned professional. He'd been double-handling Bailer himself, a twelve-year veteran of the company and no stranger to the heat, in less than ten minutes. Murphy had observed from the rear-view mirror during each stop along the northern third of the valley – Bailer panning out to the left, Kaltenbrunner to the right, each to his heap and back again. But by midway through the evening John had been finishing off his own piles from the oncoming lane, hurling every bag into the compactor, stomping back through the road, and clearing what remained of Bailer's mess without comment. Bailer was beside himself. He initially spoke highly of John's perform- ance, but he couldn't help but feeling somewhat uncomfortable, almost insulted by the mercilessly cold-shouldered silence to which he alone had been subjected for the past six hours. John hadn't spoken one word to him all night. He'd remained silent for the entire round. He'd gone about his duties quietly, with the green jumpsuit pulled over his torn street clothes and the all- weather hood folded back in a tight knot. He'd leapt to the ground at each stop, pitched sacks of trash into the churning compactor two, sometimes three at a time, then run ahead to secure the next load before Murphy could make a lock on him. He'd singlehandedly hoisted heavy furniture that would have taken other crews two of our finest members to handle. He'd never hesitated when a bag broke open and dumped moldy pizza and glass over the pavement; he'd scooped up the remains and let fly in one fluid motion. The three of them had rolled north along the valley walls, up and down Barrow Creek road to the cabin district at Sparrow's Height. At some point Bailer had kindly asked to have a look at one of John's acquisitions just before it was forfeited to the compactor. It was a bowling trophy or mem- orial plaque of some kind to which Bailer had taken an instant liking. He'd asked John if he wanted to keep it for himself, to which John had replied with a curt sweep of the hand and a harsh No. Bailer had set the plaque on the front seat next to Murphy, feeling sorry he'd asked.

The only other exchange of any kind which had gone between them had occurred the moment a renegade boxer came charging out of a yard on East 4th St., intent to kill. On spotting the advancing dog, Bailer had dropped his load and scampered off into a bush. But John had remained behind. He'd quietly dropped his bags, assumed a squat-haunched Cumberland judo stance of some sort – one foot forward and the other drawn to strike – and, at just the right instant, lashed out with a perfectly angled drop-kick to the jaw. The boxer had gone yowling back into the yard in a quadriplegic scurry. John had then turned and continued his work as though nothing had happened. When Bailer had finally peeked out from his hedge and crept back toward the gate, he'd found John already mounted, impatiently awaiting his return.

Bailer had never seen anything like it. He was personally ashamed and felt strangely cheated by the rest of us. We were seated at a triple table at the Dick listening to him go on about it. Though his story did sound interesting, we had to figure it was just another Bailer epic, nothing new. Bailer had a well known knack for embellishment; he'd once claimed to have targeted and killed a groundhog – *shot it right between the eyes* – from five hundred yards (five football fields) with a scopeless .22. Whenever he launched into one of his yarns we just sat back and enjoyed the show. Whether he knew it or not, no one put much stock in his claims. On that particular night it should have been no different. But for some reason it was. No one knew exactly why or how, but something was out of place. For one thing, it was highly unusual to hear Bailer relay an account at his own expense that way. And he *did* look crushed, there was no denying it. It was strange. Bailer epic or no, it left some of us to wonder.

By halfway through the next week all doubt on the matter had been dispelled. On Wednesday night Burt Clayton pulled his compactor into the lot with Kaltenbrunner and Irwin on gate. They had finished the second route – the southwestern factory circuit, probably the nastiest – over an hour ahead of schedule. John had now completed each route in its entirety at least once, meaning he had personally worked alongside of almost every hand in the yard, with the exception of the heavy-machinery operators. We had seen him at work. We had watched him go.

No one was calling Bailer a con man anymore. Bailer himself was babbling like the court fool with a thousand 'told-you-sos.'

There were mixed feelings all around concerning John as the new addition to the staff. On the one hand, the drivers were lining up early in hopes of getting paired off with him for the evening, thereby making it to the taverns in time for the tail end of happy hour. All they had to do was drive faster and turn in earlier. They didn't have to deal with him one-to-one. It was different for the gate hands. Though everyone agreed John was faster and more efficient than any greenback we'd ever encountered, those who had to work at close quarters with him unanimously maintained that the tense, hateful silence all around him made for an unbearably long six hour run.

His opening weeks in our company appeared to be more of an awakening to prior knowledge than a compulsory education. Everything fell right into place for him very quickly, just as it had begun to down in the sewers and in the convenience store a month earlier. We had never seen someone so terrifyingly driven in all our lives. Several of us had approached Wilbur to ask what seemed to be the problem. Had he lost his whole family tree in a twelve car pile up or something? Problems with the wife? Was it drugs? Was he out on parole? There had to be an explanation. From the rear-view mirrors of the compactor pits he appeared to be taking out a lifetime's worth of bloodlust on a few random bags of garbage. He evidently had it *in* for someone or something, and we weren't entirely sure it wasn't us. We half-expected him to crack on one of the rounds and steal off with a compactor for a street trashing spree. He made everyone terribly nervous.

While veering around sharp corners he would grip the overhead gate rail and let his feet trail behind in the open air. He had a way of dismounting at a precise moment of deceleration so as to reach the next heap at a trot before the compactor had come to a full stop. It took him no more than six seconds on average to load five bags from a pile situated to the rear of the rig, ten for one adjacent to the cockpit. In coming upon oblong furniture or discarded equipment, instead of waiting for another gatehand to assist with its loading, he would either stomp each object to pieces and load it separately, or plow it to the compactor in a crashing series of somersaults. When patrolling the farmer's markets, cattle ranches, and fast food stores, he was often elbow-deep and without complaint into the same mounds of gristle that left the rest of us retching. At the hospital he slung polyurethane bags full of foreskins and bodily growths without hesitation. Even the double-lined butchers' bags from the meat shop didn't faze him. It was as though he had seen it all before. He remained on gate through the late night thunderstorms, emerging at the end of the night every bit as soaked to the bone as the rest of us, but appearing somehow invigorated in spite of it all. We could see it in his face – not just at closing time, but all through the rounds. His brow remained knotted as a crow's talon as he scanned ahead of the moving rig for some sign of activity. He kept his eyes wide open and took everything in – mailboxes flying by to either side of the road, every door in the neighborhood passing in rapid succession. He spotted family picnics and class reunions along the way, packs of huntsmen kicking up pheasants in the fields, groups of freight runners huddled at the filling station, coots and woodchucks in the roadside ditches, on and on . . . He watched it all go by, then dropped to the ground to hurl yet another batch of tightly wound sacks into the compactor – twelve stops a street, ten streets a neighborhood, four neighborhoods a route, one route a night, five nights a week (one way to live, one way to end it).

Back on the balcony, his and Wilbur's nightly sessions took a turn. As they sat there, side-by-side in their bog-slag sanitary jumpers, their dialogues gradually shifted from beet-pulp feed cuts for the common ewe to potential compactor malfunction and the impracticality of the existing route circuit. They were on the same turf now. They shared the same cast of characters and the same basic duties in common. They paired off their nightly plunder in ranked competition. They inconclusively diagnosed Kuntsler's speculated neuroses. They discussed the rest of us too: we were to discover much later that, though John rarely spoke a word in our company, he'd been prying our life stories out of Wilbur to the last detail. He'd gotten a lock on everyone but Kuntsler, and fittingly enough, Kuntsler had had a lock on everyone but him. As polar opposites, those two had been removed from one another thus far: John remaining out on the rounds, and the old man shacked up with his paperwork, oblivious to the meanderings of his employees. Those being the existing conditions, very little direct confrontation could've been expected in the first stretch.

However, Wilbur knew perfectly well that, like it or not, John was having a tremendous impact on the rest of us, one which would eventually have to be brought to the old man's attention in one way or another. John himself may not have been aware of it. Kuntsler certainly would have been the last one to know. It was only Wilbur, and possibly one or two of the operators who were able to pick up on the unmistakable hike in productivity among the gatehands. We were all working our fingers to the bone at a maddening rate in order not to look bad in comparison. We hadn't seen anyone tear into the slag more ferociously since Dennis's last year as a dope fiend, and even then Dennis had been fueled by pharmaceuticals, trash food, and congenital imbecility. To the best of everyone's knowledge, John was no drug addict. He was a greenback juvenescent. Which made the fact that he was running circles around the rest of us all the more unbearable.

At the close of every evening we hit the Whistlin' Dick fagged and fashed to the point of collapse. Our joints were in agony. Our backs were bent. Most of us were quietly incensed with Wilbur for having brought this curse upon us, although confronting him on the matter would have involved owning up to something to which our pride was not yet ready to concede. As a result, Wilbur got an undivided cold-shoulder for a while, one he picked up on right away and which did nothing but add to his already escalating sense of dread. It can't be said he harbored any concrete regrets for having recommended John for the job, but all the same, it usually wasn't until the gates had been drawn for the evening and those two had driven home to the relative safety of their balcony that he was really able to loosen up, knowing at least one more day had gone by without a complete and total blowout.

*

The rounds continued. June hit with a crippling heat wave that was to kick off a four and a half month regional drought. Before it was over the golf course would be a scorched plateau, the autumn harvests in peril. The heat made for particularly rigorous work-conditions on our end. In addition to the community's overall yield being much higher, the rate of putrefaction among organic disposables – yard clippings and food scraps which comprised 15 per cent of the seasonal haul – was accelerated by the rise in temperature and made for both terrible odors and inordinately high fly breeding. Handling the livestock scraps became almost unbearable. Our poorly ventilated work suits made us subject to potential heat stroke. In the past, the summer heat had always slowed the rounds to a crawl, but now, with John on the crew, we suddenly found ourselves doubling our efforts beyond the norm – to what end we weren't quite sure – and sweating like tub cattle on the killing floor.

John carried on, seemingly impervious to everything. He downed crate loads of pasta and watched himself fill out in the mirror. His muscles began to tone up again. His chest thickened. He was soon bringing home his own share of loot from the rounds – high school trophies and war medals from the retirement home, family scrap books and wedding gowns, old rifle parts and fishing rods from the cabins on the outskirts, discarded records and children's toys, pots and pans, vintage pornography, wine bottles, street signs, boxes of wigs and baby-boomer maternity clothing wrapped in yellowed newspapers and moth balls. All of us had similar stockpiles in our own homes, making for cramped living quarters and rigorous spring-cleanings. One of the obvious and only fringe benefits of our occupation was the acquisition of an occasional jewel. In the next few months John would gather, among other things, one antique Corona typewriter that would bring one hundred and fifty-five dollars from the farmer's market, two operable color televisions, a pouch of what appeared to be genuine Shawnee hunting arrows, a pile of Studebaker hubcaps, a working rotary beater, and an original secessionist flag from the Confederacy.

Again, working the rounds did have certain material advantages, but for the most part they were so rare one had to plow through a mile of slag to get to them. Otherwise, our occupation was undeniably one of the lowest on the ladder, particularly in a place like Baker where the 'trash man' – the very term induced an instant gag reaction – was afforded little more respect than a sewer-line wetback. For every one cookie-wielding widow who hobbled off of her stoop to bestow us with a wrapped assortment of her latest batch, there were at least three hundred belligerent locals raring to mock and humiliate one of the green niggers to his deathbed. We were lambasted on every round. It had always been that way. It was part of the job. There was no point in fighting it, or so we assumed. We were *filthy animals and ought to be treated as such*. We heard it from Kuntsler every night. We heard it in the taverns, from the factory rats, the pork shack staff, and not least of all from one another. It had grown to be accepted as common knowledge, and along with that acceptance had come the same feelings of liberation, deliverance, and even bliss known to anyone who's ever been screwed beyond all hopes of recovery.

Curtis and Irwin had once been drenched in pig blood while clearing the disposal pit at Keller & Powell. They'd been standing at the base of a loading ramp filling a roller cart with entrails when two steerhands from the abattoir had crept to the overhead railing and deliberately dumped a twenty gallon tub from the latest kill over their heads. Irwin had caught the blast square in the face, while Curtis had been saturated from his waist down. The two of them had emerged from the incline looking like mortar-blast victims. Curtis had then charged into the main building for God knows what kind of retribution, only to be met by a jeering mob of cattlehands. He was driven out the door in a crossfire of manure and told to head back to the bread line where he belonged. His formal complaints were never acknowledged.

Another time the fifth route had been temporarily boycotted for fear of sniper fire. While traversing Old Mill Road on the north end, Murphy had been the first to have his tires blown out by trigger-happy sportsmen positioned in the tree stands at the edge of the game reserve. Over the next two weeks a rash of gunfire had lit out to all sides of the property, immobilizing three separate compactors and leaving every operator on edge. The assault had eventually tapered off with the close of deer season, but the public taverns had come alive with promises of renewed fire the next time around. Fortunately, no compactor has since been fired upon, which can be directly linked to a crackdown following one sportsman's arrest for assassinating the mayor's dog.

Another time one of the operators, Christopher Dockett, a surly ex-cook for the merchant Marines who is no longer among us, was accused, prosecuted, found guilty, and sentenced to twenty years in prison for a crime he didn't see, never could have formulated, and certainly didn't commit. According to the prosecution, on the night of November 30, 19—, Mr. Dockett left his compactor, approached the residence of Mrs. Rita Sloane, broke down the door, and sodomized Mrs. Sloane with a wooden billyclub – a charge so ridiculous it couldn't have possibly held up in any other court in the nation. Nevertheless, in Baker Dockett was jailed immediately despite outcries of protest from his fellow gate hands who insisted, even after the trial's conclusion, that none of them, particularly Dockett, had even the foggiest notion of who Mrs. Sloane was. Her address wasn't even on the landfill's roster. All the same, Dockett was imprisoned without further consideration. It was only five months later when Mrs. Sloane's husband returned to Baker from an extended trip abroad to find his wife in bed with another man that hope for Dockett's case resurfaced. In the course of the resulting divorce trial it was revealed that Mrs. Sloane and her extra-marital accomplice had gotten a bit rough one evening, leaving the former bruised and battered in all the wrong places. Together they had conspired to cover for themselves by pinning the crime on a passing trash man – a creature so wretched and pathetic that his testimony, even when corroborated by multiple witnesses, would be disregarded as inadmissable. Dockett was ultimately released, but not without being slapped with a restraining order to keep his distance from Mrs. Sloane thenceforth. He received no subsequent legal compensation for his troubles . . .

Just a few isolated incidents among thousands. As a general

rule, the average hill scrub was regarded as one of the lowest forms of life in existence. Year after year we'd been accosted at random, blasted as cellar cretins, and bombarded with compost from overpasses and storefront windows. It was commonly held that anyone on the outs needed only one quick glance in our direction to feel a whole lot better about himself. We were considered foul, expendable, and unworthy of anything but continual abuse. The one year we'd been invited to participate in the town labor fair our float had been irreparably sabotaged halfway through its construction. Though the vandals had never come forward, most locals maintained that had someone else not done it, they damn well would've seen to it themselves. *The trash man's place was on the ass-end of the heap, nowhere else.* He was expected to keep his mouth shut and roll with the punches. That's what he was paid for. He was employed by the city as a receptacle of public contempt. He was expected to be down, stay down, and never lift a finger when someone put him in place.

In that sense, John could be seen as having been doomed from the outset. Wilbur should have known that, and maybe he did. We'd all shuddered to think of what might happen the first night John was accosted by a local, as he inevitably would be. With his explosive disposition, some drastic, full-blown retaliation didn't seem at all far-fetched. But how were we, or anyone, to prepare him for it – to try to soften the blow of an assured confrontation by explaining that when it did come he would do better by himself and everyone involved just to lay down and take it? How is one to justify an ongoing policy of resignation and complaisancy, particularly to someone like John Kaltenbrunner? Impossible. It would've been easier to tell him he'd been hired on a fluke, that the landfill didn't accommodate for those with a backbone still partially intact and that if he knew what was good for him he'd pack up and walk before he got himself in trouble. But of course no one knew how to explain that either – and it would have made no difference anyway. So we kept quiet. We didn't say a word. And as could've been expected, the inevitable confrontation eventually surfaced.

*

It actually could've been a lot worse. Later on when the rest of us would begin looking to John for answers, he would encourage everyone to provoke all agitators by any means necessary. Had he encountered his own first problem at one of the production plants his response likely would've been so extreme that Kuntsler would have had no choice but to can him on the spot without any inquiry whatsover. As it was, his first cause for reprimand transpired on a much smaller scale, to everyone's benefit.

On Tuesday June 17, John, Curtis and Murphy were assigned to the fourth route – the eastern end. At 7:45 p.m. they approached the left wing of the Pineridge apartment complex on Dowler St. Halfway through their run, while pulling up to the curb of a double-chambered unit house, Murphy unintentionally bowled over a plastic big wheel which had been left in the middle of the road. Curtis peeled the flattened toy from the asphalt and pitched it into the yard, then set to work clearing the pile of garbage they had come for. Just before he and John had finished up, an obese woman of obviously German stock came storming out of a door along the row with a frying pan in one hand and a broomstick in the other. She proceeded to hurl accusations of willful and malignant property damage, swearing she would make them pay for flattening 'Robert's bicycle.' She was hysterical. She bounded over the yard in her daisy-print burlap dress, cutting an ominous nine-foot swath with the two outstretched utensils. She charged Curtis and pummeled him with the flat of the pan. She called him a bastard and swore she'd kill him, then went on to invoke repeatedly some arch-fiend or another by the name of Lester – Lester would take care of him, she spat. Wait until Lester hears about it, *Lester's gonna keeeel yooo* . . . She chased Curtis off into the road, slammed the pan on the gate rail and turned toward John.

Had she just left it with Curtis, the whole thing might've fizzled out right there. She would have stomped back inside, glared from the window for a minute, possibly made a phone call to the landfill or to Lester, and then gone about explaining to Robert that his big wheel was no more. Curtis, for his part, would have nursed the lump on his head all the way down the road, but by the end of the night he would've filed the incident away with hundreds of others just like it. Case closed.

But that's not what happened. Because she apparently couldn't settle with Curtis alone, because she felt she had to give the second gatehand a taste of the skillet as well, one of the most ridiculous episodes in the history of the company followed:

Before Murphy could see what was happening, John had pried the broomstick loose from the woman's hand and had laid her out in the yard with a massive woodcutter's swing to the backside. She went down like a targeted bison, screaming the whole way. As she groped to get to her feet, he whacked again, knocking her jellyroll diameter back to earth. Then again, and again, and again, halfway up the walk. Before Curtis could put a stop to it, John was driving her back through the yard toward the apartment at a full tilt charge. She made it inside and slammed the door. John snapped the broomstick in half and pitched it into the bushes. The woman appeared at the window screaming. John walked back to the compactor. He picked up a bag from the walk and scattered its contents all over the lawn with an unbelievably vicious scowl on his face. Curtis and Murphy were leveled. The woman kept screaming. John picked up her frying pan and threw it into the compactor. She really went wild. He added the flattened Big Wheel.

At that point Curtis snapped to and suggested they get the hell out of the neighborhood at once. They left.

Curtis and Murphy spent the next three hours in a cold sweat, knowing there was going to be hell to pay on returning to the yard. They mumbled to themselves all the way down the road, trying to concoct a workable defense for their part in the matter. They didn't come up with anything. At one point they passed a moving patrol car on 254, by which they half-expected to be pulled over, run down, and escorted to the gazebo for a public flogging. They were out of their minds with anxiety. But the patrol car came and went with the regular flow of traffic, and as far as Curtis could tell, John didn't even flinch at its passing. He didn't seem to notice at all. He was so collected that both Curtis and Murphy began to doubt their own sensibilities.

John remained quiet for the rest of the night. Curtis wanted to warn him that Kuntsler would undoubtedly be coming for him the moment they got back to the yard. As far as he could tell John didn't seem to realize what he was in for. He didn't appear to be at all concerned. Curtis would've spoken up, but after three weeks on the job it was still the case that no one quite knew how to approach John. So he kept quiet and said nothing. They finished off their round in characteristic silence.

Just as they expected, Kuntsler was waiting on his stoop the moment they arrived. He looked like a deposed general silhouetted in the door frame up there, arms crossed, shoulders twitching. John dismounted and began walking toward him before the compactor had ground to a halt. Curtis watched him go. He and Murphy exchanged nervous glances, torn between admiration for John's repose and relief at not having been summoned themselves. John climbed the stairs and disappeared into the trailer. Kuntsler slammed the door behind him.

For the next fifteen minutes a fusellade of profanity lit out from the office. As the second, fifth and first crews pulled into the lot respectively, everyone gathered around Curtis and Murphy to find out what had happened. Murphy filled us in while nervously watching Kuntsler's shadow tear back and forth behind the drawn shades. When Wilbur finally arrived with the last group, he joined us, was given the report, and set in to pacing wild circles around the yard with his head in his hands. He mumbled about having been afraid this would happen. He mumbled all kinds of things, but no one could hear a word he said over the screaming and crashing from the office.

Kuntsler was in a frenzy. John later reported that the old man had actually ripped his clock from the wall and hurled it against the closet door, then swore John himself would be personally docked for its replacement. John had remained with his back to the wall quietly refraining from comment on all but the most pointed rhetoric and privately reflecting on how much the old man reminded him of Roy Mentzer.

*

When it finally ended something strange happened.

The bellowing and tumult eventually tapered off. Silence fell over the lot for a minute or two. All of us, including the machinery operators, were huddled together beneath a cone of light twenty yards from the trailer. The only sound to be heard was the occasional grinding of pebbles in the dirt beneath Wilbur's shifting feet. The rest of us were standing stock-still, waiting for the verdict.

Another minute later the trailer door opened. John stepped out. He made his way down the stairs and began walking toward us through the blackened yard. Up on the porch Kuntsler slammed the door one last time. The whine of the bolted hinges reverberated through the lot. John continued coming toward us. When he finally stepped into the light his features lit up in a luminescent yellow glow. He stopped. He took a quick look around at everyone. Then, to the astonishment of all he did something none but Wilbur had ever thought possible, something so alien and incomprehensible that most of us would later have to doubt our own recollective capacities.

He smiled.

THAT'S HOW IT BEGAN – closing time, June 17, in the main lot of the Pullman Valley landfill: Wilbur Altemeyer and John Kaltenbrunner tooling off for a long overdue discussion on their balcony, Jeffrey Kuntsler piecing his office back together in a state of shattered nervous hysteria, and the remainder of the crew, all twenty-one of us on a mass exodus for the Bloody Bucket to dive headlong into an all night soiree still revered as one of the most knock-down, head-splitting drunks we've ever been on. It was a night to remember for everyone.

On our end, by last call most of us were falling from our stools and braying like field asses. Visions of the old Pineridge bull harlot being goat-whipped from one end of her yard to the other in a stumbling series of failed takeoffs, and thereafter Kuntsler foghorning invective all through the lot with a borderline missionary zeal, threw us into extended fits of crippling laughter. We were a tearful mess by 2 a.m. All through the night we implored Curtis and Murphy to repeat the story again and again. Murphy's version was clearly the better of the two as, without embellishing too extravagantly, he somehow managed to recount the event from a different angle on each telling. We were starved for specifics: how many times had John laid into her? How far of a stretch had it been from the road to the front door, at what angle had the frying pan impacted with Curtis's skull, what had become of the big wheel, and so forth. We hung on through each retelling in tight-fisted anticipation until the broom whacks rolled around, then erupted in an exhilarated, foot-stomping ballyhoo that left most of us doubled over and whinnying.

The night ended with six of us passed out in our pickups, far too inebriated to drive home. And in the morning, a hangover heralding the arrival of the Norsemen.

But for all our antics, toasts, boasts and proclamations that evening, what none of us realized was that the Pineridge incident – this, for appearance's sake, meaningless blowup on John's part – was to have a much more lasting impact on everyone than was immediately evident. Strangely enough, one might cite it as *the* critical turning point in events to come, though at the time, none of us could have suspected as much. At the time, especially there at first, it just stood as something to call an ongoing group toast to, something to chortle over and indulge in during nightcap sessions. It brought a good laugh from everyone. And over the course of the next several weeks, as the drought pushed on, the nightly rounds continued, and the incident itself drifted farther and farther away, it remained in place as a sidesplitting anecdote inseparable from our after-hour conversations.

However, just when, realistically, it should have begun to recede and been filed away in the dumping ground of similar anecdotes, that's when its real effects began to germinate and come to term. With that, things would take a permanent turn. Our initial esteem for John as yard novelty and object of adoration would thereby evolve into a reverence for him as literal ideal, just as, simultaneously, the mirth of our nightcap sessions would gradually give way to a much more all-pervasive air of discontent. Both would develop unilaterally, with John as the focal catalyst.

It was Don Bailer who later claimed that frequenting Baker's taverns during that season's drought was like packing into an overheated stable house to feed from the trough alongside of the rest of the swine. During the months of July and August, factory rats from all over town poured into the bars in large, downtrodden regiments. They seated themselves at the counter and along the walls. Some of them stood beneath the ceiling fans, eyes shut tight, hats in hand, heads thrown back with the oily hair plastered over their faces. Their backs were sopped with long sheets of sweat. It rolled over their noses and into their beards, off of their chins and on to the counter. They hovered over baskets of complimentary pretzels, shoveling them in by the fistful, mouth-breathing between swallows and gobbing on the floor. The constant boom of honky-tonk crackled from the jukebox's damaged speaker system, but no one seemed to notice or care in the heat. The most for which anyone could reasonably hope was to get in on the martinis before the ice ran out, and, if possible, to snag one of the tables or chairs by the main door, where the draft was good. Otherwise, nothing was very clear. The weather had deranged everyone's senses. By the close of each night, most crews were grease-splattered, disoriented and incoherent. Tempers were unusually short fused, overall capacities more disoriented than ever. For all those reasons, the change we soon began to undergo went largely unnoticed for longer than it otherwise might've.

The Pineridge incident was our central topic of discussion for the next four weeks. Our after-hour sessions became tribunals of revelry on account of it. For the majority of that time we worked ourselves into hooting fits no less excruciating than those of the first night. We drank too much and called undue attention to ourselves from all the regulars. On a nightly basis the liquor rolled, we got louder, the calls grew wilder, and the whole crew was eventually ejected. It progressed in stages that way. On hearing enthused talk of our latest gatherings, several of us who normally didn't attend decided to stop by and see what all the fuss was about, which, in effect, increased our numbers from eight or nine to well over fifteen, sometimes more. Our triple table overflowed leaving many of us standing or seated with our backs to the wall. We very quickly went from being the most bucolic, low-key group in attendance to the largest and most uninhibited to frequent the Dick or Bucket in years.

John and Wilbur never attended. We were to discover later on, under more pressing circumstances, that the two of them had taken to breaking into the landfill after closing time and continuing their balcony tangents in the yard, alone and away from the rest of us. They never dropped in on our group for so much as five minutes. John had barely set foot in the Dick since the morning he'd met Wilbur, and Wilbur hadn't pulled a nightcap session in years. They were better off alone, or so they felt. They stayed away.

But despite their absence, John himself unknowingly hung over every meeting like an approaching storm cloud. Although, again, his impact on our group had been evident long before the drought rolled around, it wasn't until the Pineridge incident brought us together in its wake that our regard for him took a turn for the reverential. He'd previously been held up as a curse and a burden. We'd all felt understandably inadequate in his presence. But now, with the image of him taking up arms at what we were construing to be the benefit of Curtis – Curtis being someone, like the rest of us, to whom John had extended little or no hospitality – he was suddenly indoctrinated *en absentia*; he remained an outsider still, a fringe-dweller maybe, the unapproachable without a doubt, but he was *one of us* now, whether he knew it or not. He'd become a hill scrub. Without intending to do so, he'd inadvertently cast his lot as number twenty-three; but being as generally inaccessible as he was, he would first have to become an *idea*, a mascot par excellence, an agent of revenge – all based, of course, on what little we had to go – before materializing as an actual flawed, albeit remarkable individual in his own right.

To begin with, we started cut-up/tape-loop style experimentation – heavily bourbon and Schlitz-possessed pipedreams that put all our least favorite locals on the butt-end of the Pineridge incident. We tried to imagine, for example, how the results might have differed had John been on hand the time Irwin was besieged by the secretary's husband at the furniture plant for accidentally loading the couple's (empty) baby carriage into the compactor. We replaced the Pineridge woman's broom with a monkey wrench, the woman herself with various machinery operators and east-side trolls, the unit house with grain sheds and storage bins, etc. We ran through the whole community and put everyone in increasingly humiliating predicaments. We took turns replacing A with B, putting C at the mercy of K for the overall effect of X. We rehashed years of incidents and affairs in search of more material. No one who'd ever crossed our paths went unscathed. All were hammered, whipped and driven to the block by a scythe-wielding John Kaltenbrunner. And as the projected scenarios progressed, a drive to outdo one another in terms of depravity took hold. Soon enough the imagery had become so graphic and demented that had someone been listening in for even one night, we all might've been flayed alive and boiled as collaborators.

But though, at first, we were only pushing for a good hard laugh with all this surrealistic indulgence, what we were to discover in a few weeks time was that by turning an all-seeing eye on every past grievance/trespass that had ever been done us – all in the interest of unearthing more material – we were consequently drudging up several painfully embarrassing memories from over the years; memories of being kicked, beaten, spat on, insulted, bombarded with rotten food, entrails, vomit and urine, of being slapped in the face, smeared with every epithet in the book, chased, bitten, targeted, scapegoated, and even shot at. Our pipe dreaming became a continual reminder that we'd been regarded as the lowest strain of pond vermin for longer than anyone could remember. We'd grown insensitive to it. Which is why the Pineridge incident, as a retaliatory act, had appeared like a shot out of the dark for everyone.

But then again, we weren't so far gone as to be incapable of appreciating the humor in the incident itself. On the contrary, what became increasingly evident as the weeks pushed on was that we'd been waiting to bust a gut along these lines for years. There had been a hole in our lives with what we were taking to be this situation written all over it. Pineridge had brought that hole to light, the end result being that, between us, an unspoken drive to re-enact the episode ourselves began tugging at our collective conscience. Starting at that point, visions of everything from pitching forty gallon aluminum bins through bay windows to storming factory lots *en masse* – by ourselves, of our own volition, no longer via some vicarious agent – beckoned to us like lurid invitations to obscenity.

Probably the first outside party to cue in on the alteration in our behavior was the tavern crowd at the Dick and the Bucket. Though all the regulars agreed we'd been acting unusually for several weeks, it wasn't until early July that they began to realize something more than just the heat had gotten into us. None of them knew what to make of it at first. We'd always been the docile group of pushovers from the landfill; a quiet, older crew, rarely responsive to direct confrontation, and always among the first out the door in the event of a brawl. It had been that way for as long as anyone could remember. But, apparently, that was no longer the case. Something had come over us. Our crew had grown to be the largest in attendance. We were drinking other groups under the table with alarming regularity. We were filing in earlier, commandeering five of the central tables, making a deafening racket the whole night through, and running the staff ragged until well after last call. And somehow, in the confusion, we'd turned mean. We were snapping at the bartenders, ogling the regulars, glaring at the doormen. When phase three rolled around and the insults started flying, we were no longer inclined to sit back and take it all. We now joined in as active participants. We fired back with equally scurrilous accusations all around. The regulars were stunned. No one had ever seen us act this way. Most of them were younger, stronger, less weatherbeaten and instinctively more vicious than we, but they were so astonished with our sudden display of backbone (or stupidity) that they kept a cautious distance. They shied away with the same uneasy revulsion most societies accord an overcrowded leprosarium. They could've easily laid us out on the spot had they wanted – that was no question – but just the sight of us gave them the creeps something terrible. The thought of striking us in our present condition had all the appeal of guillotining a company of plague-infected hemophiliacs. Fear of contagion. They kept their distance, eying us from every corner of the room. Our appearance as a group and as individuals had taken a dive. Our eyes had gone wide and protuberant, our hair was on end, our dress was more slovenly than ever. Huddled together in a tight pack with our hoods thrown back and the grime over our drawn chest flaps, we looked like the Blue Ridge militia come home to roost. *What the hell's wrong with them green niggers*, they would say. *Lost their minds, must've . . .*

better leave 'em be. Which they did, for a while, waiting for things to return to normal.

But nothing returned to normal. What started as a two-minute episode at an east side apartment complex grew to be cited as a Bull Run allegory for all of us. Our nightcap sessions continued to degenerate into outraged confessionals. Memories of the same incursions we had tolerated for most of our careers resurfaced in backlash reminiscence. We worked ourselves into raving tantrums at the recollection of up to twenty-five years of endured community mistreatment. Our conversations were overrun by the time Irwin had done this, Bailer had gotten that, Murphy had been kicked, Dennis slapped, Curtis chased off, etc. . . . and just how gratifying it might've been to round up all our antagonists, rope them with circuit wire and mow them to the hillside in unison. We were itching for a row – not just in the taverns, not just on a drunk, but during our stone-cold sober hours on the job as well. We became openly defiant with our clientele. The customary insults with which we were bombarded every night lost their impact. The same locals who'd previously ground us underfoot became gross, pathetic caricatures of sterility. We grew more tempted to tell them all where to get off, to drive by their homes without pickup. Pretty soon that's exactly what started happening: open confrontations with locals resulting in deliberate neglect of duty and ultimately leading to the lodging of formal complaints with Jeffrey Kuntsler.

Whether or not the Pineridge incident had put the old man on alert to begin with is difficult to say. It had clearly made him prick up his ears for a while, as the scathing interrogations to which Wilbur, Curtis and Murphy had been subjected indicated. But for the first few weeks, the way the developing situation would've appeared to him versus the reality of what was actually going on were two different things. The most he could've detected to start with would've been a gradual slackening of attention to his tirades, a twinge of reluctance at carrying out his orders, and possibly, though it's doubtful, an occasional smirk at his expense during roll call. Otherwise, for appearance's sake, nothing overtly obvious would've seemed amiss. At least not at first. From where he was situated, all alone in his trailer, he couldn't have noticed much.

But by the third week in July that would all change.

To Kuntsler's bewilderment, the work week of the 18th to the 22nd opened with three separate, and what might have appeared to be unrelated, complaints pouring in from the community in just as many days. All together, that was more negative kick back in reference to his employees than he'd received over the previous five years combined.

—The first report was a simple drive-by on Lester's part – an unusual 'slip up' maybe, but no big matter. Arguably unintentional.

—The second was a confrontational exchange between Kohler and a hospital side troll. Admittedly deliberate, but still justifiable.

—However, the third was unprecedented. The third was a direct threat on the part of the Keller & Powell administration to prosecute Dennis Stauffer on charges of assault and battery. The charges were partially founded, barring of course the fact that scrawny, buck-toothed Dennis, on going head to head with two steerhands in the main lot at the slaughterhouse, had been openly provoked to the point of retaliation and had afterwards been beaten senseless. The specifics didn't seem to matter to the administrative officials, and they certainly didn't matter to Kuntsler. The only thing that registered in the old man's brain was that these three incidents, one and all, represented a direct threat to his hitherto uncontested authority. The fact that they'd all occurred back to back in the same week was enough to wake him from his slumber.

In response, he reacted as might have been expected: he cracked down hard. Starting at that point he lashed out with the same scare tactics that had always worked so effectively in the past. He docked pay. He issued citations for misconduct. He fired up roll call to a medieval pitch. He assigned scowry detail – the outhouses, mill ponds, gutter duty, etc. He leered from his window around the clock. Any time more than two or three of us convened in the yard he came charging out of his office to break it up. He ordered us not to speak with one another: *Shut up and disperse*, he'd say, *You stand there, you go there, the rest of you out of my sight. Don't speak, don't even look at one another* . . . He called us idiots. He labeled Dennis a terminal junkie and suicidal failure. He called Curtis a cellar-bastard, Murphy a jailbird, Wilbur the ugliest eligible bachelor in town. The rest of us were kennel-faggots and gook-loving Jew boys. He laid it on thick, but to what end he was obviously oblivious. He was lost. With the advent of some indefinable hysteria sweeping through his yard, he doubled up on the same Paleozoic tyranny that had always served its purpose in the past. But now, unlike before, the abuse backfired. All his efforts to crush us only solidified our already mounting disgust. Instead of striking fear, as intended, his latest reign of terror only managed to muster our unanimous contempt. The bigger and badder he made himself out to be, the smaller and more pathetic he became.

While all that was going on, the catalyst of our transformation remained far out of the picture. Following the Pineridge episode John had returned to his post and carried on as though nothing had happened. Regardless of the much talked about smile of his which had caused such a stir to begin with, he had taken no real steps toward warming up to any of us. He still didn't speak to anyone but Wilbur. He still tore a scorched path around the compactor on the rounds, leaving everyone bowled over in his wake. Realistically, he remained every bit the inconvenience he'd been to begin with, only now, the same cold disposition which had formerly irritated us to no end was being championed as the embodiment of an ideal. To what extent he may have realized this himself is anyone's guess. But Wilbur knew perfectly well – with his seniority and common sense he rightly should have – and, feeling partly to blame for the mess, took it upon himself to intervene.

To begin with he approached John. Although the two of them were always open and direct with one another on every issue, Wilbur knew that without laying the proper groundwork ahead of time, John would be averse to the suggestions he had to offer. Knowing that, his pitch took a few days of calculated maneuvering to preface. In that time he did his best to

227

emphasize, subtly and without overstating any particulars, that never in the history of the landfill had one individual had a more profound impact on the crew than he. Though he was nearly two decades everyone's minor, was less verbal than the lot bitch on the Lord's day and was unquestionably every bit as ugly as Dennis or Bailer, he'd still managed to wake the blaze on the dormant hearth in little over two months. Wilbur knew this to be true. *But*, he went on to explain, there was more to it than just that. What John didn't understand, or so Wilbur ventured to guess, was that the effects of his intolerance for one pot and broom-wielding kitchen harpy were not just going to die away after a momentary spurt of group enthusiasm. Not at all. One look around indicated that it had already gone beyond that point. What Wilbur now feared was the onset of imitation – a reckless push on the crew's part to nurture and develop what were being championed as John's primary character traits: intolerance, refusal, and rage at the slightest provocation. Without proper guidance this forced transition would result in an outbreak of belligerence and confrontation between our crew and the local citizenry – a slew of irrational behavior that would belittle the conflict up to that point – all of it geared toward emulating, even fishing for the approval of, John himself. The symptoms were already clear: the increase in productivity, the numerous reports from the taverns, the quarreling on the rounds, the all-around grumbling at the mention of Kuntsler's name, and, if nothing else, the obviously thickening tension in the air. None of these factors had existed preceding John's arrival. The truth was, whether he wanted to hear it or not, he had singlehandedly created a serious dilemma. True, it may have been the farthest thing from his original intentions; he may not have opened his mouth to anyone along the way, he may not have had a demonstrative bone in his body. He very well may not have given a damn for any of us. Those were clearly his prerogatives. However, absurd as it may've seemed, his actions, intentional or no, had set the standard for what was now being hailed as model behavior. And unfortunately, that standard had snowballed. Pineridge had distilled to a parable, the parable had sown the seeds of discontent, the discontent had led to numerous confrontations, and the confrontations were just about to result in everyone being canned for some wild, as of yet uncommitted, public explosion. He had to understand that it was every bit that serious. The crew was heading for the gin ranks at a blind hysterical charge, and the truth was – which was Wilbur's main point – the only person who could do anything about it was John. Wilbur knew it sounded ridiculous, but he insisted it was true. John, having indirectly touched off the situation, was the only one who could conceivably step in and prevent it from following through to its natural conclusion. He was the only one any of us might listen to. Knowing that, Wilbur reasoned, there was only one just course of action left to pursue. He fully acknowledged that John had in no way intended to kick up the existing disorder, and therefore, strictly speaking, was not morally obligated to resolving it. But, he said, with all due consideration, turning his back on the situation now, with full knowledge of all of the above, would be stone-cold malicious.

So, that being said, Wilbur implored John by all he held dear to please, for his sake if nothing else, try and step in somehow. He could begin by ending the sulking and glowering at everyone – Wilbur himself was catching hell on account of it. He could feign interest in our activities from time to time, exhibit mild approval, say something every now and then, at least grace the crew with an occasional nod of the head. It wouldn't be *that* difficult. He was already halfway there – without ever having said a word he'd become far more influential than our director of twenty years. Look what one smile had done, Wilbur said. *Try imagining the impact of the spoken word.* Anyway, he just might've found that the rest of us weren't *all that bad.* Granted we hadn't exactly invented the powder, but we weren't deserving of such merciless unyielding contempt. We were less cognizant of our own cowardice than he realized. He gave us more credit than we were due. We just weren't that clever. His disdain for us was on par with cruelty to animals, didn't he understand? And anyway, if he did have a problem with Baker, then with all due respects, so did the rest of us. We were up against the same thing, to some extent. If John would just realize that, he'd have the opportunity of rerouting certain disaster, making life in the landfill more endurable for everyone, and maybe, just maybe, getting something out of it for himself along the way. In any case, if he didn't do something fast, anything at all, twenty-one hill scrubs would soon be stockade-bound without a clue in the world as to what went wrong, and number twenty-two and twenty-three left behind going one on one for the asshole of the year award. The time was now, Wilbur said in conclusion.

John wasn't keen on the idea for one minute. After a moment's hesitation, he hunkered down with a sullen, almost vicious response.

First off, he said, he *did* consider the majority of us to be every bit as contemptible as assumed. He claimed that anyone, including Wilbur, who shined the brass for an imbecile like Kuntsler ought to be dragged out back with Slim's bitch.

Second, if any of his actions really had caused a stir the way Wilbur claimed, it certainly hadn't been at his initiative. He was in no way responsible for cleaning up a mess he had not made and resented all notions to that effect. Period.

Third, even if he had smiled after the Pineridge incident – and he claimed not to remember having done so – it would've only been because he'd found the situation mildly amusing, nothing more. There would've been nothing deliberately provocative or subversive about it. Whoever had come up with that one ought to *come down from the trees.*

Fourth and finally, maybe we were all up against the same thing, in theory, as Wilbur had suggested. But as far as he was concerned, however the rest of us chose to conduct our affairs in the face of that was up to us – it still had nothing to do with him. All he wanted was to be left alone.

Which was, of course, not at all what Wilbur wanted or needed to hear. At the close of their first exchange Wilbur was left discouraged and at a loss. Trying to coerce John into intervening in this situation would obviously take time.

Meanwhile, in accord with his assessment, we were going out of our minds. Just as he'd claimed, all attempts at maintaining our decorum while out on the rounds had been forcibly dismissed. We were actively provoking everyone with whom we came in contact. We were hell-bent on becoming a certifiable public menace. Consequently, we withstood all effrontery with diminishing resilience. The nightcap sessions turned uglier than ever. We were often shuffled out of the taverns after close, on which we would howl in the street, issuing open challenges toward the blackened storefronts along Main. We envisioned blocking traffic, lighting fires, poisoning the city water supply, rigging Molotov cocktails, fertilizer bombs and water cannons. One night six of us went on a mailbox trashing spree with a Louisville slugger, leaving a line of wooden posts standing naked on the north end of town. We laid low for the next few days, wondering if we hadn't gone a bit too far that time. But once it became obvious that we'd pulled it off scot-free, we flared up again, more cocksure than ever. By the end of the following week we were completely out of control. Even Dennis, who, again, could only partake of alcohol at the risk of lethal paralysis, was getting flat-out despicable over club sodas and pretzels. We were acting like assholes.

One night at the Bucket we narrowly avoided full-on confrontation with a group of cannery rats, only this time, unlike in the past, *we* had been the instigators. Actually it was Irwin, heretofore the pacifist in the bunch, who hurled an empty bottle at the opposing table and got things going. The uproar that followed fell short of full-cast brawl due only to one bartender's reflex time. We were marched out the exit door at gunpoint and barred from re-entry for the next three weeks. Thereafter we made for the Dick, which, by then, had already been alerted to our approach and was waiting with all talons bared. That was where we finally got it, as we should have.

The specific details of that evening are too embarrassing to go into at length. Suffice it to say: we started a mess – we were wholly responsible – and ended up getting the hell beaten out of us in the street as a result. The steer-droppers from Keller & Powell were fed up with us. All the regulars were. They beat us so badly most of us couldn't walk a straight line for the next week. They broke Lester's nose with a Chivas bottle. They stripped Irwin to his boxers and drove him into a cornfield. They locked Curtis in a dumpster with a mound of gristle and busted glass. The rest of us they just hammered to the ground and left for the police to pick up. When three of the sheriff's deputies did arrive, they gave us a once over and claimed they didn't want to soil their holding cells with our filth. They gave us five minutes to get off the street. At the close of the night the only one to face arrest was Irwin, who was picked up in his boxers while sneaking through a roadside ditch with one black eye and a blood alcohol reading of .32. It was a disgrace. We were banned from both of Baker's main taverns, and the others – the truck stops and highway saloons – let out word that if we so much as even thought about heading in their direction they'd send us on our way with an ass full of buckshot and a fleet of pit bulls at our heels. We were cast out. And that's to say nothing of the next night when we reported for duty in the yard. As we stood there, battered, lacerated, hung over and scarcely capable of remaining on our feet, Kuntsler stomped back and forth bellowing out how we looked like a group of girl scouts who'd been raped by the yeti. We were *revolting*, he said. Not worth a hamhock at the synagogue.

After that Wilbur was all but down on his knees to John, begging him to reconsider and insisting the keg was about to blow. He was right, although John still wanted no part of it. They were at a standoff. Wilbur continued stressing the importance of intervention. John continued maintaining his right to neutrality. Neither seemed likely to budge and both wanted an end to the dialogue. It was the first tense moment of their relationship.

But at some point John suddenly stopped protesting Wilbur's entreaties altogether. Wilbur recalls it as having been a strange moment, as though out of nowhere a little lightbulb had gone off in John's head, bringing an abrupt and unexpected end to the debate. It was a Thursday evening during the last week in July. The two of them were seated on the clay-topped monolith in the center of the yard, drinking and talking as the night went on. The east tower of the First Methodist Church had just tolled out three resounding gongs through the fog when John suddenly straightened up and, without any warning, announced that he had an idea.

SO MUCH HAPPENED over the course of the next three weeks, so many new policies were implemented, so many changes came about – all of them behind Kuntsler's back of course – that by the time the old man finally did crack the case and get the big picture, he was really no longer a part of it. The ongoing futility of trying to identify and pinpoint something which continually eluded his grasp, regardless of his approach, had systematically broken him to pieces. By the night of August 17th he'd been reduced to a distraught, Lear-in-the-wild type, a sideshow exhibit in a freak circus, a wiry, melon-headed demagogue whose fiery appeals were granted no more consideration than those of a common project-tramp on a four-day crack high. He was crushed, detached, free-floating. The rest of us had more important things to tend to than paying him any mind.

The night began with the most frantically convulsive roll call he'd ever delivered. Murphy probably put it best when he remarked that all across the nation people are jailed and/or institutionalized every day for less than half of his exhibited hysteria that evening. It was more like a recruiting pitch for the SS than an occupational reprimand. Whatever happened to the old man in later years, we all agreed that if and when he ever fell on harder times there would be a spot cleared and waiting for him at the head of a failed scriptwriters' corps in some dingy back room studio in Burbank California.

At five o'clock sharp, as the last of us had just lined up in the yard, he came exploding out of his office. Coming down from his stoop and pounding over the gravel in a wobbling power walk, his beige khakis hiked up over his navel and knotted tightly around his frail ribcage, his movements spastic and convulsive so as to accentuate his facial tick, he had all the appearance of a bloated, snakebitten appendage tied off by a terry-cloth tourniquet. The sweat running from his forehead had saturated his collar and begun to crop up in random splotches all the way to his ankles. His eyebrows were screwed up, his mouth lined with a frothy film of spittle, his face swollen blue. In one fist he held a crumpled stack of papers, in the other, a military-issue police baton with a bold LAW & ORDER etched along its length. He was off his rocker indignant and closing in.

He reared to a halt at the head of the line and announced at the top of his lungs that no one, *absolutely no one* was going anywhere short of the public whipping post and house of proctal expansion until he had some direct explanations for the onslaught of complaints he'd received in the last twenty-four hours. He warned everyone to come clean at once or *law and order would prevail* . . . Before he could continue, his face seized up in a series of harsh twitches, his lips trembling uncontrollably as he stammered and choked to overcome his rage. A minute later he came out of it and resumed, but the remainder of the coming stemwinder was to be marred with similar debilitating seizures, rendering the majority of his speech unintelligible.

First, he said producing the pile of papers, the authorities had come by earlier in the day to follow up a complaint filed by Holtz's Cannery Inc. Apparently, according to the cannery's administration, some 'red-haired ingrate' from our crew had engaged two of their employees in a screaming match, at the conclusion of which said ingrate and crew had rigged one of the company's dumpsters to his compactor, elevated and inverted it, and intentionally unloaded the entirety of its con-tents into the center of the parking lot, thereby obstructing all incoming and outgoing traffic. The compactor and crew had then fled the scene, leaving the company staff behind to hand-clear the mess. The company was drawing up formal charges and intended to prosecute to the full extent of the law.

Kuntsler could barely keep his hat on. He marched up to Roy Dickell, squared off in his face, and claimed that Dickell, being the only red-haired employee on the crew, would certainly appear to be the ingrate in question, only the thing was, according to the yard itinerary, Dickell had been assigned to the fifth route during the previous evening and damn-well never should've been within a day's march of the cannery. So how could this be?

Next, both Keller & Powell and the First Methodist Church in addition to five (not one, not two – but five!) private residents had phoned to complain that no one had come by for pickup in over two weeks. Each caller had claimed to have a heap of refuse the size of a bulldozer mounting in his pit, lot or walk respectively. In the case of the slaughterhouse, several health inspectors had come by and fined the company for breach of upkeep, with further threats to close shop by force due to the massive accumulation of waste on the premises. The company was jammed to the hilt in a legal dispute it would never win and was seeking full compensation from the landfill. There was *no excuse for it*, Kuntsler claimed.

Another thing, a 'concerned citizen' had phoned in to report that at seven forty-five the night before, the three crew members operating compactor number four (license number 72J 145) had been spotted at the truck stop power-chasing beer and whisky right out in the open. This not only brought into question drinking on the job – a *dismissable* offense in and of itself – but on consulting his itinerary the old man found that, once again, compactor number four had been assigned to the second route the night before and would have had no reason to be anywhere near the truck stop. Who had been where and why?

Finally, no one was going to pull the wool over his eyes, he said. If we really thought we were being clever by covering up whatever it was we thought we were covering up we were wrong. *Wrong, wrong, wrong!* He knew something was going on. It had been made *Deliberately Clearly.* In addition to our attitudes being deplorable to the point of obscenity, we had left so many of our tracks uncovered in attempting to conspire against him that only the village idiot could possibly remain oblivious. Just that morning he'd opened the gates to find the lot bitch gone, one of the steamrollers overturned, and the yard littered with golf balls. He was no fool. He could read the writing on the wall. Someone was going to pay for it *right now*.

He paused for effect, twirling his billyclub and shifting from side to side. Never had the fact that he was almost a full head shorter than the rest of us been so evident. The look on his face prompted Burt Clayton to recall the day his uncle by adoption, a known Aryan supremacist, was informed after a successful liver transplant that his organ donor had been a Jew.

A minute later he resumed. Starting with Dennis – it's only fitting that he chose Dennis, who rightly should have been on Dickell's route the night before – he demanded the whole truth and nothing but. *Where were you, who told you to be there, and what in God's name's wrong with you?* Dennis froze up. He shot a terrified glance toward the rest of us, only to receive a 'mum's the word' signal from Murphy. He turned back to Kuntsler and shrugged his shoulders. The old man rapped him on the head and moved on to Dickell. *How'd you end up on the second route and what the hell's gotten into you?* Dickell pleaded the fifth and got Law & Order to the gut. Moving on he approached Curtis, Bailer and Lester, imploring archangels, saints and dead football heroes for each, only to receive equally empty, wrath-inducing responses every time. Five of the eighteen of us standing around in the yard had now received varying chops and blows to the head, arms and torso. Next it was Wilbur. *What in shit's going on?* Nothing. Whap. Next. Murphy. *What the Sam Hill's gone wrong?* No idea. Whap. Continuing. *We've got all night, ladies, it makes no difference to me . . .* To Irwin: *Who gave you the order to cover second route?* Jesus Christ. *Jesus Christ? Zat supposed to be a joke?* Whap. Onward. Right on down the line.

It wasn't that his blows lacked force or precision; as those things go, we'd had a taste of Law & Order in the past and it always left a hot welt all around. Kuntsler may not have been heir to the blond beast, but on the few occasions that he'd produced that stick of his, he'd displayed a remarkable familiarity with its use. He probably worked the lot bitch over with it often enough to keep in practice, so that when the time did come for its official use, he had all the right angles and calibrations down to second nature. After it hit, the point of impact often stung and burned for hours. Law & Order, as an extension of the old man's will to power, was not to be underestimated by any means. But on the night of the seventeenth we allowed the interrogation to proceed, up to a point, without putting a stop to it. We let it continue purely in order to have one last look at the hell-spawn beneath which we had toiled and waxed indignant for so many years – one last glimpse to secure and memorialize the old bastard drowning in a mire of his own self-parody before finally being chased out of the picture for good.

As it continued, he became more and more evident as the animal closing in on extinction; as though he may've vaporized at any moment, leaving a naked billyclub in the dirt and a foul stench at his passing. He was already gone, an outflanked reverend alone at the pulpit. He no longer mattered. For that reason we endured the attack, again, up to a point.

He kept going. He worked himself into a deeper shade of lavender. He threw off every battered ornament in the book: *You want a piece of the rock? . . . The buck stops here! . . . No pain, no gain . . . You play with fire, you get burned . . . Time to pay the fiddler! . . . You take a romp in the crick, you better wear your kickers! . . .* Etc. It was painfully embarrassing. He was stumbling over himself, sputtering through his haikus, screaming until the blood vessels in his eyes took a strain. At one point he nearly fell over. On regaining his footing he whirled around to hammer Jim Donnecker in the chest without even questioning him. He swivelled his head, threw back his shoulders, hacked into the gravel, twitched, and went on.

By then everyone had noticed that as thorough as he was attempting to appear, he'd somehow managed to reroute his line of fire so as to avoid John's position. Which brought to mind a question that had occurred to all of us long ago: just how aware of John's impact on the crew could the old man have grown to be? On the one hand, there was the fact that John was still with us and had not been fired, which would seem to indicate that Kuntsler *did not*, or *could not*, have suspected. That seemed evident. But on the other hand, as desperate and impassioned as he'd become of late, it also seemed that the most rudimentary overview of the situation would've clearly indicated that from the moment John had started on the job in late May, all sense of order in the yard had gone straight out the window. That seemed equally evident. A simple before/after snapshot proved all: before being twenty years of docile subservience, after being less than ten weeks of escalating anarchy. Murphy has since suggested that the old man *had* been aware of it, but that he'd feared dismissing John prematurely might've fanned the flames of discontent even further beyond his control. And maybe he took it as a direct challenge at that, figuring that as soon as he silenced the ranks, as he undoubtedly would, he would strip John of his dignity by banishing him to two weeks of gull stoning on the west end of the quarry, then firing him out in the open one afternoon as a worthless disgrace to the trade. If that really was his plan, he had even less of a grip on the situation than anyone suspected. In any case, his meandering through the ranks did somehow pass John by, as all of us noticed. He steered clear of the far corner, leaving John himself, hands jammed into his pockets, waiting for one of us to crack.

And one of us eventually did, though not quite as had been expected. Halfway through round two Kuntsler rushed up to Bailer and threatened to fire him on the spot if he didn't own up to his part in the cannery incident. Bailer looked down, bracing himself for the blow. The old man hovered in repose with Law & Order extended to one side at the perfect angle to let fly. He announced that he was going to count to three. He made it to two and was just about to swing when someone at the back of the group (it was Curtis) unexpectedly broke wind.

Silence.

Kuntsler's eyes went wider than cake plates. His neck jutted forward. His jaw dropped. For one prolonged instant he looked to be an identical replica of the porcelain lawn jockey in the mulch behind him . . .

Then it broke. The rest of us could no longer contain ourselves. We doubled over, laughing uncontrollably. We had done our best to keep it in – we really had tried. But Curtis's timing had been *too* perfect. We let go. The old man stood there, paralyzed, speechless. He couldn't move. We howled ourselves into a group choking fit, gurgled and coughed, pointed at him where he stood, wiped the tears, then crowed some more. It hurt; a person can yak himself to an early grave with only three or four similar outbursts in the course of a lifetime. It hurt terribly. But it was worth it. Someone offered to buy Curtis four rounds a night for the next ten years. Someone else said he must have been eating half of his pickups judging by the stench of it. *Stale thunder*, Dennis announced. Everyone agreed. We couldn't stop. Had the old man suddenly snapped out of it and run amok with his patootle stick, it's doubtful that even a score of direct groin shots could've brought us out of it. It would have been like riot-hosing a ward full of cackling lunatics.

In the end we just couldn't bear to look at him any more. A few of us turned to stagger off toward our rigs. The rest followed. By the time we pulled ourselves together and left the lot, the old man had finally broken out of his daze. But by then it was too late. The last anyone saw of him, he was charging back and forth through the yard all alone, screaming and beating the air with Law & Order.

What had happened was this: immediately following our expulsion from the taverns three weeks earlier, John and Wilbur had called a late night meeting in Wilbur's apartment – John's being off-limits due to long-term plumbing problems. It was there that John spoke to us in earnest for the first time. Actually, it was Wilbur who did most of the talking, but it was John's proposal which was being unveiled, and everyone knew it. At no juncture was the issue of our recent conduct addressed; it was taken for granted that that situation was well understood. Instead, the emphasis lay on an alternative route-circuit proposal which had been conceived and drawn up by John the night before. As we were later told, he'd spent six hours hunched over a lamp-lit desk drawing up a plan which he and Wilbur believed, if implemented, would have enormous advantages over the existing system.

To start with, they quickly summarized the overwhelming impracticality of the current routes. The fifth route, for example, was so conceptually harebrained it almost appeared to have been drawn up in the first quarter of the nineteenth century for a troop of horse and buggies. It reflected absolutely no consideration for the topographical layout of modern-day Baker: those assigned to the fifth spent the majority of every evening bobbing in and out of other jurisdictions and cross hatching the north end of the valley in a wildly inefficient goose run. The operating crew was always the last one in for the evening – consistently forty-five minutes later than the rest. The other routes were no less impractical. It went without saying that anyone assigned to the second had an evening of inordinately grueling labor ahead of him, whereas one on the fourth had it relatively easy. This didn't account for the fact that the two routes should have overlapped. Continuing on, every route was similarly unworkable. They were all like tangled lengths of twine in bad need of straightening.

So, Wilbur said, laying down a row of free-hand maps on the surface of his coffee table, they'd finally come up with a solution. If we would all just gather round and have a look, it would be clear to see that their proposal would save everyone time, energy and confusion. The advantages were self-evident.

Which was true. With less than a two minute examination of their proposal, the benefits were clear. By pairing off John's carefully prepared outline with Kuntsler's schizophrenic bomb graph, the possibility of a nightly turn-in hour preceding midnight began to materialize. As Wilbur claimed, the workload would be proportionately redistributed. Certain routes would still be nastier than others. That was unavoidable. But in the long run all labor would be balanced out through continual shifting. It was a simple proposal, one that would take very little to implement. If anyone had any further suggestions, now was the time – otherwise, we would all have to agree, based on our incessant bitching for the past eternity, that the plan made sense.

The room went quiet. We could suddenly hear one another wheezing, tonsils gurgling away in our gullets, in and out, catching from time to time, lending voice to our collective hesitation, boxing it in with the walls around us. No one knew what to say. Stifled coughs from the balcony between the symphony's second and third movements. There was that momentary confusion, each of us grappling with our involuntary reflex to flee the scene, each of us paying tribute to a residual fear that by even hearing out these plans we were running the risk of being arraigned for subversion and milled to the gallows. It was a tense moment – no one wanted to be the first to speak. But it didn't last long. Murphy finally let out an emphatic *hell yes*, to which the rest of us acquiesced. And that was it. There was nothing left to consider. The proposal made too much sense to reject.

Wilbur nodded and started passing out a stack of photocopies, issuing last-minute instructions as he went: everyone was to lay off the liquor for the evening, if not the week. We were to go home and memorize our routes thoroughly. All new routes were to be effective immediately. If there were any questions, his phone line would be open all night. A follow-up meeting would be scheduled during the next week. On concluding, he looked around through the room and announced that, of course, it was understood this meeting had never taken place. Everyone nodded. *Good*, he said. *Now get out of my room, it's beginning to stink in here.*

We all let out a nervous laugh, then made to leave. We filed through the room with our papers in hand, around the couch and over the spotted rug toward the door. John remained with his back to the wall, arms crossed, quietly looking us over as we passed. We walked down the stairs to the street. Outside we looked at our watches and said nothing. The meeting had lasted five minutes.

The next week couldn't have gone more beautifully. The new circuit plan worked every bit as well as had been predicted. It was almost as though John had personally worked and reworked each route with a stopwatch beforehand to come up with the most comprehensive redistribution of labor possible. Compactors one to five all pulled into the yard at the close of every evening within fifteen minutes of one another. The first and fourth route were fused with the second. The new third was unrecognizable. The fifth no longer impaired our equilibrium. The heavy-machinery operators now plowed over more even, malleable loads. And everyone signed out earlier, much earlier. With the exception of the three or four hours Wilbur had to spend on the phone putting the proposal into layman's terms for

Bailer and Dennis, nothing could have gone any better. The question on everyone's mind was not so much *'how did we do this?'* as might be expected, but instead, as in the case of quitting smoking or finally putting a long-overdue end to a faltering love affair, *'why didn't we think of this any sooner – what took us so long . . .?'* It was almost *too* easy. Arriving at the resolve to stop deliberating and just act had been the difficult part. Following through was proving to be simple.

And what's more, it kept us occupied and out of trouble during our exile from the taverns. All through the first week we were so tied up with learning the new routes, there was scarcely a minute to be lost quarreling with the locals. The Baker Lay receded from our view for the time being. We had no time or energy for the same disputes we'd been seeking out only one week earlier. All our focus was redirected toward the task at hand. We steered clear of needless confrontations.

However, as well as things may have been going, John and Wilbur knew better than to expect the temporary ceasefire to outlive the month. They knew the hooks were too far into us for that; as soon as our new routes became second nature, they fully expected a resurgence of all the bickery and belligerence from before, only this time it would be furtherly endorsed by a self-righteous sense of accomplishment and common purpose. The outbreak which would then naturally follow would be formless beyond compare. It would be counterproductive to everything they'd worked for. The disaster they'd attempted to avoid by absurdly simple means would be exacerbated ten fold. They knew that. Hence the primary topic of discussion at the next meeting.

On Saturday night, just as planned, we met for a second time, this time in Murphy's back yard – an untended half-acre plot of weeds and evergreens located two miles south of Baker. Just after sunset Wilbur and Murphy lit a bonfire in a twelve foot pit to the rear of the house. The rest of us dragged seven cases of Schlitz to the edge of the pit, nestled down in the dirt, cracked open the first round of cans, and waited.

Lester had just gotten his nose brace removed earlier in the day. Some of us were chiding him as to his appearance, saying he ought to get into brawls more often: the farmer's tan pink from the gauze strips flattered him. *Gentleman Jim Casanova*, someone said. Lester fired back with a few good-humored retorts of his own, particularly in regards to Irwin's indecent exposure rap. Everyone was in fairly high spirits.

John came out of the house at a quarter past ten. He fished for a can in one of the coolers and sat down next to Curtis. He pulled a stack of papers from his belt. Although we certainly hadn't made a full breakthrough in relations with him as of yet, everyone had to agree that over the past week tensions had eased off considerably. Some kind of contact had been established. We still weren't convinced he genuinely cared for any of us in the least. That remains the case to this day. But in the midst of the recent transitions – August having been a busy month – he had come down from the cross, to some extent. He had stopped to have a word with some of us on two or three occasions – nothing particularly noteworthy: a few reconciliatory remarks and inquiries as to what we thought of the new routes. He'd had a laugh with Curtis one night over some seedy acquisition or other retrieved from a pile of rot at the mayor's home. He and Wilbur had even christened Murphy to one of their balcony sessions, though the rest of us knew nothing about it at the time. None of these exchanges had been overly warm, but they had made for a somewhat more relaxed, or at least less stifling all-around atmosphere, without which the success of the meeting we were about to hold would have been in dire jeopardy from the outset. If John's partial opening up to us had been deliberately strategic, it had served its purpose nonetheless.

The meeting which followed differed from the first in several regards. To begin with, John did the majority of the speaking this time, as the next proposal called for a more direct, strongarm, uncontestable presentation than Wilbur, being one of us from time immemorial, ever could've delivered. He began with a five minute open-forum on the preceding week, which resulted in everyone's complete, unreserved approval of the new routes. On calling for any suggestions he was offered none. On calling for complaints, nothing. On calling for any reflections at all, silence.

We never were the most articulate bunch in town. But John seemed reasonably satisfied and wasted no further time getting right to the point.

His next pitch, in so many words, ran as follows:

It was high time we on the landfill staff took a few basic situations into our own hands, as by now it had become perfectly clear that we, as public benefactors, were and always had been on our own. The first step would be to recognize that though Jeffrey Kuntsler was a living abomination of and by nature, some of the treatment we were accorded by our clientele was equally unacceptable. That being the case, it was time we start utilizing the minimal resources at our availability to send a few basic messages, à la Joseph McCarthy. To start off, Kuntsler was temporarily out of our reach. We had no ace in the deck in regards to him as of yet. He still ran the books, manned the phone lines, and delivered the paychecks, and we didn't have our act together well enough to tackle his platform anyway. That would have to wait. However, in regards to the Baker Lay, it was considerably different; in regards to the Baker Lay, we had tremendous leverage, whether we knew it or not. It might be said that for all our lives we'd been sitting on a powder keg to which the rest of the world was counting on us remaining oblivious. Thus far we'd done nothing but oblige that expectation. We'd allowed ourselves to be taken for granted as twelve dollar fuck dolls in an alley full of gutter tramps. We'd been walked all over at our own invitation, and the situation would never improve unless and until we realized that in full. The powder keg we were sitting on was none other than our very own landfill. Statistically speaking, every civilized society produced a bare minimum of 1,000 percent of its weight in disposables every year. Every 'civilized' citizen recoiled from that excess as from contagion itself, thereby relegating the lowest stratum of its populace to the disposal thereof. The average disposal practitioner was every bit as anathema to that society as was said excess. The common trash man had no more place in the home of respectable citizens than the garbage he had come to remove had on the dining-room rug (or the wetbacks did in the office place, the trolls in a banquet hall . . .). Every day he took up by the armful that which others would never prod with a cattle iron. By pure association he was flat on par with the disposables he was sent to retrieve. For the common yokel there was little or no distinction between the two. The couriers of debris and the debris itself were, for all practical purposes, one and the same.

But that was a generally accepted fallacy for which the trash man himself was just as much to blame as anyone. If the glaring distinction between the two – scrub and discharge – had not been defined, it was only because it had not been made perfectly clear by those in a position to demonstrate. In other words, if the trash man was equated with disposal and filth, it was because he had allowed himself to be. He had chosen the role by not refuting it. He was wholly accountable for the misunderstanding. In support of this claim, one needed only consider the nature of our services, and the hypothetical removal thereof. If one day we, for example, were to walk off the job arbitrarily, the impact on Baker would be instantaneously devastating. In a community of 4,000, each member of which produced 3.2 pounds of personal waste per day on average, an accumulated excess of 6.4 tons, give or take 10 percent in either direction, would be added to the streets every twenty-four hours. Or 89,600 pounds. per week. Or 358,400 pounds (approximately 179 tons) per month. And that was just residential Baker. The factories would be another matter altogether. We needn't have been told that industrial Baker, with its inestimable daily output, would be crippled beyond legal operability within four weeks of our official walkout. But industrial Baker, being predominantly owned and operated by out of town residents, would have very little influence, even when on the brink of total mandatory shutdown, in resolving the conflict. The real powers of resolution would fall into residential Baker's courts, and residential Baker, on its end, would be dealing with an entirely different picture than its industrial counterpart. Although the second route would be transformed into a festering dumping ground almost overnight, the rate of impact on the smaller streets, the far off corners, the public parks and private drives would be considerably more gradual. The necessary impetus to mobilize and combat the dilemma would come to term only at the equivalent

246

rate of visible deterioration in the streets around, among other things, City Hall. True, a panicked drive to secure a replacement crew would be underway almost immediately, but that too, as we were well aware, would require precious time. For starters, the community would have its hands full in simply locating and contracting twenty-something odd broken souls who were ready and willing to take up post. Even in a dreg-trench like Baker, everyone knew the hill scrub was a rare breed: a forlorn, all but hopeless tunnel-rat type found only at the crossroads of travesty and resilience. He was a prize animal, one comfortably intent on performing the same duties that would make most grown men sick. He was, contrary to popular belief, by no means an abundant commodity. Applicants for employ in our own yard trickled in only once or twice a month, often less. And when they did, they usually slunk by bathed in an air of overwhelming gravity and shame – *Oh, God, it's come to this* – as though visiting a brothel for the first time in their lives. They reported for duty as the repentant felon to confession. Their youthful aspirations had been bombed out of existence. There were years of hard times riding their coat tails: that was a pre-requisite, a requirement. Without that thousand-yard stare well in place they were spurned as unqualified. They wouldn't last a day. *To handle the untouchable, one had to rank an untouchable.* With the existing lack of incentive (poor pay), securing a replacement crew could take two or three months. And even then, the mandatory eight week training period for the bulldozer and heavy-machinery operators would furtherly delay the resumption of operations. All told, a town like Baker would be more than half-buried before the new crew was in place, and once it was, who would realistically opt to tackle a mess that size at six dollars an hour? No one. Not even the wetbacks. In spite of all notions of foolish pride there was more dignity in cashing a weekly welfare check than going up against a monster like that. It was clear to see that, at least in Greene County, the trash man was more indispensable than the banker, the butcher, and the district court judge combined, and much tougher to come by. He was the only thing standing between the community at large and unprecedented ruin.

So, what John had in mind was this: from that point on we would begin sending a few messages of our own. Every one of us would have to agree, as our recent problems would indicate, that it was time to put a stop to the abuse. The days of being chastened and debased as contemptible scrap hands were about to come to an end. With the proper approach, we could deliver our message loud and clear without running the risk of forfeiting our jobs. If Kuntsler intervened we would handle him in like manner, though it would be decidedly premature to take a deliberate shot at his post as of yet. Our goal for the moment would be to state our claim in clear and concise terms: 1) we provided an indispensable community service, 2) we demanded the simple respect accorded any public benefactor, and 3) if our demands were not met – if our services were not appreciated – the community was free to seek a viable alternative. As it was there *was* one individual in Baker, an obese troll by the name of Hackert – more commonly known as 'that smelly, toothless bastard with the red pickup' – who had been licensed through God-knows-what kind of loophole to own and operate his own private dump, conveniently located in his backyard on the outskirts of town. So, technically speaking, we weren't the *only* waste disposal company in the area, though we were clearly the only one capable of handling bulk for forty miles in any direction. Hackert was our legal alibi – everyone knew him, his name was in the book. With that in mind, we could thereby afford to start chalking off a few of the more problematic locals from our routes as we were morally, though not altogether legally, entitled. Any legal repercussions would take weeks to materialize and ultimately amount to little more than a slap on the wrist. Very little in contrast to the inconvenience rendered in the interim. When enough locals got the message, we would begin to see a definite turnaround in the public's attitude. It would be unmistakable: by mocking the hill scrubs you're only burning yourself. He just might forget about you for a while.

John produced a blank sheet of paper, pulled a pencil from behind one ear and announced that he was ready to begin taking names . . .

*

There are those rare and unaccounted for moments in the course of a lifetime when a situation deviates so far out of the realm of projected expectations that those on hand have to doubt the coparcenary testimony of their senses. This was one of them. The last thing any of us could have expected if and when John finally got around to addressing our bone of contention with the Baker Lay was that he would come up with a carefully outlined battle plan in full and unmitigated support of it. We had expected a condescending lecture, a scathing reproach, anything but a wayward-ho charge. We couldn't believe what we were hearing. Had he really just proposed we start running the company ourselves, that we drop or accept our clientele as we pleased, that if the going got too rough we would just walk off the job and let Baker drown in its own discharge? Was that what we were hearing? That same hesitation we had experienced during the first meeting came rushing back end over end. There was still too much Kuntsler in the closet to take it all in at once. Open rebellion. What were we getting ourselves into? A few of us would later have to admit to having wanted to draw the line right then and there. Had Wilbur been speaking we undoubtedly would have. It was true that John's words had made perfect sense, there was no denying it. His ideas and delivery were more articulate than anything we'd ever heard. But revamping the route circuit was one thing – taking the law into our own hands was another. It was too much to register on the spot. We were disoriented and confused, which was very possibly exactly what John had counted on. The logic being: don't let them think, feed on their base instincts. Hit them hard and fast, tally the vote, call the meeting and leave them to wonder. Deliberation breeds hesitation. Hesitation breeds failure. Before we could peer around at one another he was rapping on his clipboard and claiming he didn't have all night.

Just then, to break the tension and almost as if on cue, Wilbur sounded out the first suggestion: *Keller & Powell – boycott the slaughterhouse!* With that, a sudden, involuntary groan of enthusiasm broke loose from all of us. *Yeah... Keller & Powell... Now there's an idea. Let 'em have it. Let their grit wagons heap to the fields and be overrun by muskrats. Who said that . . .?* The prospect of leaving the steerhands and pen keepers – our most bitter adversaries and recent attackers – in the lurch struck a common chord in everyone. All our hesitation suddenly vanished. The entire picture changed. The possibilities of what we were dealing with became enticingly evident.

John chalked up one motion to boycott Keller & Powell, then called for a second suggestion. All of us shifted anxiously, tightened on our haunches, and shot a quick glance around. Then the dam broke. From every corner of the group a barrage of names broke loose and came pounding down on John faster than he could scrawl them out. It was like a kennel full of baying dogs in a street flood . . . Offenbach, Dotterwich, the Dotes outlet, Brombourg, the Street light, the refinery, the pork shack, that disgusting old dodger out at Sparrow's Height (what was his name . . . the one with the mail-order bride from Taiwan?), Knopfler, Bloombach, Pollenderry lumber, the furniture plant, DMU, etc . . . It went on. With all the drunken antics of the previous month fresh in our minds, we probably could've rattled off three hundred rat-bastard candidates right there on the spot before even having to think about resorting to the directory. John sat at the edge of the pit, frantically scribbling in the half-light. The glow from the bonfire lit up his furrowed brow, his perpetually coffee-stained tee-shirt, his second-hand tuxedo pants, all of them dipping in and out of the flickering light as he worked. He never smiled, he just kept going. Someone suggested the entire Pineridge complex. Someone else said the whole second route. Before long the proceeding was totally out of control. We all had at least one or two candidates who absolutely *had* to be on the list. Dennis and Bailer were arguing back and forth. There were calls to scratch out one suggestion and replace it with another. The meeting had deteriorated into a crazed free-for-all by the time John finally lifted his pen and called for order. It took a minute for everyone to pipe down, and another to separate Dennis and Bailer. The peace was eventually restored.

The rest of the meeting was simple. John pointed out that we couldn't very well call a general strike on the whole town (yet) and therefore moved to select and determine the ten most worthy candidates from the list by way of democratic vote. This was quickly accomplished with a show of hands. Within fifteen minutes the list was complete. After one last call for further suggestions, John adjourned the meeting, adding only that, for his efforts, he requested the privilege of adding one candidate of his own choice to the list. No one objected. The meeting ended. John pulled his notes together and left the pit. He walked into the house. The rest of us stayed on, Schlitz-bound in the onion weed.

On Monday evening it was everything Wilbur could do to issue a single photocopy of the list to one member of each crew without Kuntsler noticing. The old man had grown more and more paranoid in installments, with each new stage outrunning the last, so that now, on the eve of the boycott campaign's commencement, he was whipping through the yard like a minister for the purge. Wilbur made the rounds doing a none-too-subtle series of high fives with select members of the crew, thereby handing on a tightly-folded copy of the final plan as discreetly as was possible. Each recipient jammed the paper into one pocket after the hand off and continued shuffling through the gravel as though unfazed. Kuntsler, as always, remained on his porch glaring at everyone. It wasn't until after roll call, most of us being a mile or two up the road, that we were able to open and inspect the list. It was carefully hand-printed in the exact order we had specified, only in addition to the ten candidates we had chosen by vote, there was an eleventh name on the list standing apart from all the rest: There, in block capitals with no indication of its origin or rationale was written FIRST METHODIST CHURCH OF PULLMAN VALLEY. None of us could make much sense of it. It seemed there were more deserving candidates in town. But then, none of us had ever been terminally ill. And none of us had ever been goatboys. We shrugged it off, figuring John knew what he was doing, whether we understood it or not. We didn't pay it any mind.

Anyway, we had our hands full now. In addition to still working out the new routes, we had to concentrate on not calling undue attention to ourselves during the period of transition and, at all costs, on not accidentally clearing any chosen candidate's heap. As simple as that may sound, it did cause a good deal of confusion. Each of us had our own ideas as to who *should* have been on the list, as opposed to who had actually survived the final cut. The bulk of the responsibility came to rest with the compactor operators who had to consult the list and be on their toes on approaching each given candidate's address.

With hindsight, it's a wonder it took so long for those candidates to file a report, much less that most of them did so within a single day of one another. That was almost a bit too perfect, particularly when considering the high output of organic disposables yielded by establishments like Keller & Powell. We had expected their call within the first two days. But that's not at all what happened. No one knows why it took them, or anyone, so long to complain. All we know is that in the interim our confidence soared. As everything fell into place we began to feel as though we were capable of anything, that no one in Baker could possibly stand in our way. Granted, no calls had come in yet. We had encountered no real opposition to date. The staff at the Dick and the Bucket actually had a better idea of what we were up to than anyone in town, and even they hadn't been able to make heads or tails of our behavior.

But all the same, each of us was confident that when the situation was called to public attention, as it inevitably would be, we would be ready for it. As Donnecker so aptly stated, 'If they can't fire one of us without firing all of us, then they can't fire none of us.' And so they would have to agree to our terms, which were, after all, reasonable.

Of the eleven listed candidates, five were located on Kuntsler's second route, which was not at all surprising, as the factory circuit was home to some of our foulest clientele. When the complaints did begin rolling in it was predicted they would originate in large part from this area. Which brought up a few crucial questions. As previously mentioned, the old second route no longer existed. Kuntsler's second was a patchwork conglomerate of Kaltenbrunner's first, second and fourth, meaning that if the furniture plant (now positioned in the fourth) was the first to complain, then Kuntsler's second crew appointees – almost certainly a different crew than the one on duty – would be held accountable. In addition, Kuntsler's scheduled shifts lasted for a duration of four days – twice the length of John's two – and to complicate matters even further, the actual lineup of each crew was now rotated at least twice a week. Meaning, when the complaints did start rolling in the majority of the old man's wrath would be vented toward two or three individuals who surely would have been somewhere else at the time of any reported infraction. What it all boiled down to was this: no one knew who was going to get it first, but once the trouble did start we all had to be there to stand behind one another. If so much as one person dodged out, the whole plan would be thrown out of synch.

On Thursday night Murphy's crew encountered the first opposition. They were covering Kaltenbrunner's fourth – part of Kuntsler's first – when a wily old troll by the name of Brombourg – candidate number three on our list – came bounding out of his house and huffing it up the road in hot pursuit of their rig. Brombourg was vintage white trash. He *belonged* on the list. He was a list in and of himself. He would have made the top ten in a community four times the size of Baker. We had put up with him for years. Curtis and Lester were on gate that night. When they returned to the yard at eleven they alerted John and Wilbur as to the incident. Lester couldn't help but smirk on recounting the way Brombourg had eventually sputtered to a halt on the roadside, hacking and wheezing as the compactor continued on its way with both Curtis and Lester laughing on gate. They claimed the look on his face had been priceless. But they were also sure he would be phoning in that night, if he hadn't already. Wilbur checked with the rest of the crews as he did every night, and got an all-around confirmation that the heaps were indeed sizing up in each candidate's yard or pit. All of us were warned to be ready for the old man the following evening.

But to everyone's surprise, the next night's roll call was relatively uneventful. Brombourg hadn't called in, and neither had anyone else. We didn't quite understand it, but no one complained. We felt we could use a little more time.

That night there were two more incidents. The first occurred on Wilbur's route, the fifth, when two locals on four-wheelers gave chase to the compactor with demands to follow through on their pickup in the name of candidate number six, Arthur Bloombach. Wilbur told them to stuff it and tooled off. The second occurred on Kaltenbrunner's first at, not surprisingly, the furniture plant. Clayton was driving. Irwin and Dickell were on gate. They passed the plant at six thirty. They were pushing by the main doors when a large crowd from the second shift came bursting out of the docking bay, waving and hollering wildly alongside of a mountain of excess lumber and wood shavings. Dickell waved back.

That was Friday night. With the weekend ahead we were positive Monday would be it. We even called an emergency meeting to prepare. We met on Saturday night, once again in Murphy's backyard, to discuss our options. Everyone agreed the situation had reached its breaking point. But unlike before, there was nothing else to say. We were ready for whatever was in store. Our group motto had become 'Take no shit,' which, by definition, leaves little room for elaboration. The only thing to do was get drunk, throw horseshoes, and feed on our swelling pride like a group of shield-gnawing Vikings on the eve of a village raid.

But once again, Monday rolled around without cause for alarm. Then Tuesday. And Wednesday. Kuntsler was a bit more foul-tempered than usual on each day, but that was due only to his lurking suspicions. No complaints had been filed. It didn't make sense. Murphy and Wilbur have since theorized that the candidates on our list must have figured our neglect of their residences was an idiotic mistake which would inevitably correct itself, and through that twisted reckoning, they'd put off reporting it out of sheer laziness. They would rail us for our incompetence later. That seems a likely enough explanation for an unlikely predicament, but even so, no active reasoning could explain their decision to wait *so long*. In effect, their stalling worked to everyone's detriment *except* ours. The heaps were allowed to pile up beyond anyone's control. Kuntsler continued fabricating conspiracies which could have been clarified much sooner. The existence of the new routes went on undetected. No one was getting the message. The same candidates who'd abused us mercilessly for years on end were now responding to a direct challenge with flap-jawed irresolution. The only group to benefit at all was ours, as with each passing day the situation became more and more ludicrous, leaving us on a perpetual slapstick cliffhanger (*Have you seen the parking lot at Keller & Powell lately? – Neither have they*). Had the complaints begun rolling in sooner, the magnitude of the dilemma that followed may not have been as severe.

On Wednesday night our banishment from the Bloody Bucket was officially over. At a quarter past midnight we jammed through the door to fill the rear third of the tavern in a rowdy pack. If the staff and patrons on hand had expected a shamefaced, low-key re-entry if and when we finally returned, they were met with an unexpected surprise. Bailer's opening cry for fish heads all around proved that. We were met with undivided scowls of contempt from every corner of the room.

Ten minutes before close a steerhand from Keller & Powell approached our table. He was a pugnosed gatekeeper with a pompadour. Three of his cohorts were watching from across the room. He stopped at the head of the table, singled out Clayton and demanded an explanation for our neglect of his company. It was no laughing matter, he said. The wagons to the rear of the building were beginning to breed maggots hand over fist. When did we plan on coming back from holiday? Everyone looked to Clayton, waiting for his reply. Clayton straightened up and smiled, saying something about getting back on the job the day Keller & Powell sent its steerhands to syphon the pus from his rectal eczema. Our table exploded. The steerhand dashed back to his group, humiliated. *You'll get yours*, he said. He was *goin' to tell the boys*. Which was exactly what we'd been waiting for anyway – not just the boys, but the whole administration.

Yet still, with the entire next afternoon to allow for a single complaint, nothing came in. It was ridiculous. Wilbur and John were as beside themselves as the rest of us. All our provocations thus far had failed to invoke a single phone call. Not that we minded so much; we were actually beginning to feel invincible. But knowing the silence couldn't last forever, that someone had to break down and phone the old man sooner or later, we were all beginning to itch for the unavoidable outcome. Now that we felt we had our act together, it was time to bring the situation out into the open, to *Be done with it!* as Irwin said. As a result, without consulting one another on the matter beforehand, most of us resolved to turn Thursday night into a blowout.

Dickell, Burke and Curtis more than did their share at the cannery. Holtz Inc. had actually not made our final cut and so was not officially a candidate on the list. But it was so far up there – tied with DMU in fact – that one can rest assured it would have made the top three on our next itinerary, had one ever materialized. The cannery staff was and still is comprised of foul-tempered Dowler trolls and ex-convicts. As anyone who's ever pulled even one nightly round is well aware, the moment the Holtz crew lets out on break to saunter on the lot-side staircase, they're fresh off the belt and three cans short of homicidal. For the next fifteen minutes they bombard all wayfaring pedestrians with the most outrageously hostile invective in the book. They've always been that way. They're damned and they hate it.

The confrontation that night unfolded, for the most part, exactly as it was reported to Kuntsler. On pulling into the lot, Dickell wasn't ten seconds off gate before the group on the staircase was calling him a whoreson. In response he let loose with the same penned rage all of us had been stockpiling for weeks at that point, and by so doing, had a heated argument on his hands in seconds. It went back and forth, getting uglier by the moment. One of the Holtz rats eventually got to his feet and started making for Dickell over the twenty yard stretch of asphalt. The rest of the belthands egged him on from the rear, shrieking, yea-saying, and calling for blood. But before any blows could be exchanged, Jerry Burke, who had been quietly rigging the compactor to the largest of the cannery dumpsters, veered his rig into the center of the lot between Dickell and the advancing Holtz rat, elevated the cast iron disposal box to the compactor arm's full extension, and reversed the standard deposit code to send almost two tons of scrap metal, bottles, cardboard and rusted excess crashing down on the pavement in a series of explosions. The Holtz rats scattered. Burke released the compactor clamp, allowing the dumpster to drop seven feet into the mess with another crash. The iron box went end over end, gained momentum, and pitched over the edge of the asphalt into a drainage ditch hugging the rim of the lot. It came to rest lodged in the mud on an incline. Dickell and Curtis hopped on gate. Burke throttled it out of the neighborhood at a charge.

On the north end of town it was Irwin, Bailer and Donnecker who had stopped into the truck stop for a deliberately public display of beer chasing. In thirty minutes time they made as much noise and drew as much attention to themselves as they possibly could. They then left the establishment to weave off down the road as a public health hazard. They skipped almost half of their route. By nine, having sobered up to some degree, they hit another tavern. They were four score on walking into the Bucket later on. Irwin assured the rest of us they had been spotted by at least one Methodist, and that Kuntsler ought to have received word of their outing before locking up for the evening.

The rest of us had left similar trails all over town. We'd boycotted whole streets for no particular reason. Dennis had hit on a formula halfway through his route: for every two cans, bags, wagons, etc. left out for pickup, he'd left one standing untouched. Meaning *no one* along the second half of the fifth route had received anything even closely resembling a clean pickup. In total that amounted to almost three-hundred potential complaints. Others, like Lester and Clayton had played a slapdash round of musical chairs by rearranging some of each resident's garbage cans with those of the neighbors. They had even taken a few cans on board to transplant to other neighborhoods. The resulting confusion would be sure to tie up the phone lines and spark disputes of rightful ownership for the next two weeks.

No one did much work that night. For the most part our rounds were an experiment in poetic terrorism. The heavy-machinery operators back in the yard claimed that the total load that evening was the lightest they'd ever seen, plowed or dozed in their careers. We had almost outdone ourselves. As we sat in our tightly knit group after hours, we all had to agree that that was it: if our activities of the past six hours didn't succeed in waking the dead, then nothing would.

While we were talking about it, John, Murphy and Wilbur were on the other side of town driving the final nails into the coffin. At a quarter past one, a few minutes after Kuntsler left the landfill, they unlocked the gates with Wilbur's spare key, deactivated the alarm as usual, and started wandering through the labyrinths at random. Wilbur had brought along a second-hand set of golf clubs and a pillowcase full of shag balls. He and John climbed to the highest table top and teed off among their discarded bottles from the nights before. Murphy remained below in the yard to hot wire one of the steamrollers. For the next hour Wilbur and John drove twenty balls a minute toward Kuntsler's office with a four iron while Murphy ran amok in the yard, chasing the lot bitch in circles. When it was over, Kuntsler's trailer was riddled with dent marks, the steamroller was on its side, spinning crazily in a sinkhole, and the lot bitch was off her head with the call of the wild. As they eventually turned to leave, Murphy announced that he couldn't bear to leave the old bitch prey to Kuntsler's kicks and abuse for one more day. He hustled her out of the lot and turned her loose in the fields. She made a bee-line for the edge of the forest and was never seen again.

Needless to say, that did it. Had our evening not brought in at least the handful of complaints it did, there would have been something drastically wrong. But when Kuntsler came out of his office wielding Law & Order the next night, he did so as one who'd uncovered a maximum-security plot through his own painstaking efforts, not as one who'd finally found the long trail of bread crumbs that had been left out for him *deliberately clearly*. He was proud of himself. He'd caught us in the act. Which was just fine; our concern wasn't with his self-reverential vainglory, but with how he would react now that the situation had gone farther than we had originally intended.

Our initial objective had been to boycott a few selected candidates, bring them out into the open where a simple end to our allotted mistreatment could be negotiated, in legal terms if need be. But over the past two weeks that had proven to be no simple task. We'd been forced to resort to drastic measures in order to call attention to ourselves, we had broken the law, both societal and business-related, and we had had the time of our lives in the process. So now, even if we'd still wanted to sit down and work matters out in a civilized manner our case would have been damaged to the point of indefensibility by our recent activities. Which is a moot point anyway, one that presupposes we were interested in negotiating at all. By now our objective had changed completely. The last two weeks had been too liberating to go back on. We had gone to great lengths to imminentize a situation that would have struck terror into every one of us only two months earlier. Before even discussing it, we intuitively knew what the next step had to be. We thought about it all night after leaving Kuntsler behind in the lot with his chipped billyclub. We braced ourselves for it while going through the motions of what was to be the last nightly round for quite some time. We tried imagining every facet of what was in store for the community and for ourselves on pulling back into the lot at closing time. We were barely able to register Kuntsler's decree as he stood on his porch and announced in what was intended to be a ground-splitting display of authority that Dickell, Murphy, Kaltenbrunner, and Bailer were fired, Burke, Altemeyer, Dennis and Irwin were suspended for one month, and the rest of us would be docked a full fifty dollars from our coming pay. We kept going, wrapped up in the decision we knew was now unavoidable. We climbed into our trucks and thought about it the whole way to the Bucket. We came through the door in an uncharacteristically quiet line. We marched through to the back room and seated ourselves away from the main crowd to await the announcement we knew was coming, the one John had probably been waiting to deliver from the moment our first meeting was called. It came as no surprise when he seated himself at the head of the main table, pulled a thicker stack of papers than ever before from his bag, laid them out on the wooden top and quietly stated that it was time to call a general strike on the whole community.

259

IV

CRISIS

Six days later, at 11:30 p.m. on Thursday, August 23, an unexpected slew of phone calls from concerned citizens on the south end of Baker suddenly poured into the sheriff's department. According to each report, some 'maniac' had gone on a shooting spree in the parking lot at Keller & Powell with what sounded to be a high-powered shotgun. No one knew any exact details, but from where the department headquarters were situated on East 7th St., even the deputies manning the phone lines at the moment could hear a string of shots booming out over the neighborhood to the south. They asked no further questions. Three officers in two separate squad cars were immediately dispatched to the scene. They raced across town to the slaughterhouse, stashed their vehicles in an adjacent lot, and crept around the outskirts of the perimeter in search of the reported gunman. But instead of encountering a rogue maniac, as had been expected, they came upon William Dole, a long time employee of Keller & Powell. Dole, adorned in a pair of soiled dungarees and toting a smoking 20-gauge under one arm, was pacing wild circles at the edge of the lot and screaming obscenities into the blackened expanse of the bordering tobacco field. The deputies quickly disarmed him and asked just what it was he thought he was doing. He responded by claiming he'd been appointed by the company administrators to patrol the property and ward off the coyotes from sabotaging the gristle bins. He elaborated by motioning to the scrap-lined lot behind him, which was littered with piles of decaying entrails. He swore he'd just gone inside for a cup of coffee – he hadn't been away from his post for two minutes – *and those sneaky little bastards* had come out of the field and torn the bins to pieces. They were all out there, he said gesturing to the line of trees in the distance. They were all out there just waiting for him to nod off.

Dole was in despair. He protested that he'd only been doing his job and didn't deserve this abuse. The deputies said they understood that, but that he still ought to have known better than to go on an unauthorized firing run at midnight. They confiscated his Remington, packed it away, and sent him home. The lot was left to the coyotes for the night.

The next morning Sheriff Dippold personally paid a visit to Tom Powell in the main office of the slaughterhouse. Powell was irate, claiming it had taken most of his opening crew all morning to clear the lot. The entire property had been left in such a state that his employees hadn't even been able to park their vehicles. Everyone had been forced to leave his rig in the supermarket lot across the street, and the supermarket staff was none too happy about it . . .

It had been a terrible morning for Powell. He was in no mood for chastisement. Sheriff Dippold went on to question him as to what right he thought he had to sanction the use and discharge of firearms without proper licensing. Powell, almost screaming, replied that if the sheriff's department had been doing its proper job, he never would've had to resort to such measures. He suggested Dippold head back to his office and check his latest files for petitions. There, if his secretary was worth her weight in paper clips, he would find five formal complaints lodged by Powell himself in just as many days. He would thereby be given to understand that the Pullman Valley waste disposal company hadn't paid Keller & Powell a single visit in over three weeks. No one was picking up his garbage, and no explanation had been provided for it. The phone lines at the landfill were dead. No one in town had spotted a compactor in days, he wasn't the only one . . . And meanwhile the health department was breathing down his neck around the clock. He had already been fined once, and if he didn't keep the overstuffed gristle bins under wraps at all costs the whole company would soon be facing mandatory suspension of all operations. *What the hell was he supposed to do?* he yelled.

The sheriff backed down. Instead of issuing the formal citation he had come to deliver, he ended up slinking out of the office like an ostracized carnival mule. He promised to look into the matter personally, on which Powell yelled after him: *You do that!*

So began a confusing week for Baker's law enforcement division. On leaving the Keller & Powell lot that morning, Tom Dippold took the long way back to his department building. While en route he noticed the undisturbed trash heaps lining every street in town, and as he went, Powell's words began to echo through and take root in his head. On arriving back at his office, he asked his secretary for the past few days worth of public appeals, registered mail, phone messages, anything along those lines. He expected maybe one or two memorandums in addition to Powell's complaints – under normal circumstances the sheriff's office in Baker was, so to speak, the last stop on the postman's run. So naturally, it caught him completely off guard when the secretary turned and handed him a thick stack of sealed envelopes, fax statements, and request forms, none of which had been called to his attention. They'd all been piling up in his own basket for two weeks, he was told. He nervously took them in hand and walked to his desk.

It took him an hour to read through everything. He found Powell's complaints (1,2,3,4,5) just as he'd been told, all in order. But in addition there were three from Dalewright, one from Holtz, one from Sodderbrook, and almost forty others from private residents all over town. And they were all, every last one, in regards to failed pickup on the part of the waste disposal company. Some of them even dated back to the first week of the month.

The sheriff was confused. He summoned every deputy in the lobby to his desk to ask if anyone knew anything about this situation. The deputies stood around scratching their heads. Only one of them came forward to announce that he himself, a resident of West 1st St., had put his own garbage out for pickup on Monday morning, but that, indeed, it was all still sitting there on the curb. Which explained why the Japanese had bombed Pearl Harbor. Dippold dismissed the meeting with a wave of his hand.

He next tried to phone the landfill. The line was dead. He let it ring fifteen times, then hung up. A few minutes later he tried again with the same results. Nothing. He thumbed through a directory book from his cabinet, came up with a number, and placed a call to a waste disposal office in the capital. After a long round of transfers he was finally connected with an appropriate official. But that official ended up being even more in the dark than he. Dippold's inquiry yielded nothing. He spent another fifteen minutes puzzling over selected complaints. Then he just stared at the wall for a while.

Tom Dippold was a fifty-one-year-old ex-bricklayer and former marine. He'd served five consecutive terms as sheriff of Greene County, running unopposed in each election. He'd been appointed to office by virtue of what were widely considered his three overriding merits: his intuitive grasp on local behavior, his unwavering policy of non-intervention in domestic disputes, and his lenient handling of what might otherwise or elsewhere be deemed reprehensible infractions of law (public brawling, license violations, drunk driving, etc.). In the event of being apprehended for an occasional public outburst, most locals in the valley had very little to fear from Tom Dippold. The sheriff sympathized with the idiosyncrasies of the Baker Lay. After all, he was a part of it. That was his ticket. He'd been born and raised in Greene County. He'd been schooled as a local, elected as a local, consulted, petitioned and upheld as a paragon of local values. So long as his department remained a bastion of those values, his re-election was all but assured until the day he put in for retirement. He was counted on to dispel all conflicts within his jurisdiction as quickly and discreetly as was possible. In all his years in office there had been only five felony incidents requiring full-scale mobilization of his department: two unrelated murders, one suicide scare, the burning of the Fisher farm and that outrageously bizarre holdout on the north end of the valley. Otherwise, his five successive terms in office had been a monument to inactivity. The sheriff was expected to eradicate swiftly all disputes brought to his attention; to serve as on-the-spot judge, jury, and executioner very quiet-like, *laissez-faire*, non problematic, and, above all, in the interest of the *community*, as opposed to the rest of the nation, as the two were undeniably separate entities. That was the way the Baker Lay wanted it, and that was the extent of the order Tom Dippold had always striven to uphold. As unwritten policy, what went on behind closed doors in Greene County was none of his business; but by the same token, he'd been on a first name basis with most everyone in town for ten, twenty, thirty years, and had generally taken pride in the idea that there wasn't much going on in the area that he didn't know about.

So naturally, it was highly irregular to find him in this predicament: not only at a complete loss for details on a situation apparently gripping his jurisdiction, but, moreover, lacking rudimentary identity checks on the employees of one of the valley's most fundamental outlets. Try as he did, he just couldn't seem to remember ever having known any of us personally. It was highly unusual, but it was true. Sheriff Dippold knew nothing about his own trash men. Very few people did.

He decided to send two of his men to the landfill to investigate. They left the building. Thirty minutes later they returned to report the yard gates locked and no sign of movement within. They had yelled up to the office, but no one had responded. All the machinery was sitting there unattended. The whole lot was dead as a ghost town, they said. Very strange. They couldn't figure it.

Neither could the sheriff. He spent the rest of the afternoon on the phone with various secretaries, file runners and state officials. He called Tom Powell to request any additional information. He even spoke with a receptionist at the City Hall. But he got nowhere. At the close of the day he'd made no progress whatsoever in obtaining home addresses or alternative business numbers for any Pullman Valley landfill employee. He left the office at six feeling as though he'd accomplished nothing.

*

On returning to his desk shortly after nine thirty the next morning there were already twelve messages waiting for him: three in reference to coyote attacks, one from the Whistlin' Dick, another from Holtz, four from private residents protesting or re-protesting over neglected pickup, and the rest being strangely unspecified in nature. The secretary was at her wit's end from dealing with the public. Dippold tried to calm her by preparing a one paragraph formula response, which, in a roundabout manner, stated that he was doing everything in his power to get to the bottom of the matter. He then holed up in his office and had another crack at the phone.

To begin with, the landfill line was still dead. The state official with whom he'd spoken the day before was unavailable. The receptionist at the City Hall had misplaced his request and had to consult her files. It was a bad start. Dippold sent two of his men back to the landfill to try again. In the thirty minutes it took them to return, the secretary received five more phone calls. She was becoming increasingly unreasonable. Other phones in the building started going off, private lines and all. Everyone wanted to speak with Tom Dippold, but Tom Dippold, regrettably, had nothing to say. The two officers returned from the landfill empty-handed. They were assigned to their own phones.

By noon the department had been transformed into an open-air market. First, one of the bartenders from the Whistlin' Dick came through the main doors to scream something about his alleyway dumpsters being loaded to the gunwales. He pounded on the counter and swore there were rats the size of housecats tearing through his delivery stock every morning. When would it all end? . . . No one knew what to tell him. He was eventually escorted from the office and sent on his way with a warning to pipe down. But pretty soon more protesters were approaching on foot, most of them factory owners or representatives. The lobby started filling up faster than the deputies could empty it out. The phones were ringing off the hook. The whole building sounded like a calling board for the PTL club. The secretary was incensed, openly yelling into the receiver and slamming it back into place. From across the street the main doors of the building were said to have resembled the turnstile of a New York public bank on Black Friday – one line of drawn and dejected faces going in, one line of even more drawn and dejected faces coming out. Dippold got back on the phone with City Hall. The receptionist at the main office was out to lunch. He was transferred to another office, got nowhere, and ended up with the janitor's department. He hung up and pulled crowd control for twenty minutes, then called back. The receptionist had returned. He laid into her, demanding the landfill director's file to be drawn up in the next fifteen minutes, or else. No excuses. He hung up again. He walked out to the lobby. Two of his deputies had unsheathed their nightsticks and were looming in the doorway. He yelled at them to get their heads together. They resheathed and cowered beneath his gaze. He scoffed. He turned and made his way through the crowd to the commode doors on the far end of the room. For the next ten minutes he sat in a locked stall guzzling straight bourbon from a nickel-plated pocket flask. The roar from the lobby intensified by the minute. The walls shook, the toilet paper wobbled in its dispenser. At one point he expected the fiberglass ceiling mats to start collapsing. Through it all he shifted from one leg to the other, spat at his reflection in the stainless steel handrail, and sucked down long gulps of Jim Beam. But he was really no better off than before on returning to the lobby.

That afternoon was probably the most chaotic, haphazard, wholly nonsensical four-hour stretch the sheriff would ever know – with one notable exception – in over twenty-eight years of active law enforcement duty. He would later liken it to being stonewalled in the south-side Bronx with a pickup full of white trash in Harley gear. Before it was over, one of his deputies would recommend, only half-joking at best, that they barricade the main doors, sandbag the perimeter and hose the mob into the forest. Strangely enough, that ended up being the only quasi-rational suggestion to be made all day.

Besides being every bit as uninformed on the situation as the crowd on hand, what boggled the sheriff more than anything was that everyone in town appeared to have reached a breaking point at once. Only the day before the public complaints registered by his department had been comparatively limited in number and moderate in tone. The department itself had been dead quiet. The deputies on duty had lounged about in their nylon recliners, drinking bottled water from the six gallon tap and staring out the window at the post office across the street. The atmosphere had been characteristically dull. The sheriff himself had only just gotten wind of some inexplicable break-down in public utilities, and even then there had been no real indication of its *magnitude*. Yet now, little more than twenty-four hours later, here it was in all its unbridled hideousness – an uncontrollable gaggle of country jakes on par with any renegade chapter of the Relief Army descending on his headquarters *en masse* – jamming through the doors by the dozen, filling the main office with the flatulent stench of an overheated boxcar, waving their papers, pounding on the counters, stamping their feet, screeching over one another, pushing, shoving and demanding equal, undivided attention all around. Everyone wanted answers, answers, answers, and more than just that – *a solution*. And they wanted it *now*. Tom Dippold did his best to resolve any inquiries he could (which were next to none) and ejected as many of the more unruly intruders as he saw fit (nearly everyone who walked through the door). All this while darting back and forth to his office phone, keeping his own deputies in check, and doing everything in his power to prevent his secretary from walking off the job. There was also the matter of patrolling the crowd that had gathered on the corner of 7th and Poplar. As well as the one to the rear of the building. And the fire escape. And the bathrooms and the elevator shaft (some joker was running wild with a can of shaving cream). In addition to manning the switchboard and comlink. And always the phones, they just kept ringing . . .

The long-awaited call from City Hall finally came through. It was over two hours late, but the sheriff had no time or energy left to complain. He slammed his door on the uproar in the lobby and quickly jotted down the name and address of one Jeffrey Harker Kuntsler as it was dictated to him. He hung up again. A quick call through to the number produced nothing. He made one copy for himself, then headed back out to the lobby.

He grabbed the nearest deputy by the collar, shoved the paper into his hand, and ordered him to go kick the old man out of bed, away from the flower garden, up from the cellar, whatever it took, and bring him in for questioning. The deputy confirmed the order and left. The sheriff went back to crowd control. One hour later the same deputy radioed in to report the listed address empty. No sign of activity. Dippold had to *not* scream. He instructed the deputy to return to the department at once, only on the way he was to retrieve one Bill Gibbs from the General Automotive Repair on 1st St. Gibbs was to be ordered to deliver one diamond-toothed circular saw, one power-charger, two safety-visors, and his own able-bodied person to the department headquarters ASAP. The deputy confirmed the order. Dippold hung up and returned to the lobby once again.

By that point he and his men were just about ready to begin pitching all intruders headlong out the door without questioning. An angry crowd had amassed in the street. The parking lot at the A.A.A. was filling up with suspiciously up-to-date Lincolns. Industrial administrators and representatives were crawling out of back seats, motioning to one another, closing in on the building in coordinated groups. The sheriff had never laid eyes on nine out of ten of them. Some of them were reporting coyote raids of epic proportions. Some were threatening legal action for 'executive negligence.' Others were requesting their properties be marked up for 24-hour scavenger patrol. And still others demanding rank and badge numbers of given deputies, etc., etc. – an unremitting onslaught of muddled demands, grievances, accusations, threats and insinuations, every one being trumpeted at hair-raising levels and none making the least bit of sense. It was impossible. The sheriff had never seen anything like it. None of his training at the academy, and certainly none of his experience in the field, had prepared him for anything along these lines. The crowd wasn't listening to him, and he was getting tired of trying to explain something he himself didn't understand.

After a while he stepped out on to the staircase and made a failed appeal for order. He was booed all up and down the street. He went back inside. A few minutes later he bit the bullet and authorized the use of force by his men: anyone not immediately compliant with the first direct order to leave the premises was to be forcibly removed, hoisted by the belt and collar and thrown into the road.

Thereafter the scene quickly came to resemble an annual hay-baling tournament: a rapid-fire succession of repelled attacks, bodies being bludgeoned and pitched head over heels, kicking and wrangling on the staircase, cries of police brutality. Somewhere along the way one of the deputies called for riot gear, only to be blasted as an idiot – there was no existing armory for crowd control in Greene County, he was told – no shields, no Dobermans, no butterfly nets – only one sorry old paddywagon and six canisters of nerve gas. And no one was ready to gas the crowd. Not yet. The deputies were ordered to continue pushing, barring and driving everyone out of the office as non-incriminatingly as they were able.

At some point in the confusion a lone voice in the crowd caught the sheriff's attention. While barricading one of the main doors he distinctly overheard someone yelling about one of the local trash men, something along the lines of *why don't you pull one of the scrubs out of his hole for questioning?* Dippold whirled and singled out the source. He pushed through the room and apprehended the unidentified intruder, then demanded to know what information he, or anyone, may've had on the trash men in Baker. The man responded by saying one of them just happened to live down the street from him, a few blocks over from the department building. Dippold quickly hustled his informant out of the lobby to a cruiser on the corner. They left the scene and flew down Poplar to Burt Donnecker's door.

Donnecker, at the moment, was seated in his cramped living room watching a televised bass-fishing extravaganza and eating corn meal in his underwear. He had just woken up. He almost jumped out of his skin the moment the pounding on the door commenced. He eased the volume down on the black and white Panasonic, inched over to the door and bolted it, then quietly huddled in the corner. The pounding continued. A voice on the other side boomed out demands to open up in the name of the law. They knew he was in there, it said – they could smell the corn meal. Donnecker remained crouched in his Fruit of the Looms, wide-eyed and terrified. He didn't move. After a minute he heard a tapping on the windowpane; someone was routing through the shrubs. He stayed in place. The voice boomed out some more, promising trouble when it returned with a search warrant. Then it was gone. Donnecker ran to the phone to call Wilbur.

The whole street was in a state of wild pandemonium when the sheriff arrived back at the department. Every police scanner in town was jammed with panicked correspondence. A slew of spectators had flocked to the scene to investigate. Two arrests had been made – one for attempted assault, one for breaking and entering (repeated intrusion). The elevator walls were caked with shaving cream from floor to ceiling. The main doors were under siege. An unidentified helicopter was circling overhead. The deputies in the lobby were out of their minds. The secretary had disappeared. A crew of newscasters were floodlighting the doorway and reporting live from the scene. The sheriff was accosted by a group of ferret-nosed correspondents with boom mikes and hulking black cameras the moment he stepped out of his cruiser. He shielded himself and rammed through the crowd without comment. He made it by the press, through the main body of intruders, up the stairs and between the main doors. Once inside he ordered the immediate removal of all intruders on penalty of imprisonment. It took five minutes and one more arrest to clear the lobby entirely. Once the last of the crowd had been ejected he bolted and barred the main door – a flagrant violation of national law – in clear view of the looming cameras. One of his men tried to warn him of the potential repercussions of such an act. The sheriff balked, claiming if these weren't extenuating circumstances, then, *honey-baby, there never would be*. It was like Tet all over again.

The deputies were thrashed senseless. Their jackets were torn, their hair blown and dishevelled. Some were leant on desk tops to keep from keeling over. They looked as though they'd pulled a round as crash-test dummies. Outside the crowd was

273

cahooting, pounding on the glass and kicking up trash. The lobby was wrecked. Paper and tin cans were strewn out across the floor. The water dispenser had been overturned. There was shaving cream in the typewriter keys. It would take days to piece everything back together.

One of the deputies asked what came next. The sheriff straightened up as though to say *Right then. Next. Well . . . What does come next?* For a minute there he looked every bit as lost as the rest. But he soon snapped out of it by turning to his first deputy – the one he'd sent to Kuntsler's home – and asking if Bill Gibbs had been located. He got an affirmative, and a minute later Gibbs was summoned from his hiding place in the utility closet. The sheriff heard a rustling around in the mop basin. A broom fell out of the doorway and hit the floor. Then Gibbs meekly stepped forward, pale and trembling, clad in an all-purpose utility belt and toting the requested material.

All right, Dippold said, it was bad enough that the rest of town seemed to be one step ahead of them on whatever in God's name was going on, but if the press actually beat them to the draw, they were done for. They would be the laughing stock for miles around. So this was the plan: the deputies would sit tight and hold down the building. The doors were to remain locked to everyone, regardless. Since the secretary appeared to have gone yellow, one of them would personally have to put a call through to Pottville for reinforcements. Which meant dealing with Jake McPhearson, and that would prove no easy feat in itself. Also, a search warrant for 725 South Poplar was to be drawn up at once. They could work out the details later. In the meantime, he and Gibbs were going to slip out the back door, drive to the landfill, and saw the gates. They were going to break into the yard and dig up some concrete explanation for this mess by any means possible. Everyone was to stay calm, maintain full contact with him by radio, and, no matter what, keep the press at bay. Was he understood? He was. He nodded. And one last thing, he said on turning to leave – from then on and forevermore, they were to damn well let him know any time the public complaint basket heaped to the rim as it had that week. He couldn't be everyone's babysitter.

He and Gibbs left.

Once in his cruiser, the sheriff fishtailed the first corner and leveled out to an open 70 m.p.h. charge down Hauser St. He was deadset on eluding the press, but in the process of beating a hasty retreat from the premises he managed to scare the few remaining sous out of an already terrified Bill Gibbs, and to come within a hair's breadth of leveling a troll football match in full procession on the corner of 11th St. He switched on his emergency lights and continued. They rolled into the landfill lot a minute later. Dippold got out of the car and carelessly bullhorned a few demands into the yard. He then tossed the horn into the backseat and ordered Gibbs to get to work. By that point Gibbs was shaking uncontrollably. The sheriff rapped him on the side of the head and told him to pull his act together – *people were depending on him*. He set to work as best he could.

But he wasn't one minute into the job – sparks from the circular saw showering in every direction, power-charger humming, face mask donned and all – when a lone figure, some kind of outraged thicket gnome in reich attire, came bounding out of a mobile-home unit situated just inside the compound. Gibbs did a double take. He watched as the figure came down from the porch and veered toward him at a discombobulated stomp. He disconnected his charger and backed away from the gates. He tried to alert the sheriff, who was momentarily leant against the open cruiser door corresponding with a deputy back at the department. But before he could do so, the figure loomed into full view and bore down on them both. They gave with a start. This, Gibbs had to assume, must have been the much-talked-about director of the landfill and source of public misery number one, though by the looks of him, whatever his legal title may have been, he was not currently presiding over much of anything. He was all alone in fact, stammering unintelligible gibberish in the empty lot.

Gibbs wasn't able to make out a single word the assumed director spat forth in his opening attack, nor did he have much luck deciphering one coherent statement from the screaming match that followed. As far as he could tell, Tom Dippold and the man called 'Cussler' – or something along those lines – launched into an obscure, pre-Mesopotamian code of combat/ debate which had long since vanished from all the books, one which utilized inarticulate guttural howls and pained gesticulations of genital flagellation. He didn't understand any of it. And it raged for over ten minutes, back and forth and back and forth, seeming to go nowhere. It was only toward the very end that common English was brought into play at all, and that only for what Gibbs took to be the closing argument. Apparently, the sheriff had finally broken down and made a direct threat to arrest and book the director for obstruction of justice pending his refusal to comply with some specified demand. But the director wasn't having any of it. He told the sheriff not to waste his time – they couldn't hold him on anything and they both knew it. Tom Dippold had gotten what he'd come for – he had received his answer in black and white. Now it was time for him to get used to the idea and clear out.

With that the Cussler/Director/Thicket-gnome unit turned and traipsed back toward his office, leaving Tom Dippold in a flabbergasted stupor and Bill Gibbs with his power-charger dangling. He climbed the stairs and disappeared. That was the last anyone saw of him for quite some time.

The sheriff took the slow route back toward the department. He was in no hurry to return to the crowd, not after his visit with Kuntsler, and certainly not with the news he was bearing. He drifted through the troll football match for a second time that afternoon, then slowed to a halt on the southern corner of West 9th and Hauser. He cut the engine. Bill Gibbs watched him remove a flask from his vest and take a long pull. He passed the container. Gibbs took a small hit and passed it back. They sat in silence parked next to a pile of overstuffed twenty gallon Hefty bags.

After a while the sheriff removed a pen and paper from the glove compartment and handed them to Gibbs. *You write, I dictate*, he said. For the next few minutes Gibbs wrote and the sheriff dictated. They finished off the bourbon and the formal press statement simultaneously. Then, with nothing left to delay them, they drove back to the department.

That night Pottville 6's six o'clock news broadcast expended over half of its air time showcasing the afternoon at the sheriff's building. All across Pullman Valley and forty miles in every direction from Koll County, television sets in private homes and public taverns alike lit up with reports of a near-riot on the streets of Baker. Sweeping aerial footage captured a thronging multitude attempting to ram the department doors. Ground camera footage had been spliced into a four minute pastiche of police brutality. There were clips of various factory representatives pitching bags of trash on to the staircase, a spotlight on the Pottville cavalry (three cruisers) arriving in full force to subdue the masses, and an impassioned outcry/lament for order by two members of the Bolling County Baptist Clergy. The report was adeptly compiled. It was the kind of Topic A, mass-appeal, high profile 'Dog Bites Man' story on which media junkies and inquiring minds all across the nation thrive. The Associated Press was sure to be ringing for master copies within the first hour of transmission.

Two thirds of the way through the program Sheriff Dippold's official statement was aired in its entirety. The sheriff appeared tattered and bedraggled on opening the department doors, stepping into clear view, and squaring off with the news crew. After a round of sporadic questioning, he straightened up and stated very quickly that he had just spoken with the head of the Pullman Valley waste disposal company and had confirmed suspicions of a general strike on the part of its staff. The demands and conditions set forth by the striking party had not yet been ascertained. Department officials were still in the early stages of the investigation. No additional details could be provided at the current juncture. However, he went on to say, all of Baker could rest assured that he and his men were doing everything in their power to get to the bottom of the matter. In the meantime, all this cavorting about and panic in the streets was serving no purpose. He thereby demanded the immediate dispersal of the crowd on penalty of severe police retaliation. He was fed up with it, he said.

With that he turned and re-entered the lobby. The last frame in the broadcast caught him scowling over his shoulder amid a crescendo of mock-sympathy. Then he was gone.

For the final sequence a collage of trash heaps from industrial and residential Baker was aired in bold technicolor and coupled by a lone correspondent's all but apocalyptic commentary: *'Who knows what fate lies in store for the citizens of this small, terrified community,'* it said. *'More on this situation as it develops . . .'*

The strike was on.

As HAD BEEN ANTICIPATED – as was mathematically ensured *ab initio* – industrial Baker became a certifiable disaster area almost overnight. One quick drive through the southwestern factory circuit proved all. To the rear and side of every building, along the outer boundaries of each lot, in the ditches, at the base of every lamp post, in the disposal pits, the break areas, on staircases and loading ramps – everywhere you looked – sprawling ranges of scrap and debris sat oozing and withering in the heat. Each particular industry yielded excesses of varying size and composition, which, when taken one after another, made for a drastically incongruous visual impact on the overall landscape. As an example, in contrast with the more cumbersome loads generated by the furniture plants and novelty warehouses (up to 900 lbs. of excess per day) the paper plant's daily output was relatively modest and inoffensive, whereas right next door Keller & Powell or Frugal Bean Inc. were shoveling out the tainted lard and hide trappings by the wagon load, bringing their parking lots and perimeters alive with swarms of large black flies and hungry rodents. One pass along the northern half of Pollup Road was sure to bombard any passing motorist with an overload of visual stimuli: to the right a scattered pile of damaged crucifixes cluttered atop a long row of blue bags and bundled packages, to the left seven red dumpsters overflowing with rusted scrap metal and broken glass, just ahead a thirty yard wall of ominous black bags stacked high enough to conceal the building to its rear, and beyond that, all the slag and rot of the cannery. And one always had to keep an eye on the road – the first reported avalanches occurred on Kuntsler's second route, for obvious reasons.

The capitol inspectors who'd originally cracked down on Keller & Powell had indirectly been the driving force behind the group retaliation of factory representatives the afternoon Sheriff Dippold's building was stormed. In mid-August the state health department, on receiving alarming reports in regards not only to Keller & Powell, but to Dalewright, Frugal Bean, and Blaine enterprises as well, had sent four routine inspectors to Baker for the purpose of monitoring and investigating the situation. Those inspectors had spent the majority of every day badgering company representatives, overseers and administrators. They had gotten to operate on a first-name, albeit strained basis with individuals like Tom Powell. They had spent long hours in each factory and had reportedly appeared to revel in the unmistakably disagreeable effect they had on everyone. But before too long, other industries had begun to demand their attention as well, increasing their daily obligations four-fold. By the last week of the month they were personally making the rounds to eighteen different offices every twenty-four hours. They claimed to have made an attempt to contact the landfill administration themselves, though in one way or another their efforts had been unfruitful. No one believed them for a second. They were despised by all. The industrial administrators, otherwise and normally warring parties, had thereby struck up a correspondence with one another, openly bewailing their persecution under the health department. They had worked themselves into a network and had ultimately moved on the sheriff's building in unison. Hence the sudden siege on the 25th, hence the appearance of the dam breaking open all at once. Industrial Baker had pulled forces and moved on its own.

Residential Baker, on the other end, hadn't had cause for equal alarm. It's safe to say most of the Baker Lay didn't know what was going on until Pottville 6 or the *Daily Herald* alerted them to the fact. True, many of them hadn't received their standard pickup for two weeks prior to the official announcement of the strike, and maybe some of them, particularly those employed by the factories, had even begun to wonder. But relatively speaking, the streets of Baker were not that bad off yet, certainly nothing in comparison with Kuntsler's second route or the truck stops and convenience stores along the highway. There were really only eight to ten bags piled up in front of most private residences by the turn of the month. The heaps hadn't even grown together yet. There was still a ten yard stretch of drought scorched grass separating each pile. One given resident's garbage remained easily distinguishable from the next.

Which isn't to say that once the strike was official there weren't immediate repercussions throughout the neighborhoods. On the contrary, from the moment the sheriff made his statement on the evening of the 25th a wave of reactionary hysteria let loose through residential Baker, most of it prompted by the 'Thousands Flee!', second-coming type media coverage. It was probably mob-kindled dread more than anything which lead to an outbreak of one of the area's oldest problems: illegal dumping.

On the morning of the 27th both the sheriff's department and the City Hall staff were overrun with complaints from farmers, citizens and landowners residing all along the banks of the Patokah for twenty-five miles in either direction of the valley. There were reports of hatchbacks full of trash being dumped in corn fields, dozens of bags washing up on the riverbank overnight, full boxes being thrown from open windows on back roads, etc. One Bolling County farmer claimed to have run four jeeps from his tobacco field, but not before an ungodly mess had been deposited in the middle of his unreaped harvest. Each caller was infuriated to the point of speech impediment. It had to end at once, they all insisted. Otherwise a few choice citizens of Greene County were going to wind up mysteriously missing.

In dealing with the calls, Tom Dippold was loathe to discover that the City Hall staff was directly forwarding most of its own obligations to his department. He got on the phone to raise Cain and reduced three secretaries to tears before finally being transferred to Mayor Boll. Mayor Boll thereby instructed him to pipe down and put some troops out on patrol. He would take care of the rest. Consequently, the mayor went on the air to condemn the dumping, and the sheriff's deputies went on the riverbank to pick apart waterlogged garbage. That night the six o'clock news ran clips of certified police officers sifting through piles of coffee grounds and kitchen disposables in search of home addresses. The broadcast concluded with the mayor posting a $300 fine for illegal dumping and $50 reward for any information leading to the arrest of its perpetrators. The results were conclusive: the deputies managed to retrieve fifteen or twenty electrical bills from the mess, while seventy-three Benedict Arnolds phoned in to rat on their neighbors. The total number of fines issued came to fifty-one. Thereafter the dumping tapered off to a minimum, but in its place came forth an alternative retrospectively referred to as the 'Tidy War.'

The tidy war, as a dilemma confined to residential Baker alone, would wage for precisely as long as it was tenable (no more than three weeks) and, on conclusion, would give way to the first unified drive toward resolving the strike. Throughout its duration it would see the initial wave of animosity and self-interest among the Baker Lay gradually evolve into an undivided acknowledgment of communal damnation and a need to mobilize in the face of it. It would end the moment it became clearly unwinnable. Its participants would then scramble to salvage what remained of the sinking community ship.

But that resolve was a long way off, and many developments would come to pass in the interim. The tidy war, for all it was worth, was really just a prelude, a half-assed preoccupation taken up by homeowners in the early hours of September when it was still the case that no one quite knew what to think or whether or not to take the strike seriously.

It began with Mayor Boll's penalty campaign which effectively ruled out illegal dumping as a viable alternative. That was during the first week in September. Once the locals came to terms with the fact that they could no longer get away with tying their refuse up in a bundle and pitching it into the river as they pleased – or, very simply, once they realized they were stuck with the waste they generated – a cut-throat drive to outdo one another in terms of maintaining, or *tidying* up their own accumulations commenced. All up and down every street in town they began to appear, grappling with their heaps in an attempt to scale down and minimalize the apparent output of their own households. Most of the battle was waged by housewives or homebodies who remained holed up in their kitchens and parlors all day long. They were spotted creeping down from front porches to rearrange the mess as discreetly as they could, then tiptoeing back inside to the window to compare and contrast their own piles with the immediate neighbors'. Meanwhile those neighbors, who'd been looking on from their own windows the whole time, soon emerged in like manner to re-enact the process themselves. As each bag, chair, or lumber scrap was innovatively consolidated and reconsolidated toward achieving the least frightful outward appearance on the block, nearby onlookers and prying eyes were leering from darkened windowpanes and calling down quiet curses on one another.

The streets were soon teeming with tidy-war combatants, most of them sneaking out to their piles one at a time. In the event of two or more combatants crossing paths at once, a round of strained felicitations would be exchanged, whereupon each party would then do his or her best to maintain an air of nonchalance while strolling through the yard, tending to the hedges, checking the mail. At the first available opportunity they would bolt back inside to damn the luck and wait their turns once more. They would begin to wish hateful misfortunes on one another, conjuring the coyotes, praying for hurricane winds, dreaming of sabotaging every pile on the block in the dead of night. And just when one individual combatant would finally conclude that his or her monolith, pyramid or bulwark had finally stacked up to put those of all the neighbors to shame, someone else would hit on a new formula and throw the scales out of whack again. Mass rearrangement would ensue. The battle was in a continual state of renewal, particularly as the weeks pushed on and the growing piles to each homefront became increasingly unmanageable.

Every night when the 'man of the house' type arrived home from the factory or office he was instantly relegated, before dinner, even before sitting down to his customary can of Busch at the kitchen table, to go out and do battle with the heap on the lawn. It made for many a disgusted roadside apparition toward the end of rush hour: factory rats and managerial accountants alike, decked to the tee in the gear of their trades, ineffectively beating their trash with rake handles, desperately trying to compact the load, some of them even repacking bags in an attempt to cut down on the displayed excess.

After dark, front-porch lights and walk lamps were constantly clicking on and off as each household went on scavenger alert. The worst case scenario for any conscientious homeowner was to have a pack of coyotes tear into his heap while he slept. No one rested easy during the tidy war. All day long the homebodies waged a quiet battle, after work the blue collars lined the street to put the finishing touches on the family stack, and all through the night the combatants slept on pins and needles with their ears pricked up for the slightest sound of disturbance. That's how it began.

While all that was going on, Sheriff Dippold was waging his own war. Somehow, in the midst of the current disorder, he was being sought out to redress grievances over which he had no legal authority. For example, he had no authorized right or obligation to negotiate with a striking party, other than one originating in his own department. He was also in no way obliged to hear out complaints and demands of disgruntled factory owners, to update the press, or to correspond with state health inspectors under any circumstance. It just wasn't his job. Even if he'd wanted to intervene, all the above-listed concerns called for powers beyond his allotted command. Yet somehow, here he was paying tribute to every affected party in Baker with the consent, approval and even full-on recommendation of the technically accountable departments. In addition to tending to the already harrowing overload of obligations and responsibilities for which he *was* liable (routine patrols, dispelling congregations, the shameful and degrading dispatch of his deputies to the river-banks, and so forth) he was spending two or three hours of every day on the phone with bureaucrats in the capitol, he was making daily statements to both the *Herald* and Pottville 6, he was dealing with all the sound and fury of industrial Baker in its entirety, he was raiding homes of suspected trash runners like Burt Donnecker, only to find the premises vacant, and he was doing everything in his power to ascertain the striking party's as-of-yet unspecified demands. In full, he was doing everyone's job *in addition to his own*, and personally taking all the flak from the press, the public, and the factories as a result. He'd been forsaken. No one gave a damn for his predicament. No one, least of all the responsible officials, wanted any part of it. The secretaries at the City Hall, being intellectually on a par with a school of mill-pond guppies, did nothing but complicate matters when consulted. Their own superiors probably knew less about the situation than they. Mayor Boll consistently sidestepped all inquiries by making hollow, inconclusive pledges to 'look into the matter' himself. The state sanitation inspectors, for all their outward airs of compliance, had thus far failed to honor even the simplest request, that being to provide the sheriff's department with a list of the landfill's employees. Everyone had given him the runaround – transfers, transfers, transfers, and more often than not flat-out denial. Someone else was always to be consulted for further information, someone just one line over, someone currently unavailable, someone eternally out to lunch. It was a nightmare.

But the pressure on Tom Dippold did eventually subside, to some degree.

On the morning of September 6th his department received an unmarked letter in the mail. On opening the envelope and laying its contents out over the desk, the sheriff at long last came upon what he'd been racking his brains to acquire for nearly two full weeks. It was a printed list of demands – the full terms and conditions of the strike as drawn up and initialed by our crew. It was the only public statement of its kind we were to make in over ten weeks. It had been finalized at our last meeting, arrived at amid a cacophony of drunken debate. Its eventual presentation to the appropriate officials had been inevitable, though its actual delivery had been intentionally delayed for the sake of effect. The idea had been to give the community a clear idea of what it was up against before it had a chance to weigh its options; to prolong the outcome by one or two weeks so that the message being sent was all the more emphasized by the visual evidence on hand. That had been the original idea, and the results had come through accordingly, though, in actuality, the strike was still only in its infant stages of development. One way or another, it didn't really matter as far as the sheriff was concerned. All it spelt out to Tom Dippold was a dose of much-needed relief: a chance to lighten his own load, to get the press off his back and finally get the ball rolling in the appropriate courts.

Once the cards were in, the media went wild: with the dumping under wraps, the tidy war in full-swing, the strikers' terms declared, and all of Baker rapidly evolving into a snake pit for dysentery, nothing could've stemmed the ensuing blitz. The *Greene County Herald* and Pottville 6 hadn't had a better scoop in years. Their work was cut out for them. They had at their disposal a whole network of outraged industrial administrators. They had a local populace at the end of its rope. They had a bewildered sheriff and his floundering deputies. They had an evasive mayor who was only ever witnessed fleeing reporters from fifty yards in the distance. They had an impenetrable City Hall. They had more visual material than they could possibly compile. And now, to top it off, they had a name which would prove more invaluable to their ratings than all the reigning ayatollahs and mahatmas the whole world over: the name of Jeffrey Kuntsler.

Every night at six we were glued to our television sets for the latest update. This became our own little cornerstone ritual: we might've drunk till dawn and slept till four, but no active force in creation could've torn us away from the news at six. We were almost insanely serious about our broadcasts.

In the beginning we banded together in groups of three or four to every household – some of us to Bailer's, several to Clayton's, a few more to Irwin's, and the rest, without fail, to Murphy's. John and Wilbur always remained in Wilbur's apartment.

We spent the hour immediately preceding each broadcast poring over the morning edition of the *Herald*. We bought stacks of copies for the purpose of decorating our walls. We clipped and laminated every photograph, report, editorial and cartoon we could lay hands on. Some of them were priceless – Pineridge trolls in nightshirts chopping through the slag, tidy-war combatants shielding their faces from the camera, factory rats filing by piles of moldering debris, etc. The editorials and letters from the public were even better. Someone referred to Baker as a living compost heap. Someone else made a direct threat to the mayor. One concerned citizen even suggested, in all seriousness, that the police department be put on the streets to fill in for the hill scrubs while the strike was underway. Everyone was revolted. We were unquestionably the only crew in town having a laugh.

The papers were good – all credit where credit is due – but the news at six was impeccable. The most candid, brash and unapologetic photograph to be found in the *Herald*'s archives paled in comparison with the grotesque panorama of trash-picking, protesting and vitriolic commentary compiled by the newscasters every day. There was very little comparison between the two agencies at all. The *Herald*, on the one hand, as a Greene County publication with a daily circulation of no more than three thousand, tended to be more partial to the 'plight' of the Baker Lay, and generally regarded the strike as a 'crisis.' It was actually David Cooke, a local editorialist and sob-sister of moderate renown, who first coined the term 'crisis,' which went on to become *the* blanketing title of the whole affair.

Pottville 6, on the other hand, as an agency of Greene County's long-standing arch-rival, having nightly exposure to in excess of 70,000 viewers, was appreciably less sympathetic. In fact, one might even say that all of Koll County was actively reveling in the dilemma from day one. From where we sat, the nightly broadcasts actually resembled a pre-game pep rally, preliminary card-stacking for the upcoming playoffs. As Pottville 6, the circumstantial bully pulpit, saw fit, and to the boundless rage of the Baker Lay, the hype was clearly in favor of the Hessians. That was probably the one factor that infuriated most locals more than anything – to have to sit back in their living rooms and watch their time-honored nemeses jeer, laugh, and mount the sickly ass from a safe, comfortable, and not least of all *clean* distance . . . It was too much. Baker was at a loss for a comeback to the abuse, and Pottville 6 spared no efforts rubbing it in.

Every night at 6:01 sharp the commercials ended and the program began. After a brief round of introductory remarks the newscasters would quickly launch into strike coverage. The opening lines were always so dismal and gargantuan that many of us were left to wonder if the scriptwriters hadn't spent the afternoon combing the Book of Revelations for ideas: 'UNTOLD DEVASTATION IN THE STREETS OF BAKER THIS AFTERNOON,' 'TRAGEDY AND MAYHEM INSIDE THE WALLS OF PULLMAN VALLEY,' 'FOR THE THIRD WEEK AND RUNNING NOW, GREENE COUNTY FINDS ITSELF A SINNER IN THE HANDS OF AN ANGRY GOD . . .' And so on, a new scarehead every night. This was followed by the first of several gut-wrenching collages: detailed closeups on the Sodderbrook gristle bins, paranoid faces peering from storefront windows along Main, the elementary playground at recess amid windblown heaps, fly and maggot-ridden excess in industrial Baker. Next there were any updates on the negotiating process, which always amounted to a wave of contradictory and unverified reports. Then there was a four or five minute special presentation outlining various aspects of the history of waste disposal in Greene County. One night the construction and ownership of the landfill was discussed, another night the existing route circuits and speculated yield of each. They even ran a special on Hackert – the aforementioned private disposal practitioner with the red pickup – but they weren't able to extract one intelligible statement from his interview (his remarks were sub-titled). All this with continuing footage and commentary. Then there was the first commercial break.

Two minutes later the broadcast would resume with another collage – more industrial Baker, more paranoid faces. Then came the moment when correspondents took to the streets directly for interviews with the Baker Lay. This was usually the most erratic, unpredictable segment of the broadcast, as everyone in town seemed to have a different attitude toward going on record, or more specifically, going on record for Pottville. Some regarded it as an unconscionable act of betrayal and shied away at all costs.

But others, for reasons of their own – some probably starstruck with the idea of being on television under any circumstance, others appearing genuinely moved to the point of public outcry – took to the cameras without hesitation. They blathered and bloviated their way through numerous defamatory accusations – some of them outright lying about their own predicaments, and all positing the blame for the disaster on local politicians, the police, the courts, the landfill, and ultimately one another. Whether dressed in their Sunday suits or robed in their shop threads, they were cold, outraged, sickened and indignant.

The interviews often stretched on to the next commercial break. Once the break did roll around, we tended to slacken our attention for a minute or two. We came out of our dazes to run to the icebox, to laugh amongst ourselves, to predict the next installment in the broadcast. At Murphy's, Dennis and Dickell held headstand competitions for running bets. At Bailer's the television was muted for the duration. John and Wilbur kicked back in their lawn chairs, puffing heavily on stale Cuban cigars. Wherever we were, we relaxed for a minute, but the moment the commercials ended we were all ears again. The third and final sequence was always the most important.

As the broadcasts resumed, the heart of the matter would at last be addressed. *'Just what is going on in the Pullman Valley landfill?'* the newscasters would ask. *'To find out, we now go live to the scene . . .'* or *'In hopes of unearthing some clue, we turn to our field correspondents . . .'* On which a crowd of reporters would be pictured huddled at the base of the locked gates in the yard. The camera's eye would sweep the vacant lot and come to rest on Kuntsler's trailer. A chorus of demands for a statement would go up.

Thus far, on John's direct orders, we had remained far out of the picture. John had pointed out long beforehand that once the strike did get underway, the community would be incapable of mobilizing unless and until it had a specific party to blame for the disaster. Public opinion would be the key factor in getting the ball rolling. Once the culprits had been identified and declared, then and only then would negotiations be cleared to proceed. Knowing that, we were to grant no interviews. There were to be no pamphlets or marches, no manifestoes, no demonstrations of any kind. We were to stay out of the taverns – no exceptions. We'd already made enough of a name for ourselves as it was. We were to keep the lowest profile possible, to remain unavailable for comment, to vanish. By so maneuvering our way out of the spotlight and allowing someone else to fall into it, the press, the authorities and the general public would have no choice but to demand an explanation from Kuntsler. And we all knew perfectly well that the moment the old man opened his mouth and unleashed the same bile-rot invective we'd been hearing for years, the community would have all the responsible party it would ever need. All we had to do was shut up and let Kuntsler speak. He would do the rest. And if things went according to plan, Baker might even cast its sympathy with us.

But for the first two weeks the old man didn't even come to his window. No one knew what he looked like. No one knew anything about him. His identity was open to speculation and naturally took on mythical configurations in his absence. Most locals pictured a reclusive bog griffin hunched over a paper plate. Rumors began to circulate that he was actually dead up there in his trailer, bowled over and decomposing from a self-inflicted gunshot wound. No one knew what to think for quite some time.

But the speculation finally ended on the afternoon of the 5th, when a press crew inadvertently caught sight of him at his window. It was a beautiful shot, one that would be aired over and over throughout the coming weeks: Kuntsler's soured countenance like mangled pot roast between the blinds, cussing inaudibly and waving off the reporters with a closed fist. It couldn't have been more perfect.

He didn't appear again for four days. The first clip was run repeatedly and managed to brand its way into the public's memory, invoking mixed reactions all around. Some locals were willing to wager the old man was understandably upset, was working his fingers to the bone to settle the dispute, and so had that repellent air about him. *Executive fatigue*, they called it. Others weren't so sure; others couldn't exactly put their fingers on it, but knew for certain that they didn't like what they saw. In any case, all lingering reservations as to his actual character were effectively banished with his next appearance.

On the night of the 9th, Pottville 6 correspondents managed to lure the old man from his trailer at long last, though the resulting interview, if it could be called that – it was really more of a quadriliteral rampage – had to be prematurely cut due to the excessive profanity. The main newscasters thereby made a formal apology for their lack of discretion and promised to roll the interview as soon as it was appropriately doctored up. Which it was by the next night, though when rolled in its entirety, Kuntsler's tirade was so marred with audial dingbatted maledicta and dubbed gaps that whatever it was he'd been trying to convey was reduced to an incoherent chain of articles and prepositions amid a succession of sustained beeps. Not one clear idea came through in the whole statement. When asked if he had read the conditions of the strike put forth by his employees, he responded by saying #@$% yes, he'd *&%$ well read the @#$% terms those &% $# #$%@ %$#@ had #@$% together, but that he'd be @#$% to the $#%& before he'd @#$% $@#% to consider #$@#. He went on to call the sheriff a #$@% of a #@$%, the mayor a % $#@ with a @*@#, and his ex-employees a bunch of $%#@-*$*# #@$%. All the while flailing in and out of the camera's view and lunging at any reporters who drew too close to the gate. Before turning to head back to his office he made one last statement to the effect that all of Pullman Valley could $#@% well %$#@ in its own %$$@ for all he %$#@. He wasn't responsible for #@$%.

In effect, that broadcast brought the first phase of the strike to an end. Before its transmission all was confusion and indecision. After its transmission all was confusion and resolve. The cast of characters was in. All the main components had been declared. From one end of town to the other the sudden realization hit that under no circumstances was the dilemma about to go away on its own.

THAT SUMMER'S DROUGHT remains on record as one of the most devastating in the state's history. With daily temperatures still averaging ninety-five degrees in the shade by the close of the second week in September, nearly every meteorological record in the book had been broken. The public reservoir was two thirds empty. The autumn harvest was in peril. Most crops had been scorched beyond cultivation. Tap water all across town was brackish and granulated. A state-wide water conservation drive was underway, one which strictly regulated each household's allotted gallonage. Greene County certainly wasn't alone in resembling a sepia-toned pothole, but unlike the rest of the state, Baker was in the midst of a waste disposal strike, and the existing quandary was only exacerbated by the heat.

Again, even under normal circumstances the rate of decay among organic disposals is accelerated with a corresponding rise in temperature. All discarded food, lawn clippings, excess grease, etc. tends to generate a hideous stench when left out in the open for more than a few hours. Meaning that after four full weeks of pile-up in the streets of Baker, the whole valley was by now wafting out like treated bait to every species of scavenger for twenty miles around. As might've been expected, those scavengers soon responded by coming up from the sewers and down from the skies by the multitude.

To start with, as the steerhands at Keller & Powell had pointed out, industrial Baker was dealing with maggot breeding on a byzantine scale. Swarms of loud black flies were descending on the gristle bins in ungovernable waves. They were fogging the parking lots, devouring hides and entrails in thick humming carpets. They moved from lot to lot, pile to pile, spawning in the rot by the millions. It wasn't uncommon to come upon five or six fistfuls of vermin to each torn bag. They were everywhere – in common wastebaskets, in the gravel, lodged in tire treads and radiator grills, some of them still in the larval stage, others beginning to sprout wings and appendages. Once grown they took to the air and multiplied exponentially. Their numbers grew with each passing day.

In initially attempting to deal with the epidemic, some of the factory owners hit upon the revolutionary idea of coating the gristle bins with rock salt. Hired hands were ordered to dump twenty pound bags over each heap, then to sit back for a day or two to monitor the results. In the end, the salt only corroded and sometimes partially liquified the decomposing excess, which, in effect, did nothing but add to the stench and bring more flies. Next they tried liquid ammonia, but that just made matters worse. They finally broke down and began dousing their loads with authorized pesticides. But no matter what they tried, the flies always returned with a renewed vengeance, and the factory owners were left with almost unrecognizable heaps of semi-embalmed and truly monstrous looking toxic rot. It was heinous beyond description. Someone likened it to turning an open flame thrower on a road kill.

The flies soon lit out for new territory. They were expanding their field of operations. By halfway through the tidy war they descended on residential Baker *en masse*. All up and down every street in town the Baker Lay were witnessed swatting at their garbage and resecuring contaminated bags. The alleyways behind Main St. were blackened with swarming clouds. Windshields were splattered, wipers jammed. Children were seen running directionless circles in church lots, swinging tennis rackets in wide arcs for hours on end. Venus flytraps and treated paper sold off the shelves and had to be put on massive back order at the Dollar General. The school halls were bombed with disinfectants. Mandatory inoculations were administered in all public agencies. The Methodist Church's annual outdoor bake sale was canceled. Saturday afternoon hot-dog vendors were forced indoors. The port-o-lets at the construction sites were ruled off-limits. The list went on: every facet of community life was in one way or another affected by the epidemic of diptera. And the flies weren't the only scavengers to respond to the call. They were the first of the lot to appear in great numbers, and they might be said to have enticed the others to some degree, but they were in no way the most troublesome, and, all things considered, might have been dealt with conclusively had the problem begun and ended with them alone.

But of course it didn't. As time would evidence, they were only the scouts foraging ahead of the main ranks – the main ranks being a horde of turkey vultures, buzzards, sewer rats, gulls, coyotes, wild dogs, groundhogs and woodchucks, each of which approached in a different manner, from a different angle or altitude, at a different time of day, and with varying means of acquiring sought-after refuse. Each scavenger, it almost goes without saying, also held a different rank on the evolutionary ladder of life – the preconceived pecking order, the hierarchical lineup on the totem-pole – that is to say, each invoked a different response (repulsion, disgust, fear) among the locals which was not always in strict accord with the actual threat it represented. As an example, one nest of maggots always struck more terror and revulsion into the heart of most area residents than the appearance of twelve turkey vultures perched atop the neighbor's heap. In some ways, for aesthetic reasons if nothing else, that's understandable. But the fact does remain: one nest of maggots might easily be crushed underfoot, whereas a single grown vulture has within its talon's grasp the raw power to snap a grown man's arm in two.

Once the flies began nesting in residential Baker, the onslaught of carrion looters which had already begun to plague the industries followed close behind. Starting at just after dawn every morning, anyone in the valley could've taken one quick look overhead to find ten or fifteen birds of prey slowly circling at varying altitudes. These lice-infested monsters, with their coal black eyes and craning necks, often stood at over two and a half feet in height, with six foot plus wingspans. On dive-bombing runs they could swoop downward at ninety degree angles and work up terrifying velocities before leveling out for the kill. In addition to devouring any semi-digestible refuse left behind by human sources, they ate maggots, rodents, lawn clippings, and had even been reported to stage attacks on lone coyotes. But the coyotes, for that matter, usually banded together in packs and were nocturnal by nature. They were also cowardly. One porch light flicking on was enough to send a whole pack of them tripping off into the fields. Everyone knew that, but they still invoked panic, partly due to the frightful mess to which they were capable of reducing any organized heap in a matter of seconds, and partly due to apocryphal tales of regional explorers having once been attacked, torn limb from limb, and devoured on unfrequented back roads. The coyotes and wild dogs were loathed more than any other scavenger, with the notable exception of the rats.

The rats were the absolute worst. As the years have passed and the strike has dimmed to a controversial, at times painfully embarrassing topic of inquiry and debate, the one visual image which remains fixed in everyone's mind, the one detail which has survived all subsequent revisions and which invariably stands out from all the rest in the memories of those who were present, is that of a slew of filthy grey sewer rats dragging their oil-slicked carcasses through the streets of Baker by the score. It's the one image on which everyone seems to agree, incidentally the one image no one's been able to put to rest. And it's no wonder: the Baker Lay were able to deal with chicken hawks roosting in their elms. They endured the coyotes as best they could. They handled the muskrats in their drainpipes with relatively little complaint. But no one in the nation would have fared any better to wake up one morning and find a nine inch sewer-rat nibbling on a live maggot at his doorstep. There are certain universal thresholds.

Around the clock it ran: the flies teemed twenty-four hours a day. The birds of prey operated from dawn to dusk. The ground-hogs, gophers, muskrats and boll weevils appeared shortly before noon and ran loose until dark. The rats emerged just after sundown and stayed on till first light. The coyotes and dogs operated from about eleven to four. The combined mess generated by all these groups soon brought huge flocks of starlings, gulls, and from no one knows where, standard urban street pigeons. By the first of the season Baker had become a parasitic zoo, an all out battleground of feuding scavengers. They were everywhere. They tore into the garbage at all hours of the day. They dragged full bags into the road to scatter the contents in every direction. They picked through the mess in search of squashed apples, soured milk, moldy bread, brown cabbage, anything. Every heap in town was crawling with them. The streets were annihilated. There was busted glass everywhere, streaks of mayonnaise mixed with the remains of ashtrays, tea bags and eggshells, green macaroni, maggots breeding in cooking grease, gulls ripping at paper plates, woodchucks running by with used sanitary pads in their jaws, vultures eating field mice, owls eating sewer rats, starlings eating maggots, and more flies every day. Pottville 6's interview with Ted Drake, a local dog-catcher, just about summed it up. Drake, a long-time resident of Baker who was presently finding himself up against the worst case scenario imaginable to any member of his profession, claimed that what we had here was a bona fide case of the food chain gone haywire. The strike had brought the trash, the trash had brought the maggots, the maggots had brought the rats, the rats had brought the dogs, the dogs had brought the dog-catcher, the dog-catcher had filled the kennel, the kennel had overflowed, the dogs had been put to sleep, their bodies had filled the body-bags, and the body-bags had ended up right back out on the street, bringing more flies, etc. *ad infinitum* . . . It was a no-win situation, he said. And there appeared to be no end in sight.

The short-term effects were numerous. First, the tidy war was finally relinquished as a lost cause. Which would have come about anyway, with or without the influx of scavengers. The visible display to each household was now numbering from twenty to thirty bags on average, and no one seemed capable of keeping up with the spread. The scavengers provided a welcomed excuse to give up. From then on, most residents just focused on keeping their own trash from being tracked back into the house. The rest was damned for all it was worth and left to fall into the streets by the column. The Baker Lay had more important things to think about now, things like drawing up petitions, putting pressure on the powers-that-be, steering clear of rogue sewer rats, and arming themselves for any potential conflicts to come.

The traffic was another problem. As most curbside heaps had now grown to over three feet in height for twenty yard stretches at a time, and with the scavengers running amok and turning the streets into a hazard zone, most roads in town were becoming increasingly unnavigable. The pile-ups were collapsing into through lanes faster than they could be cleared. There were broad impasses at every juncture. Some motorists stopped to clear their paths before continuing on, but others just barreled over the mess and left it scattered in every direction. Carburetors were being jammed. Tires were blowing out. There were nails, glass, metal scraps and road kills everywhere. Drivers were veering wildly into oncoming lanes to avoid avalanches. Five trash-related accidents were on file by the close of the month. Try as the authorities did to keep the streets clear, they were continually outrun by the neverending redistribution of excess. Homicidal roadways were.

There was also the matter of several factories facing imminent shut-down for breach of sanitary upkeep. With the strike dragging on indefinitely, preserving minimal safety standards had become a near-impossibility for those industries dealing in any organic disposables whatsoever. Sodderbrook, for example, with the state inspectors still bearing down on it, had been forced to hire temporary hands for the purpose of shielding the gristle bins against the incursions of the coyotes, buzzards, rats and starlings. All around the clock, five stick-wielding wetbacks stood guard over the dump site to play human scarecrow at $5 an hour. The same held true for other industries and outlets: Holtz, Keller & Powell, the Dairy Queen, the pork shack, the convenience store, most any outlet which discarded semi-edible material. It was a *severe economic burden*, or so the corporate administrators claimed. They began lobbying for notarized gun-warrants.

As the *Herald* reported, all licensed firearm distributors in the area – department stores, sport shops, and even the Baker Bait Shack – made unprecedented gun sales toward the end of September. And the marked rise in sales was not solely attributed to industrial Baker's court-ordered authorization to take up arms temporarily, but also to the initiative of private, scavenger-fearing residents all over town. With the rats and the maggots and the dogs on the loose, it seemed everyone not already in possession of his own private arsenal made a direct bee-line for the nearest depot. They poured into the gun clubs in unbroken lines, raving about turkey vultures and home defense. Some of them had never fired a gun in their lives. Colts, Remingtons and Winchesters were brought down from their racks by the score. Shells of every conceivable caliber were bought up in cases. Deer targets and cleaning kits were swept from the shelves. The firing range was soon backed up for hours on end. On the weekends it was only available by appointment. Many locals whiled away long afternoons on their front porches, disassembling second-hand rifles and training their children to lock and load. After dark, whole crews of heavily armed neighbors lined stoop after stoop drinking whisky and waiting for the coyotes. It was ter-rifying by anyone's standards. The police department was losing its grip. Shots were ringing out through the neighborhoods at all hours. Responding deputies were arriving on scenes of reported gunfire to find two or three dead coyotes and an ongoing lake of trash, but no one in sight. Door to door inquiries, when responded to at all, always came to nothing. No one knew any-thing, no one had heard any shots. The deputies would go on their way empty-handed ... But twenty minutes later more blasts would ring out on the other end of town. Again, the deputies would race to the scene to re-enact their inquiry. But for all their efforts, they never made a single arrest.

It wasn't so bad during the daylight hours. From dawn to dusk the only gunfire to roar through Baker was issued by the industrial representatives' licensed sharpshooters, and with most of them being seasoned huntsmen, very little concern was expressed that one of their shots might stray from its intended mark. In fact, from the moment they were appointed to the rooftops throughout the southwest, the only inconvenience rendered by their daily dispatch was not so much the noise pollution or the nerve-racking intensity of the barrage – the public grew to accept those sacrifices as compulsory – but more so the matter of if and when they did tag an overhead scavenger, just where it might come down. With many of the factories being positioned right alongside of the highway, there was nothing to prevent a wounded turkey vulture from spiraling out of the sky and thumping down on the hood of a passing motorist. The resulting shock could make for enough momentary loss of motor skills behind the wheel to land the vehicle in a roadside ditch. Otherwise, the marksmen who replaced the gristle-bin crews, with their pockets full of ear plugs, their inexhaustible supply of turkey shot, and their seemingly inborn resilience to prolonged bloodshed, were regarded as Grade-A public benefactors.

During the daylight hours, residential Baker remained devoid of fire. Most locals waited till dusk to take up arms, and in the meantime redirected the residual momentum from the tidy war toward securing their own legislative means of scavenger control. In the same manner the industries had pushed for the appointment of certified marksmen – via organized lobbying – the Baker Lay now took to the courts with demands for author-ized mass extermination. And they had very little trouble securing it. Everyone, including the members of the court, was sick to death of the scavengers. It was widely held that before negotiations could proceed, before any legislation in regards to the strike could be considered at all, the streets first had to be restored to order. Classic Baker reasoning: if it moves, chase it; rid the neighborhoods of coyotes and maggots, and cooler heads will somehow prevail in the drawing room. It apparently occurred to no one, at least no one who came forward and said as much at the time, that beating around the bush with this exces-sive deliberation was wasting precious time and steadily allowing the community's condition to worsen. Had anyone stopped to consider, it might have been pointed out that whole days were being invested in scavenger hysteria, while the root of the problem – *the actual pile-up itself* – was growing every hour. The longer the public waited to address the central issue – the more decoys it veered to eradicate, the more red-herrings it left the path to pursue – the more impossibly cluttered every dimension of the slate became. It was that proverbial work rat mentality of taking one thing at a time, as opposed to going straight for the jugular, which reduced Baker to a dysfunctional bureaucratic quagmire in no time at all.

In any case, the request for county-wide extermination was approved. The court order went through. On September 25th the schools and nurseries were closed for the day, the roads were temporarily blocked, and all pedestrians were ordered to remain indoors from eleven until two. Shortly after noon the choppers appeared, right on schedule. All through the valley the walls and support beams of every structure rumbled on their foundations as two twin-engined helicopters with horizontally mounted pesticide dispensers made repeated low flying passes over the rooftops. Whole families watched from barred windows. Throngs of locals filled the stores along Main. The sheriff's department was packed like an air-raid shelter. All eyes were glued to the skies. With each chopper's pass, a fine, milky-white spray slowly settled over the streets, lending the whole landscape a slightly frosted look. It stank like a cross of ammonia bleach and table mustard.

To some degree, the extermination actually worked. The effects didn't outlive the drought and weren't entirely conclusive to begin with – most scavengers being notoriously adaptive to hostile elements – but in all fairness, it must be said the streets did quiet down for a week or two. It wasn't until mid-way through the next month that another pair of wild dogs would be spotted scrapping for a hamhock at the pork-shack doors. Neither would the groundhogs and woodchucks be found sifting through the rubble at high noon. The only rats to be seen would be crippled with ingested toxins and only able to hobble along in a paralytic stupor. As for the rest – the vultures, gulls, sparrows, crows and boll weevils that had ripped each heap to shreds – they would temporarily take haven in the woods to the north. They wouldn't leave, they would be spotted roosting in the trees and hiding in the shrubs at all hours of the day, but they would keep their distance from the streets for a little while. A momentary ceasefire, or at least a temporary delivery from the elements, was clear to settle over town.

But for all that, it was too little too late for most of industrial

Baker. For factories like Sodderbrook, the damage had already been done, and no pesticide campaign was about to reverse the effects. On the morning of the 28th the poultry plant was officially closed. It was the first factory in town to go, probably due to its unparalleled yield. With autumn having arrived and the holiday season drawing near, the company was only three weeks away from resuming its maximum output itinerary. It had already braced itself for the coming increase in productivity. The temporary hands were in place and the storage houses were overflowing. But so, unfortunately, were the gristle bins – unmanageably so. The dump site to the rear of the building had become a nauseating, one hundred and fifty yard lake of gore. Acceptable upkeep of the perimeter was no longer even remotely feasible. In excess of twelve thousand pounds of organic remains per day had been amassing in the dumpsters, bins, sacks and even standard issue cardboard boxes adjacent to the docking bay for almost five weeks at that point. The plant closed with a whimper and thereafter stood quiet with only the muffled screaming of twenty thousand turkeys in the storage building drifting over the expanse of Gwendolyn Hill.

But Sodderbrook's mandatory shutdown didn't end there; that is to say the real impact its suspension of all operations was to have on the community only began the moment the main doors were closed for the duration. In effect, the company's interdictory lockout brought about the introduction of two new factors to the already turbulent and overcomplicated situation. The first and most obvious was the 'wetback problem.' Nearly seven hundred unemployed Latinos wandering the streets with nothing better to do than convene in the alleys and play stick ball in the church lots while the rest of the community was up to its neck in refuse and red tape made for a good deal of added tension all around. The Baker Lay were nervous and trigger happy as it was. The last thing in the world they felt they needed, on top of everything else, was a potential uprising of the minorities. And that wasn't the end of it. The second factor was the introduction of a new strain of super-scavenger, one entirely immune to the pesticides, one which would go undetected at first but one which, on discovery, would prove a thousandfold more anathema to the community than all the others combined.

At 8:40 a.m. on October 1st, Sheriff Dippold received an emergency call from Paul Overholt, head of Sodderbrook's human resources department. Overholt was in a panic. His voice squawked through from the other end of the line, claiming someone had broken into the plant's storage house the night before. Someone had invaded the premises, busted all the padlocks, and driven half the company's stock off into the surrounding fields. *There were turkeys everywhere*, he said: $30,000 worth of live, steroid-fueled merchandise wandering the valley at the height of fowl season. It was a disaster, he moaned, *a terrible disaster*. He was in tears. He'd broken down on his office floor and was screaming into the receiver like a jostled infant at the foot of a long staircase. Tom Dippold told him to pull himself together – these histrionics were getting them nowhere. He would personally send a crew of deputies to the plant straightaway, not to worry. But in the meantime Overholt was to get on the horn and round up as many wetbacks as could be found. There was no time to lose. The sheriff hung up and went to work.

Overholt had not been exaggerating. That afternoon, as eleven Baker deputies worked alongside of thirty-seven net-toting Hispanics and three or four plant operators, literally thousands of twenty to thirty pound gobblers – more than could ever hope to be recovered – were found roaming the valley in disoriented flocks. They were everywhere, from the deepest reservoir at Ebony Steed to the highwayside veteran's league on the south end of town. There were eight hundred of them grazing over Gwendolyn Hill alone. The banks of the Patokah looked like a thriving bird farm. The valley walls were crawling from foot to crown.

The game reserve lit out like a thunderstorm. Gunfire went up from every tree stand and bush hovel within the perimeter. The moment word let out to the rest of the community – someone had placed a call to the 93.5 *Morning Madness* program to announce the dilemma – dozens of sportsmen started clocking out of the factories early. By noon the game reserve's main lot was filled to capacity, and the groups were still rolling in by the caravan. It was later estimated that somewhere in the neighborhood of six hundred and fifty turkeys fell prey to hostile fire in one day alone. All over town they were strung out over car hoods and front porches in large bundles. The ones which somehow managed to escape execution, motor vehicles, turkey vultures and plant reconnaissance patrols found a new home in the forest to the north. Others just wandered out of the valley and were never seen again.

At about five thirty, while most of his deputies were still out hounding down the merchandise beneath the ever-watchful eye of Pottville 6, the sheriff received another alarming call, this one from Bill Tulk, a Greene County farmer, in regards to some son of a gun or other who was pitching a bonfire in the middle of his cornfield. The sheriff rolled his eyes and promised to send yet another patrol. He gathered four of his six remaining men to come along and investigate the report. They all drove to Tulk's estate, two miles west of the town line. On pulling up to the main house they indeed spotted a billowing plume of smoke drifting out of the cornfield, just as had been reported. Tulk had no idea of who the arsonists may've been. He knew very little, only that the fire had started the hour before, and that at one point he'd heard a round of strange laughter drifting over the field. Otherwise he had no clue, though if he'd had to put money on it, he said, he would've bet the intruders were juvenile delinquents or crop thieves.

Sheriff Dippold, looking noticeably exasperated, pushed his Careras up on his nose and motioned his men to position. By that point he felt like a full-time community charwoman. Between sending his men out to pick through the trash, rounding up turkeys with filthy, uneducated wetbacks, and being openly mocked by the Hessian media every night, he had recently been subjected to the most brash, niggardly treatment he ever hoped to know. And now, to top it all off, he was about to go down on all fours in a scorched crop to sneak up on what

303

would no doubt end up being a group of kids swilling dirt beer around a weed fire.

But though the sheriff and his men, while creeping through the corn that afternoon, only expected to enact the routine round up of five or six inebriated juveniles, the scene they actually came upon in the middle of Bill Tulk's field would remain with them as one of the most appallingly hideous spectacles they would ever encounter. Even now, years later, Tom Dippold is visibly shaken up at the recollection of it. And it's no wonder, most people would be, as, instead of discovering a handful of carefree, Schlitz guzzling yahoos in Cardinal jerseys as had been expected, the sheriff and his deputies pushed through the stalks and into the clearing to find no less than fifteen genuine, stoop-shouldered, hunchbacked, disease-ridden and massively deformed Patokah-side river rats seated around a flaming barrel, slobbering over scorched turkey remains. The 'sick bastards' hadn't even bothered to remove the feathers from the bird. They were just tearing into the carcass with their fingers and holding raw chunks over the blaze until the skin had singed around the edges. Their faces and beards were mopped with sauce. They had wiped their hands on their already filthy, torn undershirts. The youngest of the lot, having seven or eight successive generations of inbreeding evidenced in the almost Cro-Magnon like contours of their skulls – the sloped foreheads, elongated jawlines, high-set cheekbones and cavernous eye sockets – were smeared in their own excrement and wrapped in soiled rag diapers that looked to have been left in place for the last two years. The whole clearing stank of death; anyone who's ever been at close quarters with a river rat can only imagine. Anyone who hasn't, *can't*. The only comparative analogy that can be drawn is to say that for the sheriff and his deputies, it was much like being the local Avon lady sent to a cannibal camp on a daisy-plated delivery bike. It was the last thing they ever expected to encounter in their own jurisdiction.

They stood there, trembling, incredulous. The river rats stared back. For one minute it was quiet enough to hear the weather-vane shifting on its rod back up at the house. The half-devoured turkey remained on its side. Smoke went up from the barrel. No one said a word.

Then it broke. To every side they dove into the corn at once. Dirt flew up. The barrel was kicked over. They panned out and away from the clearing, smashing through the stalks at a wild charge. The deputies took off after them. The whole field came alive like a Theakston fox hunt – stalks uprooting, ankles twisting, deputies cursing, bodies falling. Somewhere in the mess Deputy Biggs managed to hook one of them by the collar. Elsewhere, the sheriff dove-tackled an elder. But the rest got away by a long shot. They had vanished within thirty seconds. Tom Dippold and his men were left alone with their grease-splattered captives, feeling sick and itching all over. One of the deputies vomited. The rest just stared into the dirt muttering *god damn, God Damn, GOD DAMN!* over and over.

The first thing they did on arriving back at the department was strip, hose and delouse the prisoners. They didn't bother reading them their rights. They couldn't have booked them anyway. Neither had any form of identification on his person. They were both completely illiterate. The younger of the two could barely speak, and the older one had never even heard of social security. As far as anyone could ascertain, they had no names.

The river rats – or the 'original possum-skinners' illegitimate descent,' as they're more selectively known – live and dwell far out on the heath, away from the rest of civilization as we know it. There are a few known camps in Bolling County, and one or two in Burke, but Pullman Valley is too densely populated for them to risk settlement in our midst. Most camps are buried in the remote outbacks of Appalachia, independent of the rest of the nation in almost every sense. They are beyond what is commonly considered poverty-ridden; most of them live with no money whatsoever. Many have never laid eyes on a dollar bill in their lives. They're wholly self-sufficient. They settle in ruined trailers and deserted lumber sheds in the wilderness. They eat catfish and wild onions. They do not attend schools. They don't stray into towns. Area hospitals generally won't admit them – when one takes ill he either perishes or recovers of his own constitution. To the best of anyone's knowledge they're not on file anywhere. They're not taxed, they're not called up for drafts, they don't vote, and they're completely ineligible for financial assistance of any kind. Their existence as a group is almost universally undocumented.

But despite their invariable reclusiveness, citizens in towns like Baker *do* know they're out there. Throughout the years they've been spotted frequently enough to confirm their continued existence, yet seldomly enough to lend them that ghoulish, otherworldly aura. In addition to theories that they've progressively bred themselves out of and away from the rest of the species and can no longer be regarded as human at all, it's also maintained that they murder and devour wayfaring travelers, that they rape common livestock, that they brand their young with red-hot wires, and that they're crop thieves indisputable, every last one. They are the *boogie man* in places like Greene County, only, unlike other homespun absurdities they actually *exist* in the flesh, and, as such, strike fear into full-grown adults as well as unruly children. Sheriff Dippold knew that for a fact. He was well aware that if word got out that even two river rats were being held for questioning in his department building, much less that a whole company of them had been found convening this side of the valley walls, Baker might very well lose what precious little remained of its dwindling grip. He realized the importance of keeping the news of their confinement under wraps; to add to everything else it seemed he'd now become the minister of propaganda as well. He was more than half tempted to drive the suspects in custody out to the farthest reach of the valley for a quick round of Oklahoma justice. It might have been better for all concerned, he thought. But at the same time he was convinced it had been the river rats who had broken in to Sodderbrook the night before, that they had somehow gotten word, through whatever aberrant subterranean network, that the plant had been closed and that the storage house was standing unguarded, stuffed to the gills with thousands of plump, ripe birds for the taking. He wasn't about to act on anything without first interrogating the prisoners. Then maybe, he reasoned, with a solid confession to back him up, the rest could be dealt with in kind. Those were his intentions.

But for all his reasoning, that's not how it worked out. What the sheriff failed to take into consideration, for plausible reasons, was 'The kiss of Cumberland' or, more selectively, 'Bog womp justice' – the river rat code of retribution. Tom Dippold had never heard of any such thing. Just the idea of it would have struck him as ridiculous. Never in a thousand years would he have suspected that the group he and his deputies had stumbled on that afternoon might've actually had the audacity to creep back into town and raise hell in response to the incarceration of its brethren. The idea would've seemed obscenely far-fetched through and through. The sheriff was much more concerned with the prospect of Bill Tulk or one of his deputies leaking word to the press and making public the coverup he was so earnestly attempting to maintain. His concern lay with internal security, nothing more. Again, a grave miscalculation.

At twelve thirty that night three separate trash heaps on West 5th St. were set ablaze simultaneously. The correspondence crew for Pottville 6, which was by then lodged in a southside motor inn on a semi-permanent basis, rushed to the scene just in time to catch several area fireman extinguishing each blaze with portable foam dispensers. A group of alarmed locals was standing by, gagging from the stench of burning plastic and pesticide fumes. The event made for five or ten minutes' worth of solid footage, complete with scathing testimony from bloodshot, infuriated locals. No one knew who had started the fires. No one knew much of anything, only that, as the firemen stated, some kind of lighter fluid had been used, and therefore, it had to be assumed, each blaze had been set intentionally. With that, the main correspondent wrapped up the report with a closing statement. Then the whole crew packed up to head back to the hotel room, where the editing equipment was lying in wait. But they didn't get that far. Twenty-five minutes after the first rash of fires was extinguished, seven more went up on 11th St. Again the news crew rushed to the scene, again the fires were hosed down, and again no one knew anything. Plenty of accusations were made –

one resident was willing to wager the fires had been set by Pottville sports fans administering their customary round of pre-playoff vandalism. Someone else was sure certain members of the area's Latino community were behind it all. One bystander even suggested that Jeffrey Kuntsler had been out on the prowl with a can of gasoline and a book of matches ... Everyone had definite, purportedly well-founded suspicions he was willing to state on record. But when it came down to it, no one had actually seen anything. Whoever was running loose with the flint kit – he, she, them or it – had thus far gone undetected by a dozen squad cars out on patrol, two or three hundred self-appointed watchmen, one roving press crew, and a growing crowd of borderline-homicidal locals – all within one five square mile perimeter. And it got worse: every time one series of fires was extinguished, another would go up a few streets over. The crowd would swoon, the firemen would grumble, and everyone would proceed to the next point of infraction at an erratic canter. It went on like that all night.

It wasn't until after four that they finally let up. With one hour of darkness left before sunrise, the arsonists, whoever they may have been, at last appeared to have gone on their way. The streets slowly quieted down. The crowd ambled home. The Pottville 6 crew packed up their equipment for good – they had fared better than anyone that evening: with twelve hours remaining to compile and edit a four minute report from over two hours worth of prime footage, their work was already cut out for them. They were elated. On rolling away from the smoldering remains of the last fire, they all agreed the night could not possibly have gone any better ...

But halfway down the road to the hotel, as though not already furnished with enough material to keep the networks tied up for the coming week, they were graced with a scenario that would later put their already formidable report in the running for national correspondence awards. To this day it remains nearly incomprehensible that the only individuals to catch sight of the river rats that night *just happened* to be the members of a press crew, who *just happened* to have had operating cameras on hand at the moment. It hardly seems likely ... However, it's generally regarded as even more unlikely that any existing makeup crew this side of Flint, Michigan could have spontaneously rigged a theatrical troupe into so closely resembling a pack of Appalachian inbreds in mid-flight, as was recorded.

Whatever the case, their full report ran as such:

On turning the corner of 9th and Bigler at an estimated 20 m.p.h. run, the driver of the Pottville correspondence van saw something shoot out into the road ahead of him. He slammed on the brakes, bringing the vehicle to a halt less than two feet shy of certain impact. Looking up, the crew then found itself face to face with a 'repulsive looking eunuch' of some sort robed in what appeared to be a patchwork of torn feed sacks. The figure remained in place for several moments, frozen stiff and leering in the 200-watt flood of headlights. Then, without warning, it whirled and took off. The crew broke out of its trance and gave chase. A backseat technician managed to get a camera rigged and rolling just in time to catch the figure turning the next corner and joining a group of its presumed accomplices in the shadows of the Pollenderry lumber yard. The driver reared up again. For the next twelve seconds the cameraman rolled a detailed closeup of twelve panicked figures of similar description scrambling over one another in heated retreat. As the clip was later aired in its entirety, the group blew apart to every side, torn hospital shirts, filthy rags and most notably corroded fuel cans trailing behind as they went. The image terminated with the last five or six disappearing into the fog together. Then they were gone. The correspondence crew was left alone in the darkened yard wondering 'what in hell's vestibule' they'd just witnessed.

When word let out that the river rats had come to town, the Baker Lay, as might have been predicted, lost it. Everyone had been snowballing toward complete and total breakdown for weeks already: most locals, having long-since gone on full-time red alert, had proceeded up to and vacillated on the brink of collapse for longer than anyone would've thought possible. Given the circumstances, they really had held up under an enormous strain with uncharacteristic fortitude. Other communities might not have fared as well ... But once it was announced that the river rats, those abominable trackside degenerates, had actually infiltrated and wreaked havoc in our midst, all remaining notions of levelheadedness were forcibly eradicated. From that day forward, Greene County shifted into the equivalent of the Whistlin' Dick's phase three: unrestrained paranoia and belligerence on a grand scale. It was felt to be bad enough that the streets had become a hotbed of insurrection, that fights were breaking out in the marketplace, that long-time and otherwise hospitable neighbors were hurling death threats from porch to porch, that the courts were drowning in their own bureaucrap, that more factories were closing every day, that packs of wetbacks were loitering on the corners, that the police department had grown to be regarded as impotent, that every stoop in town was lined with stiff-collared gun freaks and dying geraniums, that the roads had been devastated beyond functional use, that heaps of toxin-coated refuse were piled up over the parking meters and traffic cones, that the forest was crawling with famished scavengers, and that the press had turned Baker into *the* state honky farm – all those factors were bad enough to start with – but with the realization that, on top of everything else, the dregs of Appalachia themselves had penetrated the inner sanctum and were now conducting a full-on slag torching campaign right out in the open, with that realization intact there was nothing left to hold on to. Thereafter Baker took the plunge.

MEANWHILE, WE WERE going through our pot-pie hell.

It's already been pointed out that we'd been glued to our television sets every night, that we'd hollered and hooed to the Pottville broadcasts and imbibed ourselves cross-eyed with clockwork regularity. Granted that's all true, but it's really only one side of the picture. The rest was a bit more bleak.

To start with, there was the matter of money. Or the pressing lack thereof. Even when gainfully employed, it'd always been a task in and of itself making ends meet on our salaries. No trash man has ever carved the court bird at yule. Our careers at the landfill had been an ongoing struggle for the acquisition of the bare necessities, one in which a single day's absence from the rounds might've made the difference between two and three meals a day for an entire week. Hence, any prolonged illnesses had always been the kiss of death. Irwin had once been down with pneumonia for eleven days. He returned to duty twenty pounds lighter and half-stricken with scurvy. He looked like death in a top hat. It was sickening. His cupboards and icebox had stood empty the entire time he was away. Once the remains of his last paycheck had diminished, he'd been left doling out his sacred collection of buffalo nickels at face value to buy Holston's cream of wheat and tomato soup. His whole set had been bartered away at a fraction of its actual worth, all for a small bag of essentials. The rest of us had similar stories. The point being: if eleven days on the mat springs had reduced Irwin to hocking the family relics, it can only be imagined what six weeks without a single paycheck was doing to the rest of us. It wasn't easy. We had started out by pulling our funds and purchasing almost three full shopping carts of budget noodles and Ma Krantz pot pies at three for a dollar. Most of them were stored away in the icebox in Murphy's kitchen, which had become our unofficial group feeding trough. We had already broken into the supply by midway through the second week. Every night Murphy put a huge pot of water on to boil at five. For the next few hours, ten or fifteen of us would straggle in to load up on carbohydrates and wonder bread. At first there was enough red sauce and garlic to go around. Then we were down to vegetable oil and salt. Then just salt. One thing about pasta: it tends to have more long-term palatability than, say, canned sardines or Little Debbie snack cakes, and *most definitely* than pot pies. By the fifth week of the strike those Ma Krantz pot pies had eaten a hole in our gullivers three inches thick. They were inducing involuntary gag reactions all around. We'd effectively poisoned ourselves for life. Even now, after all these years, we're incapable of being at close quarters with *any* Ma Krantz product. Just the smell of those preservatives is enough to make our stomachs lurch. It's much like an Ellis Island refugee's post-voyage, lifelong aversion to salted herring.

The pasta wasn't so bad. We were still managing to feed ourselves after spare change for everyday accoutrements like gasoline, chewing gum and pub draughts had been exhausted. We were acutely conscientious of our daily expenditures. Some of us had lost a few pounds (Dickell) but we had made it thus far without considering giving in.

Other daily impediments were boredom, inactivity, and isolation-induced cabin fever. With our prime directive being to remain far out of the public eye, all of us had no choice but to hole up in our flats and wait, hour after hour, day after excruciatingly endless day. And that meant no alcohol: our beer funds, limited as they were, were reserved entirely for the post-transmission soirees. And even those funds had dwindled. During the afternoons we slept, cleaned house, talked on the phone, smoked cigarettes, and, of course, watched television. We indulged in more early morning game shows and weekday matinees than we would now readily admit. Some of us even got hooked on soap operas. It was *that* bad. There are very few more hopeless spectacles in all of creation than Dennis Stauffer scratching his balls on the La-Z-Boy while wrapped up in *The Days of Our Lives*. It was sick. But we had no choice. We couldn't go out. There was too much gunfire and confusion in the streets. So far we'd pretty well managed to elude the press. The reporters and correspondents had left us alone and, just as planned, stuck with Kuntsler. The old man had more media value anyway, more than the rest of us combined. Somewhere along the way – toward the end of the third week maybe – he had taken to granting lengthy interviews to anyone who came his way. He undoubtedly believed he was doing himself a favor, even stating his claim to the public's approval with all this spread-eagle oratory. He had become the quintessential anti-poet, the 'high priest of public damnation,' the 'blatherskite of cock and bull,' the 'arbiter elegantiae of bilge.' He actually looked to be enjoying himself somehow. Which was understandable in a sense: twenty-five years of well-rehearsed roll call and the resulting compendium of pedagoguery had elevated him to an almost Coughlinesqe stature. And now he had a fresh audience – with thousands of viewers who had never had a taste of his whip looking on, he was basking in the moment as his own *magnum opus*. He was unleashing the same old shopworn Kauderwelsh, failed thunderbolts and choice billingsgate culled from the witch hunt which had grown stale, ineffective and tiresome to the rest of us years earlier – everything from *I wouldn't piss on you if you were goin' up in flames*, to *Twelve dead wetbacks ain't nuthin' but a good start* . . . No one in town was spared his high-flown indictments. Again, the mayor was this, the City Hall staff was that, the rest were a bunch of pathetic so and sos . . . And the public was eating it up, though not quite as the old man intended. Well before the river rats made their first appearance, Kuntsler had become public enemy number one all across the board. He had type-cast himself as the Antichrist. No one ever leapt to his defense. Some locals even began to confess that if they had to work under that, they would've been striking too. *Christ, he was disgusting* . . .Which, of course, didn't hurt us one bit, though it did re-emphasize the necessity of our keeping quiet. That meant continued isolation, more neverending hours behind doors. More maddening inactivity. It was only at just after dawn (the night hours having become too dangerous to risk public exposure) that we were able to venture out of doors at all. When we did, we would comb the streets, poring over the carnage like proud fathers. The generated mess really was unbelievable. It surpassed even our expectations. In little more than a month and a half Baker had metamorphosed into a teeming cess pit that made the landfill itself look like a courtyard on the Riviera. It was as though the community drain had been plugged abruptly, and all the undiluted excess had come cascading over the rim in ceaseless, putrefactive waves. It served as an effective reminder of what lurked behind the backdrop at any given juncture: what went in, came out, and what came out, when left unattended, went nowhere. To every side it sat accumulating, settling under its own weight, pitching over in scattered clumps. It stretched over porch stoops, lined doormats and staircases, littered gravel drives and public walkways, always shifting with the continual burrowing of unseen scavengers. Porcelain swans and bathtub virgins were tarnished with mustard and cooking oil. Flower gardens and cactus beds were littered with old rags, fishing line and medicine bottles. Grape vines and walls of wild ivy clung to stained fenceposts, stripped bare and scorched black. Basketball rims and yellowed military flags hung over packed dumpsters, overflowing garbage cans and crumbling styrofoam coolers, into the roads, under parked cars, throughout sewer ducts and curbside pine boxes. We examined everything until the first of the morning rush hour began to roll. Then it was back inside for everyone. The only other time we strayed outside was to creep across town to Murphy's or Bailer's. That was usually at about five. Our nightly gatherings were always the high point of the day, the only relief to be had from the crushing boredom. Without them we very well may not have made it.

The night before we received the first call from City Hall, we threw our biggest bash ever. The date was October 4th. Everyone, including John and Wilbur, had gathered at Murphy's house in time for dinner.

That evening's Pottville broadcast was superb. The programs were getting better every night. By then Channel 6's field operatives were choking their way through live commentary. Locals were being filmed staggering by with handkerchiefs clutched to their faces. A good deal of the first pesticide coating had been buried, meaning the scavengers were beginning to reappear. There was talk of a second extermination. The trash was piled up in long undisturbed ranges. The river-rat clip was run repeatedly. The mayor, the sheriff and various City Hall representatives were being bombarded with indefensible when-did-you-stop-beating-your-wife questions. More fires were breaking out, though apparently these were being set in imitation of the first wave: someone had spotted several adolescents out on the prowl with a blowtorch. The broadcasts would go on like that for almost twenty-five minutes. We would sit around in Murphy's den laughing ourselves hoarse.

That night Bailer made a motion to fly the coop indefinitely – to leave town and let the strike follow through to its natural conclusion. He was beaten with recliner pillows and thrown from the porch, then left outside, banging on the windows and pleading for readmittance. He was granted none. The program continued. Donnecker and Keller soon got into a squabble over a bag of pork rinds. Then Dennis tripped over the coffee table on the way to the kitchen. A minute later Irwin spilt milk on the rug. Everyone was warned to pipe down or face joining Bailer. Everyone piped down, but we couldn't stop laughing.

While all that was going on, several of us couldn't help but notice the way John was standing off to one side, arms folded, shoulders thrown back, the light from the television flickering over his face. He didn't make a sound throughout the entire program, but the look about him said a good deal more. It was as though each transmitted image were gratifying him more thoroughly and on a deeper level than the rest of us. True, we were enjoying every minute of it. But John was enraptured. He had the look of one who'd just come into a lifelong inheritance. Wilbur claims he was like that every night, that all throughout the strike John was on a rocket-fuel high unlike anything we'd ever seen. He remained captivated from beginning to end. To look at him one could've easily been persuaded that he was not at all intent on resolving our walkout any time soon, that he actually might've agreed, in all seriousness, with Bailer's tongue-in-cheek suggestion to let it drag out for a year or two. He almost seemed in dread of the prospect of a forthcoming resolution. It was disturbing – *inspiring, exhilarating, enticing* all at once, no doubt – but *disturbing* as well.

The broadcast concluded with yet another caustic spiel on the part of Kuntsler, followed by a quote from Ecclesiastes. Then there was a hasty five minute recap of what was going on in the rest of the world – if anyone cared – the 'John Garfield Still Dead' coverage of issues like foreign wars, hostage crises, national politics, etc. Then it was over. The television was switched off. We filed out of the den and into the yard, where Bailer was sulking in the grass. The sun was just going down.

The evening's supply of alcohol – for lack of a better term – was provided by Curtis. There was no beer to go around. We were out of money. Curtis, having known that for over a week, had been talking up his fabled home-brew-in-preparation: a truly vile concoction of apricot rinds, orange peels and nectarines which had been fermenting in a makeshift still of plastic bags and coat hangers. It was absolute rotgut. Moonshine. A hundred per cent flammable. It was the most rancid swill we'd ever tasted, more like a cross between paint thinner and cow manure than anything. Curtis claimed five shots could blind a grown steer to the walking stick. It wasn't really alcohol. It was a drug. One didn't get drunk – one got whacked. We drank it anyway. The effects were instantaneous. Within thirty minutes, horseshoe tosses were straying fifteen feet from the mark. After an hour we were slurring uncontrollably. Murphy recalls feeling as though all five senses had been thrown into a vegetable blender. It was much like the sound emitted from a length of sheet metal – a constant *wahwahwahwahwah* that left his depth perception scrambled and his head on the brink of implosion.

No one remembers many details from that evening. Somewhere along the way there was a fight, though no one's exactly sure why or between whom. At another point Lester, Irwin and Dickell were apparently seized with the undeniable urge to streak, and ended up tearing around the yard, buck naked and screaming – even leaping straight through the six foot flames of the bonfire and singeing every hair on their bodies. They were rounded up and forcibly re-dressed. And one other thing – halfway through the night Dennis was caught sneaking into Curtis's swill with a paper cup. Several of us scolded him for breach of the doctor's orders. But he fired back that he hadn't had a drink in almost four years and that we were hardly the doctor's orders in our state. No one had the gall to argue with him. Dennis went on his first drunk in years.

The only detail everyone remembers in full – besides Wilbur's oboe recital – is the pig chase: first, because it was unforgettable by nature, and second, because by way of it John got closer to opening up to us as a group than he ever had or would in all the time we knew him. The whole idea was his to begin with. Thanks to Curtis' home brew he was every bit as obliterated as the rest of us.

As it went, shortly before midnight he apparently hit on an idea. He managed to coerce Bailer into coming with him on a 'mission.' The two of them quietly left Murphy's property, unannounced. Bailer had no idea of what they were doing. They crept through the field to the west and approached a nearby farmhouse by way of the forest's edge. Bailer remembers John getting his leg wrapped up in barbed-wire while climbing the stable-yard fence. It took them a minute to dislodge him, during which time John remained dangling upside down, laughing hysterically. Once he was free he tripped across the yard and disappeared into the stables. For the next minute there was a squealing and rustling from inside. Then he reappeared, hustling a twenty-pound piglet across the stretch at a stumbling trot. He hoisted the animal over the wire to Bailer, then leapt the fence, unhindered this time. They headed back to Murphy's through the woods.

Once on the outskirts of the lot, John disappeared toward the house. Bailer remained behind a wall of overgrown shrubs, restraining the pig and doing his best to keep quiet. He still had no idea of what was going on. Sitting out there in the dark all alone, he began to worry. It seemed to him that our shindig had already gotten a bit too weird, what with all this nudity and tearing about. Things were bizarre as it was, but if this pig was really intended for what he'd begun to suspect . . . He didn't quite know how he was going to break it to John that he didn't go for this sort of thing. And it didn't help any when John finally reappeared with a tub of vaseline he'd retrieved from the shower closet in Murphy's basement. Bailer froze up. He wanted to protest, but before he could do so John had gotten down on his knees and begun smearing the animal down thick, over the nozzle and down to the hoof. Bailer watched for a minute, confused. Then he started to get the picture.

The first thing the rest of us remember hearing was an anguished cry from the woods. We all dropped whatever we were doing and stood stock still. It sounded like a wild bitch being raped by a black bear. Wilbur let out a quick 'What the hell . . .?' Then the pig came shooting out of the bushes. It veered into the yard, lighting up in a translucent pink glow from the firelight. It stopped, looked around, turned a confused circle, then started scrambling for a way out. We took off after it.

The next five minutes are a blur. Picture twenty-one annihilated hill scrubs bowling over one another in hot pursuit of a terrified, petroleum-lubed swine. Four months earlier we'd been drowning our perennial sorrows with nothing but the same long, deleterious road stretched out before us indefinitely. Now, here we were, one season later, ripped to a tee on the community soap box, unemployed, drunk on lighter fluid, the subjects of heated public dispute, stumbling through an untended lot on the heels of a stolen pig. There were a few choice events that justified the strike on aesthetic grounds alone. This was one of them. Before it was over, Burke had a sprained wrist, Dennis had come within a foot of falling into the fire, and the pig had gone into hyperventilatory convulsions from sheer terror. It was Clayton who finally caught it. The pig was fumbled into the mulch by Irwin and Dickell, and it inadvertently rushed straight into the arms of Clayton on the uptake. Clayton technically won the chase, but he never heard the end of it, particularly from Dickell. As a prize he was awarded six frozen pot pies and a nickel-plated carving knife. He threw the pies into the fire, but kept the knife.

*

No one made it home that night. There was no reason to leave, and driving was out of the question. We remained seated around the fire finishing off Curtis's brew and dropping off like flies. Murphy, Wilbur, Donnecker and John played a long round of poker in the dirt, then passed out with the rest of us some time around five. Murphy remembers being the last one awake. Lying on his back in the grass, he hadn't been able to make the big dipper stop spinning overhead. On sitting up to clear his head, he had taken a slow look around and had been overcome by a strange feeling of tranquility. The yard had been littered with paper cups and trash. The fire had died down to a glowing bed of embers. The rest of us had been snoring, beached around the pit with our tongues lolling out. He had had the feeling that no matter what might've come from there on out, be it hard times, starvation, total failure, imprisonment, whatever, that though we might've awakened the next morning smeared in dirt and vaseline, covered with insect bites, sick to the floor with crushing hangovers, that we might've stumbled home to hole up in our shacks for another round of cabin fever all over again – that no matter what came to pass in the coming days and years – that night had been something no one would ever be able to take away from us. It was ours now. We would carry it with us for the rest of our lives. And though no outside party would ever understand its intrinsic worth, it wouldn't matter. We would understand. We would know. We had been there. We had seen. That was all the proof we would ever need.

WILBUR RECEIVED THE FIRST CALL from City Hall in the middle of the next afternoon. Actually, as the secretary with whom he spoke insisted, she'd been calling all morning – not just Wilbur but every name on the list. None of us had picked up our lines in all that time. She'd begun to wonder. She'd gotten worried; something had seemed drastically out of place – *where had we been?* She was in a terrible state. Wilbur was caught off guard by the overabundance of matronly concern. He could hear the receiver grinding along her jawline on the other end. He pictured a frail, trembling tussle-wench seated at a mahogany desk being borne down on by an office full of stiff-collared lunatics. It did nothing to ease the pounding in his head. He straightened up and told her to state her case.

Apparently, she said, the city council had drawn up a settlement pitch of some sort, an offer we'd 'definitely be interested in.' A meeting had been called to session that afternoon to finalize the proposal. Our representatives were to join the assembly in the west wing of the main building at 4:30 sharp, at which point we would be briefed in full. Until then no further details could be provided; the secretary was not at liberty to elaborate. Could we be counted on to attend? Wilbur told her we'd be there, but on one very important condition: there was to be no press on hand. *No press.* If any of us caught sight of so much as one reporter, the lecture hall would stand empty. Was he understood? He was. He hung up.

John was downstairs in the shower closet. Wilbur pushed by the stack of tires in the hallway, then pounded on the door. A gurgle sounded out from beneath the running water on the other side.

Wilbur yelled in to pull it together – they had an appointment to attend. There was a pause. The water stopped. John's matted head came poking out from behind the door. *Say what?* Wilbur repeated himself, saying he had no details.

John considered for a minute. He ran his gaze along the cracked walls, with his shoulder pinned to the door jamb and matted head dripping water over the dirt-stained hall mat below. Then he snapped to. He told Wilbur to go back upstairs, to get on the horn with Murphy, find them a pair of sports coats from the closet, and mix up a cauldron of Alka Seltzer. He would be up directly.

Murphy was there in less than an hour, dressed in an old blue tuxedo that had never been worn. John and Wilbur were similarly bedecked for the occasion – coats and ties, hair combed back, the works. It was something to see – something we'd *never* seen. Three ditch diggers geared to walk the plank in the guise of dignitaries. Their garb was actually more of a cynical gesture than anything, partly due to the fact that no matter how well dressed they may have been, nothing could've kept the hill scrub from seeping through the cracks, and also because, despite the fact that this was the moment they'd been waiting for, they had serious doubts as to the validity of the council's alleged proposal. Granted, it wasn't at all surprising that the appropriate officials had moved to contact our group so soon: the strike had reached full pitch, the community was in serious trouble. It only made sense that a drive for resolution would have long since gotten underway. No mystery there. But still, the idea of an acceptable proposal having been arrived at in full seemed decidedly improbable. John couldn't help but feel someone had jumped the gun, that this offer, whatever it might have been, was unlikely to amount to anything more than rhetoric. They were prepared for a wasted afternoon.

At twenty past four they headed out.

The 'meeting' – or so it was called – lasted less than five minutes, the first three of which John, Murphy and Wilbur spent trying to locate the west wing doors (the building ran from north to south). They were in the process of routing through the courtyard when a pale, bent looking man in an oversized suit tapped on the first-story window frame from inside, motioning them toward a pair of double doors they had already tried and found locked. They walked back over and were escorted into the building by yet another secretary. They were led through a green-carpeted hallway toward a secondary assembly room. Once inside they were shown to their seats, three of six identical oak chairs situated at one end of a long steel banquet table. On the far end of the room seven uniformly heavyset city officials were seated under an electric fan, looking grim and unamused. The walls around them were lined with portraits of dead white men; preceding generations of district court judges and five or six group department photos. Over the main fireplace, a twelve point buck. Along the floor, an imitation Persian rug. The whole room smelled like a cedar-framed burial casket.

There was a quick round of introductions. Each of the seven council men announced his name and rank in a hurried, none-too-friendly tone, after which they all leaned forward and demanded to know exactly with whom they were speaking. The secretary made a note: Altemeyer, Kaltenbrunner, Murphy. Formalities complete. Moving on . . .

The eldest of the council men, a silver-haired Robert Mitchum look-alike, went into dictating a round of preliminary Choctaw straight out of the book of Mormons. He was seated third to the right at a fly rod's toss from Murphy. Whatever it was he was saying was drowned out in the expanse of the chamber. The room had originally been designed to accommodate for unamplified discourse and debate in the early half of the nineteenth century. In those years the halls and interior might've been filled to capacity, but two feuding orators on elevated platforms still had the advantage of the natural acoustics to sustain their exchange. Their voices projected over the crowd and ricocheted from wall to wall like a trapped canary. It served its purpose under those conditions. But in other situations, as in the case of the current meeting – a private, more low-key affair by definition – a single voice was very easily rendered unintelligible, garbled into a sustained wall of noise that sounded to be reverberating from the lip of a sewer tunnel. John, Murphy and Wilbur couldn't understand a single word that was being said. They were about to announce as much when the secretary moved forward to present them with a copy of the 'formalized proposal.' Robert Mitchum kept talking. John took the paper in hand. Murphy and Wilbur peered over his shoulder from either side. All three read the paper at a glance. They flipped it over. The back was blank. Nothing. Just as they'd suspected. They stood up and made for the door simultaneously. Robert Mitchum seized up. The room went quiet. There was only the sound of the doorknob unlatching as Wilbur turned it. Then the council exploded. *What was the meaning of this*, one of the voices demanded. *Just what did they think they were doing?* Wilbur walked out. The secretary started forward. Murphy walked out. Robert Mitchum came speeding along the length of the table in an attempt to bar the door. He grabbed John by the collar. John tore himself free. He turned back toward the council and stated that the next time they called us in for a proposal, they would do best by everyone to have a general game plan in mind. They knew our demands. They had all the time in the world to get it right. He turned and walked out.

That should have been the end of it. Had all gone accordingly, it would have been back to the drawing board for everyone. The council would've carried on deliberating beneath mounting public pressure, we would've returned to our homes, Kuntsler would've continued anathematizing himself into the deepest pit of the public mortuary, and the polarization of community senti-ments would have distilled to the appropriate essence required for a unilateral settlement. That had been the original idea, and that had been the way it had proceeded up till now. Had it continued on course, the strike might have been over and done with in another week. A tangible end had already loomed into view. Relatively speaking, Baker was almost there.

But that's when the city council botched everything with a grievous blunder still regarded as the most inept mismanagement of authority on anyone's part throughout the entire crisis. At the conclusion of our 'meeting' that afternoon, had Robert Mitchum and Co. paused to reflect on the precarious nature of the situation, they would have undoubtedly kept their mouths shut. They would have gone back to whatever it was they had or had not been doing over the previous weeks. They would have done several things, but filing a report with the *County Herald* would not have been one of them. Under no circumstance would they have contacted the press. Their logic in doing so eludes us to this day. We have no idea what they could've been thinking, what they possibly expected to report. Maybe they were set on publicizing the notion that they'd initiated the first coordinated push for resolution, that they were doing their best under the existing circumstances but that the striking party was being notedly uncooperative; that they had come up with a comprehensive settlement pitch, but had been spurned by the scrubs. All these attempts to save face would've been annihilated under the most rudimentary inquiry, reducing the council's decision to alert the *Herald* to an act of either reckless stupidity, or deliberate masochism. Or both. Either way, a tangible motive was sorely lacking. It made no sense at all.

As for their 'comprehensive settlement pitch,' their 'coordinated efforts:' their proposal had been the joke with no punch line. It had failed to address or even acknowledge our most fundamental demands. Of which there were three: 1) the unconditional removal of Jeffrey Kuntsler, 2) a ten percent increase in maintenance funding, and 3) a complete and total overhaul of the existing health insurance policy. The council's offer had made no mention of any of these issues. Kuntsler's name hadn't even appeared on the paper. The whole thing had been an ill-conceived list of empty commitments and half-assurances that our case would be looked into pending our immediate return to duty. It could have been drawn up by a group of uninformed school children. It was an insult at best, unworthy of the paper it was printed on. By presenting it to us, the council was declaring itself even further behind in the game than we had suspected, and our estimation of its ability had been low to start with. The same conclusion would have been apparent to the public as well, even the Baker Lay. Had the *Herald* printed our original demands side-by-side with the council's proposal, the results would have been irreversibly damning to the City Hall's already battered reputation. It was certainly nothing to which any group in its right mind would ever opt to lay claim publicly. They had no case, and it was blindingly evident.

Nevertheless, go to the press they did, and through unforeseen circumstances actually *were* spared the brunt of the backlash. This would be our first major setback in the course of the strike, the point at which the bulk of the power was unexpectedly wrested from the relatively safe court of our control and pitched headlong to the mob. It would effectively take a good deal of public pressure off of Kuntsler, bring us into the picture as active, well-defined participants, and dispel the community's previously indivisible assessment of the situation. Just as John predicted, the moment we got involved, things fell apart.

As it worked out, the *Greene County Herald's* staff, on receiving the report from the city council that evening, first decided to consult the public access files for additional information on the given members of the striking party: Altemeyer, Murphy, Kaltenbrunner. Drawing up each dossier, they set to work in search of any additional details that might beef up the article. Wilbur's record was relatively clean – one drunk and disorderly, three unpaid parking fines, and one property dispute of unspecified nature. No real media value there. Moving right along, Dale Murphy was another matter: one conviction for third degree murder resulting in a two and a half year prison term, followed by another short term for skipping parole. That was good. That was very good. Something could be done with that. Then they moved on to John. The moment they opened up the Kaltenbrunner file it was all over.

The *Herald* hit the stands the next morning:

> ### KALTENBRUNNER SAYS NO
> it read.

> ### KALTENBRUNNER SAYS NO
> #### CONVICTED FELON OPTS TO CONTINUE STRIKE, REFUSES SETTLEMENT

All across town the edition hit doorsteps, supermarkets, company lounges and office quarters. Seven fifteen and hot off the press:

KALTENBRUNNER SAYS NO

The *Herald* staff had been up all night, setting and resetting the type to perfection. An additional 1,500 copies had been run to compensate for projected demand. The presses had been left in place in the event of having to run additional printings. For the second time that week, the *Herald* had an expected record-breaker on its hands, only now, unlike the river-rat coverage, they had beaten Pottville 6 to the draw. They had snared the lead themselves. They had access to a more immediate and complete information base on the matter. The whole story was more fit for print than transmission, and for the first time in the head-on media war, the *Greene County Herald* felt itself pulling ahead in the race.

The article made next to no mention of the council's settlement pitch, or the refusal thereof. The emphasis lay instead on announcing, in the most grisly, panic-inducing manner possible, that a chapter of Baker lore thought long dead had come back to haunt the community; that the main perpetrator in the infamous north end holdout of five years past – that psychotic farm boy in rags who'd open fired on police only to be gassed from his wreck and hauled off in the paddywagon – that emaciated chicken rancher with the beat-up face who'd supposedly been admitted to a ward in the capitol and had never been heard from again – that one, everyone in town remembered him – had not only returned to Baker almost two years earlier, but had been living in our midst ever since, and was now personally spearheading the disaster plaguing the valley.

KALTENBRUNNER SAYS NO

Kaltenbrunner? Kaltenbrunner who? That was bound to be the first question on everyone's mind. In anticipation of the confusion, a complete rundown on John's known history had been provided in detail. They printed everything – the Bait Shack/Troll collision, the assault of a hospital-employed cleaning maid, the premature expulsion from Baker High, the desecration of his homestead, the firing upon of a Methodistmobile, holding his own mother *hostage* at gunpoint, blowing out the windshield of a state patrol car, the subsequent incarceration and work release sentence, everything. The *Herald* staff had arranged the layout accordingly. Two thirds of the front page was plastered with the police file mug shot of John in custody – the one taken immediately following the holdout – our beloved goatboy as a fifteen-year-old basket case leering straight into the camera with delirious, jilted eyes. No journalistic sensationalism was required to generate the impression that this was a certifiable lunatic.

It was terrible.

Word was out within a matter of hours. By noon there wasn't a soul around who hadn't heard about it. Everyone was shocked and revolted. Of course the locals remembered that holdout. It was legendary by then. At the time of its occurrence it had caused the biggest stir to be felt in Greene County for years. Every barber shop and public tavern had been alive with the word, every town crier bowled over and extrapolating. That same shot had been printed in the same publication for the same general audience. No one had forgotten about it. It had become a cornerstone of local lore.

But at the same time, it was also considered over and done with by then. Very few specifics in regards to the incident had been ascertained in the first place, and the few subsequent follow-ups had yielded nothing concrete. The last anyone had heard, that kid, whoever he was, had been locked away in a state dungeon, never to be heard from again. Case closed. Until now, Wilbur Altemeyer had been the only individual in town, besides the graduate, aware that that forgotten farmhand had ever been released, much less that he had returned to town and that, in fact, he and John Kaltenbrunner were one and the same. No one suspected as much. The *Herald*'s decision to run the article spelt out serious confusion and trouble for everyone. The strike, which had come to be regarded as a clear-cut, black and white matter of *Us vs. Them*, Kuntsler vs. Baker, Baker vs. Scavenger, Industry vs. Regulator, etc. now slid into an indefinable grey zone in which no party could possibly get its bearings. John had prepared us for our own role in the walkout in similar terms by pointing out that the average local's sense of identity was defined through being pitted in rigid opposition to other, altogether outside forces. *Us vs. Them*, he called it. As a rule, two residents on 3rd St. usually had no reason *not* to loathe one another, except when conspiring against someone or everyone on 1st. All of 1st St. felt much the same in return, except when regarding residents on the other side of Main. The other side of Main, in turn, abhorred all that was not the other side of Main, unless and until the conversation took a turn toward Pottville, in which case all of Baker was at once reconciled and reunified in the face of the common enemy. Following that pattern through to its natural conclusion (region to region, state to state, nation to nation) would ultimately culminate in a *War of the Worlds* type scenario, which is probably the only way the Baker Lay ever could've been coerced into fighting alongside of the Japanese. From the neighbor's goat in your garden to the mother ship descending on the league of nations, it was *Us vs. Them* to the bitter end.

But now, with the *Herald*'s October 6th studhorse screamer, that was all about to change; now, in place of the manichean standoff – the Kuntsler vs. Baker – there was only the good, the bad, the ugly, the lesser of five evils, and the absolute worst. This multi-polarization of community sentiments was sure to delay, even cast serious doubts over the heretofore presumably inevitable outcome of the strike, i.e. certain victory on our end. Among other things, the KALTENBRUNNER SAYS NO edition would lend credibility to Kuntsler's previously dismissed assertions that his ex-employees were a group of leathernecked ruffians. A good deal of public pressure would thereby be eased off of the old man and redirected toward us. With the official announcement that John Kaltenbrunner, our alleged leader, was a militant goat roper and confirmed psychopath, the overall picture in Greene County was muddled beyond anyone's comprehension. No one knew what to think anymore. Whom to praise and whom to blame? River rats, Kuntsler, wetbacks, city officials, wild dogs, deputies, and now hill scrubs. The only way it could have been any more confusing for the community is if one hundred and fifty switch-hitting urban liberal vegetarians had come tooling into town on hot pink scooters. The only way it could have been any worse for us is if Dennis had been sent to the council meeting in Wilbur's place. That would have made for the all-time winning combination: one psycho, one convicted murderer, and one junky.

The ox was in the ditch but good.

As for us, beyond the evident shift in leverage and all it entailed for our cause, the actual unveiling of John's identity may have caught us slightly off guard, but it can't be said we were all that surprised. We'd always thought there was something paranormal about him anyway. That would appear to go without saying. Everyone in the landfill had a story. Everyone in the landfill *had* to have had a story. Otherwise he wouldn't have been there. That's a given. However, to anyone on the outside world, John might have appeared to fall into the same category as the rest of us – a living wreck, a castoff, an expendable, a degenerate. But right from the beginning we'd intuitively known otherwise. From his first night on the rounds it had been evident, as it would've been to anyone with a trained eye for these things, that John's particular case wasn't quite that simple. There was something more to him than run-of-the-mill desperation. If nothing else, years of hands-on experience tends to enable the common scrub and like untouchables to cue in on varying degrees of mileage and hardship in select individuals. There's a certain manner in which a grown man pitches a can of slag into an operating compactor, a certain rage or resignation in his bearing as he does so, that provides indispensable first hand insight into his character. Wilbur once claimed he could tell how many failed marriages a new addition to the crew had been through just by the way he handled his bags on the first round. It's not always that simple, but in essence, that's the way it works. In John's case it had been overwhelmingly evident right from the start. No one could've guessed the full extent of what he'd been through, but judging by his performance and the air around him, there was little doubt it had been a long, strange ride. That had been our first impression, and now, with the

Herald laid out before us, our suspicions were confirmed in graphic, chronological detail. The mystery was unraveled. The ideal had finally been given form. For the first time since we'd met him we were one hundred percent convinced he was royalty.

But John didn't take it so well. As far as he was concerned, the KALTENBRUNNER SAYS NO edition was an irremediable disaster. Its publication sent him on his third and final quarter trashing rampage, from which not one article of furniture in his flat survived.

It was sometime before noon – Wilbur had just pulled himself out of bed – when the crashing started. The floorboards and walls of the apartment building were paper thin as it was – any time one's neighbor so much as coughed, one could hear the phlegm coming up. The downstairs neighbor flushing a toilet made the overhead lamps sway. Everyday footsteps shook the walls. Wilbur could even cue in on late night troll disputes from two floors up. The audibility had made for occasional interesting listening over the years, particularly when the newlyweds from Pottville had moved into the room downstairs for an extended plaster-pounding sabbatical. It had been advantageous at times, but with John's erratic sleep habits and his tendency to let fly with cooking ware in times of distress, Wilbur had lost more than one night's sleep over the past two years. Fortunately, he was awake when the clamor started up that morning, and so was able to throw on his bathrobe and rush downstairs without delay. He kicked open the door in time to catch the tail end of a desk lamp in mid-flight toward the corner sink basin. The lamp exploded on impact, sending the torn remains of the Japanese block-print felt shade falling to the floor with the shattered porcelain. Wilbur was barely able to get a grip on the situation before John turned and went for the desk, grunting like a wild animal. Wilbur rushed to intervene, having no idea what was going on. For the next several moments they grappled over the table top like two prairie dogs for a cow pie. Wilbur tried to assuage him, saying hold on, hold on, cool down now, what's the problem? But John didn't want to listen. He didn't seem to be altogether there. He looked as though he'd seen a ghost. Wilbur finally coerced him into having a seat and spitting it out. John slammed his back to the wall and slid down on his haunches, chest heaving. What had gotten into him, Wilbur asked. John made a horrified gesture toward a newspaper on the floor. Wilbur walked over and picked it up. He sat down on a chair. He read the article.

When he'd finished, he folded the paper, leaned back and let out a long sigh. They both sat there without speaking.

Outside the sun was beating down on the streets. A group of wetbacks had congregated and begun to drink on a porch stoop beyond the filling station. They were kicked back in lawn chairs, olive-skinned beer guts protruding over their belt lines. A portable radio had been propped up in the window, filling the street with a muffled short-wave transmission from Pakistan. Five or six of their young were playing in the trash. The rest were languishing in the sun with big, toothless grins. Wilbur could see them from the window. They seemed to be enjoying themselves out there, unlike the rest of the community. There was an air of leisure about them, something that said all was well in spite of the mess. Wilbur turned away. He brought his gaze back to John's overturned living quarters. He looked around through the room. The landlord, that old gum-diseased ratchet packer from Dale, would surely have a conniption if and when John ever decided to move on from his flat. The room had been in bad shape originally, but now, after all this time, it was wrecked beyond recall. Every wall had one or several gaping holes in it, some from chairs and crutches, some from clenched fists, two or three from repeated head butts. The ceilings and floor were no better. The kitchen stove was busted. There were roaches everywhere. The sink was piled high with every dish in the cupboard, some of them caked with almost an inch of burned grease, others full of billowing mold. Red sauce was splattered and crusted over the cracked tiles. The closet door had been ripped from its hinges. The toilet had never been repaired from the blow it had been dealt four months earlier. Since then John had been using the port-o-let at the filling station every time nature called – that, or, in the case of fluids alone, one of the many empty quart-sized malt liquor bottles littering the room. Every surface in the flat was lined with them. They were set up and knocked over in long rows. Their contents had begun to change color and congeal in large globules, like cooling margarine. The floorboards had been saturated and resaturated over the months. The whole room stank like a public urinal. With one look around Wilbur couldn't help but feel John had successfully transformed the face of an entire community into an extension of his own slovenly housekeeping practices.

After a while they began to discuss the situation. John was almost in tears. Twenty-four hours earlier, everything had been right on track. The council had beckoned, and he'd been preparing our response. No one in town had known anything about us, and that had been for the better. All had been going according to plan. Yet now, one day later, there it was in print: not only an end to our anonymity, but a shameless, mass-exposure of his own personal history, one which he'd always done his best to conceal, and one which the Baker Lay, even if properly informed, *never ever ever* would've been able to understand. He felt as though there ought to have been a law against such misrepresentation. He was angry with himself for having provided the council with their names. He claimed he should have known better. He claimed he shouldn't have attended the meeting at all. He was babbling, vacillating between self-disgust and guilt. Somewhere along the way he tried to explain that there were certain details from that holdout that he'd never shared with Wilbur, details that were no one's business and which were hard enough to live with by himself, much less to see a local tabloid ride the ass to market over. The reality of that situation had been a thousand times worse than the papers ever could've made it out to be, he said. The pressure would have killed most of these clodhoppers now gawking at the front page. Sure, he knew that, but it wasn't easy being the only one. It was unforgivably insulting to have to sit by and see the whole thing trivialized into palatable sewing circle mush.

Wilbur did everything he could to calm John down. He agreed the situation was bad; the stakes had just been raised right out from under us, and there was no point in denying it. But maybe that wasn't so surprising – we couldn't have expected our wagon to purr like a kitten the whole way through, he said. We'd been remarkably fortunate so far, very possibly *too fortunate*. Considering all that might've gone otherwise, we'd been spoiled by the lack of opposition. Had things gone any better, we'd have been raring to take on the whole state by the close of the season. The important thing now was to keep our heads together. We'd come too far in this mess to lose our cool at the first sign of trouble. John may have been understandably distressed by the public attack on his character, but when he came around, Wilbur was sure he'd agree.

With that, Wilbur straightened up. He told John to sit tight and stay indoors for the afternoon – venturing outside just might seriously endanger his well-being. In the meantime, he was off to pay a visit to the rest of us, who were probably in need of a few explanations. *Not to worry*, he said (Wilbur's trademark remedy for any situation), he *would take care of everything*. He would probably be back in time for dinner. Until then, he recommended John take it easy, try to get some sleep.

He left the room. John remained behind, slumped over on the floor with his back to the wall.

That night, while Wilbur was out dropping in on the rest of us, John came within a hair's breadth of being beaten to death in his own home.

As it went, he spent the afternoon sulking around the apartment, rereading the *Herald*, and listening to the wetbacks fraternize across the street. By nightfall his concentration was shot. He missed the news at six. He could've caught a recap at seven thirty had he wanted to – by then every station in the state was running a nightly special on Baker. But he wanted no part of it. He couldn't have borne to see his own ravaged face light up on the screen, followed by another uninformed rundown on the holdout. It would've been too much. And anyway, the power had been cut again. He had no electricity. He had no choice. He sat there in the dark doing nothing.

It must've been around eight when he heard the trucks pull

333

up to the curb outside. His ceiling lit up with the glow of high-powered headlights. The roar of six-cylinder engines rumbled through the room. The motors and lights were cut simultaneously. It was quiet. He didn't pay the momentary disturbance any mind; it hadn't sounded like anything particularly out of the ordinary, and he wasn't prompted to move to the window to investigate. Even on hearing seven or eight car doors slam and a host of footsteps pattering over the walk, he remained in place, unfazed. It was only when he became vaguely aware of some activity going on outside, voices and movement at the base of the building, that he began to wonder. He got up from the floor and stuck his head out the window to have a look. Down below a haggard pack of sloppy-drunk factory rats were rooting through the mailbox and milling around in the yard. They were geared in torn overalls, crowned in greasy service-station caps, and armed to the teeth with bottles, bricks and broomsticks. There were at least six of them, none of whom he recognized. He'd never seen them before in his life. No sooner had he looked out than one of them let out a yell and pointed to him. The rest looked up. *There he is*, they said, *there's the sonofabitch!* He saw the first brick coming. He dodged back inside just before it hit the window. It smashed through, clipping his shoulder and pitching him backward over the desk. He hit the floor. Busted glass rained down over him. A joint outcry went up in the yard. He rolled over and groped through the room toward the corner as the first wave of trash and cinder chunks came flying through the open window frame. He curled up beneath the sink. Handfuls of refuse, wood blocks and beer bottles continued coming in. A lead pipe exploded through the second window. More glass spread over the floor, more trash followed it through. He dug his back into the sink pipes. A bottle shattered against the wall above him, filling the basin with razor thin shards. Scraps of metal ricocheted through the room. A flower pot came through. Something hit his head. He reached for his jaw and came up with blood. That was it. *Enough.* He crawled out of his corner. A broken bedpost came down on his back. He collapsed and hit the floor. A teapot collided with his skull. An aluminum storage can slammed into the fire escape by the second window. He got back to his knees and made for the kitchen through the fusillade of compost. He regained his footing by the sink. He grabbed two bottles of stale piss from the floor. He took one stifling whiff of each, almost lost consciousness, then crept to the window's edge. He stood there with his back to the frame letting the group in the yard wear itself out for another minute.

At some point the barrage let up. Two or three voices went back and forth through the settling silence. *Shit, Bob . . . You think we kilt 'im?* one asked. The rest grumbled uncertainly. *I dunno*, came the final reply, *Let's find out . . .*

They gathered around the front door to smash the lock.

Just then the troll threw open his dining-room window and hollered at the crew to clear out. He wasn't having any of this, he let them know. They told him to keep his fat troll ass out of it, or he'd be next. *They had a score to settle.* The troll rapped on his sink basin with a wooden bat, saying they'd invoke the wrath if they kept up. The group jammed together around the window, firing back insults and lunging through the open frame. Porch lights flicked on all up and down the street. Someone started yelling from two yards over. Several neighbors ran through the filling station lot.

While no one was looking John peered over the ledge, singled out the biggest member of the group, wound up from dead center overhead, and knuckleballed the first bottle straight downward. It shot past its intended target and exploded on the walk. The whole group was sprayed from boot to face. They screamed. One of them fell over in the grass. The wetbacks went up with a cheer. John leaned all the way out the window and let fly with the second bottle. *Sploosh.* The group broke out of its stupor and stumbled for cover, soaked to the bone and partially blinded.

At that point the conflict became irrevocable. The factory rats took position behind the wall, to the rear of their pickups, down the walk. The wetbacks stomped and shouted on their stoop. The trolls lined up at their window screaming for help. John remained in the open frame until he caught a woodblock square in the face. He staggered back into the kitchen with blood surging from his nose. More trash sailed into the room. The screaming down the street doubled. He pulled himself together, gathered every bottle within reach – the line on the counter, the set on the refrigerator, the bunch on the floor – and lined them all up against the wall where he could reach for them one by one.

What followed was scarcely discernible to the human eye: a whirlwind of flying projectiles, death threats and obscenities, darting back and forth in the street, bottles erupting on the pavement, urine sloshing in the gutter, lacerations and bloodletting, trash cans overturning, garbage and refuse flying in fistfuls and heaps, broken windows, cuts and bruises, mother bashing, steel pipes, overturned recycling bins, strips of rubber tubing, corroded paint cans, etc. Everything short of gunshots. At some point one member of the group tried to scale the drainpipe and release the retracted fire ladder. He was beaten with a two by four and dropped two stories into the rose bushes. John went on to pitch a brick toward one of their pickups. It sailed over the power lines, smashed through the windshield and tore into the interior upholstery.

When he ran out of bottles he ripped the window frame from the panel and hurled it downward. Then he threw what remained of his iron lamp. Then the radio. Then the dishes, the coffee pot, the wok, his secessionist flag, a broken TV, several hubcaps, his chair, all the loot from the rounds, finally the rest of the trash lying around on the floor. At length he found himself empty-handed and backed into a corner. The room was empty. He had nothing left, and the group outside knew it. He could hear them laughing in a sick, wounded pack. They yelled up that they were coming for him. They crowded around the stoop and began ramming the front door. The flimsy red wood buckled and cracked. John looked around the room desperately. He ran into the kitchen. He tore the refrigerator cord from the wall and maneuvered the old general electric to the first window in awkward lurches. He tipped it over and let go. The group down below scattered. The large iron box came falling out of the sky, going end over end with the door wide open, throwing ketchup bottles and tin foil in a wide centrifugal arc. The crash was heard for miles. Every dog in the neighborhood went off its rocker. The wetbacks let out like a football league. The group in the yard looked genuinely terrified for the first time. They stood there, dumbfounded, stupefied, until the sirens started coming from the east. Then they snapped out of it and climbed over the refrigerator back up to the door.

John grabbed his coat and ran out of the room. He stumbled and fell over in the hallway. He regained his footing and bounded up the stairs to the top flight. Wilbur's door was locked. It was a dead end. There was no ladder to the attic, no window, nothing – just one locked utility closet at the end of the hall. He heard the front door on the ground floor finally give, followed by a stampede coming inward. He braced himself and charged for the door. It tore and gave way when he hit, falling inward and lodging on a forty-five degree angle amid the cleaning solvents and mop pails. He was thrown back into the hallway. He groped to his feet. He pried the door from the closet and climbed up on the iron sink inside. It took three direct blows to dislodge the ceiling hatch. When it gave he pulled himself up and threw his legs over the rim to the blacktop gravel roof. He jammed the hatch back into place. He threw a broken burger grill over the top of it, then took off across the roof. He heard several squad cars roar to a halt in front of the building. He didn't stop to look. He leapt from one blacktop to the next, passing high brick chimneys, ventilation pipes, and meter boxes. He kept going until he came to a ledge. He reared up and looked down. Three stories below a line of dumpsters was sitting there, lids wide open. He thought about jumping. He thought better of it. He looked around again. He could hear a small war going on back at the apartment building. His chest was wheezing like a blast furnace.

The sloped escarpment of the church's red-tiled roof was stretched out below him, one alley's breadth and a ten foot drop away. There was some kind of pole protruding from the incline halfway up. He considered it. It wasn't so far off, he decided – a *reasonable* stretch. He set his sights on it. He backed up, took a deep breath and emptied his head, then threw himself forward. He felt his feet leave the roof, the gap yawn up beneath him, the momentary suspension, the pivot in free fall, the beginning of the drop, the acceleration, the roof rising to meet him . . . then *slam*, the jolt tearing through every limb in his body, the rebound, the slip, the tiles scraping over his torso, the slide, the arm going out, the feet kicking over the roof ledge into open air just as his fingers made contact and clamped down on cold metal.

It was an awkward landing – a bit off to one side and bad on the right ankle – but he somehow managed to come out all right on the other end. He found himself sprawled out face down on the tiles, hanging by a weathervane. Sheets of cold sweat ran into his eyes and burned. He tried to catch his breath. He'd absorbed the brunt of the landing with his mid-section. The wind had been knocked out of him. He was fairly sure his left shoulder had been dislocated. His face was bleeding profusely. He knew he was going into shock. He did his best to stop the uncontrollable shaking.

After a minute he managed to inch his way up the roof toward the stony protrusion of the left tower. He made it to the far side, where the roof ended and hung out over the street. From there he could see the squad cars with their flashing lights halfway down the block. All of Geiger was lit up in a phosphorescent storm of red and blue. A large crowd had gathered in the lot of the filling station. The wetbacks were still on their stoop. The whole scene looked like a boarding house fire drill. He wanted to stay and watch it unravel, but he was standing in clear view of everyone and shaking like a leaf at a forty foot drop from the street. He knew he had to remove himself, to get out of sight.

There was a small window with dilapidated wooden shutters situated in the middle of the column behind him. He strained to reach for it. He managed to knock the left flap in. He crawled through to the cramped black interior. He replaced the shutter in its frame, then, with only a momentary wavering beforehand, collapsed into a heap of himself. And there he remained, stretched out on a small landing at the top of a spiral staircase, for the next two hours.

For the first stretch he was conscious only of the need to remain conscious. Somewhere in his mind he knew that succumbing to shock and passing out unattended in that position could lead to a quick end. He forced himself to control his breathing, to keep his eyes open at all costs. It was difficult. He almost nodded off at one point. An expanding blanket of pinpoint static began to engulf his vision, creeping inward from the periphery. He concentrated on preventing the two fields from merging to form an unbroken wall. He managed to do so without blacking out entirely.

After some time his senses started returning, one by one. He was first conscious of the smell of candle wax and mildew all around him. Then he began to feel the pain – his shoulder above all, but also his foot, his jawline, his nose, and eventually the cuts over his whole body. Next came the sound of the diminishing racket down in the street – car doors slamming, the crackle of police radios, random shouts from onlookers. Finally, his vision adjusted to the pale light coming through the cracks in the shutters. By the time he was fully restored to his senses, most of the conflict back at the apartment building had tapered off. The squad cars had been jammed full of his attackers and had rolled away to the precinct, the trolls had managed to maneuver the refrigerator off of their walk and into the street, the crowd had dispersed and gone home, the landlord had been awakened from a deep sleep and was trying to make sense of the police report, a self-appointed clean-up crew was groaning in the yard, wondering where to begin, and the various cuts on John's body had coagulated into hard knots as he sat in the dark realizing once and for all that Baker, after failing to crush him by every roundabout means imaginable, had at last resorted to attempting to murder him in cold blood. And it had failed. He felt flattered and exultant. For the first time in his life he felt he had lived up to Isabelle's primary contention: You cannot kill that which refuses to die.

Three of the four cigarettes in his pocket were soaked. The last one was all right. He dug it from the pack, tore off the filter, and spent five minutes getting the lighter to strike. Once the cigarette was lit he puffed heavily and squared himself away. He braced his feet against the opposite wall, pressed his back into the stone, and gripped his left bicep with the opposite hand.

*

He relocated his shoulder.

He had to suppress the impulse to scream for what felt like hours. He remained on that initial, excruciating plateau – soaked to the crotch with sweat, jaws clenched, eyes upturned, head slamming back against the wall – until the initial pain began to subside and give way to a dull, nauseating ache. He came down out of the delirium in successive waves. It took some time to level out. He knew his pecks and triceps would be bruised to a deeper shade of lavender for the coming weeks, but he took solace in the fact that he wouldn't have to go to the hospital. He told himself that was the most he could ask for.

Once the pain had become remotely tolerable, he decided it was time to leave. He got up. He carefully scaled down the stairwell, running his hand along the damp stone walls all the way to the ground floor. He fumbled through the dark until he found a cold brass knob on a door leading to the sanctuary. He opened it and walked through. It was pitch black inside, but with the cool air against his skin he sensed the enormity of the room all around him. He pushed his way through the dark. He lit his lighter on reaching the first pew. He continued down the aisleway to the rack of votive candles by the pipe organ in the front of the room. He lit the candles, one by one, until the walls and ceiling were revealed in the pale, flickering light. A gigantic mosaic of the resurrection spanned the length of the ceiling, just above the rafters. He stared up and followed it from one wall to the other, then down over the cedar trim, the stained-glass windows, the porcelain statuettes mounted to the wall over every pew, along the felt-lined aisleway and back to the altar.

Situated directly behind the secondary podium, an oblong mass sat draped in white sheets. It looked like a shrouded printing press or cotton gin of some sort. He climbed the stairs and approached it. He drew back the sheet. Underneath he found a red drum kit. It looked drastically out of place sitting there among all the macabrobelia, as though old Tom Devil himself had marched in and left his calling card for the reverend. He looked it over. On the outward face of the 24″ kick drum a message had been printed in gold letters with a radiant sunset and fluttering posterboard doves behind it. He stooped to look it over. 'BROTHER LOVE AND THE OBEDIENTS' it read in a wide arch. 'BROTHER LOVE AND THE OBEDIENTS,' with a subheading: 'HE HAS RISEN.' John paused to reflect. Where had he heard that name? He combed through his memory until something caught. The Obedients? Hadn't that been the gospel quartet who'd raided his hospital room while he'd been strapped up in traction from the docking bay accident? Hadn't they been the nauseo-etherealists who'd prompted him to outbreak with that virulent bile about the creek-side baptism? They had. They were the ones. How could he have forgotten? He stood up and looked around. A cold shudder went through him. For the first moment since he'd hit the roof outside he realized where he was. *He was in the Methodist church.* This was the home of the crone. Coven central. The lair of the beast. He suddenly expected the roof to cave in on him, the rafter beams to crush him to the floor, the pews to topple like dominos, the wooden effigy of the carpenter to climb down from his rack over the pipe organ and finish him off where he lay. He felt sick. He had to get out of there. He turned to leave.

But on the way to the main doors something caught his eye. There was an old wooden chest propped up on a black footstool to the rear of the sanctuary. He paused to look it over. A small laminated donation card was clipped to an open slit in the center of the lid. It was a collection box. He walked over to it. He slowly lifted one end with his right arm. What sounded to be a heaping pile of coins shifted and slid down the incline inside. His eyes lit up. He ripped the chest from the stool. It hit the floor with a crash. He dragged it down the aisleway toward the altar, cutting the carpet to shreds all along the way. He tooled with the lock by candlelight. It wouldn't give. He tried to pry the hinges. He attempted to work the screws loose from the wood, to lay into the sideboards with his boots. Still, nothing. He sat down and glared at the box. The room around him seemed to be watching as he operated; with every passing instant he felt like a vampire being furtherly immersed in holy water. He got up again. He managed to hike the box up on to the main altar. His left arm was useless. He braced himself and squared away. He brought the box crashing down on the steps. The lock gave. A

341

shower of coins and bills sprayed out over the floor. The box tumbled on to its side, tipping the votive rack back toward the drum kit. The candles hit the floor and scattered in every direction. John howled. He got down on all fours and started stuffing handfuls of bills into his pockets, his socks, his underwear. It had to have been months since they'd last emptied out the chest. There were hundreds, thousands of dollars in bills alone – so much green, so much cash money. Coins and bills and Lincolns and Jeffersons, Kennedy, Washington, Grant, the whole cast of characters barring Franklin. Beautiful sweet green bushels. More money than he'd ever seen . . . It was only a portion of what he was owed – he knew that for every fifty-dollar bill tucked into his pocket there had been twelve articles of furniture swept away from the farm. It would've taken two dozen collection boxes that size even to begin squaring up the debt. It was no equal figure payoff by any stretch of the imagination. But it was a start – a start to which he felt well-entitled.

While shifting through the payoff and loading up, he was inundated with memories of those avaricious necrophiles cleaning out his homestead piece by piece. He saw Hortense with her clipboard riding herd over the movers, the crones raiding his icebox and devouring the leghorns, his mother in the corner with her bulbous face turned away from him in scorn. He saw everything in one spiraling flash. He'd never gotten a shot at evening the score with the crones. The only time he'd spoken his mind at all, Hortense had torn him to pieces and left him for dead. Thereafter she'd split town and never bothered to return. He didn't even know if she was still alive. He couldn't count on her ever receiving word of this robbery, and even if she did, he couldn't rightly take credit for it without landing himself in jail. It was a catch-22. The victory was his, but no one could ever know. Which seemed to be par for the course.

It was right about then when he first smelt smoke. Something was burning. He straightened up and looked around. Over in the corner a thin black rivulet had begun to course upward from the floor. One of the candles had rolled under a drawn curtain. The flame had begun to lick the fabric. A long black singe mark was spreading over the patchwork. He looked at it. Other candles were burning to every side. He gazed around. He looked at the altar, up and down the aisle, at the busted chest, at his reflection in a silver goblet to the left of the second podium. The fire caught. He thought of Hortense. The curtain started to burn on its own. He let it go.

He turned back to the chest and gathered as many of the remaining bills as he could. As he did so the flames continued crawling steadily upward. An acrid cloud of smoke began to fill the room. He stuffed a handful of change into each pocket to keep the bills weighted down. He collected the last of the Washingtons and forced them into his boot. He stood up. He routed through the first pew for a hymn book. The flames started to roar. He threw a book through a side window. It shattered. He crawled through the hole to the alleyway, spilling change from his loaded pockets over the pavement. He scaled an iron gate at the end of the alley and dropped into the street. He crawled off to a stoop to wait.

A thin plume of smoke coiled out of the shutters and wafted over the cupola high up in the east tower. The neighborhood was quiet – no one but the wetbacks in sight, and the wetbacks had drunk themselves almost blind by then. He sat on the bakery stoop watching the smoke gradually thicken. No one seemed to notice. It wasn't until it started seething from the cracks in the main door frame and hazing up the street that a pair of walklights clicked on. By then the church windows had begun to light up from inside. A woman's scream eventually cut the air. After that it was only a matter of moments before the street was filling up with bleary-eyed and horrified locals. The smoke poured out of every crack in the building's facade, drifting through open windows, kitchens and bedrooms throughout the neighborhood. Pretty soon another sizeable crowd was on hand. John curled up in his mining coat with his head hung low, doing his best to remain far back in the woodwork, away from the crowd. He knew he shouldn't have been there. As of that morning, he was the most high profile figure in the county. And there he was, wide out in the open at the scene of a public emergency. He knew he should have cleared out immediately.

Had anyone recognized him, he'd have been caught red-handed and most likely torn limb from limb. He should have left. But he couldn't resist the spectacle. As he later claimed, it was like witnessing the birth of his own child. He was caught.

The fire engines could be heard sounding off from the west, then the north, then west again, merging into one gigantic wail as they approached. The few deputies who had arrived beforehand had already tied off the area in front of the cathedral and were keeping the crowd in check as they waited for the trucks. Most of the smoke was still billowing out of the windows high up in the east tower. The pewter cupola with the cross positioned on top was concealed from view. The only flames visible as of yet were the ones devouring the wooden double doors encased by the enormous stone arch and bracketed by the twin marble columns to either side of the main entrance. But a low rumble and an orange glow illuminating the stained glass and projecting a multi-colored depiction of the last supper on to the walls of the houses across the street indicated a huge blaze within.

The fire trucks arrived. They squared away in the street, jammed together in an awkward line. The sirens cut. Firemen leapt out of cockpits and down from ladders and began running to and fro. They had just gotten their hoses in place and were ready to begin when the windows finally blew, exploding with the roar of a cannon blast. Thousands of shards of hot stained glass rained down in the streets. The firemen ducked and scuttled through the shattered remains of the last supper, checking their hoses for damage and pulling shards of the apostles from their overcoats. A whole new lake of smoke spilt out from the gaping window frame above. Inside, a wall of flame was consuming the resurrection. The mosaics on the opposite wall crumbled and fell off in long slabs. One of the main doors finally gave and toppled end over end down the front stairs and into the street. The firemen leveled a hose at the doorway and blasted. As the water chewed into the fire, a new, more acrid and black smoke rose from the sanctuary into the sky. John saw his shutter fall from all the way up in the east tower. He followed it to the ground where it crashed in the courtyard at the foot of a statue of the virgin.

He got up. It was time to go. The church was ruined. The crowd was broken. The trash was still in place. In the course of one evening he had repelled a direct attack from the factory rats, sacked and burned the lair of the beast, and was walking away with his pockets stuffed, knowing he would never die: The River Jordan wasn't big enough.

He left the bakery steps and made off down an alleyway to the south.

It was just after midnight when Murphy and Dennis, seated in Murphy's den watching a news flash of the cathedral fire, heard something moving around in the kitchen. Murphy grabbed a five iron and ran to investigate. He pushed open the door to find John, cut to ribbons and caked in blood, leaning over the pantry sink by the back door. His clothes were torn, his skin bruised in deep black pits, and his whole body laced in a grimy brown film. Murphy stared at him in disbelief. John stared back.

He hobbled to the coffee table. He took off his jacket and draped it over a chair. He began removing handfuls of crumpled bills from his pockets. Dennis pushed by Murphy, looked at John, recoiled, and said Damn, he looked like shit. John took off his shoes – more bills on the floor, out of his socks, up from his belt line. He piled them up on the table in a mound. Once he'd finished unloading he sat down, took a deep breath, and ordered Dennis to find him a cigarette. Dennis disappeared into the living room.

Murphy sat down at the table. He and John took another look at one another. Murphy explained how we'd all been worried sick – Wilbur had gone home that night to find their apartment building fragged to oblivion with the troll staggering through the wreckage like a bereaved Italian mother. When he discovered John had disappeared, he'd naturally feared the worst. He'd driven straight to Murphy's in a panic. The rest of us had gone out to comb the neighborhoods. We'd been looking for him for hours . . .

Dennis came back with a Winston. John lit up. He leaned back and exhaled, then said no, everything was all right. It had just been one unbelievably weird evening, that was all. Anyway, we had to replenish the beer funds somehow, didn't we . . .?

Before the rest of us returned that night, Murphy sat Dennis down to count the money, then pulled John into the den alone. He closed the door. He turned and started rooting through a breakfront drawer, saying there was something he wanted John to have on permanent loan. John stood watching with his arms at his side. Murphy found what he was looking for. He came up with a faded leather pouch. *Just in case*, he said, handing it over. John looked down. He unfastened the strap. It was a loaded .38.

ON LATER BEING QUESTIONED as to the acquisition of the fertilizer bomb used in the incineration of the river-rat camp, the
seven Ebony Steed employees responsible for the Patokah dam
disaster adamantly insisted they had acted on their own; they
had formulated and executed the whole plan themselves. It had
not been a company related endeavor. Their superiors had not
authorized or approved the distribution of the charges used in
the blast. Right down to their sentencing they held true to the
fundamental righteousness of their decision to act. Their cause
had been just, they maintained; it was the lack of preliminary
foresight, the gross miscalculations in the heat of the moment,
that led to the disaster which followed. They ended up pleading
temporary insanity, citing extenuating circumstances as due
cause for momentary loss of reason.

Courtroom testimony revealed that in the late hours of
October 8th, the defendants were gathered at a table in the
Whistlin' Dick public tavern. At approximately 10:30 p.m. a
passing resident entered the establishment to announce that the
First Methodist Church was on fire. The tavern quickly emptied
out, most of its customers, including the Ebony Steed crew,
being intent on rushing to the scene of the fire to join the crowd
already on hand. As the council for the defense maintained, that
crowd was clearly enraged over what was being taken for
'another river-rat burning' – this one far worse than all the
others. When the roof of the church then unexpectedly collapsed
at approximately 11:05 p.m., the estimated twelve ton bell tower
on the north end of the building toppled into the street and
flattened a Ford Bronco belonging to one Richard Cale, a
member of the group in question. Cale then flew into a rage and

had to be restrained by his fellow employees. He was witnessed screaming about how he was going to 'kill them sonsabitches' by twelve individual bystanders. Though he was said to have eventually regained his composure to some extent, none were left with the impression that he'd been fully restored to his senses when last seen being forcibly hustled away by his companions.

William Shuck, one of the two munitions experts employed by Ebony Steed, admitted to having been the first one to suggest the bombing. After leaving the scene at 4th and Geiger, he reportedly turned to the group to announce that he personally had knowledge as to the whereabouts of a river-rat camp to the west of the valley. He claimed to have caught sight of a large settlement in the Bolling County National Forest while on a hunting expedition six months earlier. He was relatively sure he could relocate the camp, even in the dark, and therefore, in the name of penalty and repentance, recommended the group set out directly. Everyone agreed. They piled into their pickups and drove to the Gwendolyn Hill reservoir. Shuck used the gate code known only to himself and five other employees to infiltrate the property. He acquired one fifty gallon barrel of ammonuim nitrate, one roll of blasting cord, and several charges from the powder vault. When questioned on his decision to select and utilize such an inordinately high amount of raw material, he admitted to having been privately aware that 'that much ANFO could blow half the county to the moon.' He admitted there had been no excuse for his lack of discretion. He had personally rigged a charge large enough to vaporize a river-rat camp and all its inhabitants ten times over. Once again, he deferred his poor judgement to temporary insanity.

With the material acquired, the group then set off for the Bolling County forest. Within an hour they had located the camp, but in the process of motoring through the unpaved outback in search of it, they'd made enough racket to announce their arrival and scare off the rumored inhabitants long before-hand. They arrived to find the camp deserted. There was only an assortment of rusted wire cages filled with starving gobblers and wild hares at the base of a rotting mobile home. The group got out of their pickups, removed their rifles from their cockpit gun racks, and set to work shooting up everything in sight. They killed all the livestock. They gutted the onion patch. They razed the interior of the bus. They smashed the flower pots and bird cages. They shot the wood-stove full of holes. At one point Cale swore he heard laughter in the woods around them. He fired into the dark at random until being restrained by Shuck.

They finished off with what was left of the camp. Their vehicles were then removed from the clearing. Shuck rigged the fifty gallon barrel to one of the trailer's support beams. He ran a wire one hundred and forty yards into the woods and primed the shot. The seven of them stood at a distance, staring toward the camp through the flood of headlights. Shuck threw the switch. The roof of the mobile home sailed into the sky. It pin-wheeled in a flaming arc one hundred yards over the treeline, then came down in the river like an earthbound meteor.

When the smoke cleared, the only thing that remained of the camp was a $15' \times 17' \times 25'$ scorched pit. The group purportedly felt no remorse. They all felt justice had been done, and congratulated one another accordingly. They were positive they had performed a community service for which they would be publicly praised. It was only halfway down the road to Baker that a few of the neglected preliminary blast calculations began to creep into William Shuck's head: a fifty pound fertilizer bomb necessarily requires a 1.2 mile safety clearance radius from its point of detonation. On consulting a road map from his glove compartment, he was suddenly hit with the realization that the river-rat camp they had just annihilated was located no more than .5 miles to the northeast of a one billion gallon capacity hydroelectric dam. At that point Shuck was said to have almost lost control of his vehicle.

Four hours later, the group was arrested. But by then a third of Bolling County was already underwater.

The front page of the next morning's *Herald*, as a round the clock, full-staffed accomplishment, was subdivided into three cover stories: the Clearwood dam disaster, the burning of the Methodist church, and the free form raid on the Kaltenbrunner home. Each story was briefed in a 6″ × 18″ vertical column, including photographs and primary captions. The dam disaster took precedence over the others in terms of sheer magnitude. The reservoir's main fore-bay had ruptured, a jagged fault line had opened up along the dam wall, releasing an estimated 100,000,000 gallons of blockaded river water every hour. Bolling County had been flooded. Several small vehicles had bobbed away from riverfront homesteads. Swing sets were hanging from tree limbs. Whole families were trapped in attics. The corn growing district looked like a cat-tailed swampland. Area residents had been evacuated. The total damage estimate, though untallied as of yet, was expected to run well into the upper half of the seven digit range. That's not including repair costs, court fees, hospital bills, and governmental subsidizing for crop losses. The restoration of Bolling County would probably require a two hundred page account to cover in full, something we don't have room for here. Suffice it to say, the Ebony Steed operators responsible for the blast were bound for lengthy prison terms, as were the six locals apprehended in the raid on the Kaltenbrunner home, and the two river rats recently announced to be in custody in connection with the Sodderbrook intrusion.

From that point on, the daily editions of the *Herald* came to resemble, as the rest of this account could very easily grow to resemble, an occupying army's crime log in a city under siege. Day after day increasingly abnormal behavior broke loose from every corner of the valley. More arrests were made over the next two weeks than at any other point in Baker's history. The Sheriff's holding cells overflowed. The county jail was filled to capacity. Tom Dippold made a formal request for federal assistance, terming Baker a qualified war zone. His request was denied, ostensibly due in large part to his bad phone manners. The only out of town officials to respond to his plea were two or three sociologists from a state university who were compiling a doctoral thesis on mob-generated violence.

The strike continued.

—On October 9th, seven unspecified minors were arrested in

connection with a series of trash fires. Though dressed in carnival get-ups so as to resemble Patokah-side river rats, they later laid claim to the collective title 'The Sons of Kaltenbrunner' and readily admitted to having spray-painted their logo on the underside of the 254 overpass, right next to the notorious 'SCOOL SUCKS.' They were released with a pending court date for arson and underaged drinking.

—On October 11th, a knock down brawl of unprecedented magnitude erupted in the Bloody Bucket. The fight was allegedly sparked by frustrated Keller & Powell employees who were flagged by the bartenders after stirring up too many quarrels in the course of one evening. Responding deputies reported to have arrived on the scene to find the brawl completely beyond their control. They had no choice but to let it rage without intervening. Afterwards, they lent a hand in cleaning up the mess.

—On October 12th, a dead cat was nailed to the door of a southside tenement house occupied by seventeen Central Americans. Every Toyota on the block was found chalked up with racial epithets, defecated on, and coated in gallons of molasses. Sixteen tires were slashed in total. No arrests were made in connection with the incident.

—On October 14th, at 1:30 a.m., a tree squirrel got into a main electrical generator outlet on 2nd and Groll streets, disrupting the power throughout Central Baker for over two hours. In the ensuing blackout, a rash of burglaries broke out along Main St. Bay windows were smashed, rack locks were busted, and an estimated $16,000 worth of various merchandise was stolen from twelve different display cases. Four arrests were made before the repairmen could finish scraping what was left of the squirrel from the generator box with a putty knife.

—On October 15th, two area residents were arrested for hotwiring and making off with a steamroller from the Pollenderry lumber yard. On being questioned, both suspects admitted their guilt, but insisted they had planned on returning the machinery just as soon as they had flattened the colossal accumulations of debris lining their front walks. The steamroller was returned. Pollenderry pressed charges anyway.

—On October 16th, two of the visiting sociologists were man-handled out of a street side sandwich shop, locked in a portable latrine, and tipped into the street with a splash. Their attackers claimed to have been fed up: all day long those 'clipboard-toting academians' had sat there taking notes and studying the behavioral patterns exhibited by the locals. Most residents had begun to feel like lab rats in someone's sick experiment. They'd warned the sociologists to clear out while they had a chance. The sociologists had ignored the warning. Hence the attack. Sheriff Dippold refused to press charges, saying he probably would have done the same himself. The sociologists left Baker humiliated.

—On October 17th a massive demonstration at City Hall deteriorated into a full-blown riot, resulting in eleven arrests, two hospitalizations, and $4,000 dollars worth of street repairs. A makeshift committee of concerned citizens assembled under the direction of the Baptist Church descended on the building at 11 a.m. to picket and protest the council's perceived incompetence. What was initially intended to be an unconfrontational rally quickly turned sour. By 1 p.m. an enormous crowd had flocked to the scene, and in the confusion, several of the new arrivals took to pitching bags of trash over the main gates into the yard. Cries went up for 'Death to Kuntsler,' 'Death to Kaltenbrunner,' 'Death to Dippold,' 'Death to The Council,' and most of all, 'Death to The Strike!' The council summoned the authorities. Within ten minutes, Baker deputies arrived on the scene geared in their newly acquired riot gear. The crowd was ordered to disperse. The order was ignored. The deputies were soon being bombarded with trash. They unsheathed their nightsticks. The trash kept coming. They gave one last order, then gassed the crowd. In the confusion that followed, two protesters – one being an elderly widow – were clubbed unconscious. The crowd subsequently dispersed, leaving the sheriff and his men, a handful of reporters, the Pottville 6 crew, eleven cuffed agitators and two hospital-bound casualties.

The list goes on. Whether it was a resurgence of illegal dumping, the full-force return of the scavengers, more wrangling and bickering, muckraking, mudslinging, fighting in the streets, breaking and entering, property damage, assault and battery, resisting arrest – any way one looks at it Baker had become an open air battlefield. The papers reflected as much. We've got every public arrest on file laminated in our scrapbook, but the list is far too extensive to allow for an unabridged rundown. Side by side, the complete list would wrap the interior of Wilbur's apartment twice over. The only welcome news to come out of mid-October at all was the long-awaited end of the drought, and even that was foiled by the torrential three day downpour that followed in its wake. By the time the rain let up, the streets had been transformed into a foul soupy bog and replenished breeding ground for sewer rats. The coyotes and turkey vultures returned. An estimated 768,000 pounds of trash was lining the streets of residential Baker alone. It was piled up over ten feet high in places. The charred remains of the Methodist church were crawling with woodchucks. Everything was in shambles. It was at that point, on the eve of the Pottville/Baker playoff, that the main Channel 6 correspondent made his renowned observation, against a backdrop of decay, that all of Baker appeared to be awaiting the arrival of the four horsemen.

BROOKS COUNTY DEPUTY Darryl Kratz would testify under oath five months later that, though every officer in attendance had been adequately forewarned, neither he or the responding deputies from his jurisdiction had any *real* inkling of what was in store on the night of the 21st until the moment that first wave of Pottville fans came careening into Baker like a parade of wailing fire trucks. Up until then, he would maintain, their expectations had been dismal, to say the least, just as their fellow officers from four other jurisdictions had been left equally on edge by that afternoon's long-winded precautionary harangue from Tom Dippold. They'd all been alerted as to the volatile, potentially explosive state of public morale currently pervading through Greene County. They'd been assured that by evening's end they might very easily find themselves up against any calamity known to defenders of the public trust. The sheriff had even stated, in the most clear and sober terms he was capable of mustering, that as bad as the situation in Baker may have appeared on the nightly news, the hands-on reality of it was infinitely worse. The whole valley had become unpredictably insane, he said. A 'jack-bastard's asylum' were his exact words. The deputies had taken his advice at face value. They had braced themselves for disaster long before embarking for the gymnasium lot on West 5th St. While en-route to their posts, they had seen stoop after stoop to either side of the slag-ridden street lined with bare-chested locals getting piss mean drunk. Small crowds had been gathered around flaming barrels on corners and in back yards. Beer cases had been stacked up six feet high and diminishing. As the cruisers had rolled by, long rows of faces had turned on them in scorn. One of the Tanner County deputies had remarked that they looked like hedge grinches in a four alarm blaze. They didn't speak, they spat; they all appeared to have been charred in pottery kilns.

Once parked on the outskirts of the lot, the deputies had remained in position for over an hour watching barbecue smoke drift through the neighborhood, oil-slicked rats scuttle over the cracks in the walk, and at one point, a box-office ticket wench and a downtrodden janitorial crew rigging an electronic advertisement board over the admissions window, after which the crew had disappeared in a trail of power lines, leaving the suspended board flashing in a panoramic, lite-brite display:

TONIGHT: BAKER WILDCATS VS. POTTVILLE HAWKS: TONIGHT

The sign had remained in place and any deputy like Kratz with prior knowledge of regional events had shuddered at the sight of it. It was a well known fact that, even under normal circumstances, a Baker/Pottville playoff was, legally speaking, nothing to be taken lightly. In the past, these annual showdowns had led to thousands of dollars worth of pre-game vandalism, numerous disrupting feuds in the stands, and on occasion, full-blown rumbles in the parking lot. As a rule, the entire state, and more – the whole of the corn belt – was dead serious about its basketball. It was the provincial battle chariot, the coal rat's warhorse, and in the case of Koll and Greene Counties, the existing rivalry was nothing short of fanatical. Over the preceding week Tom Dippold had been reminded of that fact the hard way.

The sheriff had been opposed to holding the game on home grounds from the outset. With Baker in its present condition, and with the Channel 6 newscasters having greatly exacerbated already aggravated tensions between the two communities for eight weeks and running at that point, the idea of actually going through with the scheduled game seemed downright suicidal. It would've been like running the New York marathon through a Cambodian minefield, he'd insisted. He'd refused to play any part in it. He hadn't been prepared or willing to have massbloodshed on his conscience for the rest of his career. On the morning of the 17th he'd made his official announcement to the press: The game was canceled.

Bitter cries of protest went up all through the valley. In the course of the following forty-eight hours, twenty-seven lengthy petitions had been hand-delivered to the department building in rapid succession. The *Herald*'s Tom Fuchs had hailed the decision a 'flagrant violation of inalienable human rights.' The county athletic commission had gone into an uproar. The *Pottville Daily* had branded the sheriff a yellow-bellied coward. The Baker Lay had taken to the airwaves. No one had approved of the decision. It was widely held that the community had actually endured the crisis in stride. The prospect of the sheriff imposing a last-minute injunction on the one event most locals felt they had left to look forward to was not about to be tolerated.

By the afternoon of the 19th the cancellation had been overruled by the city council. Tom Dippold had been publicly reprimanded for attempting to exercise authority beyond his command. For once, the sheriff had had to agree: *Hell no, the decision had not been his to make*, he openly admitted over the air. *More than half the decisions he'd made over the preceding weeks had been pawned off on his department by the legally responsible agencies . . .* He was glad to see the City Hall pulling its own weight for once, it was just a shame it had taken a basketball game and not a myriad of potentially life-threatening situations to prompt them into doing so. He was disgusted with everyone. He wavered before the cameras like a Pineridge wife beater on a nasty drunk, saying Go ahead, hold the game, but when the heads started rolling he and his deputies wouldn't be to answer for the mess . . .

Everything had been put back on track. The game had been cleared to proceed. The morning of the 21st had rolled around with clear skies and an open forecast. All through the a.m. a crew of hired hands had cleared the walk of the highwayside gymnasium, piling compacted rubbish from the gutters and parking lot into two separate dump trucks. The trucks had then been driven to the public school and unloaded on the outskirts of the playground, just as authorized. It had taken the crew five hours to clear the perimeter, after which the popcorn stands had been wheeled into place. Long multi-colored streamers had been draped over the glass paneling and ventilation ducts toward the roof of the building. Inside, electricians had gone to work on the scoreboard. Sound men had tested the P.A. repeatedly. A group of janitors had hand-swept the aisles. Two Baker mascots had taken to cart wheeling over the main floor in preparation for the evening.

Tom Dippold had spent the afternoon on the phone trying to round up reinforcements from surrounding communities. He had managed to acquire unspecified pledges of assistance from Brooks, Tanner and Blaine counties almost immediately. Needless to say, he hadn't bothered contacting officials in swamp-fallen Bolling, who'd have probably just as soon emptied out their jails on Baker. He'd also spent a harrowing twenty minutes engaged in a screaming match with Pottville Sheriff Jake McPhearson, who had taken personal offense to a press statement put forth by Dippold two weeks earlier and was now threatening to refuse the dispatch of even one of his deputies for the purpose of patrolling the game. In the end, McPhearson had given in, saying he would see what he could do.

By five the reinforcements had arrived: a total of sixteen deputies from four jurisdictions. Tom Dippold made no attempt to conceal the fact that he had hoped for at least twice that number; including his staff and his own somewhat less than able-bodied person, he had at his disposal a total of thirty-five ill-equipped and thoroughly wary officers for the purpose of monitoring and controlling a projected crowd of six thousand. He was not at all optimistic. He had summoned everyone together in the lobby for a quick briefing.

First off, he'd said, there wasn't enough riot gear to go around. He would've apologized for the lack of provisions, but he was already owed one too many apologies himself and couldn't even pretend to be overseeing this operation of his own accord. Therefore, he was in the same boat as everyone – probably worse off, as he was personally sure to catch hell for any and all mistakes made that evening. And there *would* be mistakes made that evening. He assured everyone that regardless of the Baker Lay's insistence that it would be able to comport itself for the playoff, its oath was no more reliable than the standard outpatient's claim to rehabilitation. Greene County was out of its mind, he said. *In-sane.* He hoped everyone understood that. The deputies were dealing with a highly unusual situation here: Baker had become an un-patrolled, un-indoctrinated, undeclared police state in every sense. The mob ruled: law enforcement in Pullman Valley had grown to require the necessary overlooking of what would otherwise be considered grievous offenses, and the implementation and enforcement of, strictly speaking, unwritten laws. The county jails and holding cells were packed beyond legal fire-hazard capacity. The courts were backed up for months to come. Underage drinking and mass jay-walking were the least of anyone's concerns. No arrests short of a misdemeanor had been made in weeks. The prime directive for the evening was not ticketing pinball drunks or teaheads – there was nowhere left to store them – but rather, keeping the brawls to a minimum and the guns in the clear. Without additional assistance, that was the most they could hope for.

With that the deputies had been dismissed. Twenty-three squad cars had rolled out of the department lot in unison. The deputies had driven through the devastated neighborhoods to the southeast, had crossed the highway at 5th St. and had rolled into position in and around the gymnasium lot. And there they had waited.

Darryl Kratz maintained that the first group to arrive on the scene had gathered along the eastern fence at 6:45, roughly twenty minutes after nightfall. They were 'kids' mostly, adolescents in nylon jerseys standing out in the open, drinking beer out of long-necked bottles, arguing amongst themselves, and donning the customary hometown-green face-paint. By seven their group had grown to a small crowd. From down the street figures had begun to appear beneath the light-poles in packs of four and five at a time. Troll families had hobbled down from front stoops. Wagons had come by and pulled up to the curb. Wooly-faced factory rats had staggered out of their passenger seats to urinate on the patch of grass lining the sidewalk. Pretty soon large groups were coming from every direction. A line had formed along the north wall.

At seven fifteen the parking gates had been opened to the public. The ticket men had assumed position. A line of cars had started rolling in. Money had changed hands. Traffic guards had signaled motorists into place on the south end of the lot. One of the guards had yelled at a group of delinquents scaling the fence and shaking so violently that the entire framework had begun to bow. The guard had been ignored. Someone had lit a Roman Candle. Elsewhere a bottle had smashed on the pavement.

Deputy Kratz had watched the scene unfold with a queasy, though not altogether overwhelming, feeling of dread welling up in him. He would later admit to having had mixed impressions there at first. The beginning *had* been strange, he would claim – one of the more eerie spectacles he'd ever witnessed – but certainly not as strange as the sheriff had led them to believe. Granted, the crowd had had a certain something otherworldly about it – there *had* been that air of pressurized containment hanging over the scene – but still, right up to a quarter past, he could hardly believe this was the irrepressible mob over which the whole state was in such a tither. It had seemed to him that rounding up and subduing everyone on hand could have been accomplished with relative ease inside of an hour's time. He had begun to suspect that the Baker law enforcement division really was every bit the bastion of ineptitude it had been made out to be.

But it was right about then that the first wave of Hessians had rolled into view. With that, Kratz's confusion had been dispelled.

The first noise he remembered hearing was something akin to a fleet of F-16's approaching from sea. It had cut the air over the parking lot in a gigantic roar, jolting every officer upright in his seat and silencing the crowd from one end to the other. Everyone had stopped to look north toward the churchyard and the Main St. Federal Bank, beyond which the rumble was steadily growing as it approached. Then, out of the gap, there it was – there came Pottville in all its clamorous glory, throttling down 254 in a lumbering procession of pickups and town wagons, car horns blaring, mufflers roaring, lights flashing, passengers straining out of hatchbacks three at a time. They forded by the bank lot hurling open-throated obscenities as they came – cries of 'Trash Pickers!' 'River Rats!' and 'Good God Damn this place stinks!' They pitched open sacks into the churchyard by the dozen. They weaved their vehicles in and out of the passing lane, barreling over the remains of the latest avalanches. They whacked at the highwayside accumulations with broom-handles. Long before they'd made a screeching right turn on to 5th St. and leveled out to a charge, the Baker crowd had begun to boo and cuss. Deputy Kratz had seen an instantaneous transformation come over the crowd he'd been patrolling thus far. To every side of his cruiser the assembly of what had been mildly rambunctious Wildcats fans had suddenly metamorphosed into a mob of wild-eyed ber-serkers. He had rolled up his window and stared around in disbelief. Bodies had shot through his headlights in contorted profusion. Howls had gone up, unidentified objects thrown overhead. From where Kratz had sat watching, the whole thing resembled a raid on the holy temple, with the crowd as the money lenders, the deputies as Pilate's elite, and the overhead full moon as the celestial host.

Six of us were gathered in Murphy's den when the televised coverage began. Every enterprising sponsor in the area had made a bid for air time with Pottville 6, the result being that the pre-game rundown was riddled with more commercial breaks than actual commentary. The game was estimated to be going out to over seven counties and thirteen municipalities, for a total of 125,000 viewers. It was the largest televised local sports event in the area's history. All through the state taverns were packed, households were tuned in, graveyard shifts were running special transmissions over empty shops. Drink specials were being advertised on long red banners at establishments like the Bloody Bucket. Wildcat/Hawk flags had been posted to either side of 254 from the overpass to the hospital. This was the moment everyone had been waiting for, the culminating point and fruition of nine straight weeks worth of an unrestrainedly con-frontational media-blitz. Everyone with a vested interest in the affair, which was just about everyone within a day's journey of the valley, was sure to be watching.

As for the outlook on the game itself – if anyone cared – the running predictions were the same as they had been every other year: the Wildcats would lose miserably. Pottville, being a community of twelve thousand, had almost three times the student body of Baker from which to draw. Their team consisted of over twenty 6′3″ barbarians who'd been held back for so many remedial grades, that by the time they entered their freshman years in Terrence High, they were sporting full-length beards and were primed for highway work. Many of them grew up in a neighborhood on the outskirts of Koll County known as Buzzard's Roost, aka, 'The Wasteland.' The Wasteland was somewhat of an open-air halfway house, a colony of drunkards and convicted felons either in hiding, fresh out of prison, or directly bound for. The great majority of Pottville's criminal element and, incidentally, the cream of its athletic league came straight out of Buzzard's Roost. It was often said that when the Hawks were feeling cooperative, they'd take the time to dribble around their opponents; otherwise and under normal circumstances they simply laid waste to everything in their path and dealt with the penalties as an afterthought. They had taken the regional championship for six of the previous eight seasons – they were undisputed in the area – but they were usually fouled off the court in the early rounds of the state games.

Baker, on the other hand, had no wasteland from which to draw. At least not one that yielded seventeen-year-old, 220 lb. future jackhammer operators. In all its history it had only gone to the state games once, and that arguably by default. Once there it had lost out in the first round. The Wildcats, all seventeen of them, weren't much to look at.

But all that assuming anyone cares; on the night of the 21st none of the fans really did. The game wasn't being viewed or patronized by virtue of its athletic merit. In the past, the responding crowd had been half the size it was that night. The broadcasting had been limited to the two respective communities and had been subsequently documented with all the enthusiasm of a Sunday afternoon billiards tournament. The allure had always been in the warring crowds. No star player had recently entered the ranks of either team to render this year's event any different. No surprise victory was anticipated. Combat was. The truth is: the game was no more than a side show. The real interest lay with the spectators and what might happen.

From where we were sitting, at least the six of us in Murphy's den – Murphy, Wilbur, John, Curtis, Bailer and Dennis – more than half of the crowd looked to have filed into place by seven thirty. Dennis was getting a kick out of the preliminary commentary and was providing his own barnacular interjections over the voices of the sportscasters. Murphy, Curtis and Bailer were hunkered down on the couch guzzling imported lager and looking unenthused. Wilbur was on the phone with Donnecker.

John was pacing. Since the evening of the raid on his home, he'd become more restless and introverted than ever. In two weeks he had worn a solid path over the hallway carpet, into the den, around the coffee table, back through the hallway and into the kitchen. He'd stopped drinking beer and switched over to coffee. He'd gone through two and a half tins of ground espresso in ten days. Somewhere along the way, he'd confided in Wilbur that ever since his accident at Sodderbrook he'd been having terrible migraines every day. He figured that at some point during the raid he'd managed to sustain a concussion, maybe during the leap from roof to roof or possibly from the tea kettle that had clipped his skull, as the headaches had gotten so bad as of late, particularly when he drank, that he'd had trouble even speaking. His insomnia was at an all time high. He'd switched over to coffee to dull the ache, but by so doing he'd ended up smoking even more than usual and annihilating all hopes of ever getting a decent night's sleep. He was also having trouble eating, probably due in large part to his body's continual state of dehydration from the caffeine. He'd lost a considerable amount of weight – weight he didn't have to lose in the first place. Large black bags had appeared under his eyes. He was pale and undernourished; also short tempered – he'd begun to snap at the rest of us for no apparent reason. Wilbur had offered to take him to the hospital, to which John had replied that it had been the hospital that had damaged his head to begin with. Under no circumstance would he return to 'that chicken-soup institution.' It was out of the question. He would live with the headaches.

He'd stayed in Murphy's flat for sixteen days. Every afternoon he'd disassembled and oiled his .38 over several pots of coffee. At night he'd tossed and turned on the cellar floor with an old red blanket and a matted down pillow spread out beneath him. He'd remained in the cellar until the floor had been flooded during the storm. Thereafter he'd moved into the den upstairs to spend all his time pacing around the house and staring at the wall in silence. He'd only left the property on one occasion since the 7th, and on that one occasion he'd done so with four of us guarding him like watchdogs. All for a trip to the supermarket. It had been ridiculous. We'd had to sneak into the IGA during churchgoing hours just to load up on the essentials without running the risk of being spotted. As far as Baker knew, John was either gone or dead. He hadn't been sighted in public since the raid. On the practical side, the sacking of his residence and his resulting absence had redirected community pressure back toward Kuntsler where it belonged. It had cost John every earthly possession, the risking of his life, and the sustainment of numerous bodily injuries, but he'd successfully thwarted the attentions of the press. The raid had become an *embarrassment*, something no one wanted to acknowledge or admit. John had managed to get the *Herald* and Pottville 6 off our backs before either agency had really had a chance to lay into us, but he had done so at the expense of his own home and corporeal freedom. He was still hated – it's doubtful he ever would've been able to assume residence in the community again – but the aversion to Kaltenbrunner ultimately paled in comparison with the aversion to Kuntsler. The Baker Lay were by now convening at the landfill gates in murderous packs every afternoon. The sheriff was having to put the main lot on constant patrol to ward off bloodshed. To the extent that anyone was still capable of passing judgement in Greene County, the old man's fate was already sealed. The confusion was total, but within its precarious auspices several conclusions were emerging as steadfast inevitabilities; foremost being the assurance that Jeffrey Kuntsler had to go. The old man no longer had a prayer. Everyone knew it was only a matter of time before he'd be exiled by necessity. Baker officials had long since outdone themselves in terms of procrastinating the unavoidable. Settlement, by local means or otherwise, was imminent. All other avenues had been exhausted. If federal troops had to step in before the courts were able to resolve the dilemma, then that's what would happen. Either way it would only be a matter of days now, one week at the most. The crisis was over. We had won. All that remained was a basketball game.

Such must have been John's mindset that night when he came stomping out of the kitchen, positioned himself between the television and the rest of us, and made his unanticipated announcement.

He was going to the game.

Everyone but Dennis looked up. Wilbur dropped the receiver from where it was cradled between his chin and shoulder. We all stared at John. He stood there, saying nothing.

Was he *out of his mind?* Curtis asked. What was he talking about?

John straightened up and repeated himself. That's right, he said, God dammit, he was going to the game! He was sick of being holed up like an animal. If he had to stare at those ugly blue-papered walls for another minute or hear so much as one more convalescent wisecrack out of Dennis he was liable to charge out into the yard and start shooting up the neighborhood. This quarantinement was driving him up the wall. He couldn't take it anymore. He was going to the game. If any of us wanted to come along, then the time was now that the end was nigh. Otherwise, he'd see us later.

He almost made it out the door before we were able to stop him. Murphy gently barred his way and told him to hold on, what was this all about? *What about our 'low profile?'*

To Hell with it! John responded motioning to the television set. *Look at those monkeys*, he said. A sweeping pan of the Baker stands lit up on the screen. They were *finished*. They'd been *murdered*. There was nothing left of them. They couldn't touch us now. The strike was over. As for our anonymity, we'd just paint our faces green like all the rest. No one would be able to tell the difference. It would be easy.

We sat there staring at him.

Well? he demanded.

Against our better judgement, and to our regret even now, we somehow conceded to his plan. Looking back, we realize we probably could have talked him out of it. It wouldn't have taken much. We could have driven him out of town for an evening of mild entertainment where no one knew his face or name from Adam. Or even better, we could've watched the game and drunk our fill on the house in any of the Main Pottville taverns. We would've been toasted as heroes all over Koll County . . . But John didn't want to go to Pottville. He wanted to go to the game. He wanted to sit out in the open with the same crowd that would've just as soon torn him to pieces. He wanted to *smell* the carnage. It was his idea of a good time, we suppose. And unfortunately, we went along with it, three sticks short on enthusiasm though we were. We had grown to accept John's judgement as rule. Just as on the night when he'd come stumbling through the back door with all that cash stuffed into his briefs, or as his bombshell announcements at each meeting had at first seemed devoid of rhyme or reason, we had learned not to question him. By then, we trusted that he knew exactly what he was doing. All his predictions thus far had been dead accurate.

At any rate, that's how we've since attempted to justify our inexcusable shortsightedness in agreeing to accompany him to the gym.

The sheriff assigned Darryl Kratz and Tanner County Deputy Wilson Groll to the main doors to conduct the preliminary searches. He deliberately avoided placing his own men or the Pottville deputies in any situation requiring direct contact with the crowd. Most of the deputies inside the gymnasium were from Brooks, Tanner and Blaine counties. The rest remained outside along the street and to the rear of the building. The reasoning behind the dispersal of troops was sound: Tom

Dippold was correct in assuming the likelihood of conflict would be reduced considerably by placing seemingly disinterested officials at the doors to conduct the mandatory weapons check. With the crowd in its current state, the possibility of a Wildcat being patted down by a Pottville official, or vice versa, was not likely to bode well for anyone. That being the logic, Kratz and Groll were appointed to the post with orders to maintain a guise of 'relative neutrality.' They did so, and for the most part, the line was filed in without cause for alarm. In the first half hour only two confiscations were made: one ankle-strap boot knife from a Hessian's pair of combat boots, and one bundle of quarter sticks wrapped in a makeshift Hawks banner. Otherwise, the only disturbance from the line was a minor scuffle that broke out toward the west wing of the building at 7:50. The sheriff's men hustled the combatants – four in total – out of the line and into a group of paddywagons on the corner of 5th and Geiger. They were all released with a warning after twenty minutes.

Tom Dippold was seated in his cruiser at the corner of the highway. Pottville wagons were weaving off of 254 on to 5th by the hundreds. Crowds of the Baker Lay were gathered along the fence hurling one-fingered salutes toward the incoming vehicles. The noise was nerve-shattering. The whole block was wafting out like a drunk tank. The sheriff felt terribly isolated sitting there all by himself, even though he was really only thirty yards from the nearest deputy. That was the position Curtis, John and Bailer caught him in when they passed: sealed off from his company, trapped in his cruiser, fidgeting with his riot gear and looking sick with nervous energy. *There's the sheriff*, Bailer said. We pulled by and shot him a glance. Tom Dippold didn't notice.

Curtis took a ticket from the parking attendant, then wheeled his pickup into the lot. Murphy followed up to the rear. Both vehicles were parked on the southwestern end, four rows in from the fence. The rest of us sat tight while Dennis struck out to find a tube of face paint. While he was gone, Murphy dug an old dingy sweatshirt out of his hatchback and threw it to John. John pulled it on and wrapped the hood over his head. A minute later Dennis returned with a tube of green paint he'd bought from a Wildcat for a dollar. Pretty soon our faces were smeared thick, and to our relief, each of us appeared comfortably unrecognizable. Wilbur looked like a Mardi Gras scat-queen, Dennis a Tennessee hillbilly, and John the purgatorial raftsman. With a quick look at one another, we relaxed considerably.

John left his .38 in the glove compartment. He knew the deputies would be conducting searches and there'd have been no quicker way of announcing ourselves than being apprehended in possession of a firearm.

We walked over to the gates, then up the street to the main doors. It was a rough wait in line. We kept expecting someone to blurt it out. *Hill Scrubs!* they would yell, then beat us into the pavement. But after a while it was clear no one had noticed. The Baker faces were green, the Hessians bright red, all lined up in a row. We fit right in. We made it through without any problem.

Stepping inside was a different matter. Wilbur later recalled that moment as having been like entering an Athenian auditorium for a Sunday afternoon massacre. From the moment we pushed through the doorway into the hot, crowded hallway inside, the pandemonium of the parking lot gave way to its actual source and allotted each of us, for the first moment since we'd walked out on Kuntsler, irrefutable proof of the *odium proletaricum* inherent to the corn belt which had been unleashed and catalyzed to fruition by way of the strike. Not that we hadn't already been intimately familiar with its every manifestation; long before John had walked into the picture we'd weathered and endured it as a way of life. And since then John himself had been attacked in his home, the whole community had gone off the deep end, and the press had documented every detail along the way. We knew exactly what lay behind the curtain. We'd endured it for years. But it wasn't until we stepped through the main doors that evening to be overcome by a blast of hot air, the roar of the crowd over the marching band, and the sight of the two insanely hysterical multitudes railing at one another in the stands that its full magnitude finally registered.

The only patch of seats left on the Baker side were positioned high up in the stands toward the eastern wall. We pushed through the crowd from the main entrance and within a few minutes all six of us were in place. From there we had a good view of the court.

The Wildcat cheerleaders – the Chicklets – were attempting to size up a pyramid in the center of the floor. Wilbur remembered two years earlier when one of them had fallen from that position and broken her wrist in clear view of two thousand spectators. She'd been subsequently ostracized out of the league and had last been seen operating an Interstate toll booth on the north end of the state. Fortunately, this year no such disaster befell the Chicklets, as had that been the case, the game might have come to an even more abrupt end than it did. The pyramid sized up, the mascots shot by, and each side of the crowd let loose accordingly.

High up in the rafters a carpet of red and green balloons was hugging the ceiling over the scoreboard. Several hired technicians had cleared the ceiling of bird nests earlier in the day. A group of confused pigeons was fluttering about in the balloons and over the suspension wires, looking for a home. Wilbur ran his gaze along the ceiling and down the wall, past the time clock, to a second-story window frame where the heads of the county athletic league were looking on from their observation box. Down below a popcorn vender was wrangling with a group of Hessians. The opposite stands were alive with war cries. Twelve foot banners were stretched along entire rows, being hoisted and waved by up to ten persons at a time. The logos were brutal: HATS OFF TO BAKER POLECATS — CESS PIT DELIVERANCE — KUNTSLER FOR PRESIDENT — PHEW! – SMELLS LIKE A RIVER RAT IN HERE — BAKER = TRASH, etc. One group of Hessians were dressed as garbage cans. A twenty foot banner of a coiled strip of steaming feces covered in flies had been nailed to the opposite wall. Numerous chants were going up – BA-KER STINKS! BA-KER STINKS! Over and over. It was merciless. The Baker crowd was at a loss for a comeback. It had no choice but to sit there and take it. It was true – *Baker did stink*. It couldn't be denied. The abuse was simultaneously objective and pejorative. It rang true and left the Wildcats fans all the more enraged. There was nothing they could do about it. They were helpless. Had they anticipated this beforehand, they probably wouldn't have pushed to override the sheriff's cancellation of the game to the extent they did. That realization appeared to be hitting them now. Wilbur could see it in their faces: *Maybe this wasn't such a good idea after all.* They were miserable and ashamed, but trying to veil their disgrace with a forced show of enthusiasm. Running his gaze across the rows of Hessians, then over to the Baker Lay, then back to Pottville again, Wilbur was struck by several obvious differences between the two crowds in the very same manner Darryl Kratz had been left speechless on comparing and contrasting his own fellow deputies with those serving under Tom Dippold. When paired off with the Baker Lay, the Hessians had the overall appearance of a group of well-oiled boarding school graduates, even though the socio-economic distinction between the two communities was virtually undetectable. The conduct of the Hessians may have been ruthlessly belligerent, but there was still a relatively light, carefree air of indifference about them; partly because they could rest assured the Hawks would mop the floor with the Wildcats in the first quarter, but mostly due to the fact that they'd been leading normal, functional, stress-free lives for the previous two months. At the end of the night they would pile back into their wagons and drive north to clean, well-lit streets. They would turn in for the evening with smiles on their faces, having mocked and humiliated the Baker Lay to the whipping post like never before. End of story.

The Baker crowd, on the other hand, looked as though it had been through a war. All up and down the eastern stands the attire was slovenly, postures were slumped, and individual faces looked sick and delirious. It was as though everyone in town had gone on a two year grease diet. Darryl Kratz had noticed it in the department lobby earlier in the evening. The Tanner and Blaine County deputies had reported for duty trim and fit, whereas Tom Dippold and his men had stood around pasty-faced and battered as emaciated ghouls. The only question which remained in regards to everyone in the valley, both deputy and Wildcat fan alike, was: had their levee broken entirely, or had one last reserve remained intact the whole way through? Was there still a breaking point left in them? Could one final outburst be mustered from the ranks before they resigned undivided? To look at the crowd, Wilbur was left uncertain. Yes, they were making lots of noise. Sure, they were stomping and screaming toward the opposite stands without enough sense about them to pound sand into a rat hole. But how much of the enthusiasm was Dutch courage, and how much of it was genuine blood lust? Wilbur couldn't tell. For all his years in Greene County, he still wasn't sure. The only thing he, like Deputy Kratz, knew for certain was that the citizens and officials of Pullman Valley appeared to have veered farther from the beaten path than ever before and were now like some exiled desert tribe wandering the tundra in search of its misplaced heritage. It was self-evident in their every gesture. It was even manifested in the Wildcats themselves, when, after another ten minutes, the marching band pushed into a crescendo and the team came pouring on to the court from the locker room gate. The whole gymnasium erupted in a cacophony of boos and cheers, stomps, chants, and handheld air-horn blasts. If nothing else, it was the largest reception ever afforded any Baker athletic team; but in spite of the crowd's roar, nothing could've concealed the fact that the members of the team itself were stone cold terrified. One was left to suspect, as they fell into place for the customary round of free throws, that it wasn't so much the prospect of going up against the Wasteland's finest which left them pale and trembling, it was more so the tremendous pressure they were now operating under, the enormous expectations bestowed on them by their *own* community that brought to mind the Colombian football player who'd been lynched by his own compatriots for lackluster performance in the World Cup. Even when the Hawks made a similar entrance from the other end of the court, the Wildcats' concern lay not with the lumbering Cimmerians from Buzzard's Roost who now opposed them, but instead with the chaotic, lurching mass of their own home court. They had the look of those condemned to dance before the executioner.

The preliminary free-throws continued. Each team coiled over the floor in a serpentine chain, sinking bank shots, three-pointers and lay ups. The few remaining seats along the opposite wall filled up. Four referees, two from each community, were introduced over the loudspeaker. More amplified gibberish came through the P.A., after which all were ordered to rise for the national anthem. What followed was an almost treasonous rendition of the 'Star Spangled Banner,' one interrupted repeatedly by shouting and horn blasts. The only individuals to be seen observing the intended silence were a few veterans in the lower stands, the fifteen or sixteen deputies along the first tier, and the two teams. No one else cared.

When the anthem concluded, the full roar commenced. The cheerleaders panned out to position and pulled for one last cry from their crowds. The Hessian mascot did a somersault. The Pottville 6 news crew squared away in its pit. The clock was set to go.

The game itself lasted for a total of eleven minutes and twenty-one seconds, which was probably six minutes longer than it should have. Including three official time outs, one quarter break, two penalties for traveling, one clock-stopping suspension for poor sportsmanship, and the time required to issue two red cards, the whole event, from start to finish, was twenty-five minutes in length. That's to say nothing of the crowd related disturbances; within minutes a wide path had been cleared for the deputies along the first tier leading to the west exit. Before the quarter bell sounded, at least thirty-two spectators had been escorted into the alley and pitched into one of the wagons waiting on the corner.

Surprisingly enough, the Wildcats actually won the tip-off. Not so surprisingly, that was about the only thing they won all night. The rest was a slaughter, both athletic and corporeal. The Pottville defense was an almost impenetrable bulwark. Its line was consistently taller, faster, and more aggressive than the Wildcats'. From up in the third tier it was difficult to follow the game's progress at all. What little we did manage to gather via breaks in the crowd was perfectly in accord with the projected outcome: the Wildcats were up against the wall with the opposing centers boring in, the guards rebounding their every attempt to break away, and the majority of the game unfolding on the far end of the home court. By the third minute into the game the score was 12–3 in favor of the Hawks, and the Wildcats had racked up their three points only by way of free throws. It was five minutes before Baker sank its first legitimate shot at all: an admittedly beautiful three pointer by junior Kevin Stills, who'd been bivouacked at half-court by four looming Hawks and had no choice but to let fly with a seemingly foolhardy overhead toss. It was one of only three legitimate shots the Wildcats would make all night, the only three-pointer of its kind. The moment it swished through the net, the Baker Lay exploded. It was the moment they'd been waiting for, mired in their pit like captive animals. The marching band flew into the alma mater. The locals hooed and whinnied themselves into a standing ovation. From where we sat, we could see Stills beaming with pride, though looking a bit surprised with himself for actually having made the shot. He retreated down court as one delivered from the gallows.

One minute later he was trampled underfoot by two Hawks who'd obviously, by anyone's standards, targeted him, arguably on direct orders from the Pottville coaches. He was hauled away in a stretcher with a season-ending injury. That was when the fouling began.

From up in the stands we could see the Baker referees suspending one of the two Hawks responsible for the injury. The suspended player, Blaine Rehack, a 6'7", 235 pound senior with all the mass and majesty of Kull the Destroyer, threw back his tangled black hair, raised his arms to the Pottville crowd, and mimed a mock-sympathetic violin recital. The Hessians roared. The louder they laughed, the harder the Baker Lay lurched. All around us the hatred was welling up. There were cries for 'Kill that bastard!' and 'Skin the coach!' But for the most part the referees took the brunt of the blame – and not just those from Pottville, but from Baker as well. Murphy, who'd been trying to outline the rules of the game for John, as this was the first game John had ever attended or had the patience to sit through in his life, explained that the refs always caught hell from the crowd, regardless of the call. Which was true. One had to be a sucker for punishment to put in for referee detail in Pullman Valley. As a rule, the ref was *never* right. When he made a call against the home team he was a turncoat. When he made a call against the visitors it was never thorough enough. No matter how clearcut a given infraction may have been, his ruling was always and without exception railed as an act of betrayal, just as he himself was shunned as a conspirator. He was in league with *them*. He was the voice of authority where it was least desired. He couldn't win. Despite the obvious need for his appointment, he was hired on and treated more as a doormat for the crowd's wrath than an athletic monitor. On the occasion that he actually did miss something or made a bad call, he was blasted as a moron and an idiot, and often even made to pay the price outside of the arena later on. Everything from public insults to raids on his property generally limited his career to a period of three or four months. After that he either quit of his own accord or was run out of the league by force. The turnover was neverending.

Rehack eventually returned to the bench, pulled on a sweatshirt, and sat there smiling through a round of back slapping and congratulations. The four refs convened in the center of the floor to clarify their decision. The clock was stopped. The Wildcats were huddled together discussing something. The Hawks were lumbering about on the other end of the court. The Baker Lay didn't let up for a second. After a minute one of the Baker refs nodded to the others and walked over to the scorekeeper's table to state their decision. Rehack was suspended from the league for two weeks. The other player was issued a red card. The Wildcats were allotted two foul shots. A massive grumble went up on both sides.

Senior Dwight McCaffrey missed the first shot, probably due to the peripheral bombardment from both crowds. While lining up the second, he was suddenly clipped by a full Pepsi can that came flying out of the Pottville stands. Without hesitating he retrieved the can and line drove it back into the crowd. It hit a Hessian seated in the fifth row, prompting a large group from above into rushing the floor. McCaffrey seized a coach's chair from the sidelines and held it overhead. One of the Hawks shoved him from behind. McCaffrey came around swinging. He

373

missed. A group of Baker factory rats ran over the court to meet the Pepsi crew at mid-point. Everyone in the gymnasium rose at once. The deputies managed to intervene before the two groups could reach one another. At least ten individuals were subdued and escorted outside. McCaffrey was ordered out of the game. The Pepsi can made its way back on to the court. Someone threw a caramel apple at a Pottville referee. The gym was a mess. It took another minute for the crowd to settle down, after which McCaffrey's replacement missed the second shot.

The clock resumed at 6:51. The Wildcats were down two players, the Hawks one. In the next ninety seconds there were three more fouls. The game was deteriorating into a rugby match. The Hawks were feeding on the crowd's roar, converting it into aggression. The Wildcats had gone from being quietly apprehensive to outwardly resentful. One could tell just by looking that they hadn't asked to be the centerpiece in this dispute. They were hating every minute of it. It was bad enough going up against the Hawks under normal circumstances. But now, to make matters worse, their opponents had become exhibitionists. And it was no wonder: with a seventeen point lead and every couch potato for miles around tuned in, they could afford to throw away a few shots for the sake of effect. While retreating down court, they began randomly stonewalling the Wildcats without notice: on at least three separate occasions, all of which went unpenalized by the refs, the Hawks covered their opponents up close, to a point, then suddenly reared up and allowed the Wildcats to slam into them with all the unbridled momentum of a full charge behind them. Not only were the Wildcats thereby knocked to the ground, humiliated and embarrassed, they were individually warned or penalized as well. It was dirty play.

At 8:36 one of the Hawks fouled a Wildcat in mid-air during an attempted three point shot. He technically should have been suspended from the league with Rehack; the attack – a driving forearm to the torso – had been blatantly deliberate. It was completely inexcusable. Nevertheless, it warranted only a red card. On hearing the decision, Baker's coach Brody tore on to the court and went head to head with all four refs at once. He squared away in their faces and stammered himself blue to the ears. For a minute there it even looked like he might start swinging. The crowd egged him on. The refs shook their heads *no* and pointed him back to his seat. He yapped on like a rabid animal. They gave him an official warning. He threw up his arms and whirled around. The Baker Lay hissed as he made his way back to the sidelines, cursing and spitting.

Once again, the peripheral distractions were overwhelming enough to thwart the first free throw. While the second was being lined up, the group of Hawks fans who were dressed as garbage cans suddenly 'lifted their lids' – as the *Herald* would term it – that is, they lined up to the rear of the net to expose their bare backsides to everyone. Before the deputies were able to hustle them from the scene, another fight broke out by a popcorn stand along the northern wall. Eight more deputies ran to break it up. The stand was almost overturned in the scuffle. There looked to be at least seven fans from each community tumbling over one another in an indefinable battling mass. The northern wall was the hot zone, the borderline between the two crowds. Only the drunkest, burliest and most belligerent from each community dared position themselves in its midst. Nothing but a single three foot aisle separated them. It took several minutes to re-establish the most threadbare semblance of order.

With twenty-four seconds remaining in the first quarter, the opposing crowds were teetering on the brink of collapse. Paper bags, chocolate donuts and strings of lit firecrackers were raining down on the floor. Everyone was standing, stomping and wailing. An unbroken line of offenders was being herded toward the gates by the deputies. The head of the Baker sports commission made a failed appeal for order over the loudspeaker. No one paid it any mind.

During the final moments of the quarter, one of the Wildcats sunk a beautiful lay up from inside. The scoreboard crawled two notches. The Baker Lay howled. But the gap was hardly narrowed. When the final bell sounded the score stood at 24–9. The first quarter was over.

*

Out in the parking lot, Tom Dippold's problems continued. With the ejected fans being pitched into the alleyway faster than he and his men could cuff them, three of the four paddywagons at his disposal had already been packed. To make matters worse, several of the disputes which had begun inside were now continuing behind the locked wagon doors. The sheriff had wrongly assumed that without a crowd there to bear witness to and encourage each confrontation, the warring parties, when holed up in an eight by twelve mobile cell, would naturally cease with the hostilities. Therefore he and his men had just packed the wagons at random without any consideration for the lineup. Each vehicle now held from ten to twelve ejected fans who were thrashing around in the interior like a bucket full of Maryland crabs. The sheriff hadn't counted on the fights continuing. He quickly discovered, as the brawling resumed and the walls of each wagon banged and rattled from within, that the fisticuffs they had dispersed in the gym were more than just cases of chest-pounding crowd play; even without the audience there to cater to, it was clear the Baker Lay and the Hessians were genuinely out to bludgeon one another senseless. The sheriff realized he had to segregate the detainees or face possible manslaughter charges. Doing so was no easy task.

On opening the wagon doors, the deputies found the occupants inside kicking and mauling at one another in the dark. The moment the streetlights flooded into the cell, several bodies shot out and made a break for the highway. They were chased, tackled, and dragged back to the corner. The red faces were roped off from the green, then filed into place. It was a miracle none of them had been seriously injured. One wagon had contained nine Wildcats fans to only three Wastelanders, who, despite the odds, had more than held their own. There were a few bloody noses and welted skulls, but otherwise, everyone appeared to be intact. They were all stuffed back into the wagons, kicking, cuffed and screaming.

The sheriff barged into the unoccupied admissions booth to put an emergency call through to the West Tanner County precinct. Sheriff Bob Dix had been waiting for his call for the past ten minutes. His whole department was watching the game on the television as they spoke, Dix said. Not to worry, ten of his deputies and six from Blaine County were already en route to Baker. He had to admit, he went on to say, earlier on in the day he'd been convinced Dippold was just being overly paranoid. But now . . .

Never Mind That! Dippold screamed. What he needed now was one hundred heavily armed men, six paddywagons, and a fleet of attack dogs. The gym was about to go. He ordered Dix to get on the horn and get to it. He hung up. Then he dialed Pottville. Jake McPhearson answered. *What can I do for you?* McPhearson asked lazily. Dippold exploded, telling him to cut the shit, he knew exactly what was going on: his jurisdiction was running hog wild over Baker, and if he didn't move to send at least twenty men to the scene at once, he'd be answering for it in court later on. McPhearson laughed on the other end. Just how much later might that be, Sheriff? he asked. We talkin' *years or decades?* McPhearson then leafed through his memos to produce a two week old article from the *County Herald*, which read:

SHERIFF DIPPOLD PRONOUNCES
POTTVILLE LAW ENFORCEMENT *STERILE*.

He was less than one paragraph into quoting the article when Tom Dippold hung up.

Halfway through the five minute quarter break Dennis set out for a caramel apple. He was back in two minutes, having proceeded no further than five yards down the congested aisleway. The stands were impassable. He stood over his seat, looking around nervously. After a minute he announced the same thing all of us had been privately thinking: *This place is gonna blow*, he said. *Maybe we oughtta git . . .* Looking around, it would have appeared that, again, Dennis was somehow the voice of reason in disguise. The chants from the opposite stands were getting more ruthless by the minute. The quarter break was turning out to be every bit as loud as the game itself. To every side there was talk of storming the floor, executing the referees, sacking the Pottville athletic bus, etc. The Baker Lay were in an infuriated stupor. And it was only getting worse. Judging by the roar, there was no

377

way the game would make it to half time; and on top of that, our face paint was beginning to run. Our beards and necklines were saturated green. The hill scrub was bleeding through. None of us wanted to leave, but we knew sticking around might prove to be a terrible mistake. We compromised for our indecision by vowing to leave three minutes into the next quarter. Our final error.

At the conclusion of the five minute pause, the Wildcats came back out of the eastern gate looking anything but rejuvenated. Coach Brody had obviously dragged them over the coals in the locker room. One of the players later admitted to having suggested they just take up the poleaxes and get it over with – stop pretending they were conducting anything less than full-on gladiator warfare. The rest of the team had grumbled in agreement, despite Brody's livid criticism of its performance. By the time the Wildcats were back on the court, it was clear to see that they felt forsaken by everyone – their coach, the referees, certainly their own fans. The only question they appeared to be seriously considering was: Why are we doing this? *Why go on?*

The Hawks sauntered out like homecoming kings. They didn't trot on to the court – they walked. Making their way over the floor in that manner, they looked like trolls garbed in red tunics stumbling to the icebox for a cold burger. Their own fans pulled a twenty yard wave the moment they entered, and didn't stop hooting until the lineup was assembled at mid-court.

The band cut with a wave from the ref. The clock was reset. Another failed appeal for order piped through the loudspeakers. The air horns, garbage chants and traffic cone bugleries resumed.

Forty-six seconds into the second quarter, Wildcat center Bobby Long caught a two-handed pass square in the face while attempting an interception. He was knocked to the floor howling and bleeding through a busted nose. He left a trail of blood over the court all the way to the sidelines. On the bench, a responding medic did his best to tend to the injury while shielding Long from the bombardment of trash coming down from the Baker stands to the rear. A mock pity party rose from the Pottville crowd. Long's replacement assumed position. The game continued.

At 1:15 Hawk rear guard Donny Glok scored a twenty yard overhand three pointer from down court, prompting the Hessian body into a mass rendition of Taps. The Baker Lay thrashed in the stands. To every side the jeering and insults rose up in a deafening chorus: The Pottville cheerleaders were waving goodbye, bon voyage, and so long, sucker. The Hawk mascot was scratching his ass like an orangutan. One Hessian was darting back and forth in the stands, gesturing toward a red banner labeled POOR LITTLE POLECATS with a plastic pointer. The news crew was panning over the crowd repeatedly.

Tensions during what was to be the final minute of the game – from 1:15 to 2:20 – escalated non-stop. The activity on the court was almost indiscernible toward the end – two opposing teams stumbling around in paper bags, soda cans and trash with a hailstorm of caramel apples cutting the air overhead. The Hawks were a full thirty points in the lead, but no one seemed to care anymore. The real battle was being waged by the opposing crowds; the game had become a corner-exhibit, a prelude to the main event. No one was even watching. All eyes were fixed on the opposite stands, everyone braced for the inevitable. Trash was being hurled in every direction. The popcorn vendors were packing up out of fear for their lives. Six deputies were climbing through the aisles on the northern wall. Isolated scuffles were breaking out on every tier. Packs of factory rats were pushing through the stands toward the court. Masses were moving in group undulations, surging, waning, falling apart and regrouping in greater numbers. And always the roar, the deafening clamor that rose and intensified in pitch until no one could make out a single word being spoken, spat or bellowed by even his closest companion. This was the last snapshot of the evening before everything fell to pieces: there they were, Pottville and Baker, two neighboring communities which prided themselves in their own supposed good sportsmanship, charity, levelheadedness and neighborly concern, unveiled as an hysterical mob of naked apes and misanthropes.

The final play was a disaster. At 2:14 one of the Pottville referees was clipped by a soup can that came flying out of the Baker stands. The ref whirled and engaged in a shouting match with a group in the front row. The clock was somehow left running, even though the other refs, being temporarily distracted by the conflict, turned away from the game to assist their colleague. The court was left unmonitored for the next five seconds, just long enough for one of the Pottville guards to trip up an advancing Wildcat with a highly illegal leg sweep. The Wildcat's feet came out from under him. He hit the floor with a thump. The ball flew off the court. Everyone in the gymnasium *except* the referees saw it happen. The Baker Lay screamed foul. The Hessians howled for joy. All four refs turned to find one downed Wildcat with a bewildered looking Hawk standing over him, shrugging his shoulders as though to say *who, me?* The clock stopped.

Somewhere in the next few moments Curtis distinctly overheard John saying *here it comes*. The refs convened at mid-court to question the two players. The Wildcat was visibly enraged, the Hawk smooth-talking and passively aggressive. A group of scorekeepers ran out on the floor to interject. The trash came down from every side. The refs shrugged their shoulders. They hadn't seen anything. They couldn't penalize an infraction they hadn't witnessed. *Here it comes*, John repeated. Death calls went up to every side. The marching band stopped. The chicklets huddled together. The mascots shuffled to and fro, as though plotting their escape routes. The Baker referee squared away at mid-court, raised his arm toward the scorekeepers' table, and motioned the official decision.

NO PENALTY.

From where we sat it all appeared to happen at once. No sooner had the signal been given than the entire patron body had the drop flap pulled out from under it. The melee ensued. The Hawks and Wildcats flew into a rumble at mid-court. The northern wall lit out with uninhibited combat. The referees took cover. A team of medics weaved over the floor. Deputies scattered in every direction. The sheriff's men swarmed in from the alley. The mascots bolted for the emergency exit. Six fire alarms blared out along the walls. Before anyone could move to intervene, the two crowds had broken open and flooded the floor, merging at mid-court to form an indistinguishable swampland of flying chairs and pack brawls.

The last image transmitted over the air was that of a surge of bodies from both stands following up the benchside replacements in storming the floor. Thereafter the signal was disrupted when a Wildcat was pitched over the railing into the news pit. $7,600 worth of transmission equipment was destroyed. The newscasters stumbled over one another to salvage the remaining material. The overhead sprinkler system activated automatically, dumping a twelve year old reserve of filthy, contaminated emergency water that smelled like rotten eggs and Limburger over the whole gymnasium. It coated the soundboard, the cameras, the boom mikes, and everyone on the court, in an oily paste.

We're still amazed that we ever managed to make our way to an exit at all, much less that we did so within two minutes. Between our spot on the third tier and the nearest gate there was a fifty yard run of bedlam. Our first reaction would have been to huddle together against the wall and wait it out, but with the sprinkler system gushing that hot, corrosive reserve water over everything, we, like the rest of the crowd, had no choice but to make a break for it. Our recollection of actually doing so is hazy. Visibility was minimal. The only details we're able to recall in common are being soaked from head to toe, ramming down the aisleway in a six man chain, the fire alarms blaring down on us, our face-paint running, bodies jostling to every side, seat cushions soaring, the constant whack of bone on bone, fist to jaw, foot to ribcage, the masses clotting every exit door, the continual feeling that we were about to be blindsided, the deputies clubbing Hessians and Hawks, Wildcats, trolls, factory rats – the poor footing, puddles on the court, bloody noses, high-pitched screams, mascots falling over one another, fighting on the ground, fighting in the stands, fighting along the wall, beneath the bleachers, in the band pit, everywhere. Trying to get through it all was like plotting one's course through hand-held footage of a barnstorming run. It was impossible to follow. No one knows how many injuries were inflicted inside the gymnasium, as the crowd soon spilt out to the parking lot, where the real battle was already underway. Our group didn't make it to the west gate intact; we lost Wilbur and Curtis somewhere along the way. Both Murphy and Bailer, who were each at least sixty pounds heavier and three inches taller than John, managed to shield him through the mob. Dennis, who was doing his best to lead, was the only one who saw the Baker referee being carried out the door by a group of factory rats.

There were already five or six hundred fans in the parking lot before we made our way out. The battle was in full swing. Baseball bats and tire irons had been retrieved from hatchbacks. Hoods were being smashed and stomped. Windshields were blowing out. Ten man groups were writhing on the asphalt. Cheerleaders were running by. Whole waves of Hawks were scaling the fence, kicking and whacking at the Wildcats below, throwing themselves over the top, and making off into the surrounding neighborhoods. The highway was blocked. A Hessian ran by with a stolen tuba. A Hawk was seen beating two members of the marching band. The Pottville mascot was stripped naked and whipped with belt handles. Tires were being slashed, headlights busted. Fans were locking themselves in their cars and curling up in hatchbacks. Engines were roaring. The traffic guards had deserted. Horns were blaring, police sirens, the fire alarm inside. More groups kept pouring out of the gym.

It was impossible to find our way. Somewhere in the mess Bailer relocated Wilbur, but he lost John and Murphy in the process. No one knew where Curtis was, and Dennis had been missing from the moment we stepped outside. Murphy and John were left alone. They crouched down and scuttled through the crowd toward Murphy's pickup. They made it halfway through the lot without a problem. But just beyond the flagpole they wandered into an isolated rumble. Before Murphy could manage to maneuver their way out, John was sucker-punched and knocked to the ground by a towering Hessian. Murphy laid the Hessian out with a driving forearm. He was then set upon by the others. Under normal circumstances, his attackers might have woken from a two-day coma in traction after he got done with them. Behind that docile, bovine exterior of his, Murphy's *other* self, the one that had landed him in prison years earlier, the one that could've torn through a roomful of grown men to all but his own expense – *that* Murphy – the one he always did his best to keep under wraps at all costs, would've had no problem cleaning the pavement with the whole group. However, at the moment he was trying to keep watch over John, and he couldn't very well act as bodyguard *and* one man army simultaneously. In the end he failed as both.

Before he was able to free himself, the group of Wildcats fans off to his left suddenly froze and hissed to one another – *Kaltenbrunner . . .! Ain't that Kaltenbrunner . . . ?* Murphy's assailants backed off for a minute. He turned toward the Wildcats fans. They were staring at something behind him. He whirled all the way around. John was there on the ground, trying to get to his feet. His hood had been pulled back. The paint had washed away. His face was exposed. Everyone was looking at him. *GOD DAMN IF IT AIN'T!* someone said. *THASS KAWDENBROONER!!!*

Murphy remembers broadsiding the group before they had a chance to lunge. He went down along with them screaming at John to *Go, Go, Go, Get out of here!* John took off. He leapt on to the hood of a town wagon and bounded from roof to hatchback down the aisle toward the fence. Within seconds his name was being bellowed all through the lot. Anyone in a position to stop and look saw a spindly legged apparition charging over the hoods on the south end with the beginnings of a sizeable crowd welling up on his heels. The rest of us, wherever we were, saw it happening. We made off in his general direction, but cutting through the crowd was dangerous, difficult, and slow moving. Murphy was tied up in an 8–1 brawl and couldn't get free. Wilbur and Bailer were chopping through scuffles with a stolen pile jack. Dennis was probably the closest in the bunch, and even he had to contend with a thirty yard bog of impenetrable mayhem. John was alone. His only hope was to reach Murphy's Chevy without being snared. Which he did. Barely. He managed to throw open the door and reach for the glove compartment just as a group of factory rats loomed up behind him. He had his thumb on the compartment latch the moment they got a hold of him. They ripped at his legs and ankles, trying to overpower his grip on the interior arm rest. It took four of them to drag him from the cockpit. He hit the ground face first and took a boot to the ribs before coming around with the .38. He leveled the barrel in a straight armed brace. The group standing over him drew back. He inched to his feet with his back to the Chevy. The group continued to widen around him. As some of them later reported: Before he broke out of his stance, scrambled over the fence, and disappeared across the highway, he looked them all over, and muttered something about killing the fatted calf and arming the aware . . .

By the time Sheriff Dix's reinforcements arrived on the scene, the riot had spread over the northern half of Baker. The Tanner County deputies recall rolling across the overpass and into town as having been akin to entering a front-line artillery assault. Every road was a blockaded impasse of fire trucks, battling crowds and traffic jams. Off to one side, pickups bowling over trash heaps and spinning figure eights through front lawns. On the other, Hessians and factory rats feuding in the trash. Up ahead groups of Hawks and Wildcats being crammed into squad cars three and four at a time. Elsewhere fires breaking out. Outnumbered groups being pummeled blind, benches, dumpsters and community monuments overturned. Between eight-thirty and ten p.m., every crossing in town was alive with the same pandemonium and lawlessness that raged all through the valley that night. One might've easily gone astray from one corner to the next. It all looked the same.

No one knows how the wetbacks got dragged into it. Some locals maintain 'those nasty spics' were just waiting for the moment, and that they even incited the whole melee themselves. The wetbacks, in defense of their community, would later refute those charges by claiming most of them had just been sitting on their porch stoops the moment the mob came around the bend on to 3rd Street, and that they were involuntarily dragged into the riot through no fault of their own. One way or another, whether they acted in defense of their families, or if, indeed, they were fed up with the dead cat treatment and needed no further incentive, the wetbacks were quickly incorporated into the melee as active participants, were arrested, pitched into the wagons, driven to the slaughterhouse, and herded into the killing pens alongside of everyone else. With the county jail overstuffed and the department cells filled to capacity, Sheriff Dippold had no choice but to requisition the Keller & Powell building as a temporary holding facility. The more unruly detainees from every community, not just the wetbacks or Wastelanders, were cuffed to separate holding gates, out of one another's reach, all up and down the west wing of the building. The rest were packed into the main pens with eight hundred pound steers breathing down their necks.

3rd, Main and 5th streets were by far the hardest hit areas in town. When the final figures came in three weeks later it was revealed that over $65,000 in property damage had been inflicted on the seventy-five yard stretch of Main Street bracketed by 254 and Geiger alone. Three hundred and seventeen arrests were made in just over two hours. There were six gunshot wounds, four stabbings, and in excess of four hundred sustained injuries of varying severity. Three reports of sexual assault were filed. Seventeen trash fires were extinguished by the Greene County fire department. The Baker Bait shack was burned to the ground. There were nine unrelated auto accidents, the last of which involved four separate vehicles and one getaway. Two hundred and sixteen windows in residential Baker were shattered. The number of downed mailboxes, trampled flower gardens, slashed tires and busted wind chimes went un-tallied. All but four establishments along Main were heavily looted. The list goes on to include numerous accusations of police brutality, breaking and entering, attempted murder, miscellaneous property damage, and most notably, an attempt on the part of ten Baker factory rats to lynch referee Dwayne Jacobs. As the Blaine County deputies credited with intervening at the last possible moment testified, they arrived on the scene at 6th and Geiger just in time to find Jacobs, with the noose already tightened around his neck, being hoisted overhead, kicking and screaming, just moments before the group on hand was able to pitch the other end of the rope over a tree limb, pull it taught, and tie it into place.

It's all on record. The completed files on the melee occupy three full cabinets drawers at City Hall, all of which remain open to public access to this day. Probably the only surprising detail anyone with enough patience to plow through it all would be apt to discover is that, miraculously, somehow, no one was killed.

It was the longest evening in the valley's history. Everyone involved dealt with the melee from his own little corner, and everyone, from the lowliest troll to Mayor Boll himself, has been trying to recover ever since. Literally hundreds of charges would be subsequently dismissed from the courts on grounds of some obscure, antiquated 'mass-hysteria' clause skillfully resurrected from the state law books by overworked defense teams. On the positive side, the court's overload would thereby reduce standing judiciary obligations to a 'mildly unmanageable deluge.' But not so conveniently, the majority of the pending disputes would then be turned over to the public arena, where they would be subject to chronic embellishment and revision. Before too long, factory rats who'd been overpowered and beaten senseless on the night of the 21st would be claiming to have taken out twelve Hessians with a tire iron singlehandedly, then walked to the Dairy Queen for a nightcap. It's the same delusional miscarriage of cold hard facts which has led to the post-mortem mythology surrounding John Kaltenbrunner. No one seems capable of owning up to what everyone *knows* and what the records reflect: namely, that over a period of nine weeks, the citizens of Pullman Valley them-selves – and themselves alone – went from 1) quiet desperation to 2) outward hostility to 3) all-out, ungovernable insanity on a cast of thousands, and that, in the end, they managed to botch, bungle, thwart and hideously disfigure everything they came in contact with along the way. They've got no one to blame but themselves, yet the idea of taking credit for anything as disas-trous as the Baker/Pottville melee is anathema to their collective pride. Consequently, they seek out all available scapegoats in hopes of pardoning themselves, both individually and on the whole.

With the completion of this account, there are now three avenues any genuinely inquiring mind might opt to pursue in getting to the bottom of the crisis. The first, as has been mentioned, would be the public access files, predominantly comprised of police reports, news clippings, departmental memorandums and miscellaneous registered complaints. Though consulting the official records might prove worthwhile in some regards, most disinterested parties would probably find the material tediously inconclusive. The alternative, the second avenue, would be to hit the tavern circuit, where the residents who were actually in Baker at the time might provide their own version of the story, depending entirely on the mood they happen to be in at the moment, the company they're keeping, and, of course, their current blood-alcohol level. This approach might prove more consistently entertaining, and even somewhat more insightful, though one should again bear in mind that the accounts acquired from the tavern regulars will most likely be bastardized derivatives of what were only half-truths to begin with. At any rate, in both cases the most pivotal character in the whole affair will be grossly misrepresented. Neither the *Greene County Herald* or the Baker Lay ever knew the first thing about John Kaltenbrunner. To date, no worthwhile record of his existence has been accessible to anyone, yet considering the crisis without considering his role therein is like bypassing Bonaparte in a study of the battle of Austerlitz. Without opening the complete Kaltenbrunner dossier to the public, no comprehensive understanding of the crisis will ever be attained. Hence this account: an attempt to merge the public files, local lore, and the balcony barnyard epics in one highly readable, chronological, factually based recap as compiled by the green-nigger/hill-scrub contingency of Pullman Valley. Other alternatives could very well surface in the coming years. The resources certainly exist. Everyone in Baker has a story to tell. Getting it down on dictaphone would be simple. The oral history might sell a million copies in paperback, right alongside of *Jonathan Livingston*

Seagull. The east-coast critics would label it a 'redneck inferno.' Charity collections would pour in from south of the Mason-Dixon. West-coast independents would prattle on about negative Karma in the corn belt. It would be a nationwide overnight sensation, a hot potato potboiler, but it would accomplish nothing. It would, in all likelihood, destroy everything toward which we've worked.

In the end no one is more fit to tell the story than what remains of the Baker 22. We were the only ones who operated from inside the whole way through. Though alternative accounts may have since been doctored into greater marketability, and though we admittedly only knew John for a few short months, no one else has even a smattering of the actual facts *and* the resolve to stick to them.

As for the rest of the October 21st melee, it's all on file and much too lengthy to go into beyond what's already been covered. The specifics could drag on indefinitely. The only thing left to consider in detail is the remainder of our evening and a few subsequent notes, whereupon this account will have served its purpose.

In brief, while the rest of the community was in an uproar that night we spent almost three hours combing the streets in search of John. It took us twenty minutes to regroup and escape the parking lot, after which Curtis and Bailer hit separate pay phones to put out the word. Within minutes, the rest of us were on the move, incensed though we were at having been left out of the evening's activities.

We looked everywhere. We hit all of John's familiar haunts – the coal yards, the cemetery, the refinery, along the riverbank. We couldn't find him anywhere. Most of the rioting had died down by eleven, and he was still missing. No one could tell us anything. He hadn't left a note at any of our doors. Murphy's kitchen was empty. The last anyone, namely Dennis, had seen of him, he'd been heading across the highway with a loaded gun in hand. For the second time in three weeks we were fearing the worst, only this time our suspicions felt far more substantiated, almost certain. Something was terribly wrong. By midnight we were openly assuming he'd been either arrested or hospitalized. Or worse. We were screwed. Wilbur was the one who finally bit the bullet and walked into the sheriff's office.

The department lobby was wrecked. There were papers and crushed tin cans all over the floor. One of the ceiling fan's rotary blades had been bent, causing the whole thing to wobble and bang on its axis repeatedly. The two deputies sucking at cold coffee in the center of the floor looked too worn out to notice. So did the sheriff. Tom Dippold was seated in a far off corner that no longer looked to be the designated pulpit of a department chief so much as it did a cleaning maid's washroom. He had the air of an itinerant sharecropper who'd at long last, through some final deprivation, been rendered unshockable. He was slumped back in his chair, staring into space and chewing absentmindedly at an unlit stogie. A long trail of ashes was scattered over his belly. Wilbur remembers him looking like a sedated bluegill there in his recliner. He was completely unresponsive at first. He didn't look up, didn't move, didn't appear to be there at all. It was only when Wilbur stated explicitly that a friend of his was missing and that he was worried that the sheriff seemed to register a voice at all. Maybe he would know the name, Wilbur said. He was looking for John Kaltenbrunner.

Tom Dippold looked up. It can't be said he flinched. It can't be said he lurched, jostled, grimaced or winced in the slightest. All that can be said is he looked up, which is, however, probably more of a reaction than any other name in town could have gotten out of him at the moment. He slowly stared Wilbur over from a thousand yards in the distance. After a pause, he went back to his spot on the wall and mumbled quietly that John was in the hospital.

Wilbur drove across town to the Baker General. The waiting room was a nightmare. There were deputies everywhere, Hawks and Wildcats in slings and wheelchairs, trolls and wetbacks sprawled out on the floor, skulls wrapped tight. A continual wailing was emanating from the emergency room and drifting through the halls. The loudspeakers wouldn't stop. Nurses and doctors were running in every direction. Deputies were uncuffing detainees for treatment. There were pools of blood on the seats, stains on the carpet. Wilbur put in his request with a receptionist but had to wait for an available M.D. until after 3 a.m. Before then, no one could tell him anything. The pay phone had been disconnected, and he didn't dare leave the lobby for fear of missing his turn. He sat there for hours.

Finally, an overtaxed surgeon on a smoke break came out to have a word with him. After a brief exchange, Wilbur was issued a temporary pass and motioned down the hall.

The elevator was out of service. A technician was working on the lift gears in the open shaft. Wilbur took the stairs to the fifth floor, then found his way to room seventeen. Baker deputy Keith Gates was standing guard over the door. Wilbur showed him the pass. Gates looked him over and demanded identification. Wilbur produced his driver's license. Gates took a careless look at the card, then handed it back, saying there was *No Way* anyone was getting in to see the suspect. Direct orders. Wilbur asked what had happened. Gates drew back and asked if he was serious, if he really didn't know. He really didn't know.

As Gates then explained, and as Wilbur was to verify in greater detail later on, John, after fleeing the gymnasium parking lot earlier that evening, had not been able to shake his pursuers, and, as one was all that had been needed to sound the general alarm, had managed to attract another crowd on the other side of the highway. By the time he rounded the corner of Main and 254, the group on his heels was reportedly twenty strong and growing.

He ran into the Whistlin' Dick. The regulars inside were busy screaming at the bartenders to fix the television set. The game had been interrupted when the picture had suddenly jarred to one side, blurred over and gone black. Since then the screen had been dead. One of the doormen was up on the counter switching channels. The crowd was giving him hell. In the midst of the unrest, John came stumbling through the main door. All eyes followed him as he fell over a table, hit the floor, got to his feet, ran to the far wall, and pressed his back to a pint rack. The moment the mob came through the door he started shooting.

The subsequent chaos was unprecedented in the history of Greene County tavern brawls. Over the years the Dick had seen everything from full-scale police raids, to F-3 tornado warnings. But none of it had ever been on a par with that evening's stampede. The crowd on hand evacuated within moments, but not without annihilating everything in its path. Tables went over, screams cut the air, pitchers crashed, shots boomed out. The jukebox was overturned. Speakers were torn from the wall. The cigarette machine's display case was smashed, busted glass and spare change showered over the floor. A mound of bodies sized up, jammed together in the doorway, kicking, gouging, trampling and pulling at one another. A grizzly skull fell from a rack and tipped across the pile of thrashing limbs. A motorcycle helmet was thrown through the front window. Bodies followed through after it, dropping from the sill into a pile of bags in the street. The burglar alarm went off. John was seen climbing up on the counter, kicking a tap, and firing over the top of the room at random. The last regular out the door saw him tear the seven foot rowing oar from its rack over the row of whisky bottles, destroy over half of the house liquor supply in one sweep, then bring the flat end down on the register, sending it toppling to the floor with a crash.

From across the street his spurned attackers, the infuriated bar staff and the flabbergasted regulars watched him through the open window frame. He looked 'bewildered' standing there on the bar, rowing oar in hand, beer surging over his pant legs, and the tavern in shambles all around him. One minute later the first wave of combatants from the game came tearing around the corner, and before anyone had time to prepare, the looting and combat along Main was underway. Somewhere in the mess John snapped out of his daze, hopped down from the bar and ran into the street. He was hit by a passing squad car. His .38 rattled off into the gutter. He pitched over, unconscious.

Wilbur didn't know whether to believe it or not. But as he would soon discover for himself, with the exception of numerous details concerning the demolished hubcap collection, the broken clock, four sustained fractures, etc., all had gone exactly as Gates claimed. John was now to remain under guard for the duration of his treatment. Afterwards, he would be shipped off to a state penitentiary for a 'long holiday.' Gates was noticeably unsympathetic. He advised Wilbur to pick his friends more carefully from then on. Wilbur knew better than to ask for a break. He was sent on his way, feeling helpless. He had a terrible feeling. Just earlier in the week John had sworn he'd never go back to the hospital. He had long-since stated his case against prison, saying he'd opt for suicide if and when it ever came to that again. Wilbur had believed him.

On the way to the stairwell, he brainstormed for any available options. He looked up and down the hallway, past the nurses station, the open elevator shaft, the cleaning closets, any avenue that might serve as a potential escape route. But he couldn't find anything. He looked back toward John's room. Gates was staring at him. There was nothing he could do. He walked down the stairwell and left the hospital.

It's been ten years now. Baker's changed a bit. A few more industries have settled in. Several families have come and gone. We've lost some of our original crew to one thing or another. Everyday life has gone on for those of us who lived through the melee, but it's never really been the same. As it is, not a single day goes by in Pullman Valley that John isn't somehow, directly or indirectly, brought to everyone's mind. Even now, after all this time, we still find ourselves wondering for hours on end just what it was that went through his head during those last few hours before making his break from room seventeen. At times we're certain we can see the whole thing, as though we'd been there ourselves, we can see it all. We can start from the moment he regained consciousness and let it roll forward like an old 16mm newsreel. We can see him opening his eyes, looking around in confusion, wondering where he is, then jolting upright the moment it registers. The indubitable look of disgust. We can see him tearing the catheters from his forearms, twisting himself free from the straps, crawling out of bed, and pacing back and forth beneath the light fixtures with his turquoise nightshirt hanging all the way to his knees and the rear flap hanging open to expose his pock-marked ass. More disgust. Walking crooked circles through the room, looking for a light switch, checking the barred windows, the door. Finding himself trapped. Going over every possibility until finally hitting on a plan. Then setting to work immediately, dismantling the bed frame, securing one of the iron leggings, wrapping it in a pillowcase. Buttoning his ass flap and beginning the long wait for the nurse on duty to come by on her routine check. Remaining in that position, crouched to the right of the door, running his fingers over the pipe, going mad with impatience, pain and nicotine withdrawal. Tightening his grip over the pipe, watching his knuckles go white, relaxing for long enough to let the color return, then clamping down again. And his heart rattling away in its cage. The sickening smell of disinfectants, old paint, rubber tubes and infirmary sheets. The bedpans clanging in the tubs outside, the nurses gabbing away at their stations, the telephones sounding through the hallways, the thin crease of light beneath the door spilling over the floor and dying out in the darkness, all of it, everything, all the grisly little details that were bound to have culminated and sent his mind racing wild, working itself into such a state that by the time the jangle of keys finally did sound out behind the door, he had to have been as charged as a Castillian bull that had been locked in the darkened vaults of the corrida for two full weeks before being turned into the ring in a disoriented rage. Whatever his state of mind may have been before the door was opened will remain a matter of conjecture, but the events that followed are all on record.

Deputy Gates didn't have time to know what hit him. John had pummeled him senseless and was halfway down the hall before the nurse was able to peel herself from the spilt remains of the TV dinner and let out a bloodcurdling scream. The nurses huddled around station number five reportedly heard the ruckus, followed by the slap of bare feet charging in their direction over linoleum tiles. They saw a flashing streak of turquoise and rubber tubing fly by, heading in the direction of the broken elevator doors. They yelled out that the lift was out of service. But by then he'd already taken a quick left into the open shaft. He fell two floors and crashed through the roof of the jammed car below. He landed on an emergency repairman inside who was seated with his back to the wall eating a ham sandwich. The repairman was astonished. John garbled out a quick apology, then hobbled out of the car and down the hallway to the emergency exit, trailing behind a generous flow of blood from a gash that had opened up along his left leg. A third-shift janitor was the last member of the hospital staff to catch sight of him. The janitor recalled a blue-sheeted white boy with torn catheters dangling from every appendage scaling down the fire escape and hobbling off into the night.

There were three more sightings, all in a row, which seem to indicate he took the adjoining alleyway running parallel with Poplar all the way into town. At approximately 4:23 a resident of the Linkhorn trailer park phoned the sheriff's department to report a wounded river rat on the loose in her flower garden. Eight minutes later another call came in in regards to 'some hoodlum' scouring the town square's fountain floor for wishing well change. Finally, at 4:40 a graveyard clerk at the convenience store reported that a badly injured, soaked to the bone, half-naked 'customer' had just barged into the store, slammed a bloody fistful of change down on the countertop, and demanded a pack of cigarettes. He'd then left the store and had been last seen heading for the river.

Just after dawn at 6:47 a.m. on October 22nd, Baker deputy Calvin Dirk found the body curled up in the weeds beneath the Patokah overpass, with six crushed cigarette butts in the dirt all around it.

AFTERWARDS

THE RECEPTIONIST AT THE HOSPITAL, having looked over the previous evening's logbook, gave the authorities Wilbur's name and address for the purpose of identifying the body. Two deputies came to his door just after sunrise. He listened to what they had to say, then left them in the hall while he dressed. He had a cigarette at the coffee table and tried to clear his head. He hadn't slept. He'd been walking the floors for hours. Now that the deputies had arrived with their announcement, he'd have just as soon continued the pacing as put in for one more episode in the most outrageous night of his life. He thought for a minute that if he turned his back on everything, pretended none of it was happening, left the deputies by the curbside and the phone off the hook, it would all cease to exist somehow. The deputies' suspicions would never be confirmed if he refused to go along for the ride. In that manner, the body would never be identified, the reported death would never be verified, would never have actually happened. The past, that which had already gone, couldn't come to be if he flat-out refused to catch up with it. It was like coming to terms with one's involvement in an unexpected car crash: one moment you're gazing out the window without a care in the world, the next – BAM – there you are, pinned to the dashboard in a pile of yourself with a fanfare of sirens, medics, and public officials running circles around the twisted remains of your vehicle. Above all you're wondering what happened, but more specifically, just how it happened *so fast*. Your first reaction is to think – wait a minute, let's try that again, if we can just back it up a few seconds and take two, I'll get it right this time around. Nothing can have changed that fast.

No momentary slackening of attention can be *that* irreversibly damning.

But it is. One instant is all it takes. After that there's no going back.

Wilbur eventually gave up and walked out the door. The squad car was waiting for him in the street.

He stared out over the devastated streets from the back seat on the way to the Patokah. The driver left the highway at the overpass ramp. The car pulled into the rail yards and parked beside two other black and whites and one ambulance. Wilbur got out and walked through the gravel. He passed a line of freight cars. He walked over the tracks to where two deputies were marking off the body next to a burlap stretcher. One of them pulled back the sheet and looked to him. Wilbur nodded. The medics covered the body, hoisted it on to a stretcher, and carried it off. Someone asked if he needed a ride. He said no. He walked down to the water and sat on a rock. A minute later the entourage was gone.

Two tugboats were docking on the opposite bank. A pale grey light was coming up over Gwendolyn Hill on what promised to be an overcast morning. All through the fog the scavengers were beginning to crawl from their nooks. The pigeons were coming out from the underside of the bridge. Muskrats were scurrying through the cattails along the riverbank. A wave of vultures appeared from the woods and soared by, bound for the freshly churned feast in the streets. Before long the highway was warming up with the first wave of traffic.

Wilbur remained on his rock, thinking about nothing in particular. He was exhausted. The last twelve hours had rendered him insensitive to all but the lapping of the current against the dock pillars at his feet. Everything else was too much to comprehend for the time being. He'd been overloaded – too much input, too many things he'd never seen or done before, not the least of which had been identifying a body. That, in particular, probably wouldn't have settled well had he been in his right mind. Under normal circumstances he might have gone on a tear; might have drunk himself blind, hit the back roads, shot up the yard, whatever. But sitting there on the morning of the 22nd, he just didn't have it in him. He was spent. It would take three nights of solid sleep for the real shock to set in, and several months beyond that for the shock to follow through on its natural course: from shock to remorse, remorse to anger, and anger, finally, to acceptance. That was the way these things worked, or so he'd been told. That was what he had to look forward to. He opted to savor the catatonia while it lasted.

All around him the first wave of calm to be felt in days was settling over the valley. A group of dockworkers was lounging on the pier across the way. The hum of incoming traffic drifted over the Patokah. Off to the right and up the hill from the opposite bank a large yellow generator stood fenced in on a tripod where the Kaltenbrunner farm had once been. It was a nine hundred yard stretch from the old elm where John had stacked wood as a ten-year-old to the matted patch of grass marked off in the clearing a few feet behind Wilbur. From point to point, it wasn't much of a run, but by Greene County standards it was another country.

Even though Wilbur was scarcely capable of putting together more than two coherent thoughts that morning, there were a few fundamental predictions for the immediate future on which he could've banked with reasonable certainty.

He knew, for example, that, just as John had predicted the night before, the strike would be over within another week. Which it was. Starting that very morning the Baker Lay would stumble out of their houses as abject, craven-faced zombies to wander through the rubble toward City Hall, where hundreds of locals from every point in the valley would be amassed to put the final, unconditional clampdown on the council. The council would eventually crack under the pressure, and after exhausting all other options, would at last present our crew with an acceptable settlement pitch. That would be on the evening of the 25th. Baker would have been an official police state for three days by then. After minimal deliberation Kuntsler would be ousted and exiled to some remote mining town in Alabama, never to be heard from again. The landfill's official directorship would then be offered up to the candidate of our choice. For reasons of competence and overall ability, it would be an obvious toss-up between Murphy and Wilbur. Not so predictably, Murphy would decline the offer, for reasons of his own, leaving Wilbur at the helm as our new crew executor.

His first act in office, before anything got underway, would be to demolish Kuntsler's mobile home with a fleet of steamrollers. The remains would be flattened and buried with the latest deposit on the west end of the yard. Thereafter he would oversee the construction of his own office, the interior of which would be lined with ornately framed press clippings from the strike. All around the room they would run, beginning just to the right of the doorway and continuing along the western wall, behind the desk, over the oboe rack and clear to the other side of the doorway, ending with the final clip announcing the settlement, which would be enlarged and boldly mounted to the inside of the door, where he could gaze upon it from his chair. Following that there would be a long-awaited hike in pay for everyone, effective immediately. A new coat of paint would go over the forklifts and compactors. Several company policies would be abolished. Roll call would be discontinued. As standard procedure, all inter-departmental conflicts would, henceforth, be settled by way of dueling – via clenched fist or shot glass, depending on the severity of the dispute – after which, as a rule, all would be forgotten. Murphy would go on to organize company picnics, complete with obstacle courses and potato sack races, to be held at the landfill, in the state park and along the banks of the Patokah every other month. We would all receive new suits and an extra week of paid vacation for our unwavering allegiance through the strike.

Consequently, a rejuvenated, almost idyllic atmosphere would begin to roll through the yard. The days of fretting over the rounds would be over. Our time at the wheel and the hours in the taverns would become tolerable, almost rewarding. It would be a fine enough ending for buck and wench, barring, of course, the inconceiveable nightmare of the cleanup itself. The cleanup would demand over five weeks of solid, king-hell nasty overtime, for the sake of which a full trailer of military surplus chemical warfare suits would have to be shipped in at the company's expense, a community-sponsored crash course in emergency desanitation would be hosted by a resident authority on toxic waste, and two nurses from a nearby clinic would be sent by to administer a round of mandatory inoculations. What would follow would stand forevermore as the most indescribably wretched series of rounds we would ever pull in all our professional careers. But afterwards, the streets would be restored to order, and the long, arduous haul to recovery would at last be underway.

Other, more long-term outcomes Wilbur might've accurately predicted on the morning of the 22nd include:

—A five year ban on homeground Baker–Pottville athletic events.
—A whopping 11 percent increase in county taxes for the next two years.
—The eventual reconstruction of the Whistlin' Dick, albeit under new ownership.
—The five year imprisonment of the six Ebony Steed employees responsible for the Patokah dam disaster and the consequential flooding of Bolling County proper.
—Tom Dippold's landslide defeat in the next election.
—The majority of the city council being voted out of office within fourteen months.
—A temporary, though drastic cutback in Sodderbrook's existing labor force due to massive loss of stock.
—An incalculable number of imprisonments, fines and community service obligations being sentenced or issued to participants of the October 21st melee.
—The two year construction of a new Methodist church being scrutinized, heckled and ridiculed by area Baptist, Episcopalian and Catholic communities.
—The town treasury being depleted to the point of bankruptcy after seven weeks of community reconstruction.
—More insurance rackets than could possibly be listed.
—The replacement of the Baker General's lift car.

—The instant revocation of industrial Baker's firearms licensing.
—A pending lawsuit from a state university for the brash mistreatment of its field operatives (the sociologists) during the month of October.
—The imprisonment of the two river rats already in custody, as well as four of the six factory rats responsible for the raid on the Kaltenbrunner residence.
—A host of miscellaneous personal disputes – everything from petty bickery to 'post-traumatic' demands for financial compensation – being brought to the attention of local courts and rendering Baker a virtually uninhabitable firing line for the next six months.
—And, not finally, but most importantly on our end, the advent of a whole new code of conduct/courtesy to be allotted the hill scrubs of Pullman Valley.

In the same manner John was given his space following the burning of the Fisher farm, we would henceforth be avoided when at all possible, and quietly deferred to otherwise. It might be said most locals would hesitate even to think too loudly in our presence from that day forward. Over the next decade we would only be dragged into one knock-down brawl, and that due in large part to a case of mistaken identity. Never again would we have problems with the Pineridge bull harlot type. We would grow to be loathed and abhorred more universally than ever, but now the contempt would be intermingled with enough terror and respect to keep everyone at a safe distance. Which, the Baker Lay would eventually realize, was all we'd ever wanted in the first place.

Anyone in town could've made the same fundamental predictions before the strike was officially over; most of them had become foregone conclusions by or before the melee.

But other eventualities were not so immediately foreseeable. Some would take time to come to term, and could not have been accurately forecasted on the morning of the 22nd. Even with a workable knowledge of local affairs, it would've been difficult to predict *if, how, when* and *to what extent* the Baker Lay would be willing to botch the records in their forthcoming drive for acquittal. That would take time. A cushion of at least two or three years would first be required for the smoke to clear from the crisis, after which the long-term damage might be more easily assessed. How much public shame and disgrace would linger on after the fact? How much would dissipate? How much of it would find a home? How much of it could be forgotten, rationalized, justified, sublimated, contextualized? How much mass exposure could the community learn to live with? What particular events and individuals would be scapegoated most severely? And when they were, how far would the coverup go? There was really no way of telling at the moment.

It would take Wilbur himself years of reflection to put everything into perspective. His concern would remain primarily with John, firstly because he had a pretty good handle on everything else, but also because when and if the post-crisis fabrications did begin to surface, the majority of the public's wrath would be pawned off on those *in absentia*, the 'dead ones,' those condemned to stand trial without defense: Kaltenbrunner, Kuntsler, Dippold, Robert Mitchum. The least Wilbur could do, for his part, was be ready for it when it came. He owed that to John. We all did. And still do. John withstood one too many specious character assassinations in the course of his short lifetime to have to be posthumously memorialized in railway-miscarriage/river-rat terms. We venture to say he deserves better.

Wilbur would have his work cut out for him. He would already have his own notes stacked up in a pile on the kitchen table. He would know exactly where to go to follow up the rest of his leads. He'd find Roy Mentzer in a wheelchair as an unusually early admission to the Pottville retirement home. Elias Kauerbach would still be stationed in a third-floor office room at the feed mill. Tom Dippold would be right up the road in an isolated cabin at Sparrow's Height. John's peers would be tracked down through their graduating yearbook. Even the crones would be available for comment. Compiling interviews would be no great challenge. Deciphering fact from fiction *would*. Fortunately, Wilbur would have one last ace in the deck which hasn't been mentioned: on the evening of October 6th, after the apartment had been raided, the church had burned, and the rest of us had returned to Murphy's to find John battered but intact, John had quietly pulled Wilbur out into the yard where they could speak privately and, wired on adrenaline to the point of madness, had finally come clean with the full story behind the holdout. He'd told Wilbur everything, exactly as represented in this account: from the sackful of puppies to Hortense's prurient incursions, the existence of the vault to the final and crushing revelation of Ford Kaltenbrunner's alleged depravity (which, incidentally, remains unverified to this day). Wilbur had been the sole confidant of this confession and had never intended to publicize any of its specifics. He would remain true to that resolve for years. But with the eventual formulation and propagation of the campfire creation theories – John as anarchist, John as heretic, etc. – he would be left with no option but to come forward with the details. The truth would have to serve as the better of two evils.

Until then Wilbur would have years to ponder all the paradigmatic injustices, consistencies, and paradoxes from the whole of John's known existence:

—The paramount injustice would emerge as the fact that, in the end, John's all time nemesis, Hortense Allenbach, received governmentally subsidized funding at his expense straight up to and two months beyond his death. Hortense would never be seen in Pullman Valley again, but the checks would continue to go out to her, wherever she was. John may have eventually settled up with Baker, but he never got a crack at the viper omniscient.

—The primary consistency would be that Wilbur's first and last impressions of John were identical, meaning that from the moment Wilbur found him groping in the mulch on that cold February morning to the final scenario beneath the overpass by the Patokah, no more explosive a personality – one around which things just naturally seemed to combust spontaneously – ever graced the valley.

—And finally, the chief paradox would lay in the fact that John, after a lifetime of pitting himself in rigid opposition to everything Baker epitomized, ultimately fulfilled one of the community's most fundamental directives: the challenge issued to every young man to surpass or outperform his father in one way or another. Meaning, Ford Kaltenbrunner may have failed with an Ebony Steed labor strike, but John Kaltenbrunner, his son, – the dragonslayer's first born, who'd repeatedly been deemed unworthy of his heritage – succeeded with his own.

The rest of us would have time to come to our own conclusions. Starting with that evening in late May when he first rolled into our landfill in his torn pants and black orthopedic shoes, we would rehash every memory at our availability in search of some clue as to how one of such tender years and awkward disposition ever could have walked into our lives, turned them upside down so completely, then quite suddenly left us behind to figure out the rest on our own. In time we'd begin to realize, or at least to *believe* that right from the beginning we'd somehow known we would one day be called on to tell his story. Why else would we, an otherwise characteristically unobservant lot, have watched him so closely? What could we have been looking for? We had to have had some idea. Or maybe it was just that John was the most remarkable oddity any of us had ever seen, and that we couldn't very well take our eyes off of him. One way or another, we would continually have to turn back the clock to that first night, when Wilbur pulled into the lot and parked his rig on the north end of the yard just before starting time, and out from his passenger seat hopped this angry looking kid with a mangled face and a funny haircut who brazenly peered around at all of us. We'd start from that point and let it roll.

We'd find ourselves running back to him in times of need, back to his bony-assed howl in the wild as our newfangled antidote for ordinary madness. Any time the everyday grind took an inordinately high toll, when a compactor broke down, taxes came in, a shoelace busted, a W-2 was lost, an inspector dropped by, the sink was clogged, the trolls started screaming, the landlord phoned for overdue rent – all the 'a's, 'b's and 'c's of just

405

getting by that might send any reasonably sensitive soul charging into the fields in his nightshirt – time to run back to John: to remember how he'd kicked and lashed his way through one disaster after another with all the accumulated confusion of a life gone wrong from day one boiling to the surface at once. Boiling to the surface for us; beckoning us to unload our own bile into its chamber pot, then walk away new men. Brought back to earth with another clean slate to soil at the continuing expense of a dead farm boy.

John's final contention: in the face of having to walk the plank, it was still our prerogative, our inalienable right, to pull an ass-backwards cannonball on the way to the shark-infested waters below.

Our immediate surroundings would serve as a continual reminder of his impact. His route circuit would remain intact. His blue leather mining coat would hang suspended from a wall hook, just over the main vault in Wilbur's office. A single .38 calibre bullet would remain lodged in the wall at the Whistlin' Dick, clearly visible to anyone who could sneak a peek behind the mounted quail above the jukebox. His memory would manage to keep itself alive, not just among us, but all through Greene County. We'd think of him in every dirt bar in the land, see his face in every pack of smokes, his downcast gaze on every factory floor from here to Jerusalem, his open-throated cry sputtering in the frying pan as we burned our Grade-A bacon henceforth. We'd hear his name in every gunblast, in the clinking of glass mugs, the stench of the Whistlin' Dick, the crackle of pork rind wrappers, the roar of yellow tractors, bobbing sheep, burning barns, the morning angelus, smoldering cathedrals, overturned forklifts, carrier pigeons, chicken shacks, hog houses, corncribs, knock-down brawls and broken toilets. And above all in the barnyard we carried with us and could no more escape than ultimately buy into, the barnyard we went gallivanting into all four corners to elude, but just ended up taking with us wherever we went.

But for the time being nothing was finished. And nothing would be over and done with at the riotous conclusion of the 'funeral' four days later – when the paddywagons would finally pull away from the cemetery with all of us kicking and screaming inside. When Wilbur would fall over into the corner with the cuffs biting into his wrists and the blood in his eyes, trying to recount the day's events from the moment he had gotten out of bed that morning. And even before. How, on the previous evening – two hours after the final settlement papers had been signed at City Hall – he'd dusted off his only dress suit and hung it from the coat rack with the polished pair of alligator shoes situated against the wall down below. How he'd dressed himself at 8 a.m. that morning, struggled with the necktie, and run a comb through his hair for the second or third time that decade, then stood before the mirror, going up and down, thinking about how ridiculous he looked, and hoping, for that reason, that the rest of us wouldn't make a habit of dying off. And how he'd driven to the market to meet Murphy as planned, and had found him by his Chevy, decked out like a genuine lady-killer. How they'd argued with the butcher in the doorway of the meat shop until a price had been settled on and the pig had at last been dragged out from the kitchen. And the way it had chortled and drooled at the end of its rope as they paid up and somehow managed to maneuver it into the back seat without soiling their suits. And then had driven across town to the St. Francis of Assissi resting ground, running fifteen minutes behind schedule. How they'd left their rigs on the hill and walked through an aisle of corroded marble crosses and ebony plaques down to where the company in mourning was gathered and waiting. And the big blue coffin by the hole in the ground. And everyone in attendance: six duty-minded, wholeheartedly oblivious Methodist crones, a group of reporters from the *Herald*, four or five bystanders we'd never seen, that wily old gravedigging troll with his assortment of shovels and spades tastefully laid off to one side, and then, of course, us, all twenty-two of the hill scrubs. How Father Furmas Dick (no lie) who had never met John and knew nothing about him, delivered a nauseatingly magniloquent eulogy that was just about as touching as the front-page coverage of John's death had been three days earlier. And how Father Dick had assured everyone that John was in a better place now. And how

Wilbur and the rest of us had done our best to stomach it by trying not to listen and allowing our gazes to wander over the stratum of rooftops to the west. And how a neighborhood dog had yapped on through the entire service, tearing back and forth on its choker chain just beyond the cemetery wall. And how Father Dick had eventually concluded his insufferable jeremiad by unveiling a wire cage and setting two doves free to fly off into the sky – presumably intended to signify the spirit's liberation from earthly bondage – even though both birds simply ended up fluttering ten yards up the hill and perching themselves on the bottom limb of a nearby tree, where they remained for the rest of the afternoon. And thereafter began reciting from a prayer book, volleying to and fro with the crones, the only members of the company versed with the text. And how Wilbur had quietly disappeared at that point, making his way up the hill to prepare. How he'd pulled off his coat, removed the tub of vaseline from a brown paper bag, opened his passenger door, and wrestled the pig over to a large headstone, out of the company's view. And the old watchman who'd come up the hill a minute later demanding to know what the Sam Hill was going on. *This is a Sacred resting ground!* he'd said. *And this is a last will and testament*, Wilbur had replied. And the way the watchman had recoiled, crossed himself, and hightailed it back to the front gate to summon the authorities. And how Wilbur had finished the task just as the service had concluded, and the rest of us had waited down below rolling up our sleeves and looking toward him. And how he'd stood and given the pig a swift kick to the flank that sent it charging down the aisle. And how, at that point, everyone in our group had broken away from the doom and gloom and panned out after the pig, leaving the crones, Father Dick, the reporters, and the troll alone and befuddled. And how closely what followed had identically resembled the chase before – everyone colliding and falling and sliding and chasing after the hot pink blur, wiping out roses, smashing into headstones, barreling over reporters and bystanders, until the squad cars finally shot through the gates and raced up the hill, their sirens screaming. And how, at the last minute, Murphy had gotten everyone out of his hair, slammed Donnecker and Dickell out of his path, tore the rest of us from the pig, charged up the hill toward the grave after it, got a hold of its hind legs, and hoisted it overhead with a scream. And then got his first nightstick to the gut. And then another. And how two deputies had dragged Murphy and the pig to the ground, flailing away until the rest of us jumped in and everyone went over, one grappling pack of obese animality. And how John's casket had been knocked from its pedestal and pitched face down into the plot with a crash. And everyone had hollered and leapt headlong into the fracas, and Wilbur right along with them, until one of the deputies had gotten a hold of him, raised his nightstick and spewed something nasty about *God damn scrubs* before coming down with the big crack that sent Wilbur to the place of a thousand little lights at the end of one dark tunnel. And how he realized, while there, that John was not in a better place at all, that by then, if anything, he'd just found a new job, had landed himself a spot on a production line, had taken up the pick axe, was tilling fields, digging ditches, commandeering jackhammers and riding steamrollers: toiling away till his back was broken, then out the door to the riverbank all over again, just like always. Clockwork of a higher dementia. And the way Wilbur had come to, face down and handcuffed in a patch of his own blood, only to see one of the deputies desperately trying to woo the pig with saccharine-sweet overtones. And how the pig, after regarding him mistrustfully for a minute, had finally turned tail and charged straight into the grave. And how one of the deputies had yanked Wilbur up from the ground and slapped him around until Wilbur looked up and announced that he shat in all their mothers' milk. And how he'd heard the pig kicking and scrambling around on the underside of John's coffin down in the hole as he was led toward the big wagon, inside of which the rest of us were thrashing around like incarcerated behemoths. And how they had maced Murphy and had brought him up alongside of Wilbur as they beat the rest of us back into the tank and pitched those two – the last two – inward. Then slammed the doors. And how, when Wilbur had gotten to his feet, he had looked through a small rectangular slot of light in the wagon door and had seen the troll standing all alone beneath the two doves up on the hill.

And how, as he turned and joined in on the kicking and screaming, and the paddywagon had begun to pull away from the cemetery-in-shambles which would be the final installment in a ten week media blitz, he knew for certain that nothing was finished, that John was not in a better place, and that an object in motion tends to stay in motion. A lord at rest tends to roll in his grave.